BY
DIKSHA BASU

The Windfall

DESTINATION
WEDDING

DESTINATION WEDDING

A Novel

DIKSHA BASU

BALLANTINE BOOKS

NEW YORK

2021 Ballantine Books Trade Paperback Edition

Copyright © 2020 by Diksha Basu
Book club guide copyright © 2021 by Penguin Random House LLC

Published in the United States by Ballantine Books,
an imprint of Random House,
a division of Penguin Random House LLC, New York.

BALLANTINE and the HOUSE colophon are registered trademarks
of Penguin Random House LLC.
RANDOM HOUSE BOOK CLUB and colophon are
trademarks of Penguin Random House LLC.

Originally published in hardcover in the United States by Ballantine Books,
an imprint of Random House, a division of Penguin Random House LLC, in 2020.

LIBRARY OF CONGRESS CATALOGING- IN PUBLICATION DATA
NAMES: Basu, Diksha, author.
TITLE: Destination wedding: a novel / Diksha Basu.
NEW YORK: Ballantine Books, [2020] | Identifiers: LCCN 2019056842 (print) |
LCCN 2019056843 (ebook) | ISBN 9780525577133 (acid-free paper) |
ISBN 9780525577140 (ebook) Subjects: LCSH: Domestic fiction.
CLASSIFICATION: LCC PR9499.4.B376 D47 2020 (print) | LCC PR9499.4.B376
(ebook) | DDC 823/.92—dc23
LC record available at https://lccn.loc.gov/2019056842
LC ebook record available at https://lccn.loc.gov/2019056843

ISBN 9780525577133
Ebook ISBN 9780525577140

Printed in the United States of America on acid-free paper

randomhousebooks.com
randomhousebookclub.com

246897531

Book design by Barbara M. Bachman

For Mikey

DESTINATION
WEDDING

JFK Airport: Their Flight Is Delayed Due to Technical Reasons and Everyone Is Secretly Wishing Airlines Didn't Announce That and Make All the Passengers Nervous

"I CANNOT BELIEVE MY MOTHER IS HERE WITH HER BOYFRIEND and I'm here alone," Tina Das said to her best friend, Marianne Laing, in the British Airways business-class lounge at JFK. Tina, in the hope that she would be able to sleep through the first leg of the flight to Heathrow, had rimless glasses on instead of her usual contacts. She never needed much makeup thanks to her thick eyebrows, which had been a liability when she was younger but were very fashionable now and gave her face all the drama it needed. She was wearing black North Face sweatpants that cinched at the ankle, a gray, long-sleeved T-shirt, and black-and-white Adidas sneakers. It was hot in the lounge so her Guess fur vest was hanging off the chair behind her.

A bowl full of nuts was on the table in between them. Tina picked up a handful while staring out of the window and tossed them all into her mouth and started chewing before she realized she had eaten several whole pistachios, with shells. The hard, cracked pieces pierced her mouth and she spat them out. A grumpy old man appeared out of nowhere with a broom and shook his head at her as he swept up the pistachio shells.

"I didn't know they had shells," Tina said apologetically.

The man said nothing but kept looking at her as he swept, his broom knocking her foot aside.

"It isn't my fault," Tina said to him again but he didn't respond.

The man walked away and Tina turned to Marianne and said, "At the price of these tickets, the nuts really shouldn't have shells."

Marianne was applying lip balm and laughing. She was so good at putting on makeup that it was hard to say whether or not she had any on, but the smattering of brown freckles across her nose was visible and, despite the fact that it was November, still had a velvety brownness they usually acquired over the summer because she had recently been to San Francisco for Tom's college roommate's wedding. Marianne was wearing similar sweatpants and a plain black long-sleeved T-shirt, and a red shawl was draped over the back of her chair.

"We're like world-weary businesswomen who travel internationally twice a month and are just so over it," Marianne said. "I feel like I should be impatiently clacking away on a laptop but I have no work to do this week and I bet Tom's fast asleep."

Marianne looked down at her phone and the itinerary that had been sent by the wedding planner.

"It feels like we're going to have a lot of free time," Marianne said. "There aren't that many events listed here. I thought Indian weddings had days and days of events."

"I think these days most people just pick and choose what parts they want to do. Shefali wanted to walk down the aisle in a white dress but my aunt put her foot down and said she could pick and choose what she wanted but she couldn't change religions," Tina said. "We'll have time to explore the city, though."

Marianne nodded as she cracked open a pistachio and ate it and played with the shells in one hand.

Their flight was two hours late so they were on glass number three of champagne and plate number two of mini sandwiches. Even on Tina's decent income, these business-class tickets were prohibitively expensive. She had managed to book an economy flight using her own money and then used her miles to upgrade herself. Tina was the vice president of development for Pixl, a streaming network for which she sought video content, a term she hated but a job that paid her enough to live alone in a two-bedroom apartment overlooking McCarren Park in Williamsburg, Brooklyn. Her work was frustrating—ideas forever on the brink of becoming television shows but nothing concrete yet, nothing complete, nothing finished. Her enthusiasm for projects always waned as more people got involved and ideas gradually got altered and then shut down altogether.

At Pixl, Tina was in charge of finding content from India so she had been back a few times over the past five years. But it was always to either Delhi or Bombay, where she stayed at a Taj Hotel, took a car and driver everywhere, and partied with producers from all over in rooftop bars and seaside clubs that could have been anywhere in the world. And then she returned to New York City without having seen much of actual India.

Tina Das was conceived in India but born, nine months later, in Columbus, Ohio. Three months later, like her father, she held a coveted American passport. Her mother stubbornly held on to her Indian passport and Green Card. For the first eight years of her life, her parents took her to India every summer and they stayed with her aunt and uncle, the parents of Shefali, the bride, in New Delhi. In the eighth summer, her father got malaria and spent two weeks in Holy Family Hospital and decided, on the flight back, that he didn't want to return to India next year.

"Let's go to London next summer instead," Tina remembered him saying on the flight back that year. He had lost weight and his belt was looped tightly around, his pants bunching at the waist. Back in Ohio, he bought new pants, without pleats, Tina had noticed, and the following summer they went to London, then they went to Ubud, then Stockholm, then Buenos Aires, then Tokyo, and even Colombo the year before Tina left for Yale, but never back to India. Her mother went once when her mother died in Calcutta, but that was all before the divorce.

Last year, Tina had come tantalizingly close to green lighting a reality show that would have featured the best musical talent from around Asia and put them together with a Bollywood music producer to create a band. She had found a K-pop singer from Seoul, a dancer from Ho Chi Minh City, two beatboxing brothers from Sri Lanka, a drummer from Dharavi, the Bombay slum, and a female spoken-word artist from Lahore, but the project fizzled, and Tina had gone home frustrated and depressed and worried about her career. She was still upset that it hadn't moved forward and now all except Sid, the drummer, were committed to other projects. The K-pop singer had joined a reality television show in Singapore as a judge, the two beatboxing brothers had moved to Berlin, the spoken word artist was seven months pregnant and focusing on fashion design, and the dancer from Vietnam was performing with a cruise line in Halong Bay.

Tina felt bad about having let Sid down. Sid, with his easy confidence and priceless bright smile. Sid, who was tall and slim and had a rough beard and laughed easily during the audition and wore his pants baggy and who, back in New York, Tina thought about often— what his life was like in India, who his friends were, who his family was. He was immensely attractive—his confidence, his swagger, his inaccessibility—and he often crossed her mind. After his audition, he had lifted his shirt to wipe the sweat off his face and revealed a perfect set of abs and dark hair trailing into his boxers. Tina had shaken her head, laughed, and called a lunch break.

He had stayed in touch with her and checked in often to see if the show might get back on track and she never had any good news to give him. He had started working part-time as a personal trainer to make money while working on his music. But Tina knew that personal training was just enough money to survive, whereas the show would have allowed him to move his mother out of their slum and into a concrete apartment, and she felt awful that she had let him down. Honestly, he'd said "slum," but she wasn't quite sure what he'd meant. Was it one room in a slum? Was a slum by definition a room? A shack? She had marveled at the sheer size of the blue-tarp-covered expanses of Dharavi she had flown over while landing in Bombay, but she couldn't actually visualize the homes within it. She didn't know how to ask and she didn't want to show up at his doorstep with a camera, even though that would obviously make for good television. Maybe this was why she was struggling to get her projects off the ground—reality television often felt too invasive for her.

When she told Sid she was going to be in Delhi for a week, he had immediately said he would come from Bombay to see her "just to touch base." Tina was dreading seeing him on this trip, dreading looking into his handsome, eager eyes and telling him that there was still no show and no other talent. It was easy to feed Sid fake hope over email but she knew she would have to tell him the truth this week. She would put him in touch with everyone she knew in Bombay in case they wanted to hire a personal trainer, she decided; it was the least she could do for him.

Since she was meeting Sid, Tina could have tried to expense this trip as well but her boss, Rachel Sanders, knew the bride and knew Tina would not be doing any work. But maybe it was time to talk to Rachel about booking her business class for all her future work trips. Sheryl Sandberg said she should lean in, after all. Not that Tina had read the book but really the title told her everything she needed to know. Was Sheryl Sandberg still an appropriate role model or was that over now, Tina wondered. It was hard to keep up sometimes.

It was nearing 11 P.M. and the lounge was gradually emptying out and Marianne and Tina were the only ones sitting at the round tables close to the bar. A bored bartender was leaning behind the bar playing on his phone, and a few others, mostly men in business suits with laptops open in front of them, sat at the tables or on the large armchairs near the floor-to-ceiling windows that spread across the entire far wall. Across the lounge and the empty tables and dirty dishes and folded newspapers, in one corner near the food station, sat Tina's mother, Radha Das, and her boyfriend, David Smith. Tina's mother looked exactly like Tina was likely to look in twenty-five years—her hair, still thick, was in a low bun, carefully colored to hide any hints of gray, and she wore no makeup except a dark brown lipstick. She was slim and had a long neck and looked like she could be one of those "real women" models for the Gap or Uniqlo, a younger Rekha maybe—her mother had that Bollywood glam even though she never watched any Bollywood films. David looked like he belonged in a catalog for eyeglasses or high-end sweaters, maybe Viagra—he was wearing jeans and a black T-shirt, a black jacket on his carry-on suitcase next to him, and Tina could never get used to how all-American David looked. How on earth was her mother, her Indian mother, dating a man like this all of a sudden, Tina wondered. Not quite all of a sudden—two years—but Tina still wasn't used to it. David was the kind of man you took a hiking selfie with, maybe with a big golden dog included.

"Have you noticed that all mixed-race couples are forever taking hiking selfies? What's that all about?" Tina asked Marianne. Marianne was white, as white as could be. Marianne and her blond hair and light blue eyes, but her last name—Laing—threw everyone off even though it was Scottish, and seemed to confuse Marianne herself.

For the last four years Marianne had worked in a test prep kitchen for *Five Senses* magazine. She worked with a team that developed and tested recipes, plated them, photographed them, named them, and wrote the recipes. She had initially been the one hired to write the recipes but now she largely focused on the plating and display of the dishes for shoots. Marianne had a confident aesthetic when it came to her work, and she always seemed to have a strong preference for exactly which way the asparagus should point. Her mother had dedicated the walls in one room of Marianne's childhood home in Bethesda to a collage of pages from the magazine that featured Marianne's work.

Marianne had grown up far more comfortably, with a swimming pool in her backyard and annual summer holidays at their home in Mallorca. Her father was one of the original creators of IMAX films and her mother was a columnist for the weekend section of the Bethesda *Herald*, and now her parents did little other than travel the world wearing pastel-colored linen.

Being blond and from Bethesda would have been so much easier than being brown and from Ohio, Tina thought.

"And it's usually the brown person who posts the picture online because you just know they wouldn't generally go hiking—no Indians go hiking—but the minute they go slightly uphill with a white person, they feel so fit and outdoorsy, they have to post pictures online," Tina said.

"Are you being pissy about David coming to India?" Marianne asked. "Because you and I went hiking last summer and you took a thousand pictures."

Tina looked over at David again. The worst part of this all was that Tina found him attractive. She looked away.

"He's like what I imagine Colin Wrisley turned into," Tina said.

"You remember his last name? That was so long ago! He has three kids now and they all play lacrosse," Marianne said.

"You played lacrosse that entire spring too! Didn't you even try out for Yale's team?"

Marianne shook her head and laughed. She had. She had fallen head over heels for Colin Wrisley and started playing lacrosse—she hated it and was terrible at it—and going to ice hockey games and wearing sports jerseys. That was sophomore year, and that summer he was hiking to Everest base camp, and Marianne said her goodbyes and left her jerseys at the Salvation Army in New Haven and returned to Bethesda and her books for the summer, and only ever saw Colin Wrisley again when they crossed paths in the hallway after her Monday-Wednesday class on women and literature in traditional China. In fact, she remembered, that was where she met Tony Wei, for whom she taught herself how to make soup dumplings. But that ended quickly when he said nothing could ever compare to the soup dumplings at Din Tai Fung, and her heart sank when she realized she had no idea what Din Tai Fung was, and since this was before iPhones she couldn't even excuse herself to the bathroom to google it quickly. And of course, on the heels of that, was Riyaáz from Pakistan—the ultimate international romance, the one who still crossed her mind, the one for whom she had once, late at night, alone in her room, tried draping a scarf like a burqa, leaving nothing visible but her eyes.

Outside, the tarmac glistened black and she could see into the oval windows of parked airplanes. A Singapore Airlines plane taxied slowly toward the runway.

"My father is on this flight too. He's obviously avoiding the lounge," Tina said. "My mother said David's looking forward to going to India because he loves doing yoga. I really wish America had never discovered yoga."

She was folding a page of today's *New York Times* into an origami swan. Three smaller origami swans—one made from a napkin, one from a discarded boarding pass, and one from a *Time* magazine cover— lay on the table in front of her.

"Don't you do yoga at that place across the street from you?" Marianne asked.

"I used to but I think I'm done," Tina said. She also watched the Singapore Airlines plane reach the main runway and thought about all the people in the plane, jostling into position, not yet feeling cramped and annoyed and exhausted. She thought about the young families in the front row with their babies in their laps waiting for the bassinets, hoping the children would sleep through the flight. She thought of the couples off on holiday or returning home after a trip through America. Maybe an Indian family with two parents and two children in high school flying home to Singapore after visiting family in Rochester and going to Niagara Falls. Maybe the mother was flipping through the inflight magazine to find a Bollywood film to watch.

Last week, at the end of her yoga class on North Eleventh Street, the slim Caucasian instructor ended the hour by sprinkling water on all the students and saying "It's holy water, the way they do in Hinduism." Tina opened her eyes—she wasn't supposed to, they were supposed to be in relaxation mode. The teacher caught her eye and smiled and nodded slowly. Tina was used to this in yoga class and she sagely nodded at the instructor and offered her a gentle smile, letting the instructor bask in her Indianness. Then Tina did the same with all the other students who bowed to one another after class, their hands pressed together in namastes. She was certain that the other students lingered during their namaste with her and she felt like a fraud—

because not only did she barely speak Hindi, she struggled to even touch her toes—but still she went around nodding slowly at everyone as if she were Buddha himself.

A few months ago, after too many happy hour cocktails with Marianne, Tom, and her ex-boyfriend Andrew at the Pony Bar on the Upper East Side, Tina, surprising herself the most, suggested dinner at Saravana Bhavan.

"I could definitely go for a tomato-onion uttapam," Tom said, pronouncing it with a hard *t*. Tina saw Marianne smile at him and touch his elbow. Tom buried his face into his brown cable-knit scarf and put his hands into his blazer pockets.

"As long as it's not too spicy," Andrew had said. "I don't want to have to run to the bathroom."

Tina felt her ears get hot with embarrassment—about Andrew and his inability to eat spicy food, but more, worse, about being Indian and having food that was associated with urgent trips to the bathroom. Marianne had grown up eating meat loaf, and her family had all-American traditions like breakfast for dinner every Sunday. Tina had tried suggesting that to her mother when she was home for winter break her sophomore year and her mother had said, "You're too old to be so cutesy, darling. We're having keema khichdi tonight. Now, open up the windows, I don't want the onion to make things smell. And take all the jackets from the downstairs cupboard and put them on the guest bed. The smell of food just lingers and lingers and I won't have us walking all over town smelling like the kitchen of that horrid Indian buffet restaurant."

"WHEN WAS THE LAST time we went on a trip, just us?" Marianne asked, flipping through the same *Time* magazine, now without a cover. "Was it senior year to Cancun?"

"Unless you count that depressing New Year's Eve we spent in Atlantic City," Tina said.

"We are definitely not counting that," Marianne said. "That was when I nearly burned down our rental trying to make dumplings. Remember?"

"I do remember. And then we ended up having bologna on white bread for our New Year's Eve dinner."

"And New Year's morning breakfast," Marianne said. "What a disaster. I'm glad we're doing this trip just us."

"I'm so grateful," Tina said. "Forget my mother and her boyfriend, I have you here and this is going to be fun."

Marianne was watching Tina's mother and David.

"I can see why you find him sexy," Marianne said.

"I should never have told you that," Tina said.

"It's the dad-bod thing. I get it," Marianne said.

"Maybe I should call him 'Daddy.'" Tina said. She laughed. "Daddy David Smith."

"You could be his hot young trophy wife. If you had kids, people in Williamsburg would mistake you for the nanny."

"No, that's taking it too far!" Tina said laughing, throwing a pistachio at Marianne. "I'd have to speak in really clear English to show I wasn't the nanny."

"And you would have to wear expensive workout clothes and always carry Starbucks."

"And then all the other Lululemon mothers would feel guilty that they had assumed I was the nanny."

"And they would all say, 'Not that there's anything wrong with being the nanny. My nanny saves my life,'" Marianne added.

"Like that mother who burst in to get the kids out of the interview with the BBC dad."

"Yes!" Marianne said. "The one everyone assumed was the nanny because she was Asian."

"I made the same assumption," Tina admitted. "But then I read that she was the mother before Andrew, and when he said that he thought she was the nanny, I used that to start a fight with him and call him racist."

"It's a wonder you two lasted as long as you did," Marianne said.

"Daddy David Smith," Tina sighed.

Marianne looked over at them again. Radha and David both had reading glasses on and newspapers in their hands but it was clear that they weren't actually reading. Seeing them made Marianne wonder if she should have put more pressure on Tom to come to Delhi with her. She had asked once in passing but followed it up by saying Tina didn't think she was bringing Andrew. Then Tina and Andrew had broken up, putting the question to rest.

A few weeks ago, she'd shown him the glittery glass bangles she had bought in Jackson Heights for the wedding.

"You're going to look so beautiful," Tom had said. "You should have this trip with Tina. I'm sure she'll appreciate that. But you will be on my mind constantly."

She had rubbed her fingers together and said, "Damn it. Now there's glitter everywhere."

Tom had gone to the kitchen and brought back a wet paper towel and handed it to Marianne and said, "This will help with the glitter. Let's go out for dinner tonight. We haven't wasted money for fun in a long time."

A little over twelve months ago, Marianne was sitting on the 6 train on the way to see her gynecologist on the Upper East Side and she was reading the previous week's issue of the *New Yorker*. She looked up to see what stop they were passing when she saw a handsome black man right across from her reading the same issue. He looked up then too, perhaps sensing her gaze, and she lifted her magazine to him and smiled.

"I'm also always at least an issue behind," the man who turned out to be Tom said. He had an earnest face, a little nerdy with his glasses and collared shirt and tidy slacks.

"I panic every single Tuesday when it arrives," Marianne said.

At Grand Central the train emptied out and Tom crossed over to Marianne's side of the train and said, "Have you ever submitted to the caption contest?"

"I have! Several times," Marianne said. "Never made it."

"I made it to the final three once," Tom said.

"You're like a celebrity," Marianne said. "I've never met a real-life *New Yorker* cartoon-caption-contest finalist before."

"We should exchange numbers. I'll show you my entry sometime."

At the gynecologist, Marianne asked to have an IUD put in.

Tom was from Newton, Massachusetts, which, she learned, was a lot like being from Bethesda but with different sports allegiances. His father was a professor of African-American studies at Tufts and his mother was a pediatric dentist, and Marianne's parents had met them for brunch in Brooklyn one sunny weekend morning and everyone got along easily, perfectly, and the two fathers even discovered that they had taken flying lessons at the same flying club outside Westchester. It was all so perfect on paper, maybe too perfect, and in any case, Tom hadn't even mentioned proposing and Marianne worried that he never would and she was starting to get itchy feet again, wondering if maybe she needed something more exotic, more exciting, and less familiar.

"HOW DO YOU MAKE these so quickly?" Marianne asked Tina as she picked up the origami swan made from the *Time* magazine cover. "I'm going to keep this."

Tina took it out of her hands and thoughtlessly crushed it and said, "Don't take that one. I'll make you a better one."

"Let's get more free champagne," Marianne said.

"Can you believe your mother is bringing David Smith?" Neel Das, Tina's father said as he approached his daughter and her best friend at the bar getting refills on their champagne glasses. He put his bag down at the table where their things were and stood next to them at the bar. He had been wandering around the duty-free shops trying to avoid his wife—ex-wife—but since the flight was over two hours late, he had no option but to come to the lounge and face everyone.

"A champagne for me too, please," he said to the man at the bar.

"It's prosecco. But still good," the man at the bar said. "Where are you folks flying to today?"

"India," Marianne said. "Where are you from?"

"Mali," the man said, as he popped the cork on the prosecco bottle and smiled at Marianne.

"I've always wanted to go," Marianne said to him.

"You have?" Tina and the bartender asked her.

"Of course," Marianne glared at her. "Timbuktu has always sounded so magical to me."

The bartender laughed even though Marianne had not meant it as a joke.

"Look at how broad his chest is. Can you imagine how handsome he'll look in Indian clothes?" Mr. Das asked, looking across the lounge at David.

He shook his head and took a sip of his drink. The three of them took their glasses and walked back to the table where they had been sitting and Mr. Das looked at the origami swans on the table.

"Why are you making the swans again?" he asked Tina. "Are you anxious? I read somewhere that most air crashes happen in the first three minutes after takeoff."

"That doesn't sound right," Tina said.

"I'll believe you," Marianne said. "Then I can relax after three minutes."

"Exactly. I download three-minute-meditation apps for takeoff," Mr. Das said. "But then I don't use it and instead spend three minutes staring at the faces of the flight attendants and then I order a drink."

Mr. Das picked up a handful of pistachios while looking around the lounge and tossed them into his mouth. He also sputtered as the shells hit his teeth and poked the inside of his mouth. He spat them out into a napkin.

"They could at least shell the nuts," Mr. Das said.

"Why did you agree to be on the same flight?" Tina asked, placing her glass down. "And why are you wearing a turtleneck? Don't they give you headaches?"

She picked up the remaining origami swans and crushed them all into a ball.

"Your mother booked my ticket as well and she thought it would be nice for all of us to be on the same flight and who am I to argue? I'm wearing a turtleneck because *Esquire* says it's dignified and makes men look more intelligent," Mr. Das said. He picked up the ball of crushed swans and tried separating them and pressing out the wrinkles. "He might look good but there's no way a restaurant manager can afford a business class ticket to India, let alone one for her as well. But how on earth does his gray hair make him look so dignified?"

"Ma probably paid," Tina said.

"Exactly," Mr. Das said. "With my money."

"You don't pay alimony," Tina said.

"Not my money exactly but family money, Tina," Mr. Das said. "Your inheritance."

"Why are you swinging your arm?" Tina asked, noticing her father swaying his right arm off the side of his chair.

He lifted his wrist to Tina and said, "Fitbit."

He had bought a Fitbit last week but discovered that it tracked steps based on movement so he had been keeping his arm swinging even when he wasn't walking in order to increase his step count. Figuring out how to maximize his step count while minimizing the number of actual steps he took was more challenging than just walking around endlessly. Maybe he would buy one of those mobiles they give infants to keep them occupied and attach his Fitbit to it. But that movement might be too smooth to register as steps. What he needed was one of those large clocks like his family used to have in Calcutta with a swinging pendulum.

"Marianne," he said. "How have you been? Where is your skinny little husband? Tell him to come along. He can still hop on a flight tomorrow and be there for the fun parts."

"Just boyfriend," Marianne said. "Not husband. And I can't imagine Shefali would be too happy about having to rethink the seating arrangements last minute."

Tina and Mr. Das laughed.

"Marianne. Sometimes I genuinely forget how white you are," Tina said. "Seating arrangements? There's going to be over a thousand people at this wedding. Nobody's sitting anywhere."

"You know, for our wedding, the invitation card said *You and your friends and family are invited to celebrate*. I didn't recognize more than half of the guests at our wedding," Mr. Das said. "Book that fellow a flight. I like him. Tina, that's the kind of man you need to meet. Marriage material—isn't that what your generation says?"

"I don't need any kind of man, Papa," Tina said. "Isn't that how you raised me? Not to need a husband or a boyfriend."

"Everyone has a boyfriend," Mr. Das said, no longer listening. "Even your goddamn mother. Sorry, I meant, even your lovely mother. Not just his chest, even his shoulders are broad. Do you think he lifts weights?"

Mr. Das twisted around in his chair to look at his ex-wife and her boyfriend again. He raised his glass at them and smiled, and David waved energetically while Radha nodded gently in his direction. Mr. Das swiveled back around and had a large gulp of prosecco.

"You're being awfully nice," Tina said. "Are you seeing a therapist?"

"No therapists for me, Tina. Living with your mother all those years was enough. I'm sure her patients get a lot from her but I personally am sick of being analyzed. That's for David Smith to deal with now."

"Then why the sudden generosity, Uncle?" Marianne said.

"Marianne, I like that you call me Uncle. You're an honorary Indian," he said.

He pulled at his collar.

"It's hot in here. Is anyone else hot? This turtleneck is giving me a headache. Do either of you have Tylenol in your purse?"

"It's so hot in here," Radha said to David at the opposite end of the lounge, near the big windows. She took off her Eileen Fisher black cardigan under which she was wearing a black, sleeveless tunic top over a pair of black leggings. While planning what to wear for the journey, she had googled "best travel outfits" and scrolled through a slideshow of celebrities in airports. How did women travel in such tight jeans and high heels?

"How do I look?" she asked David. She hadn't had her arms bare outside a beach or a bedroom in nearly two decades and the skin on her shoulder was wrinkled in a way no models in magazines ever wrinkle but it didn't matter. Let young people waste time worrying about their bodies, their perfect bodies—she was happy with this one, wrinkles and all, especially sitting here right now drinking a glass of wine with David.

"Beautiful," David said. "Better than anyone else in this entire airport."

This was exactly why she could never trust David's compliments. If she had asked Neel the same question, he would have looked at her, really looked at her, and said, "None of us can compete with the youngsters anymore but you look quite good for your age. I don't know why you always complain about your upper arms—they're only slightly big for your body."

But David always took compliments too far—she knew perfectly well that she didn't look better than young people, and by saying that she did, he undid the compliment. Never mind. The bare arms were not about him, they were about herself. It was what she told all her clients all the time—needing external validation is risky. She glanced quickly at her husband—ex-husband—sitting there talking to their daughter and her best friend. Why was Neel swinging one arm continuously? She noticed the Fitbit on his wrist. Right, his step count.

David, meanwhile, was flipping through a guidebook on India. On the cover there were three poor children smiling and showing teeth so white you'd think they belonged in Hollywood.

"Let's go sit with Tina and the others," Radha said to him.

"May we join you?" she asked as they approached Tina, Marianne, and Neel. How silly to be so formal with her own daughter and ex-husband.

"Of course," Mr. Das said. "Come, come. Have a seat. Nice to see you, David Smith. Radha, I was just telling the girls here that I am following in your footsteps. I have met someone. Well, I have met someone over email and I am about to meet her in person."

Tina drained the rest of her drink.

"Meera and Rakesh introduced me to this woman in East Delhi who runs a matchmaking agency for widows," Mr. Das was saying. He turned to David and added, "Meera and Rakesh are Shefali's parents, David Smith. Meera is my sister. They're the ones paying for all of our rooms at the club. Yours as well. You probably know that. Anyway, this Mrs. Ray has clients all over Delhi and even the United States and I think maybe Singapore now. And she introduced me to Mrs. Sethi and we've been in touch over email these past few months."

"I have to use the bathroom," Tina said, and she got up and walked away from the group.

Now her father was going to start dating. And he was discussing it so openly. She stood near the bar and looked back toward her father, still alternately tugging at the neck of his turtleneck and swinging his arm, speaking to her mother and David.

"You aren't a widow," Radha said, slightly more softly, perhaps, than she had intended.

"Widower," David said. "Male widows are called widowers. But there's so few nobody even uses the right term for them."

Mr. Das looked over at David and nodded. Smart man.

"He is correct," Mr. Das said. He lifted his glass in appreciation and continued.

"And you are correct as well, Radha. I am not a widower; you aren't dead. But there are so few male widowers that Mrs. Ray also works with male divorcés. Not female ones, though, so, Radha, you're out of luck."

"It sounds like a scam," Radha said. "And I have David; I don't need some strange matchmaker in East Delhi."

"Of course," Mr. Das said. "Anyway, this Mrs. Sethi seems absolutely lovely."

Even though he was playing it cool now, Mr. Das had also been rather surprised when his sister suggested this. But the world was changing, Mr. Das thought. He had been so embarrassed by the idea of divorce at first, thinking Indians didn't get divorced unless they were academics or artists, but clearly India had been changing behind his back if a widowed woman was running a matchmaking agency for widows and divorcés in Delhi.

Tina came back to the group with another drink and put her full glass down at the edge of the table that was filled with empty dishes and used cutlery and crumpled napkins. The woman clearing up plates and glasses came over to their group to collect the used dishes. She looked from Marianne to David and back to Marianne again and said, "Gosh, don't you look just like your father. Lovely."

"He isn't my father," Marianne said.

The woman ignored her, picked up the used plates and glasses, and said, "It's nice to see families traveling together. You have a nice trip."

"I suppose I do look a bit like you, David," Marianne said to break the silence.

"God this turtleneck is tight," Mr. Das said. "Radha, you were wise to wear a sleeveless top. It looks decent too."

"I really hope the flight isn't delayed much longer," Marianne said. "I'll go check."

She got up and walked toward the front desk to check the flight status. Poor Tina was going to have an exhausting week ahead. Marianne called Tom. He didn't answer. She checked the flight status—there were no further delays—and then tried again. He answered groggily, "What's wrong?"

"I just wanted to hear your voice once more before I left."

"That's nice," Tom said. He had fallen asleep with his light still on. He felt around his sheets to find his glasses and put them on and reached for his watch on the bedside table. "I miss you already."

"Did you turn the light off before you fell asleep?" Marianne asked.

"Of course not," Tom said. He leaned back against the wall and yawned.

"And put your glasses on the bedside table before you sleep. You're going to break them in bed one of these days and you'll be really stranded," Marianne said. "Did you confirm your dental appointment for tomorrow?"

"I canceled it, actually," Tom said. "My mother is coming down for the day and she wants to see the Oculus."

"I can't believe a train station has become a tourist attraction," Marianne said.

"I can. It's beautiful architecture. You just take it for granted because it's in New York and not, I don't know, in Budapest somewhere," Tom said.

Marianne smiled.

"Get some sleep," she said. "And take your mother to Century 21 to shop after you see the Oculus."

"It's her favorite store in the city. Then she'll try to drag me to Nordstrom Rack and we'll argue and then feel guilty and have a cup of coffee together and talk about my sister's poor life choices in order to reconnect," Tom said. "Have a good flight, Marianne. I really do miss you already. I'm going to leave my light on to sleep because it just doesn't feel right to switch it off myself."

Marianne hung up the phone in time to see Mr. Das and David marching out of the lounge. Was a life partner supposed to be a window or a mirror? Marianne wondered.

"David Smith here says I should get a pair of wireless headphones," Mr. Das said. "Want to come along?"

Marianne waved at them to go ahead and she returned to Tina and her mother sitting alone together.

"Auntie, I like what you're wearing," Marianne said.

"Thank you, darling," Radha said.

"I wish I could just embrace my thighs and wear short skirts. Not that your arms need embracing. I mean your arms are really nice," Marianne said.

"Relax," Radha said. "I know what you mean. It's easier to embrace your imperfections once you're older. You girls—although it's really very silly to call you girls now—you ladies are at a hard stage. It gets easier, I think. I'm glad you two decided not to bring your boyfriends along. This will be a nice trip for you."

"Andrew and I broke up. I told you. Remember? Anyway, I didn't think anyone was bringing boyfriends along. It's a really juvenile word," Tina said. "I'm going to go see what Papa is doing."

Radha thought of stopping her, of asking her to stay, but she knew there was no point. She and Neel had been divorced for nearly a decade and she had met David two years ago, but Tina still had her anger. She didn't seem to have the same anger toward her father, though, as he was preparing to go off and date some woman he barely knew. What was he trying to prove?

Tina was also thinking about what her father was trying to prove as she walked out near the entrance to the lounge and sat down on one of the chairs there. From here, when the sliding glass doors opened, she could look out at the main terminal and she could also look into the lounge. A woman in a dark blue skirt suit sat at the front desk, her blond hair pulled into a neat ponytail, the computer screen reflecting in her glasses. This part of the lounge was cold, near the door, and Tina pulled her jacket closed and leaned back into the chair. The woman at the front desk was probably younger than her, Tina thought. Suddenly, at thirty-two, it felt like the whole world was younger than her. The woman at the desk looked up and caught Tina's eyes and smiled. Tina smiled back.

She envied that woman, so sure of herself. This woman who knew exactly how to do her hair and wore neutral lipstick and came to JFK every day to work and probably went home to a comfortable apartment in Queens, maybe with a cat, and watched one episode of a television show while knitting a throw. She probably went to yoga classes and left actually feeling calmer.

It had been a while since Tina had done anything from beginning to end. Maybe she would teach herself knitting just to get the satisfaction of a finished product. All the television shows she developed went nowhere. She had picked a difficult career for someone who liked finished products. Everything in television was forever in progress, pre-production, production, occasionally post-production, and then rarely, so rarely, actually on-screen. She didn't know the odds when she first started. Maybe she could run a marathon to accomplish something concrete but that seemed tiring.

The woman took off her glasses, leaned back, and said, "Where are you flying to today? Are you on the delayed flight to Heathrow?"

Tina nodded and said, "And on to New Delhi from there. My cousin's getting married."

"A big Indian wedding!" the woman said. "What fun. I've always wanted to go to India. I'm jealous."

The woman looked around at the empty lounge and continued, "I get jealous of everyone who comes through here. I've never even left America. Soon, I hope. Maybe for my honeymoon."

She held up her left hand and pointed at her ring.

"Congratulations," Tina said.

"Japan is where I really want to go, though. Have you ever been?"

Tina shook her head.

"My fiancé wants to go to South Africa but I'm pushing for Japan. My second choice is Brazil but he's been there once before so that probably won't happen. Compromise, right? That's what they say about marriage!"

She looked so happy. Tina said, "Congratulations again. I hope you make it to Japan soon," and walked out of the lounge.

British Airways Flight 143, London–New Delhi

S OMEWHERE OVER TURKEY, SICK OF READING, SICK OF MOVIES, and sick of sleeping, Radha got up and walked to the flight attendant galley area to get a ginger ale and look out of the window into the dark sky. She never drank ginger ale except on flights.

There was nothing to see beyond darkness outside the small window near the flight attendants. A male flight attendant in dark blue pants and a tucked-in blue shirt was tidying up the galley area.

"Started in Heathrow or coming in from somewhere?" the flight attendant asked.

"JFK," Radha said.

"You must be tired. Ice cream?" he asked Radha.

She shook her head. He opened a small chocolate ice cream bar for himself and sat down on his seat.

"Restless more than tired," she said. She looked down the dimly lit aisle of the plane and said, "I'm traveling with my ex-husband, current boyfriend, and daughter."

"Forget ice cream. Need a whiskey shot in that ginger ale?" he asked.

"How long do you spend in Delhi?" Radha asked.

"I'm here for forty-eight hours and then doing this same route back to Heathrow," the flight attendant said. He got up to throw away the ice cream wrapper and then restocked the small wicker basket with packets of chips and biscuits. "But then I'm taking a month off and going on a cruise with my wife, son, daughter-in-law, and granddaughters. I've never been on a cruise before."

"That sounds like fun," Radha said. "A family holiday."

"I get seasick on boats," the flight attendant said. He was dreading this holiday but his daughter-in-law had planned the whole thing and his wife had never liked the daughter-in-law much and always felt guilty about it so she had agreed to this cruise and forced him to also sound enthusiastic. He would try one of those motion sickness wristbands.

A small beep sounded and he looked up and said, "Six C. Off I go. I bet they just want a glass of water."

He filled a plastic glass with water and said to Radha, "This way I'll save a trip," and went down the aisle.

Radha leaned against the bathroom door and looked at all the passengers. Next to her own empty seat she saw David's face lit up by the light of his Kindle. He certainly was handsome.

"Is this door stuck?" came Mr. Das's voice, suddenly frantic, from inside the bathroom. "Help! Hello? Flight attendant! Pilot! Tina! Anyone?"

He pushed against the door and Radha said, "Ow, no, Neel, stop pushing, you aren't stuck."

She moved away from the door and Mr. Das burst out of the bathroom and said, "That was terrifying. You know I'm always worried about getting trapped in small spaces. And an airplane bathroom would be the worst. Imagine the embarrassment of having to knock and bang and shout to get rescued and then all the passengers stare at you as you return to your seat."

"Are you nervous about going back to India?" Radha asked Mr. Das.

Mr. Das looked at her then he looked down the aisle and said, "You know people cry more easily on flights? Something about the altitude affects your emotions, believe it or not. I was watching an episode of *The Office* and nearly cried."

"Some of those episodes will make you cry at any altitude, though," Radha said.

"True."

"We were a happy family the last time we made this trip all together," Radha said.

"Ice cream?" the flight attendant, now returned to the galley, asked Mr. Das.

"I would love some, thank you," Mr. Das said.

"I love this time of a flight," the flight attendant said. "The silence, watching everyone sleeping or watching movies or reading. It's such a forced break from the world."

He went back to the galley to get himself a cup of coffee. In the third row Radha could see Tina and Marianne fast asleep. Tina's face was covered with her blanket and her arm was draped over the side of her seat.

"I'm going to put her arm in so it doesn't get knocked," Radha said to Mr. Das.

"I'm going to ask the flight attendant if he can spot a nervous flier by the way they stare at him during takeoff and landing," Mr. Das said.

Radha gently moved her daughter's arm up to her side, away from the aisle. She then covered her exposed arm with the blanket and touched her fingertips to Tina's hair. Tina, always a light sleeper, could smell her mother's perfume and opened her eyes and peered out from behind the blanket to see her walking back to her seat. Then she looked ahead and saw her father in the galley at the front of the cabin talking to the flight attendant. She could see him nodding and nibbling an ice cream bar.

Radha sat back down, leaned into David, and said, "I'm nervous about this trip."

David put his large hand on her leg and left it there.

Colebrookes Country Club, New Delhi, India: Jet Lag Is So Nice at First When You Wake up Early and Energized

OF COURSE ROCCO GALLAGHER WAS HERE FOR THE WEDDING. Why was Tina surprised? Early her first morning in India, energized from jet lag, she was sitting out on the porch outside the cottage she was sharing with Marianne for the week. There were about twenty cottages around the grassy knoll. Tina had a lilac shawl around her shoulders and was looking out onto the Colebrookes gardens trying desperately to conjure up a sense of nostalgia. Home, she thought, then slapped dead a mosquito against her right calf. She grimaced at the trace of blood on her palm, looked around, wiped it against the cushion on the next wicker chair, and scratched her calf.

She had never lived in India but she had always enjoyed the feeling of looking like everyone else here. In America, Lizzie Ainsley in middle school had thrown out the plastic fork and spoon from Tina's lunch tray one day and said, "I read a book that said Indian people only eat with their fingers so I guess you don't need these."

It was chicken nuggets and tater tots for lunch that day so Tina didn't need the cutlery but she still made a point of walking back to the steel cutlery table, getting replacements and using the fork to spear the crumbling tater tots and deliver them to her mouth.

She had told Andrew this story once, over a bottle of wine and a plate of jalapeño poppers somewhere in Fort Greene.

"I hope it's easier being Indian in middle school in America now," Tina had said to Andrew. "You know, my mother always wanted to name me Priyanka but she was worried I'd be made fun of for my name so she picked the race-neutral Tina. I bet all the Indian kids are named Priyanka now."

"Probably some white kids too," Andrew added. "But come on, being Indian, even fifteen years ago, could not have been that hard."

"My classmates used to ask if I preferred eating monkey or elephant," Tina said.

"Okay, my classmates used to say they wanted to have sex with my mother. The term 'MILF' had just been coined and my mother, well, you know how she likes tight jeans and low-cut tops," Andrew said. "Middle school sucks for everyone."

"But yours has nothing to do with your race," Tina said.

"And yours has nothing to do with your mother," Andrew said. "Look, I'm not defending what people said but sometimes you label someone racist when it's maybe just personal distaste. Like instead of saying this person doesn't like you, it's easier to say this person doesn't like Indians. I'm not talking about your middle school classmates, all kids are assholes, but I'm talking about now. Like last week when you called the barista at that coffee shop racist because she was rude to you."

"I can't believe you're taking her side," Tina said.

"There was a long line and you asked to sample oat milk," Andrew said.

"It doesn't sound like a real milk," Tina had said.

Less than a week later they had broken up.

Another mosquito landed on Tina's arm. She looked down at it, this terrifying tiny creature that was more dangerous to humans than any shark or roaring lion.

Could she pitch Pixl a documentary on children suffering from malaria or dengue? She could make the opening sequence like *Jaws* only it would be *Bites*.

A pre-winter haze hovered over the Colebrookes lawns. It looked romantic even though Tina knew it was pollution. But the thing with Delhi pollution was that it never felt sinister when you were in it for just a few days. Having constantly read about it in the news recently, she had put an anti-pollution mask in her suitcase but she knew she wasn't going to use it. On the circular lawn, a man in a brown khaki uniform and a loosely tied turban on his head lazily raked the grass.

Memories usually made things seem smaller in reality but Colebrookes looked bigger than Tina remembered. Shefali's family used to come here every day, and whenever Tina had visited India as a child, she used to love being invited to play tennis or feed the horses and then have masala cheese toast, slices of creamy Black Forest cake, and bottles of fizzy, sweet cream soda. It all felt so decadent, the way the butlers wore uniforms and called them Miss Tina and Miss Shefali even though they were nine years old. Shefali's father's side of the family had been members for generations. It was next to impossible to get in now, Shefali's father always bragged.

"It's not about the fees," he said. "This isn't one of those horrid new clubs where you can just pay your way in. You need to have history—ideally have a road in Delhi with your family name on the sign. These new-new clubs, they're available to everyone and their mother and the staff act snooty and there's no sense of hospitality. You know that new Saket Recreational Centre? An undercover journalist discovered that key parties were being organized there."

"What are key parties?" Tina had asked. Nobody answered, and it had taken Tina half a decade to find out.

On the far side of the grass stood a row of cars—mostly white Ambassadors and some black, expensive-looking cars with tinted windows. Birds chirped high up in the neem trees and horns beeped faintly on the main road but, at 6 A.M., it was decidedly silent and peaceful. Except for the sudden *thwack* of pigeon poop landing on Tina's chair millimeters from her arm. Tina looked down at the white splatter and considered moving chairs but then remembered she had just wiped mosquito blood on the other cushion. "Never mind," she told herself. "This is the charm of India. Home."

Her father always said that Indians believed a bird pooping on you to be a sign of good luck, Tina remembered. What a country of optimists.

Maybe Pixl would go for a documentary on global superstitions. No, that would blur very quickly into religion and somehow offend everyone.

Her peaceful contemplation ended when a dark blue Jaguar with tinted windows thumping music came speeding down the drive, churning up dust. It stopped in front of one of the cottages a few doors short of Tina's. Two tall men stepped out, both wearing jeans and button-down shirts, one tucked, one half-tucked. One of the men held a cigarette, but that was all Tina could make out from where she sat. The dark Jaguar pulled ahead and came to a stop in front of Tina. The passenger-side window went down and Karan, the brother of the groom, stuck out his head with hair so perfectly gelled that a tornado wouldn't budge it.

"Tina's here," Karan said.

From the driver's side, cigarette in his mouth, Pavan, the groom, ducked down and said, "Welcome! Shefali said you were arriving last night. Settled in? We would stop and chat but I was supposed to be home about . . ." Pavan looked at his watch ". . . four hours ago, and Shefali keeps threatening to call off the wedding so we need to go."

Tina had always liked Pavan, even though she was surprised at how quickly her cousin had decided to marry him.

"AT SOME POINT, YOU'VE just got to do it," Shefali had said. "I'm not crossing thirty without a ring on my finger like some sad sack. I don't want to get a cat."

This was just over a year ago at the farmer's market in Williamsburg. Shefali was holding a hibiscus iced tea in one hand and the huge diamond ring on her finger was catching the bright autumn sunlight perfectly.

"I know . . . you're almost forty," Shefali added. "But, I mean, it's different for you."

"Thirty-two, Shefali," Tina said. "I'm turning thirty-three."

Shefali stood looking at some sprigs of lavender.

"Sure," she said, absentmindedly twirling the ring on her finger. "I need to get this tightened. It'll be a disaster if I lose it. But I told Pavan exactly where to get it so I could just replace it pretty easily if I had to—not that my parents would be happy about that. You know how it is for old people—if you have to buy two rings, you better be able to show the world both rings or at least somehow let everyone know you bought a second ring that was just as expensive as the first one. But anyway, what I meant was that it's different for you because you've chosen different things."

She gestured vaguely around and Tina shook her head at the ease with which Shefali knew she could replace a forty-thousand-dollar ring.

"You want to live alone and be a New Yorker and make a point and you're happy doing all that," Shefali continued. "I wish I could be happy doing that but I want the boring stuff—I want to change my name and be married and have a home with vases that always have fresh peonies, you know? Pavan's grandmother has a greenhouse full of exquisite flowers."

She glanced at a slim black woman standing near them carrying a beautiful baby, face out in a BabyBjörn, his chubby arms reaching for everything.

"I want that," Shefali whispered. "Look how beautiful she looks."

Tina turned to look and the baby caught a fistful of her hair and tugged.

"Ow!"

The mother grabbed the baby's hand and started slowly undoing his fingers while laughing and said, "Balthazar! No pulling hair. I'm so sorry."

Tina just stood there waiting for the baby to release her and Shefali said, "Not a problem at all. We were just admiring you and your baby."

The woman smiled at them and kissed the top of her baby's head. She handed over eight dollars for a small brown sachet of dried lavender and walked away, two strands of Tina's hair clasped tightly in Balthazar's fist. Tina rubbed her scalp and inhaled a lavender sprig deeply. Wasn't it meant to help you relax?

"YOU'VE BEEN SPOTTED," Karan said, glancing up at the rearview mirror. "Reacquaint yourself with our friends, Tina. We'll see you later in the day."

With that, the Jaguar pulled away and Tina looked up to see the two men walking toward her. The one with the cigarette in his hand, she saw now, was unmistakably Rocco Gallagher. Could she retreat back into her cottage, pretending she hadn't seen him? She had to; she hadn't even brushed her teeth yet. She squinted her eyes, as if the sun was blinding her, and nodded at them the way, she imagined, one would nod at a stranger in the distance. Escape at hand, she took two confident steps backward, and fell over a potted bougainvillea. The pot broke into pieces and Tina landed squarely in the spilled soil, the crushed bougainvillea nestled into her armpit.

TINA HAD LAST SEEN Rocco two years ago in London when he had slipped out of her room at the St. Martins Lane Hotel early in the morning.

She'd agreed to meet Shefali in London on her way back to New York after a weeklong business trip to Bombay. By coincidence, Shefali had been on her way to Nice to partake in a vintage car rally through France. Tina had worked the whole flight to finish a partnership proposal for an ad agency in Bombay—this had also never come to fruition. The VP of the ad agency gave birth to twin daughters and Tina never heard from her again—and hadn't slept. She'd landed at Heathrow Airport early on a Thursday morning and gone straight to the hotel in Leicester Square, stopping only for a sausage puff and a cup of coffee. She fell asleep for the remainder of the day, waking up at dusk to a slew of text messages from Shefali wondering where the hell she was.

Shefali was waiting for her at the bar downstairs with a very handsome white man and a long-limbed Pakistani-British woman who was a comedian of some repute on her way to do a stand-up set in Covent Garden. Tina wondered, as she often did, where Shefali found friends like these. She never saw Zahra, the stunning Pakistani woman, after that night but the handsome man turned out to be Rocco, from Australia, lately of Bombay, who Shefali had met at the previous year's car rally in Lausanne. The rally kicked off at the Château d'Ouchy, and Shefali and Rocco had shared the driving of a small white and green Morris Minor convertible for the first twenty-four hours and hit it off enough to meet again for a pre-rally drink in London. Two glasses of Sauvignon Blanc later, Zahra the comedian had to head to her show and Shefali wanted to go with her. She asked Tina to come along but Tina said she was too exhausted for stand-up comedy and begged off, staying at the St. Martins Lane hotel bar with Rocco for another drink. From there, on Rocco's recommendation, they ended up at the Boheme Kitchen and Bar sharing a French onion soup and a porterhouse steak. Rocco had ordered, and Tina remembered how odd she found it that he wanted to share soup so soon after meeting.

Tina also remembered how much he made her laugh that night, how little he was interested in kissing her, and how interested this had made her in kissing him. After dinner, they had walked past a man on the sidewalk auctioning off a box set of perfumes, a cluster of women gathered around him shouting out numbers. Rocco had rushed up to the group and shouted out ten pounds, twenty, twenty-five, all the way up to fifty, at which point he won the box set of perfumes and handed it to Tina as a gift.

"To remember this magical night," he said, right as a double-decker bus turned a corner inches away from them. "May every London cliché come true."

Tina put the perfumes in her purse, quite charmed by this impulsive bidding, but when they went back down the same street a little while later, they saw the perfume seller sitting on a sidewalk with the other people who had been bidding, all drinking beer.

"I was cheated. They were all in on it. Come on," Rocco said, grabbing Tina's hand. "That's not a gift I can give you so that means we have to give all three bottles to strangers. Let's go."

Tina remembered now that Rocco had pulled her purse off her shoulder, opened it, and looked for the bottles. Inside her purse he found a small, red mesh bag that contained her makeup.

"You don't need makeup," he said. "Throw this out."

"Don't be an asshole. All men think they don't want a woman with makeup but that's just because they're too dumb to see well-applied makeup. It's the best trick we play on you," Tina said. "Give my purse back."

"You carry vitamin D pills around?" Rocco asked, taking out the white pill bottle and rattling it around.

Tina pulled her purse back, took out the three bottles of perfume, and handed them to him.

"Do what you want," she had said. "I'm going back to my hotel."

"No, wait. We bought these together, we have to get rid of them together. Don't get mad so easily," Rocco had said and for whatever reason, probably the stubble on his face, Tina had agreed.

They gave one to a woman in a tight dress standing in line outside a club. They gave one to a woman smoking a cigarette by herself outside Wagamama. And for the last one, Rocco flagged down a taxi, got in, asked the taxi driver if he had a wife, gave him the bottle to give to his wife, and got back out. A taxi driver in New York would have cursed him for that, despite the free perfume, but this British taxi driver apologized for some reason.

From there, they had gone to another bar—she couldn't remember which one now, but it was near Seven Dials and it was in a basement—and they had each done a bump of cocaine off a key, had another drink, talked for what seemed like hours, and ended up back in her room at the hotel because Rocco was staying in a hostel in Brixton, since he had spent all his money on nonrefundable accommodations along the vintage car rally route and didn't want to take a bus or taxi all the way back out there that night. They hadn't had sex, of that Tina was sure. They had kissed a bit, nothing spectacular, and both fallen into bed and asleep before any clothes could come off. No, she was forgetting a detail. Soon after they had fallen asleep, she had woken back up and walked downstairs in search of a McDonald's, in desperate need of chicken nuggets. She hadn't found any and had returned to the hotel room and looked at Rocco, marveled at his jawline, and fallen asleep again.

The next morning, in a daze, she gave Rocco her number and told him it was a pleasure meeting him and then felt relieved when he left her alone in the big, fluffy white bed with nothing to do except order room service and laze around until she had to meet Shefali for lunch. He never called. The night had lingered in her memory and from time to time she googled him. She had been fascinated by him, his way of inhabiting the world, so at ease. How he'd traveled solo through Brazil and Cambodia, how he'd been in a motorbiking accident in Ubud and stayed there for two months recovering. How he'd moved to India.

Back in New York City, she had met Andrew, who was everything Rocco wasn't, and she found that safer, if duller. On a real estate site, Andrew had showed her a listing for a "compact" two-bedroom house on a quiet lane in Portland. It had a small front and backyard, and the current owners had a bright yellow plastic swing and slide set up on the grass. In the pictures, the skies were blue and the kitchen counters were clean and Andrew had said, "I should be able to afford something like this in the future."

* * *

"DOES THIS MEAN ZAHRA might be here too?" Rocco asked now, looking around the Colebrookes driveway as if Zahra might be hiding behind a tree. "She was a stunner."

"I don't think Shefali and Zahra are still friends," Tina said, still on the ground. "But then, I didn't think you and Shefali were either and here we are."

"Here we are, indeed," Rocco said with a smile. He reached his hand down to Tina.

She looked up at him and shook her head and said, "As you can imagine, this is humiliating. Can you both turn around so I can get myself up out of this planter?"

The two men faced away and Rocco said, "You must be jet-lagged. I only ever meet you when you're jet-lagged, it seems."

"I'm fine," she said, back up to standing, brushing off the seat of her pants. "You can face me now. There's just no graceful way to get up from the ground after you turn thirty."

"Who are you here with?" Rocco's friend asked, looking over Tina's shoulder. "I'm Kai, by the way."

Kai, East Asian–looking, at least partially, was tall and handsome and wearing a neatly tucked-in shirt. He had glasses on and was the kind of guy that Marianne would start reading obscure Chinese science-fiction books for.

"My friend Marianne. She's still asleep."

"Good morning, good morning, Rocco sir, Kai sir," Rajesh, the butler, said as he bustled past Tina. "I saw you coming so I have brought coffee and toast for everyone, like madam requested."

"I didn't," Tina said.

Rajesh pulled out a small vial from his pocket and handed it to Tina saying, "Freshly pressed coconut oil for you. I noticed your elbows are a bit rough. Rub this on before you take a shower and you'll notice how smooth they become in no time."

Tina touched one of her elbows and pulled her shirtsleeves down.

"Rough elbows are common these days because you people keep your elbows against a desk all day for computer usage," Rajesh said.

"He's right," Kai said. "I do publicity for Nimo, have you heard of it? It's a Japanese beauty brand. Coconut oil and snail slime—our secret ingredients."

"Snail slime?" Rajesh asked. "Interesting. I'll have to try that."

"I haven't tried it personally but it works wonders in the trials," Kai said.

"Tina, ma'am, I'll try to get you some also," Rajesh said.

"Okay, that's enough, thank you," Tina said. She looked down at the vial of coconut oil and added in a whisper to Rajesh, "How long do I leave it on for?"

"Fifteen minutes will be good," Rajesh said and went back off across the main lawn toward the clubhouse.

"I'm still drunk," Kai said. "The hangover is going to hit after I take a nap, I can already feel it."

"Take two aspirin and drink two whole glasses of water before you sleep," Tina said.

"That's the American remedy. I'll give you a Berocca before you sleep—that's the British secret," Rocco said. "And they know how to drink and nurse a hangover better than Americans do."

Tina poured herself a cup of coffee and took some toast and was preparing to return to her room when David and her mother approached from the far end of the golf course in workout clothes. It was most unlike her mother to carry workout clothes for a weeklong trip for a wedding. The clothes looked new. And both Radha and David were wearing matching New Balance sneakers.

"Good morning, Tina. Making friends already?" David asked. "We couldn't sleep either so we've been off for a walk around the periphery of the golf course. It's all so well maintained. But now coffee and toast is just what we need. Radha, should I pour you a cup?"

"They've redone all the stables," Radha said. "And there are some beautiful, big horses. Maybe you and Marianne could have a ride. Didn't Marianne have a horse when she was younger?"

"Fred," Tina said.

"I had a horse named Gibran," David said. "Radha, I'll take you riding. The horses would love you. Remember that police horse in New Orleans that nuzzled your neck?"

Radha shook her head slightly at David and Tina said, "When did you go to New Orleans?"

"Mardi Gras," David said. "Have you been? It's terrific. I tried to get your mother to ride an electric bull on Bourbon Street but she refused."

"David, didn't you say you had to use the bathroom?" Radha turned to Tina. "Isn't it nice being back? Do you want to join our walk around the club? We came here a few times when you were young but I don't know if you remember much."

"Actually, I'm still a bit sleepy. I think I'll go in and try to sleep for another hour or two so I have enough energy for the day," Tina said. A stroll with her athleisure-clad mother and her boyfriend was the absolute last thing she felt like doing.

She entered the cottage and found Marianne still in her bed, eating toast and looking at her phone.

"Should I have brought Tom?" she asked Tina. "He just sent me a video of his niece falling asleep in her high chair. It's really cute. Want to see?"

"We can go horseback riding later today if you want to," Tina said.

"I couldn't. I miss Fred too much," Marianne said. "Someday I'll get another horse and put matching riding boots on my whole family and go out to the stables every Sunday morning. I'll stand on the sidelines with a cup of coffee and a cable-knit brown sweater and watch my children get lessons."

"That sounds like Tom's life in Boston," Tina said. "A far cry from living in a luxurious bungalow in Lahore like you had once planned. With holidays in Mayfair, was it? Isn't that where Riyaaz's family had an apartment?"

Laughter came into their room from the porch.

"Are there people on our porch? It's so early," Marianne said.

"Some of Pavan's friends just got back from a night out and my mother and David were on a little health-giving walk around the golf course. She has New Balance sneakers on. So does he. Did you know they went to New Orleans for Mardi Gras? I certainly didn't."

Tina sat down on Marianne's bed and pulled her legs under Marianne's sheet.

"Shefali got lucky, don't you think? The way their worlds merge," Tina said.

"I guess so. She's marrying a guy so perfect on paper it may as well have been arranged. But what about love and passion and excitement?"

"Does it have to be one or the other?" Tina asked.

"I don't know. Boston or Lahore? I don't know," Marianne said.

"I'm hardly someone who has this figured out but there's something to be said for matching résumés," Tina said. "Arranged marriages often work out. Love marriages often don't."

"Is that what non-arranged marriages are called?"

"Did you ever watch that ridiculous Millionaire Matchmaker show?" Tina asked.

"No, but I feel like I did because you talk about it all the time," Marianne said.

"Matchmaking intrigues me," Tina said. "Good on paper or good in bed, like you said. Can you have both?"

Marianne propped herself up on an elbow and took the remaining half of Tina's toast.

"That's what you should make a reality show about," Marianne said.

"No!" Tina said. "The last thing the world needs is another show about matchmakers. Although can you imagine how much fun that would be? A deep dive into Indian matchmaking? You know they match horoscopes? And for some really traditional people, if a woman has a horoscope that says bad luck will befall her husband, she has to first marry a tree so that her human husband will be spared."

"Does it have to be a tree?" Marianne asked.

"I think it has to be a living thing, so maybe a goat or a goldfish would be allowed. I don't really know. Most young people we know wouldn't be the kind to subscribe to that but some people do," Tina said. "But that's the problem with presenting that on a show—suddenly that becomes the narrative about India, and the next generation of young Indian kids gets made fun of in school for marrying a tree. Do you know how many kids in my school used to ask me if we rode on elephants in India instead of cars?"

"In our church, before you get married, you have to have some counseling sessions with the priest and one of the things they make you do is write down five things about each other that start with 'I love it when you . . .' and five things that start with 'I don't love it when you . . .' I can't imagine how anyone follows through with marriage after reading their partner's reviews of them. Every culture is fucked up," Marianne said.

"In its own beautiful way," Tina added. "But you never have to explain white American culture. Every Indian kid, every Egyptian kid, every Japanese kid sees a hundred different representations of it from the minute we're conscious. We all know the church wedding, the whole walking-down-the-aisle thing. But Indian weddings are a whole different deal. Can you imagine Andrew's family in Delhi like this? Did you know that at some Indian weddings there's a tradition that all the young cousins spend the first night stopping the married couple from getting any time alone together? So, like, basically, all the kids are there to cockblock them. Though we would never actually say it's about sex."

"I think that's amazing. There's too much pressure to have sex on the wedding night. I can't imagine wanting to have sex after a day spent talking to Tom's extended family."

"Fair point," Tina said.

Marianne finished her toast and brushed her hands together. "Dropping crumbs in bed is the best part of any holiday," she said.

"We can also clip our fingernails anywhere we want," Tina said.

"And let toothpaste spackle the bathroom mirror."

"And kick crumpled receipts under the furniture."

"And flip our purses over the carpet to shake out the sand at the bottom," Marianne said. "It's a wonder we aren't banned from hotels."

She reached for Tina's coffee.

"Is there milk and sugar in that?"

"It's black," Tina said.

"Why do you insist on drinking gross black coffee as if it's a per-sonality trait?" Marianne asked, returning the cup and finishing the toast. She got out of the bed and walked to the bathroom. Tina stayed sitting in her bed sipping coffee. She heard the toilet flush and the tap run, and Marianne returned to the room with her hair tied up and glasses on.

"I'm going to find myself an Indian man to marry," Tina said. "It makes sense. Andrew didn't make sense—do you know how difficult it was to find an Instagram filter that flattered both of us? He was right, it wasn't about him coming to the wedding. I just needed something con-crete to end it once and for all, you know?"

"Listen, I don't think at all that Andrew was the right guy for you but you could have just been honest with him. Telling him you couldn't bring him because your conservative Indian family would object to a white boyfriend was a bit too blatant of a lie. Your mother's white boy-friend is here. In New Balances."

THAT WAS EXACTLY WHAT Andrew had argued that morning at brunch. And he was right, of course. Tina had tried to end things with him several times before, but it had never stuck. Mostly, she'd made halfhearted attempts filled with metaphors and jokes and then she would go four or five days without seeing him before she inevitably changed her mind and sent him a text because he was fun and conve-nient and reliable. And things had sort of been hobbling along like that for almost two years.

"My mother says you're my payback for how I've treated women in the past," Andrew had said over his eggs Benedict that morning.

Tina had reached over, picked up a strip of bacon from his plate, and said, "That seems like a humblebrag but I can't quite figure out how."

"I can't keep doing this," Andrew said.

"Doing what?"

"This," he said. "Us."

A waitress picked that moment to come over, Tina remembered. Her head was shaved on one side and she had a septum piercing.

"What a gorgeous day," the waitress said. "I don't even mind working on days like today. Everything feels like a celebration. I had a group of girlfriends in here earlier this morning at the end of a night out and I have never seen a group rally so hard. They had five bottles of cava between them and then left a very generous tip."

She had leaned over the table. Tina had looked at the butterfly tattoo in her cleavage and waited in silence while she picked up the empty coffee cups and empty side plate of hash browns.

"I ate, like, three of these in the kitchen just now," the waitress said about the hash browns. "I swear the chef puts cocaine in these."

She winked at Tina then and said, "Anything else I can get for you? I'll be right back to refill your water."

"It's fine, thanks, we don't need any more water," Andrew said. "Thanks."

The waitress looked deflated as she nodded and walked away.

"Her enthusiasm was endearing," Tina said. "You didn't need to shut her down like that. I love it when people genuinely seem to be enjoying themselves. But that butterfly tattoo was questionable, I'll give you that."

"We're in a relationship, whether or not you like it, Tina," Andrew had said. "I don't know why you refuse to accept that or what you're waiting for before you decide one way or another but I can't do this anymore."

And after that day, Andrew never agreed to meeting up with her again, no matter how flirtatiously she texted, and now, here she was, just two weeks later, in India.

* * *

"I SHOULD BE DATING an Indian guy," Tina said. "Right? Should I be dating an Indian guy? From Delhi or Bombay, and then we can have children who will learn Hindi and won't have to have weird hippie names. Or Maya; they won't have to be named Maya."

"You barely speak Hindi," Marianne said.

"That's true. Did you know Hindi has different words for a good smell and a bad smell? Badbu and khushbu. I once told my father's neighbor in Jersey City that the food had a really good-bad smell."

Marianne sat down on the sofa on the other end of the room and pulled a nail file out of her purse and began to file her nails. Marianne always obsessively filed her nails. She used to bite her nails when she was younger and she had traded in that bad habit for this one.

"What's today's plan?" she asked. "It doesn't even feel like we're here for a wedding."

"The schedule is right there," Tina pointed at the coffee table in front of Marianne. The schedule, embossed in gold and covered with glitter, was next to a basket full of laddoos, dried fruits, nuts, Snickers bars, and little boxes of Frooti drinks.

"Tonight is the cocktail party at the Goldenrod Garden," Marianne said. "And then there's a haldi lunch, a day trip to the Taj, and the final night reception and wedding. That's it? Just those events? What are we supposed to do the rest of the time?"

"Whatever we want," Tina said. "Most of the guests are from Delhi so it's not one of those packed, minute-by-minute wedding itineraries. And I think they only planned the Taj Mahal trip so those of us who flew in from around the world wouldn't feel like we'd wasted our time."

Marianne took a bite of an orange motichoor laddoo. "Wow, that's rich. And very sweet. Want the rest?"

Tina shook her head.

Marianne put the half-eaten laddoo back in the box and noticed two other small boxes with her and Tina's names on them. She opened hers and found an astonishingly delicate beige cashmere stole. She took it out and touched it against her cheek. The wedding planner's business card fell out from the folds and landed near her feet.

"This is the softest material I have ever touched," Marianne said. She tossed Tina's box across the room. In Tina's box was a similar stole in black with subtle gold embroidery. Tina also touched it to her face, another business card falling out.

"This is amazing," she said. "I like your color more, though."

"Good, because I prefer yours," Marianne said, swapping.

There were two other forms on the table and Marianne looked at one.

"This is a contract of some sort," she said. "What is this?"

Tina reached over and took the paper and read it. She laughed.

"It's a waiver. It gives them the right to film us this entire week," Tina said. "Shefali must be getting a professional wedding documentary made. She had mentioned something about a trailer release."

Colebrookes Country Club, New Delhi: Shefali,
the Bride, Is Shouting at Her Facialist on the Phone
for What She Thinks Is the Start of a Pimple on Her
Chin (It Isn't, but the Facialist Packs Her Kit and
Rushes Over to Shefali's House Anyway)

MR. DAS KNOCKED ON HIS DAUGHTER'S DOOR. NO ANSWER.
One of his suitcases hadn't arrived last night so he was wearing his
underpants and socks from the journey inside out under fresh clothes.
British Airways had located the suitcase, accidentally on a flight to
Shanghai, and promised to deliver it to Colebrookes within forty-eight
hours. After lunch he would stop by one of the malls in Saket and buy
some new underpants and socks, and next time he would distribute his
clothes more evenly between the two suitcases. He was carrying two
suitcases because his sister, Shefali's mother, had made him bring her
two sets of glasses from Crate & Barrel and he had used all his underwear and socks to pad the fragile things in one of the suitcases.

He checked the time. It was 12:40 P.M. and he was meant to reach
Mrs. Sethi's house at 1 P.M.

"But, please, Mr. Das," Mrs. Ray, the matchmaker, had said on the
phone. "Please have some sense and do not arrive right on time. One
fifteen is okay. And don't forget to take something small—maybe a
bouquet of flowers or a book or some good coffee beans if you have a

favorite kind. Make it something that will reflect your personality but no wine, no alcohol. Not for a first meeting."

Sometimes Mrs. Ray wondered if this Matchmaking Agency for Widows was a fool's errand. But while talking to Mr. Das, she looked over at her new husband, Upen Chopra, in the swimming pool in Goa, and reminded herself that no, everyone deserved a second, third, and even fourth chance at love. Or, in the case of some depressing marriages, a first chance at love. Although this Mr. Das fellow sounded like he had quite amicably divorced his wife. He had mentioned that she was also in Delhi for the wedding. Mrs. Ray liked such stories. Upen pulled himself out of the pool on the other end and sat on the edge. From behind her large sunglasses, Mrs. Ray noticed him call a pool boy over and point in her direction. He then looked over at her and winked and jumped back into the water. Mrs. Ray watched him glide under the surface toward her, his back muscles tensing with each stroke. Age really was nothing but a number, she thought, as she watched her husband, fitter than any thirty-year-old in the area. Why should the fun end just because your skin was a bit more wrinkled than it was yesterday? Yes, everyone deserved another chance at love.

Which was why Mr. Das was standing outside his daughter's cottage wearing khaki slacks with a dark blue button-down shirt tucked in and inside-out underpants and socks, and holding a coffee-table book on the art of Rabindranath Tagore. He knocked again. This time finally Tina answered, looking freshly showered and wearing jeans and a kurta. Radha had always discouraged Tina from wearing Indian clothes or getting too involved with the Indian community, saying they weren't in America to separate themselves, but Mr. Das liked seeing his daughter dressed this way.

"Should I wear a tie?" he asked.

"No," Tina said, walking back into her cottage, running a comb through her wet hair. "You don't want to seem so eager. You look nice in this. It's casual without being sloppy."

"Casual but not sloppy," Mr. Das said. "That's good. What does one do when they meet someone I-R-L for the first time? That's *in real life.*"

"Who taught you that?" Tina asked.

"The matchmaker has a young assistant who does all her online work. He emailed me saying Mrs. Ray likes to speak with all her clients before their first I-R-L meeting so I had to look up the meaning."

Tina went to the mirror to get ready while her father kept talking.

"I also asked her what I should wear today but she put the phone down saying a man my age should know what to wear so then I googled some pictures of George Clooney. Anyway, long story short, here we are—and are you sure I don't need to wear a tie?"

"One hundred percent. Are you bringing her that Tagore book?" Tina pointed toward the book in his hand.

"Well, Mrs. Ray also said—" Mr. Das started but his daughter interrupted him and said, "Papa, you're already doing better than ninety-nine percent of the men in the world. I think you should relax and go enjoy this. Even if it makes me uncomfortable."

She liked being able to tell her father she was uncomfortable; if she mentioned it to her mother, her mother would jump straight into her psychoanalysis of why exactly Tina was uncomfortable and how it meant there was something in her life that needed changing. Recently she had said that she thought Tina "used her heritage"—being Indian but living in America—as an excuse to claim she never fit in when, in fact, she had the luxury of fitting in in both America and India if she would just stop complaining and make a few decisions.

"It's always easy to cast blame," her mother had said, leaning back on her red rocking chair and moving her reading glasses from her head to her eyes to page through the latest issue of the *New Yorker*.

"Roz Chast," her mother had said. "Now, that's someone I'd love to have as a client."

Tina thought her mother's clients' parents all owed her thanks for the fact that they still had good relationships with their children. Radha was so determined not to be blamed for any of Tina's problems that, unlike a lot of therapists, she committed her entire practice to never putting any of the blame on anyone's parents.

"Is this odd for you?" Mr. Das asked his daughter. He hadn't really stopped to consider his daughter in this whole thing, and when he did, he knew that she was still so angry at Radha and David that she would forgive him and accept his romantic liaisons more easily. Tina was always unfairly generous when it came to him.

"It's fine," Tina said. "You deserve happiness too."

Mr. Das nodded. Tina had always assumed the divorce was her mother's fault and Mr. Das didn't do too much to change her belief. Which was fair, he reasoned. After all, Radha now had David but he had nobody. He should at least get his daughter's allegiance. And anyway, it wasn't clear who was to blame for the divorce.

THE MORNING AFTER THEIR Yale graduation, Tina and Marianne had been sitting in their living room, empty beer and wine bottles, an overturned hookah, open suitcases, and boxes scattered around them. Their third roommate, Monika, had left before graduation to spend the summer fishing for salmon off the coast of Alaska before starting medical school in Chicago. Marianne was moving to New York, having got a job as an editorial assistant at *Good Housekeeping*. Tina was going back to her parents' home in Ohio for a few months before deciding what to do next.

They both sipped from colorful bottles of Gatorade.

"You'll be fine," Marianne said. "You're going out into the world with a degree from Yale. It doesn't matter that you don't know what you're doing yet."

"I really think I should go spend a year in India," Tina said. With her toe, she pushed a cushion off the sofa. It was yellow with red Indian embroidery on it and she had brought it to college with her four years ago and spent four years trying to like it. "Do you want this pillow?"

"You've had that pillow since freshman year," Marianne said. "It's disgusting."

Tina looked down at it and said, "I can't bring myself to throw it out. It's from Jaipur, I think. My father got it years ago. I guess I'll take it back to my parents' for now."

"Throw it out, Tina," Marianne said.

"Throw what out?" came Tina's mother's voice from the hallway. They had left their front door open, going in and out with boxes and trash. Outside, the skies were blue and the sun was shining. New Haven felt so safe and warm, and Tina was terrified about leaving. She had halfheartedly applied for a few jobs but the vague idea of moving to India had stopped her from actively pursuing anything. But then she couldn't quite get herself to move to India, it felt too foreign and too frightening so now she was doing the least foreign and least frightening thing possible and simply moving back home with her parents. She was giving herself until the end of August to decide what to do next. Otherwise she was putting herself on a one-way flight to New Delhi.

"Why is she here so early?" Tina asked, scrambling to get up, throwing the pillow back on the sofa, and kicking a few beer bottles under it. "I'm going to get lectured about the future the entire way home."

Radha entered the living room holding a Starbucks iced coffee with a pair of large purple sunglasses pushed up on her head.

"Someone asked me where Saybrook College was on the way over here. Maybe I look like a college student," Radha said. She held her purse and looked around the messy room for somewhere to place it. She sighed loudly and put it back on her shoulder. "Maybe a grad student."

"Professor is more likely. Why are you here so early?" Tina asked.

"Your father was being terribly slow and I wanted to take a walk and enjoy the morning. You know how I love being back on a university campus. Makes me feel young," Radha said.

"Papa won't know how to get here from the hotel," Tina said. "He's useless with directions."

"He'll figure it out," Radha said. "Look at you two. Oh, to be young again. Did you have a party here last night? You should have invited us. Well, me, anyway. Your father fell asleep in front of the television in the hotel with a cup of tea balanced on his belly."

Tina watched her mother walk around the room, taking it all in. She touched her fingertip to the bookshelf that was also somehow sticky and pulled it back.

"Not everything about youth is wonderful, of course," Radha said. "But so much is. The excitement. The future. Gosh, I remember when I first came to America, I used to have butterflies in my stomach all the time. Just the limitless possibilities."

Tina looked over at Marianne. Marianne looked into her Gatorade.

"I should go finish packing," Marianne said and walked toward the door.

"Feel that shoulder blade," Radha said, squeezing Marianne as she tried to leave.

"Ma, are you okay?" Tina asked.

Radha was still holding on to Marianne's shoulder.

"But the possibilities so quickly start getting limited. You make one choice and you have to let all the other choices go. I suppose you've both already sort of started this march. You're Yale graduates now, you will never be Harvard or Princeton graduates."

"There's always grad school," Marianne said, trying to slip out of Radha's grip.

Radha smiled and patted Marianne and said, "An optimist. Off you go, Marianne. Go finish your packing with your gorgeous, gorgeous shoulder blades. You women, you're not girls anymore, will run the world someday. I can't believe it's been four years since we dropped you off."

Marianne left the room and Tina stood up from the couch and continued putting her books into boxes.

"Ma, your basement is going to be completely filled with my stuff, but I'm going to commit to a plan by August at the very latest. I'll call Papa and tell him to get here by noon. I should be done packing by then."

Radha sat down on the couch and placed her purse on her lap. Outside a car went by with music thumping and Tina looked at her mother and suddenly felt scared. Her mother was looking out of the window at nothing at all.

Tina continued placing books carefully into boxes as though she might revisit *An Introduction to Microeconomics* in the future.

"We won't have a basement for you to fill, darling. We're getting divorced. And my small apartment in Manhattan barely has space for my things. Check with your father about his new apartment in Jersey City, otherwise maybe look into finding a storage unit somewhere. They come and collect your boxes, and I've heard it's quite well-priced and easy. Some of them have cute ads on the trains. Have you ever seen them? I saw one the other day that had a naked couple lying on the floor—you know, bodies entwined etcetera, etcetera—in an empty apartment and it said, 'Maybe we made storage too easy.'"

"What did you say?" Tina said.

"I suppose the ad was implying that they had put all their clothes into storage. It isn't about logic, I guess. As always, sex sells."

"Ma, stop," Tina said. "What did you say? You're getting divorced?"

"Yes. Well, technically we're already divorced but we didn't want to tell you until after graduation. Didn't want to ruin the festivities. Didn't you notice that we booked a suite for this weekend? With beds in two rooms. Anyway. I'm not moving until next week. And I think your father will take a bit longer. You know how precious he is with things like packing. But we've found good buyers already and everything is moving quite smoothly, touch wood. I've been sleeping in your old room and I just love the elm tree you can see out of your window. You positioned your bed well."

Tina had just stood there, an astronomy textbook in her hand, looking at her mother. Her legs felt weak, her stomach felt hot. Everything around her seemed to blur except, she remembered vividly, the sound of someone's flip-flops smacking against the sidewalk outside.

"Did you say Manhattan?"

"I've always loved Manhattan. The culture, the people, the crowds. And you know everyone there needs therapy so it will be good for my work as well," Radha said. "Anyway, enough about all that. Let's not waste time. Tell me what I can do to help with the packing. Is the kitchen done? I could handle that if you'd like. Just not the bathroom."

"Ma," Tina said. "Ma, why? It's not like you two are that young anymore. I don't understand. What's the point of this? How will Papa manage on his own? You have to remind him to take his statin every night."

Radha had inhaled deeply, stood up, and said, "We'll make sure he sets an alarm."

She walked over to Tina, took the astronomy book from her hand, and said, "Life is complicated, Tina. You'll see. Things aren't always black and white but we'll all be fine. Now, let's get moving. I'll go see to the kitchen."

"What about me?" Tina asked, aware that she sounded foolish, juvenile. "You couldn't have done this while I was still in college? Or after I had found a job and settled down? What am I supposed to do?"

Radha held up the astronomy textbook.

"If there's one piece of advice I can give you, it's that you won't revisit this textbook. Come on now. Moping about solves nothing."

They didn't talk about it anymore, from what Tina could remember now. Tina had always taken her mother's response, her mother's evasiveness, as proof of her guilt. Her father had arrived a little while later, unaware that Radha had already told Tina.

"Hello, my wife and daughter," he said from the entrance to Tina's apartment. At that point Tina was lying in Marianne's bed, still shocked by her mother's news. In the hallway, she heard her mother say to her father, "Stop it, Neel. I've already told her."

"We were supposed to tell her together," Mr. Das said in a clenched whisper. "Radha, what did you tell her? I should get to tell my side too."

"She's an adult, Neel. Nobody needs to take sides."

"You left the hotel early just to reach her before me. We had agreed to tell her once we got home."

"I can hear you," Tina had shouted from Marianne's room.

"WHAT ARE YOUR PLANS for the afternoon?" Mr. Das now asked his daughter.

"I've got to go meet Sid, that drummer I had shortlisted for the reality show. Remember him? I told you about it," Tina said.

Tina sat down at her dresser to put some makeup on. She had booked a hair and makeup artist for all the wedding-related events but she wouldn't arrive for a few hours. Tina studied her face in the mirror. She leaned in—was it her imagination or were the two-hundred-dollar facials she got at a loft in Koreatown once a month really making her skin glow?

"Are you excited? Do you know a lot about her?" Tina asked her father. "Mrs. Sethi, right? How old is she? How long ago did her husband die? Are you sure she doesn't just want a Green Card?"

"Tina, darling beti," Mr. Das said. "That's all for me to worry about now. I should be asking you questions and worrying about your love life. You can't spend all your time taking care of us. I know the divorce wasn't easy on either of us but you can't play the role of the parent—especially since you were, what, twenty-two when it happened? I worry that you use it as an excuse."

Tina stared straight into the mirror. Her facialist had made her a custom face pack that she had used on the plane. She had asked Chon to make her a clear mask, not a sheet mask, because she was certain she would be arrested if she settled into her seat wearing a white mask. Celebrities always claimed they put on face masks on overnight flights but Heidi Klum was unlikely to get arrested in her first-class cabin. Tina would have to message Chon and thank her; she really did look well-rested despite the long journey and dry air. Chon was from Assam but pretended to be Korean. She had giggled and spoken to Tina in Hindi one day and confessed to being Indian. Tina always went back to her for her facials and tipped her twenty-five percent and never confessed that she didn't speak Hindi.

"I'm just curious about Mrs. Sethi. This whole matchmaking-agency-for-widows idea feels a little harebrained to me. And sad."

"It's sadder to spend your days alone," Mr. Das said. "Trust me, I know. Is this Sid fellow single?"

Tina put her lipstick down and said, "It's a work meeting."

"Unexpected things happen, Tina," Mr. Das said. "A matchmaking agency for widows, for instance. What madness."

Mr. Das gave a little laugh, his obvious happiness disorienting for Tina.

"Now, listen," Mr. Das said. "Will you be walking anywhere on this date? Or can you wear my Fitbit and keep your arm swinging? I would do it myself but I'm worried it will give a bad first impression."

Mrs. Sethi's Home, K Block,
Hauz Khas Enclave, New Delhi

THIRTY MINUTES LATER, WITH HIS ARM RESTING CALMLY BY HIS side, Mr. Das, driven by Kaushal, his chauffeur, wearing a crisp white uniform, was pulling up to Hauz Khas Enclave, K Block. Kaushal used to work for a family in this same neighborhood three years ago but he had been fired when he fell asleep at the wheel and hit the divider while driving the family from Delhi to Mussoorie. He had worked two full shifts leading up to that trip. Nobody had been hurt and even the car was only slightly dented. But the husband got so angry he fired Kaushal right there, in the late evening on the side of the road, and took over the driver's seat, even though he had been drinking beer in the back. They left Kaushal there to hitchhike his way back to Delhi and told him to collect his things and leave their home before they returned in three days. Kaushal looked into their driveway as they went past and saw the same BMW he used to drive parked there and was secretly pleased that the family wasn't doing well enough to buy a new car. In the time since, he himself had moved up from a scooter to a used, old Maruti 800 to a still-used-but-less-used black Swift, so he reasoned he was doing better in life.

The streets were quiet except for the occasional schoolchild in uniform skipping down the street, an ayah walking lazily behind holding a backpack and water bottle. A coconut seller sat on the ground near a large tray heaped to the skies with coconuts. The seller was eating the silky white flesh of the coconut and it looked so inviting Mr. Das was tempted to take one in to Mrs. Sethi but he imagined both Mrs. Ray and his daughter would frown upon that. A whole coconut was an awkward gift to bring on a first date—Mrs. Sethi would have to find a sharp knife and either he or she would have to hack into it violently and try to pour the water into glasses before breaking the entire shell in half to access the flesh. No, it wasn't a graceful gift to bring; he would pick one up on the way back to Colebrookes and get the butler to split it open.

Mr. Das looked up at the window of Mrs. Sethi's apartment and noticed a head disappear. How strange, he thought, as he walked to the main entrance and rang the doorbell. In her bathroom, Mrs. Sethi heard the bell ring as she leaned against the wall near the window and caught her breath. He was here. After nearly four months of increasingly frequent emails, Mr. Das was now standing at her front door. She had instructed Anita, her most impressive maid, to let him in and offer him water or a cold drink and seat him in the dark blue armchair that faced her bedroom door so she could make an entrance. Under no circumstances was Lavina, the grumpiest of the maids but the best cook of them all, allowed to interact with him or ask him a thousand probing questions.

So Lavina was pressed up against the kitchen door trying to listen to what was happening at the front door. She had ajwain seeds roasting in a pan on the stove to make paranthas later; she reached over and turned the flame off so she could hear better. Her own husband was a good-for-nothing drunkard but at least she had the sense to lie to him about her salary and only give him a third of her money while she put the rest into an account of her own, and the day was fast approaching when she would have enough money and courage to leave him. She would remain working for Mrs. Sethi, though. She was a good employer, and since Lavina had a face that always looked unfriendly, she was rarely asked to do anything outside the kitchen, and Lavina loved the kitchen. And Mrs. Sethi always gave Lavina a sari and matching blouse piece on her birthday, and it wasn't the gift but the fact that she remembered Lavina's birthday every year which made Lavina vow to never quit.

Lavina could hear Mr. Das politely asking Anita whether or not he should remove his shoes and she could hear Anita telling him to have a seat. Anita was such a suck-up. Lavina shook her head and went to the freezer to take out red snapper to defrost for a Goan curry for dinner.

In the bathroom off the master bedroom, once it went silent, Mrs. Sethi looked in the mirror. She was wearing a dark green raw silk kurta with matching dark green cigarette pants with a green-and-gold-embroidered dupatta draped across her shoulders. Her hair was down loose and the recent mehndi that she had put in was creating subtle red highlights against her dark brown hair. Her hair looked a little fried from years of—well, years of life. She wasn't one of those women who had her hair processed much but once you get past fifty it didn't seem to matter much what you had put your hair through. She wished her younger self had known that. In her twenties and thirties she was certain she would be able to resist old age if she just made the right lifestyle choices, so she oiled her hair regularly, took her vitamins, didn't smoke, wore sunblock, and avoided fried food. But, much to her disappointment, it turned out that age didn't give two hoots whether or not you processed your hair or drank gallons of water. Age was going to do whatever it wanted to do and now, in retrospect, she wished she hadn't been quite so strict with herself. Everyone knows that death is unavoidable but aging is the sinister creeper that pretends to be avoidable and then slaps you across the face, leaving a trail of wrinkles and thinning hair. Now Mrs. Sethi was hoping her hair would start to go gray soon because she'd heard if your hair goes gray before it starts falling out it won't ever fall out and Mrs. Sethi had recently been noticing more and more strands of hair on her brush and in the drain in the mornings. She dabbed some Biotique lipstick on her lips and lifted the edges of her eyes. She was now officially attractive *for her age* but at least she had that, she decided. She even occasionally had people politely claim they would never have guessed that she had a twenty-eight-year-old daughter.

In the living room, Mr. Das was looking at a framed picture of, he assumed, Mrs. Sethi's daughter. The picture sat on the side table next to him, next to a vase shaped like a watering jug filled with half a dozen brightly colored flowers. He looked around the room at the floor-to-ceiling bookshelves filled with books and was intimidated. He didn't read at all these days—maybe the occasional business book—but nothing more. Tina kept telling him to read more but he didn't and the only reason he had this book about Tagore with him was that the guest services person at Colebrookes had bought it when he told them he needed a tasteful gift for a lady friend. Now, what if Mrs. Sethi wanted to know if he had read any of Tagore's work? It would be embarrassing. Mr. Das was sitting and trying to think if he had seen any Bollywood films based on Tagore's work that would at least give him a baseline but he was coming up blank. Before he could take his phone out and google "popular Tagore stories," the door across the room opened and Mrs. Sethi stepped into the room. Mr. Das's eyes widened in surprise at her beauty and he stood up to greet her.

"Mrs. Sethi," he said hurriedly. "Mrs. Sethi, so nice to finally put a face—a beautiful face—to your name. I brought you a book I think you will enjoy but I confess I myself have not read any Tagore and am deeply ashamed."

Mrs. Sethi laughed, charmed. Mr. Das was funny in his emails, often self-deprecating, and she hadn't been sure if he knew he was funny or if he really was just awkward and a bit insecure, and she still wasn't sure. But suddenly, right now, she didn't mind which one it was because either way it was charming. She liked Mr. Das immediately.

"Please call me Jyoti," Mrs. Sethi said. "Or you'll make me feel like a schoolteacher."

She was instantly drawn to his nervous energy, his casual yet clearly expensive clothes—not that she needed them to be expensive, but given that they obviously were, she was glad they didn't look obviously expensive. Her late husband, who had been the spokesperson for Shell India, had worn only suits and ties.

"Well, you picked well, Mr. Das, because I am a big fan of Tagore and I have heard good things about this one," Mrs. Sethi said. "Please sit. Would you like a glass of coconut water?"

Over coconut water, the conversation with Mrs. Sethi flowed as if their interactions over the last four months had been in person all along. Mr. Das wondered if, like him, she had reread all their email correspondence early this morning to make sure she had talking points.

"Has Lavina stopped using so much oil in the cooking?" he asked.

In the kitchen, Lavina was sitting near the door shredding coconut when she heard her name in this context. Well, that's rich, she thought. On the one hand, Mrs. Sethi wanted tasty food but on the other hand, she pretended she didn't like too much oil. She would fry the red snapper first tonight, Lavina decided, then drop it in the gravy. It was much tastier that way anyway.

"Yes, she takes instruction well," Mrs. Sethi said. "Not that I'm opposed to oil occasionally, but too much ruins the flavor of more subtle ingredients."

"I feel that way about butter," Mr. Das said. "I've never enjoyed the taste of butter. But if you say 'no butter,' people smile knowingly and make jokes about your diet."

"I know that far too well," Mrs. Sethi said with a laugh. "I can't tell you the number of times I've accepted dessert when I didn't want any just to avoid snide comments about the widow trying to maintain her figure."

"You have a wonderful figure," Mr. Das said. He looked away, embarrassed, and took a large sip of his coconut water. Once he had told Radha that David had a good figure and Radha had told him that the term "figure" had sexual implications. He wasn't sure if he agreed with her but now he was acutely aware that he had used that term.

"And Anita's daughter's exams went well?" He quickly tried to bring the conversation back to safer territory.

Mrs. Sethi smiled and said, "It's as if we've been braided into each other's lives for months already, isn't it?"

But despite the familiarity, there was also the excitement of a new connection, a new relationship. He noticed Mrs. Sethi's repeated habit of gently touching her left earlobe with her left thumb; a million emails wouldn't teach him that. For that he needed to be here in her living room looking straight at her. She sat with her feet tucked under, her toenails peering out, painted a light pink color. Her feet looked well-cared-for, as if they hadn't had decades of walking barefoot in India. Most women had cracked and dry heels by the time they crossed fifty but not Mrs. Sethi, Mr. Das noted. Mrs. Sethi must have regularly lotioned her feet when she was younger. He never liked his wife's feet. Ex-wife.

"Did Marianne end up bringing her husband along?" Mrs. Sethi asked. Was he staring at her toes? Was it too much, the pink nail polish too girly? She curled her toes inward, trying to hide them under her legs, feeling silly that she had spent all of yesterday at a beauty salon.

"Boyfriend," Mr. Das said. "I was corrected. But no, she left him behind. The girls are here together, which seems to be nice for them. And Radha . . . I'm the only one here alone."

"You have your whole family here. You're hardly alone," Mrs. Sethi said.

"Alone in a room at night is what I mean," Mr. Das said. "No, that's not at all what I mean. Although it's true but I didn't mean to say it the way it sounded."

Mrs. Sethi laughed and said, "This coconut water is wonderful but should we have a glass of wine? I know Mrs. Ray says no alcohol on a first meeting—date, whatever you want to call it at our age—but it's different, isn't it? We've known each other for months now."

Mr. Das was relieved and he took a few deep breaths while Mrs. Sethi vanished into the next room to get two glasses of wine. He had heard that just five deep breaths, with intent, could completely reset your brain but he wasn't sure if Mrs. Sethi was going to actually get the wine, open the bottle, and pour the glasses herself, thus giving him the time needed, or just tell her maid to bring the wine, in which case she would be back in the room before he had finished even his first inhalation. He was overthinking it, he decided. He closed his eyes and took a deep breath in right as Mrs. Sethi returned. Well, one was better than none.

SDA Market, New Delhi: What Tina (Fortunately) Doesn't Know Is That Just Moments Ago a Monkey Stole a Woman's Handbag

SUNIL, TINA'S CHAUFFEUR FOR THE WEEK, DROPPED HER OFF at the back entrance of the IIT Gate Market and watched as Tina stood uncertainly on the street side trying to cross. Maybe he should have taken a U-turn and dropped her off on the right side of the road, he thought. Tina was throwing him off this week. When his passengers were foreigners, he always made sure he dropped them off on the right side of the road so they didn't panic and get scared about crossing streets. When his passengers were Indian, he dropped them off at the most convenient spot and watched them in the rearview mirror as they confidently, often leisurely, jaywalked across the road. But Tina was neither here nor there. He had picked her and her blond friend up at the airport and Tina's discomfort in India was immediately palpable, mostly because she was clearly trying so hard to disguise it. She had spoken to him in broken Hindi last night and rattled off some names of main roads in Delhi as if she knew the layout of the city. Poor girl. The names she had used were the new names, the ones that were changed for arbitrary political reasons, not the old names that all locals knew them by.

But Sunil understood. He had moved to Delhi from Ratnagiri when he was eighteen, almost twenty-five years ago, but he still constantly worried that the terrified small-town boy was peeking out from behind his carefully crafted big-city-man persona. Should he offer to drive her around to the other side, Sunil wondered. But the entrance to the market was just fifty feet away.

And that's exactly what Tina was standing there wondering too. She wished the chauffeur—was it Sunil?—would drive away and not watch her trying to figure out a way to run across the road. She didn't want him to notice how obviously disoriented she was here. She had spoken to him in Hindi last night and had even memorized some of the main road names so he wouldn't think she was a complete tourist. They were two women in a car late at night in Delhi, after all.

She caught his eye in his rearview mirror through the back window and gave him a smile and a half-nod. She pointed at the cars and waved her hand back and forth fast and shook her head to try and communicate, "Delhi, good old, familiar Delhi with its crazy traffic. Don't worry about me, you drive off, I'll manage, I've done this before."

She waved at him hoping he would understand she wanted him to leave. Right then a large DTC bus came to a halt right in front of her and what felt like hundreds of passengers suddenly disembarked and pushed past Tina. As the crowd parted she saw about a dozen men and women in saris and salwar kameezes and pants and shirts, and one woman in a pencil skirt set with black pumps, and one man in a dhoti with two huge jute bags on his arms, all clump together in a group and cross the road with traffic swerving around them. Safety in numbers. She tried to catch up with them, run across with them, but by then the bus was moving again and the angry bus driver honked at her loudly and forced her to retreat, sweating but exhilarated.

"Stupid pedestrians," the bus driver muttered to the bus conductor, who was standing near him on the steps of the front door. "If I hit one more, I'll never get my license back, no matter how much I pay."

The man he had hit last year was fine, just a broken arm, more shouting and screaming than anything else really but a crowd had gathered before the bus could drive away and he had to wait for a policeman to come and had to pay four thousand rupees in cash before the policeman let him go. He had driven the full bus, passengers in tow, and the policeman, to a Standard Chartered ATM to get the cash.

Tina was catching her breath near the sidewalk when Sunil reversed in front of her and rushed out to hold open the back door.

"So sorry, madam," Sunil said. "I should have dropped you off on the other side of the road."

"No, no," Tina said. "No problem. Rush hour."

It was early afternoon.

"It's always rush hour in Delhi," Sunil offered. "Please, sit. It'll take a bit of extra time because the U-turn is only at the next traffic signal but I'll drop you off on the right side of the road."

Tina hesitated.

"I insist," Sunil said.

TINA WALKED THROUGH THE MARKET toward the café and looked around at the groups of young students sitting and drinking coffee and smoking cigarettes. There were young girls—some in dresses, some in salwar kameezes in bright colors, some in high-waisted jeans and crop tops that looked straight out of a Topshop advertisement. There were some young couples, and fathers chasing after toddlers. A hookah bar had spilled out onto the main market and sweet-smelling smoke rose from the colorful hookahs. A magazine seller and a banana seller sat side by side on the ground with their goods spread out on the floor in front of them. The magazine seller ate a banana.

Two women in bright salwar kameezes approached her and asked, in Hindi, "Where's the Hi-Glow beauty parlor?"

"I don't know," Tina said. "Nahin pata."

"Hm, okay," one of the girls said, also in Hindi. "We'll find it. Maria recently moved there—she does the best eyebrows in town. I've followed her here from Miracle Beauty Parlor."

They thought she was from here, Tina realized. They thought she was one of them.

"I know Maria," Tina tested. "She does my eyebrows also."

"She's very good," one of the girls said but she squinted at Tina's eyebrows. She looked at her friend and they both looked back at Tina and looked her up and down.

"I have to go," Tina said. "Tell Maria I say hi."

"What's your name?"

"Tina. But she probably knows me just by face."

The girls walked off in the other direction and Tina watched them go.

Nobody looked at Tina, and why would they? She could easily have been a teacher at the nearby college who came here every night for a cup of coffee after work. Or she could be a young mother living in one of the homes of Hauz Khas Enclave who spends the day at home with her baby but goes out for a walk every evening once her husband gets home in order to get a little bit of time to herself. Here, in this market in Hauz Khas, where she looked like everyone else, Tina could be anyone. Nobody here knew that her driver had to drive almost a mile extra to make a U-turn that would allow her to be dropped off at the right side of the road because she couldn't cross it on her own.

SID WAS SITTING OUTSIDE the café wearing jeans and a black T-shirt that said "KALE" on it. His jeans were fashionably torn and his chest had become broader from all the personal training. Tina remembered why he had stood out immediately when she held open-call auditions in Bombay. He was made for stardom. Not only did he have the physical presence that would sell on television but he was a tremendously gifted drummer. He mostly played the tabla and there was, of course, the exotic appeal of that for an international reality show, but he was equally good on a traditional drum set and a Spanish box. It was something about seeing him tilt back while drumming on the Spanish box that made Tina stop the audition and tell him he was shortlisted. She had then canceled the remaining auditions for the afternoon and gone for a massage at her hotel.

In his last email to her, he had sent her a picture of him doing pull-ups, shirtless, in a kids' playground in Bombay. He had turned it into a joke, something about scaring the kids off, but really it was obviously an excuse to send her that picture with his dark skin glistening with sweat and muscles rippling. She had saved the picture, in an album titled *Potential Casting*, but it was the only picture in the album.

"Ma'am." Sid smiled and rose to greet her. The white of his teeth sparkled against the dark of his skin. The same darkness that would cause him to be questioned at a fancy restaurant would make him a heartthrob on the screen. That was also why she was the most disappointed about telling Sid it wasn't going to happen—had it happened, had she managed to make Sid a household name, another Sid from another town in another world with the same dark skin would be able to enter fancy restaurants easily. Maybe that was wishful thinking. She was hardly going to eliminate prejudice with a reality show.

"Don't call me 'ma'am,' Sid. You know it's Tina," Tina said.

"Tina ma'am, then," Sid said. "I've ordered you a black coffee—I assumed that's still all you drink? I remember it from the auditions. This one has become a bit cold by now but I can take it back to the counter and ask them to warm it up just a little bit."

"It's fine the way it is," Tina said. "Thank you. Sorry I'm a bit late—rush hour."

Sid looked at the time on his phone.

"Your shirt," Tina said. "I went to Yale. I find those shirts quite funny."

Sid looked down at his chest and looked back up at her.

"Yale?"

"Where did you get that shirt?" Tina said.

"On Hill Road. In Bombay. I have a friend named Nishant Kale so I thought it would be funny."

He pronounced *kale* like *kaa-lay*.

"Anyway," Tina said. "How long are you in Delhi for?"

"One week," Sid said. "I've never been here before so I thought I'd see some things before I go back. And the train takes almost twenty hours so it didn't make sense to come for less time."

He had taken a train from Bombay when there were flights available that would take less than three hours? India had a slew of low-budget airlines that didn't cost that much. But clearly even those were out of his reach. And now he had paid for her coffee as well. Tina asked him about his work.

"Well, ma'am—sorry, Tina. The show did not work out so I am now focusing on the personal training. You also must be focusing on something else? God willing the show will happen someday but until then, what can you do?"

"It might," Tina said. "I'm still working on it."

She wasn't. But he was so handsome.

"You tried, ma'am. I know you tried. These things happen. Do not apologize," Sid said. A stray dog wandered over near their table and Sid leaned over and stroked it. Tina's shock must have registered on her face because Sid laughed and said, "Don't worry, I'll wash my hands. But it's sad that the dirty little things have nobody to clean them and as a result nobody touches them either. Physical touch is important."

Sid had a swagger about him that hadn't faded despite the show being canceled, Tina noted. Young women walking past were noticing him and men in more expensive clothes than Sid's were clearly irritated by his presence. He ran his hands through his dark brown hair and it flopped over his eyes like a film star's. Tina couldn't help but smile and shake her head.

"What?" Sid asked.

"You," Tina said with a smile. "We need to get you on camera."

A young boy in tattered clothes walked past the coffee shop holding a handful of colorful balloons for sale. He was licking a half-eaten red lollipop and didn't seem particularly interested in selling any of his balloons. Tina watched him watching everyone around him.

"My neighbor does that," Sid said. "Balloons. There's no money in it at all."

Tina waved the boy over and asked him for a balloon. He beamed at her and asked her which color.

"Blue," she said.

He handed her a blue one and asked for ten rupees. Tina took out her wallet and handed him a hundred. She looked over at Sid and added, "Actually I'll take them all. All six."

And she gave him a five-hundred-rupee note. The boy handed her the balloons and looked down at the money, shrugged, and wandered off into the market.

"That's sad," Tina said, hoping Sid would notice her generosity.

"Not always," Sid said. "The kid next door does it for his own entertainment. Whatever little money he makes from selling the balloons he uses to buy more balloons to sell. It gives him an excuse to hang out near Joggers Park and watch people all evening. That kid probably has nothing to do with the rest of his day now."

Tina looked up at the cluster of balloons floating over her head. She looked into the market to see if she could spot the boy and return the balloons to him. But then her money would seem like charity. Would that be offensive? Was Sid annoyed at how easily she had given that money away? What was Tina supposed to do with these balloons now?

He stood up and held his hand out to her and said, "Come on. Let's take a walk."

Tina followed Sid out of the main market down a quiet back lane running alongside a park. Under the trees that lined the edge of the road, there were six or seven motorcycles parked in the shade. On each of them sat a young couple, their backs to the world, their hands out of sight, huddled into each other, stealing kisses, touches, hidden foreplay that wouldn't lead to sex simply because they had nowhere to have sex. Tina watched the first couple, the girl's dupatta draped over both of them, their heads pressed together. From the back, they looked perfectly still, immobile. Occasionally the girl would pull her head away and laugh. She suddenly made eye contact with Tina.

The girl stopped for a moment, her privacy interrupted, and stared. *Was the couple who'd just exited the market looking for a private spot as well?* the girl on the bike thought. She looked over her boyfriend's shoulder at them and wondered what they would do since they didn't have a bike. The woman looked rich, though. Why did they need to wander back here? Why was the woman glaring at her? Maybe she was one of those married rich women who were having an affair. She wondered if they knew that the Rose Garden, just a few streets away, had benches hidden away in different spots of the garden. It was still early enough that they would be able to find an empty one. She hoped they knew, she hoped they would find a place to be together. The woman certainly shouldn't be carrying balloons in her hand if she wanted to go unnoticed. Silently, she wished them luck and returned her attention to her boyfriend, his hand now inching its way under her kurta, up her leg.

Tina looked away, embarrassed that she'd been caught looking. But nobody else registered Tina and Sid.

"In Bombay we have the sea," Sid said. "So at least you can face that, not a dirty wall. It's much more romantic. When the tide is low, you can walk all the way out on the rocks and it's like you're alone in the world. A big reason to prefer Bombay over Delhi."

She wondered about Sid's love life. She knew he shared one room with his mother and brother in Dharavi. He had once told her she must come over for a meal when she was in town next but neither of them had followed up on it. Did he date, she wondered. Did he find hidden public spots in Bombay to kiss pretty young women? Or was he married to his music, as he had claimed on his audition tape?

At the end of the road, a man stood urinating against the same wall, making use of the same privacy.

"Do you live near Times Square?" Sid asked as they continued walking down the dusty path through the trees.

"Not at all," Tina said. "I live in Brooklyn. Times Square is in Manhattan. Brooklyn is . . ."

She stopped herself. How could she describe her New York to Sid, who had only seen images? To Sid, her arrogant confidence in avoiding Times Square would seem confusing. Why live near such an iconic spot and avoid it? She thought that herself sometimes because she secretly loved Times Square even though she always claimed not to. It was true that it was too hectic during the day, with the sleazy men in character costumes trying to lure tourists to pose for pictures with them. She had once seen an Elmo with his head off standing in a corner near the entrance to the Forty-Second Street train station angrily smoking a cigarette while screaming into the phone about a failed acting audition. That was Times Square during the day. But sometimes, late at night, Tina liked to walk through Times Square by herself to marvel at the lights and the billboards and the tourists smiling, laughing, taking pictures, in awe of magnificent Manhattan. She thought of them sending back their selfies to family members around the world. She thought of them in line at security check at JFK or LaGuardia, waiting to go home to different corners of the world with memories of briefly having stood in the center of it. They would be tired by then, the high of New York City slowly being replaced by the exhaustion of it. Their suitcases would be filled with fridge magnets and little yellow taxicab replicas and dirty laundry and they would be sad that their vacation was over but also excited that at the end of this journey was their own bed, their own coffee mug, their own little place where they liked to wake up and take in the morning each day.

"Brooklyn is not that close to Times Square," she said. "But I like Times Square too."

"Make the band happen, Tina," Sid said, turning to face her with a smile. "Put my face up there on those billboards! And then I'll bring my mother for a holiday and show her I've become king of the world."

Tina laughed and promised Sid she would work on it.

"Or at least on one of those small billboards that line the streets in Delhi. My mother will be just as impressed by that," Sid said. "Actually, my mother won't even care about that. She'll just be happy if she knows she can pay her electricity bill next month."

"I'm so sorry," Tina said, unsure what else to say about his situation.

"Relax, you're allowed to laugh. You don't have to look at me solemnly because I'm poor. You know you do that every time I mention my mother?"

"Can I drop you off somewhere?" Tina asked as they reached the main road. "I have a car and driver with me so I can even drop you off at your hotel. Where are you staying?"

"Actually, I've heard the train system in Delhi is really good. If you just drop me off at Hauz Khas metro station, that will be good. Unless you want to try the train with me?"

Tina pretended she was tempted but she knew it would be crowded and hectic and definitely expose her as a local imposter so she said no, she would have to get back to the club to get ready for the night. As they walked toward the parking lot, Sid pulled out a beedi and lit it.

"Smoking unfiltered cigarettes isn't good for you," Tina said.

"Just call it a beedi, Tina ma'am," Sid said. "In any case, nothing is good for you so you might as well enjoy whatever you want."

They stood again at the edge of the two-way street. Tina was reaching into her bag to call Sunil to ask him to pull around to her side of the road. Sid left the lit beedi in his mouth, looked left and right for traffic, grabbed Tina's hand, and pulled her across the street, the balloons trailing behind her, right as a motorcycle swerved past them honking. His hand was the rough hand of someone who performed manual labor. They walked to the Mercedes and Sid went to get into the front seat near Sunil.

"No, you don't have to do that," Tina said. "Sit in the back."

She passed Sunil the balloons and he wrestled them into the front seat. *What was Tina doing with this young fellow?* Sunil wondered. Was she one of those visitors who chase around poor people thinking they're seeing the real India? Indians from abroad weren't usually that type; they were usually more comfortable hanging around with their wealthy cousins at Colebrookes or Gurgaon or Defence Colony. He had had one recent Indian passenger from Brighton who ducked down in the backseat every time they were stopped at a traffic signal to avoid looking at any beggars or street performers who might approach the car.

Sid dropped his beedi, crushed it with his foot, and got into the backseat with Tina. Tina wondered if she'd made him uncomfortable by insisting he sit with her. Unless the backseat was full, the front was

reserved for maids and nannies and helpers and, maybe, personal train-
ers.

At the station, Sid got out and Tina put the window down and he
leaned in.

"Let's meet again," Sid said. "If you have time."

"Of course," Tina said. "I'll make time. Tomorrow I'm tied up with
wedding things all day but maybe the day after. Or tonight I might go
out with some of the younger people at the wedding—you could join
us, maybe?"

"I couldn't do that," Sid said. "But call me tomorrow and I'll have
a plan by then. We'll go see something or eat something or drink something. It will be fun."

He pointed at the front seat and said, "Enjoy the balloons. And hey,
I bet that kid appreciated the money more than the balloons. I know I
would."

Then he smiled at her and added, "It's good to have you back,
ma'am."

Sunil started driving but the window was still open and the wind
made a balloon hit her in the face. Tina slapped it back to the front of
the car and leaned back and smiled. She took out her phone and looked
at the picture of Sid doing a pull-up. She imagined standing on a sidewalk in Bombay with him and eating pani puri for twenty rupees and
then, like in a Bollywood movie, getting caught in the monsoon rain
and running for shelter and a hot cup of tea, her hand in his rough
hand.

Colebrookes, New Delhi: Three Young Men from St. Stephens College Have Crashed the Wedding and Brought an Empty Gift-Wrapped Box to Give as a Present; They Do This Every Night During Wedding Season in Order to Eat and Drink Free

"WE COULD BE ANYWHERE IN THE WORLD RIGHT NOW," Marianne said.

Marianne, Tina, Rocco, and Kai were sitting in the living room of Rocco and Kai's cottage sharing a bottle of wine. The room had an artificial fire in the corner that flickered and even hissed like a real fire and made the room seem cozy and warm. But it had a setting that allowed you to turn off the heat since it wasn't quite cold enough yet in Delhi. The wine sat in a metal ice bucket on a stand, and on the table in front of them Rajesh had put out a cheese platter and a bowl of onion and spinach pakoras with a coriander chutney.

Marianne picked up the schedule of events and said, "It started at seven. Aren't we really late?"

"It's an Indian wedding, Marianne. Nobody is going to show up before ten, we're fine," Tina said. "And anyway, there will be literally several hundred people there. All we need to do is make sure Shefali sees our faces so she knows we came and marveled at the lavish decorations."

"Are you sure?" Marianne asked. "I feel weird being so late. What if they have something special planned for a specific time?"

"They don't," Rocco said. "Tonight is basically for Shefali's parents to preen a little and for everyone who is invited to be able to say they were invited. Right, Tina?"

"He's right," Tina said. "Relax. It means a lot to Shefali that we're here but Indian weddings are meant to actually be fun for the guests, not just a laundry list of events they have to show up for at a specific time in specific clothes. By Indian weddings, I mean the ones where eight hundred people show up even if my spoiled-but-lovable cousin doesn't know more than two hundred of them. It's meant to be a general celebration for the whole community."

Tina took a sip of her wine and added, "Listen to me pretending to be all knowledgeable. But Indian weddings really are actual fun."

"I remember being made to hold my pee in for a really long time when I was at my aunt's wedding when I was nine because she was just about to walk down the aisle and I'm still traumatized," Marianne said.

"Where did you get that anarkali?" Tina asked. "You had time to shop today?"

"I borrowed this from your mother," Marianne said, looking down at the outfit that made her feel like a queen, or at least a Bollywood star. "Rocco, how long have you lived in India for?"

"Five years next month," Rocco said. "Mostly in Bombay but sometimes, depending on how my year has gone, I rent a bungalow in Goa for December and January."

Originally from Melbourne, Rocco worked as an editor on Bollywood films. His career had picked up surprisingly fast over the past five years, and he now rented an airy two-bedroom apartment on the twelfth floor of an apartment building named Le Chateau on Fifteenth Road in Bandra West, Bombay's poshest neighborhood.

"And you like it here?" Marianne asked.

"You should all wish that if you're reborn, it's as a white man in India," Rocco said.

"Or a white man anywhere in the world," Marianne said.

"Says the oppressed white woman," Tina added.

"Adds the wealthy Indian woman," Marianne said.

"But when people look at me, they don't know whether or not I'm privileged and that itself is a lack of privilege," Tina said. "Like when most people see you, they see white skin and they assume you're privileged and treat you accordingly, thus increasing your privilege. Do you see that? So even if you're underprivileged, as a white man, you're still treated as privileged."

"In India it's easy to see which Indians are privileged, though—the way you dress, the way you inhabit space. It's not just about skin color," Rocco said.

"How long are you going to stay in India for?" Tina asked Rocco.

"How long are you going to stay in New York for?" Rocco asked her.

He got up and took the wine bottle out of the ice bucket and refilled Marianne's glass. He poured the last remaining drops into Tina's glass, put the empty bottle down on the low round coffee table, and sat down on the sofa next to Tina to use the club phone. The sofa, despite its neat appearance, hadn't been changed in years and it sank in the middle, causing Rocco to press into Tina.

"That's different, I live in New York," Tina said.

"And I live in India," Rocco said.

"One more bottle of the same, please, Rajesh," he said into the phone. "And two bottles of Bisleri water, cold."

He put the phone down and turned to the others and said, "Did Tina tell you about our wild night of lovemaking in London a few years ago?"

"You know each other?" Marianne asked.

"Tina ate a potpourri leaf that night," Rocco said.

"What?" Tina asked.

"Don't you remember? We ended up at that warm bar that looked like a library with armchairs and bookshelves and you ate a dried leaf out of a bowl of potpourri on the table."

Tina suddenly had a flashback to that night. She had done that. She had pretended it was deliberate and chewed and swallowed the whole thing even though it left her mouth tasting like soap. Then she had eaten a second one in order to make it seem intentional. Rocco hadn't said anything and she thought she had gotten away with it; so much so that she had forgotten about it until now.

"You're the London guy!" Marianne said. "I remember now. I heard about you. Tina tried to—"

"We didn't have sex," Tina cut her off. She shook her head at Marianne. She didn't want Rocco to know she had searched for him. "I was Rocco's second pick after the hot Pakistani comedian left."

"That's true. I settled for Tina. And her fancy hotel room so I wouldn't have to pay for a cab all the way back to my shitty room. But who knows? Maybe this week we'll finish our unfinished business."

He nudged Tina with his elbow and she couldn't help but laugh. There was a reason he had stayed on her mind after that night. He had intrigued her so much that night; she had found it so difficult to imagine his life in Bombay. She remembered interrogating him about his life, she recalled now.

"Do you get stared at a lot in India?" Tina had asked him at that bar in London.

"Not in Bombay. Not in Delhi so much either. Or Bangalore. Or the airports, come to think of it. The only time I've felt really aware of being an outsider was on a train from Benares to Calcutta but that could just as easily have been because I was tripping on bhang and thought there were miniature Mughal paintings coming alive and performing Hindustani classical music on the upper bunk across from me. But in Bombay, in Bandra, half the restaurants are owned by French people who are much paler than I am," Rocco had said.

"I've been to India for work a few times lately but I don't know if I could live there," Tina had said.

"It's not for everyone," Rocco had said. "But no place is, I guess. One of my friends I was traveling with moved to Wellington in New Zealand because he couldn't handle the chaos of

Asia anymore. I went to visit him and I couldn't stand the peace of it for more than a fortnight. Dreadfully bland. Why go to heaven before you're dead?"

Tina had looked into her wineglass and emptied the remaining drops into her mouth.

She did the same now, sitting next to him in India. He fit in here so seamlessly. How? When it seemed Tina didn't fit in anywhere, even here, where she looked like everyone else. Rajesh knocked on the door of the cottage and Rocco got up to answer. Rajesh peered in over Rocco's shoulder and saw Tina and Marianne sitting in the living room around the fire. All the Colebrookes staff had strict instructions to never turn the fires on when they were cleaning the rooms because the electricity charges were enormous but Rajesh always loved those fake fires and appreciated guests who turned them on.

"Looking handsome, sir," Rajesh said as he handed the fresh ice bucket to Rocco. He stepped in to take the other bottle and ice bucket away and looked around the room. "Everyone looking lovely."

He loved the big weddings that took over the club this time of year. In a different world, under different circumstances, Rajesh would have been a fashion designer. Whenever he worked at these fancy weddings, later at night, in his shared room at the back of the club, he took out a little notebook and drew sketches of the best women's outfits he had seen that night. He looked over at Marianne and Tina—they both looked beautiful but they weren't fashion-forward enough to go in his notebook. Rajesh bowed at them all and stepped back into the night.

There was another knock and Tina went to open the door. The bride and groom stood there, Pavan wearing a perfectly tailored navy-blue suit and Shefali wearing what could only be described as a floor-length Indian cape with gold embroidery running through it. Under it she wore skinny black ankle pants and a black crop top that showed off her slim waist. On her feet were a new pair of gold Louboutins with sharp spikes at the back that Tina had seen her buy in New York City. The towering heels made her stand about an inch taller than Pavan and she had both her arms wrapped around his torso. Shefali's hair was tied into a tight, low bun with a perfectly straight, thin middle part and her eyes were heavily lined with kohl. A large red bindi dotted her forehead. She looked stunning.

"We escaped," Shefali said with a laugh and entered the cottage. "Getting married is so much more boring than I thought it would be. We're just standing there shaking hands with a thousand people we barely know. I don't understand why my mother wouldn't let me wear a white dress and walk down an aisle."

"An old lady kissed me on the lips," Pavan said. He sat down on the sofa and Shefali sat down next to him and tumbled toward him, kissing his cheek.

"I don't blame her," she said. She wiped her lipstick off his cheek.

Shefali kicked off her heels and pulled her feet up. Pavan leaned back and put one arm around her and took out a steel flask from his pocket.

"Warm Old Monk," he said. "Cheers."

He had a large gulp and passed it to Shefali, who also had one.

"We need Thums-Up to go with this," Shefali said, wincing. "And ideally a cigarette, but my mother will have a heart attack if she smells smoke on me."

Tina looked at them, so comfortable in their Indian clothes, leaning into each other, drinking the sweet Indian rum.

"This reminds me of my college drinking days," Shefali said.

"I used to sneak Old Monk into movie theaters," Pavan said.

"Same! And into the tombs in Lodhi Gardens," Shefali added.

There was another loud banging on the door and this time Marianne walked over to open it. Outside stood Karan, Pavan's brother, broad-chested and handsome, wearing a plain black sherwani, his hair flopping over into eyes that betrayed his intoxication. He looked at Marianne and said, "Oh, hello. Aren't you stunning? I'm Karan, brother of the groom."

Marianne instinctively tucked her hair behind her ear and smiled.

Karan dropped his cigarette onto the ground and crushed it under his foot. He stepped into the cottage and stopped and looked at Marianne again and said, "You're really gorgeous."

"Wow, thank you. I mean, I didn't really have much time to—" Marianne began, but Karan walked straight into the kitchen and poured himself a glass of wine while Marianne stood in the doorway staring at him, her whole body feeling as though it would dissolve like a cube of sugar in tea.

"Shefali, I've been sent to hunt you down," Karan said. "Your mother noticed you two slipping out of the side gate."

"I can't do anything without Ma noticing," Shefali said. "Such a hypocrite. She and Papa secretly went and got legally married two weeks before their real wedding to take the pressure off and still she sends someone after me because I left the venue for two minutes."

Pavan looked at Shefali as she spoke and removed her bindi that had gone off center and put it back perfectly in place. Shefali kept talking, and Tina instinctively put her own fingers up to her forehead even though she wasn't wearing a bindi tonight. Shefali stopped abruptly and said, "Oh no, Tina, I just realized I didn't tell you Rocco was coming this week."

"No, you didn't," Tina said.

"Rocco, you never called her, did you? Asshole," Shefali said. "Tina, is this awkward?"

"It is now," Tina said. She threw a pillow at Shefali, who ducked and laughed. "Stop it! If my hair gets messy, my mother is going to think I disappeared to have sex with Pavan."

Pavan reached over and tousled Shefali's hair and said, "Then we might as well."

"You didn't say where you're going for your honeymoon," Marianne said.

Karan looked over at her when she spoke and said, "You need a nose piercing. And a nice big pair of jhumkas for your ears."

"Please, no," Tina said. "That beret you wore for six months when you were dating Samuel was enough."

"Your honeymoon, Shefali?" Marianne tried again to change the direction of the conversation. That beret really had been misguided. She had bought it at Nordstrom Rack the week after meeting Samuel, the French artist with whom she had also taken up rolling cigarettes and learning all about Toulouse-Lautrec. For a brief period there, she had had very passionate views about commercial sex work.

"Right. That's because I don't know," Shefali said. "Pavan's planning all of it. I only know that we're starting in Singapore. The rest is a surprise."

"You are setting up high expectations for the rest of your married life," Rocco said.

"And I'll meet those expectations," Pavan said. He looked over at Shefali and said, "Chalein?"

"Already?" Shefali asked. "Ek aur sip. Then we'll go back."

They took another swig each from the flask. Shefali stood up and leaned against Pavan's shoulder as she put her heels back on.

"And all of you please make sure you sign the waivers for the wedding video and give it to Bubbles. I'd really rather not have her make that assistant of hers forge a bunch of signatures," Shefali said and followed Pavan out of the cottage.

The assistant was Bubbles's driver, Ritwik, who was the only one on her staff who could read, and he was sitting in the dark with an assortment of pens trying to figure out how to ask Bubbles for a bonus for committing fraud.

In the cottage, Karan got up to leave with the bride and groom but stopped in front of Marianne and said, "Head over soon. I want to know everything about you."

Marianne nodded and started wondering what she would tell him about herself, who she could be with this handsome Indian stranger. She would tell him about her time in Condesa in Mexico City, she decided, but she would be vague and make it sound like she went there every year, instead of admitting that she had only been there once. Fancy international men loved tales of annual globetrotting, she found. Tom's family spent every summer on the Cape but that didn't have quite the same ring to it as Condesa.

After Shefali, Pavan, and Karan left, Tina searched through her email for the correspondence she had had with her boss, Rachel, when she was auditioning people for the making of the band. She found what she was looking for—the picture Sid had submitted with his initial application. In it, he was leaning against a dirty wall wearing jeans rolled up at the ankles, no shirt and no shoes. His dark skin glistened in the sun and he was smiling at something just past the camera.

"Dating app?" Rocco asked as he poured a refill for Tina.

Tina looked down at her screen, shook her head, and nibbled her cuticle. Her nail polish was chipping but she hadn't had time to get a manicure. She always wished she could be one of those women with perfectly done nails, and she tried from time to time. But she inevitably lost interest and left her gel polish on for too long and ended up cutting her nails with the polish still on and hating the sight of her hands for weeks.

"It's someone I'm auditioning," Tina said. "I think. I *was* auditioning him, anyway."

"You have a picture of the drummer? You never told me that," Marianne said with a laugh. "Show me. You're so secretive about him."

"No, it's nothing," Tina said. She locked her phone and placed it facedown on the sofa next to her. Something about that shirtless picture of Sid felt too intimate at the moment, even though Tina had passed it around her office and pinned a large printout on the corkboard in the conference room. "Let's not talk about work."

Goldenrod Garden, Colebrookes, New Delhi: One of the Bartenders Has Already Managed to Tuck an Expensive Bottle of Whiskey into His Pant Leg

"IF THIS IS THE COCKTAIL PARTY, WHAT WILL THE WEDDING BE like?" Marianne whispered to Tina as they approached the main entrance to the reception.

"You'll have to wait and see, darling," a woman with a smoky, raspy voice said behind them. "But let me just assure you that it includes a full Bollywood dance number, performed by actual Bollywood stars. Zara and Zarina are coming in for the wedding."

"Shefali knows Zara and Zarina?" Tina asked, surprised that her cousin was friends with the famous Bollywood actors.

"No, darling. She isn't friends with them but she can afford to fly them in for her wedding to pretend she's friends with them." The woman shook her head. "You're on the bride's side, I assume?"

Tina and Marianne introduced themselves to Mrs. Bubbles Trivedi, the wedding planner. In actuality, Bubbles was frantically trying to find Zara and Zarina impersonators because Zara and Zarina had canceled last minute due to pregnancy rumors surrounding Zara and Vikram Abraham, the very married cricket player.

Mrs. Bubbles Trivedi was wearing a gold sari with the pallu draped across her shoulders, and had matching gold hair, hanging loose, and diamonds sparkling all over her body. She was short and round and glamorous. When Marianne and Tina extended their hands, she slipped the familiar gold business cards into them, laden with more glitter to stick to their hands.

"You two look marriageable age. Keep my card," she said and added to Marianne, "I plan weddings anywhere and everywhere. The world is your oyster, darlings, but don't wait too long. Oysters go bad very quickly. Enjoy the cocktails, ladies."

Bubbles went past them to find Arun and Maria Goswami, the owners of India's largest e-commerce site. She had heard rumors that their daughter, Leia, was dating someone distantly related to Prince William and she needed that contract. This was really only the second wedding Bubbles had planned. The first was her own son's in Goa last year. Her daughter-in-law happened to be a fashion designer in Bombay who'd invited some real A-list Bollywood celebrities, and the wedding had been so successful that Bubbles found herself telling people she had organized the wedding with no mention that it was her son's, and next thing she knew, Shefali's mother, who had been there, called her to help arrange a similar wedding in Delhi for her daughter. Bubbles quoted what she thought was an astronomical amount, and when Meera agreed easily, Bubbles discovered it wasn't terribly difficult being a wedding planner if you had a big budget.

She straightened her diamond necklace and surveyed the crowd. This was going to be terrific for her portfolio. Once the wedding video was finished, she would buy a hundred thousand YouTube hits and promote it on social media. The rest of the hits would naturally follow.

Ten horses lined the main entrance with ten white men in some sort of uniform sitting atop them on sturdy leather saddles. They all had blond hair parted on the side and wore riding boots. Bubbles had found them all at a backpackers' hostel in Daryaganj and offered them five thousand rupees each and a free dinner. One of the men was bent over on his horse chatting with a young Indian woman in a sheer black sari. Bubbles went up to them and hit the man's boot with her purse and said, "I didn't pay you to flirt. You sit upright and look British."

"I'm from South Africa," the man on the horse said.

"Nobody needs to know where you're from," Bubbles said, shaking her head at him and walking ahead.

She checked that all the other men on horses looked suitably distinguished and then spotted Arun and Maria Goswami, Maria in a crushed-velvet, purple floor-length jacket with huge solitaire diamonds in her ears.

"Maria! Arun!" Bubbles said. "How lovely to see you. Gosh, it's been ages."

Technically not a lie; she had never met them before.

Large speakers at the four corners of the lawn played instrumental shehnai music. Kai and Rocco wandered off to the bhel puri stand and Tina and Marianne headed toward the huge, round bar in the middle of the lush lawns. There must have already been close to three hundred people milling about. Looking around, Tina realized that cocktail night meant Indo-Western wear, not just traditional Indian attire. The men were mostly wearing jeans with blazers and the women were all in some variation of Indian clothes that weren't quite Indian. On the other side of the bar, Tina could see Shefali and Pavan standing side by side and glowing. Glowing more than everyone else was. Was this really the effect love had?

They shook hands with the people they were talking to and Tina watched them stay glowing and bright as they approached some other guests, and that's when she noticed they were in a spotlight that was being controlled from behind the trees in the distance. If she followed their subtle glow carefully, she could see that they were being very strategically bathed in a soft, diffused yellow light that wasn't so bright as to be obvious but was just bright enough to let the couple shine brighter than the rest of the people in the crowd. There must have been someone tasked with keeping the light moving smoothly around with them because they maintained this perfect glow no matter where they went. So it wasn't love, it was just good lighting; at least that was something money could buy.

"I could find a husband here," Marianne said. "And come to parties like this every weekend. Maybe someone like Karan."

"You have Tom," Tina said.

"He's not going to propose," Marianne said.

"Maybe that's because you've never given him a reason to think he should," Tina said. "How can you not see that you're meant for each other? I have never seen you happier than when you're with Tom— I mean like truly, truly, deeply happy. I'm not talking about the contact highs you got with Sven or Riyaaz or Minh or Seydou—wow, you really have been around the world. Karan is your typical handsome asshole."

"So handsome," Marianne said, scanning the crowd for him.

"Extremely handsome. But you just know he's going to be another Riyaaz," Tina said. "I, on the other hand, need to find my own Pavan— someone reliable who will straighten my bindi and drink Old Monk with me."

Tina looked over at a tall, handsome Indian man standing alone, his arms crossed in front of him. His chest was broad and he looked powerful.

"Someone like that," she nudged Marianne. "He looks different from the rest of the crowd somehow."

They both looked over at the man, now surveying the crowd. Tina caught his eye for a fleeting second and smiled. He nodded at them.

"Should I go and say hi?" Tina asked. "Let's go talk to him."

They made their way over to the man, who now looked above their heads and continued staring at the crowd.

"Unavailable men are so attractive," Tina whispered to Marianne.

Tina stopped to grab a tandoori prawn off the tray of a passing waiter. She pulled the prawn out of the tail and ate it and then held the tail and looked around.

"Damn it, I didn't take a napkin. Put this prawn tail in your purse," she said to Marianne.

"No. You know I'm deathly allergic," Marianne said. "And even if I wasn't, I'm not putting your prawn tail in my purse."

"Hello," Tina said to the man. "Are you on the bride's side or the groom's?"

The tall man looked down at Tina and Marianne. Behind him, Bubbles Trivedi was gushing to Maria and Arun Goswami about their website.

"Groom," he said and looked over his shoulder at the Goswamis.

"So easy to navigate," Bubbles was saying. "And they make returns so easy by sending someone to collect the item. Thank goodness for cheap labor in this country, am I right? The silver lining of income inequality."

Bubbles laughed.

"We like to see it as an attempt to decrease the inequality," Maria Goswami said coldly.

"And how is darling Leia?" Bubbles continued. "She's grown into such a beautiful young woman. The world's eyes are on her."

Tina made eye contact with the tall man and rolled her eyes. He smiled and nodded slightly but said nothing.

"She's a character, that Bubbles," Tina said with a laugh. "I'm Tina, cousin of the bride. And this is my friend, Marianne."

"Ankur," the man said.

"Look at those diamonds," Marianne whispered to Tina, staring at the huge solitaire diamond sparkling in Maria Goswami's cleavage.

"My friend is eyeing Maria's diamonds," Tina said. "Create a diversion so we can steal it and run. And I can slip this prawn tail into her purse while we're at it."

The man uncrossed his arms, placed one hand on Marianne's shoulder, and said, "Please do not get any closer to the Goswamis."

He muttered something in Marathi into a black earpiece that Tina only now noticed in his ear. Right. He was the Goswamis' bodyguard.

"We would appreciate you both keeping your distance from Mrs. Goswami tonight," he said to Tina and Marianne. He crossed his arms again and stood tall in front of them, again looking over their heads. "We will be watching you."

"Maybe he and I are not meant to be," Tina said. "Let's go get a drink."

Fairy lights, huge balls of marigold flowers and candles gave the entire lawn a warm glow. Tina and Marianne walked toward a group of women who looked vaguely familiar. They all had long, thick black hair, skin that glowed, and jewels that sparkled on them. As Marianne and Tina reached within earshot, Tina could hear them speaking comfortably in a mix of Hindi and English.

"Tina, is that you? Shefali's cousin?" one of the women asked. Her arms were hennaed up to her elbows and gold bracelets clinked on both wrists. She was wearing a gold maang tikka in the part of her hair and her eyes were lined heavily with kohl.

"Aarti?" Tina asked. "Am I remembering right?"

"Yes! Gosh, it's so good to see you. It's been ages."

Tina introduced Marianne to Aarti, Shefali's friend from school, and the rest of the women, also friends of Shefali's. How did rich Indian women all have such great hair, Marianne wondered. Any one of these women could be married to Riyaaz now, she thought.

"I kept meaning to look you up while I was at Pratt but time just flew. Are you still living in New York? I could never. My dishwasher flooded my entire apartment and that's when I knew I was done living abroad."

"It was someone in London calling me Paki that did it for me," another one of the long-limbed women said. "I didn't even know that was meant to be racist until the guy I was with got offended on my behalf. I got even more annoyed that he thought I needed to be defended."

"You're both fools," another one of the friends said. "I'd move to London or New York in a second if I wasn't married. Do you know how much the Delhi pollution is ruining our lungs?"

"You smoke a pack a day," Aarti said.

"Half a pack," the friend said. Then she looked at Tina and Marianne and said, "But none of you Americans smoke anymore. That would be my one issue."

"She just likes to work it into every conversation that she's married," Aarti said. "Because the rest of us aren't yet."

"What are you girls waiting for?" Bubbles emerged as if out of thin air. "You don't want it to get too late. Here, take my card. Bubbles Trivedi, wedding planner."

Bubbles handed her card out to everyone, including Marianne and Tina again.

"We met earlier," Marianne said, holding out the card to return.

Bubbles ignored her and continued, "Ovaries expire, you know. I had three miscarriages myself. Although one may just have been a heavy period. Anyway, the point is that you girls need to get a move on. The brother of the groom is single."

"And he's slept with every woman in Delhi," one of Shefali's friends said.

"And half of London and Hong Kong and Dubai," Aarti added.

Marianne pocketed the second card, more glitter covering her hands.

"We're going to get a drink," Tina said. "Aarti, it was nice seeing you."

"Let me know if you need any help around Delhi. I know Shefali's probably super busy," Aarti said.

"That's annoying," Tina said to Marianne as they walked away. "It was so condescending how she offered help. As if I don't know my way around Delhi."

"I thought she was being nice," Marianne said. "And please do message her and find out where she shops. She looked incredible."

"There you are. The most beautiful woman at the wedding," Karan said at that moment, grabbing Marianne by the hand and twirling her around. "Come on, I want to introduce you to some friends."

Marianne looked at Tina, smiled, and vanished into the crowd before Tina could stop her.

Tina made her way through the glittering crowd toward Shefali and Pavan. She walked past Maria and Arun Goswami again, talking to another couple about a chartered flight to Monaco. She kept a safe distance, worried that their bodyguard would knock her to the ground if she didn't. A mixed group of men and women were discussing a golfing holiday. One couple was whispering audibly to each other about going to the bathroom for a bump of cocaine. Everyone was drinking champagne from Champagne and whiskey with large round balls of ice with no clouds. Bubbles was standing next to a group of three men saying, "It's all fun and games now but you're going to want to find a bride before the inevitable male-pattern baldness kicks in. Here, take my card."

Tina stopped at a large table filled with ice and shot glasses of vodka and oysters on the half shell. A woman about her age came and stood next to her and dripped Tabasco onto her oyster and swallowed it.

"Not bad. They flew them in from Cochin," she said and turned to Tina and held out her hand. "Swati, friend of the groom. Ex of the groom, actually. Nice to meet you."

"Tina. Cousin of the bride," Tina said.

"She's a lucky bride," Swati said. Swati was wearing a pink-and-red sari with a black blouse and black bindi. She spoke with an American accent. "Pavan's a great guy."

"Are you from the US?" Tina asked.

"Born and raised in San Diego," Swati said. "But I've been in Delhi for about five years now. I work for the UN. Vodka shot?"

Tina nodded and knocked back a remarkably smooth vodka shot. She noticed a diamond sparkling on Swati's ring finger and pointed toward it and said, "You're married?"

Swati twirled the ring with her thumb and said, "Three years. He's not here tonight, though. He's in DC for work."

"Is he Indian?" Tina asked.

"French. And fifteen years older than me and has a teenage daughter who lives in Paris. Best relationship of my life. We met here," Swati said. "You?"

Tina shook her head.

Swati didn't register Tina's response. Instead she looked over at Pavan and Shefali and said, "One more shot for me."

Tina watched her down it, wipe her mouth with a napkin, and say, "Now I can go say hi to the happy couple. I never thought he'd marry her."

Tina picked up the Tabasco to try on the oyster but too much came out. She tried to pour some off but then it looked like she had bled on the ice. She swallowed the oyster whole and tried using the empty shell to scrape the ice over the red spill. She looked over her shoulder. Nobody had seen. She quickly moved to the champagne counter right next to it and asked for a glass. Rocco came up next to her and said, "Kai found a Brazilian model from Goa and a waiter with a platter of tandoori prawns. I have been abandoned."

He opened his fist and revealed four prawn tails.

"And I need a napkin."

"I have also been abandoned," Tina said. And she added her prawn tail to his collection.

"It's so good seeing you," Rocco said to Tina. "Do you remember the bangers and mash we were so determined to find at the end of that night?"

"I do!" Tina said. "And thank God every place was closed because I would for sure have vomited if I'd eaten at that point."

Rocco clinked his glass against hers and said, "I asked Shefali about you a few times."

"We don't have to do this," Tina said.

"I really did ask her," Rocco said. "I even googled you. You got promoted last year, didn't you?"

"Now I do even less at a higher salary. It's been difficult. I've had so many close calls but ever since the project I was doing in India fell apart, I've kind of lost motivation."

Tina told Rocco about the reality show she had been trying to cast.

"I heard about that show. There was a lot of enthusiasm about it in the local music community. It would have been good," he said.

"It's getting frustrating," Tina said. "I feel like I don't have any control over whether or not something will actually happen. And when something moves in the right direction, I'm so nervous that it'll fall apart, I lose my ability to work efficiently."

"Anything collaborative can be difficult," Rocco said. "My best work, the film I'm proudest of, didn't make it past the Indian censor board and the director refused to make the changes they asked for so it's likely nobody will ever see it."

"I think I want to do something more meaningful. Something that will really impact lives," Tina said. "That sounds a little immature, doesn't it? Like what does meaningful even mean? If it were that simple, it would be . . . simple. I don't know."

Loud fireworks suddenly erupted above their heads and caught Tina off guard. She grabbed Rocco's arm and he put his hand on her hand. They looked up to see three helicopters hovering overhead holding a banner that had a picture of Shefali and Pavan. Another loud firework and the banner exploded into multicolored carnations that fell from the sky.

"Impressive," Rocco said, turning to look at her. His grip on her hand tightened momentarily and neither of them moved for a beat before Tina pulled her hand back and asked, "How the hell did they get permission to do that in the middle of Delhi?"

"I went to a wedding last year that had hired a Russian synchronized swimming team," Rocco said. He looked at Tina still looking up at the sky and added, "I saw your picture on the Pixl website. That's a great shot of you."

"What?" Tina looked back at him. "The one of me in a collared shirt? I hate that picture. I look so corporate. As if I'd wear a pencil skirt and pumps and get my hair blow-dried. Utterly misleading."

She had been wearing a T-shirt with a small Pepsi logo on it that day and the company wouldn't allow any logos in pictures. So she was forced to wear a plain, white button-down shirt that Rachel had in her office and she had always intended to update the picture but never got around to it.

"I thought you looked good," Rocco said.

"Did you see the flower explosion?" David and Radha approached Tina and Rocco, David's face lit up with excitement. "It was wild."

"I had heard something about flowers getting hand-painted and now I know why," Radha said.

"This is like a movie set," David said.

"He's too enthusiastic," Radha said with an indulgent smile.

Rocco put his hand out to introduce himself and Radha introduced herself as Tina's mother and introduced David, without adding on any relationship.

"You're Tina's mother?" Rocco asked. "Are you sure? You don't look like someone who would have an adult daughter. Now I understand where she gets her beauty."

"Aren't you kind," Radha said.

"Charmer," David said. He turned to Tina and added, "He's a charmer. Where's that accent from? South Africa? Always wanted to go."

"Australia," Tina said and looked around for her father but he was nowhere to be seen.

"Remember that Australian couple we met at the bar in Miami?" David asked Radha.

"When did you go to Miami?" Tina asked.

UNCHARACTERISTICALLY, RADHA HAD BOOKED two tickets to Miami for a weekend last spring and surprised David. She had been to Miami once before for a conference and loved it and had always wanted to go back. Ever since she had met David she had been going to spinning classes and was feeling particularly slender on the day that she bought the tickets and booked the hotel. She had then gone to Eileen Fisher and bought a white one-piece bathing suit with a zipper up the front and a zebra-print wrap and large straw hat to go with it. She had held David's hand and laughed over a glass of wine at the airport. She hadn't told anyone she was going and felt giddy with excitement on the whole flight there.

Tina had called her while she was sitting with her feet in the pool drinking a cosmopolitan with David, and Radha had told Tina she was with a client and hung up and ordered one more drink. Two young men were sitting at the table on the pool's edge and one of them raised his glass at Radha and said, "Cheers, girl. That bathing suit is working on you."

"It really is," David said. "You're striking."

Radha sat up a little straighter and leaned in and kissed David on the cheek. He put his arm around her and Radha leaned into his wide chest. Was this what she had missed by marrying a man who lived a life of the mind, a career of Excel spreadsheets? Neel never would have spent a lazy evening drinking cocktails with his feet in water. He hated his fingers or toes pruning. Holidays with Neel involved research and long walks and historical sites and knowledge and while she was grateful for that for Tina's sake, sometimes she just wanted to lounge near a pool in a bathing suit.

After two drinks that day, Radha changed into a sleeveless linen dress and they decided to stroll north up the beach for dinner at the Bazaar at the SLS. On the way there, they stopped at a bar with no people but filled with fake palm trees and tiki torches and plastic flamingoes, and David said, "Two vodka Red Bulls."

"And one heart attack," Radha said. "Are you mad? I'll stick to a vodka tonic with a wedge of lime."

"I wouldn't touch the lime at a dive like this if I were you," David said. "A Red Bull would be safer."

They both had their drinks fast and then an unfamiliar version of Frank Sinatra's "I've Got You Under My Skin" came on and David grabbed Radha's hand and pulled her into the middle of an empty dance floor. Radha laughed and allowed David to spin her around and the room blurred into pinks and greens as she danced. She had never been inside a bar this filthy and she had never had so much fun.

But then, on the beach, Radha saw the groups of young people with their perfectly bronzed skin and tight abs and long limbs and rubbed her bare arms. Two women on Rollerblades shouted out, "Excuse me, ma'am," as they sped past her. Radha looked down at her dress and stopped to pull out a shrug from her large wicker purse.

"It's chilly by the water," she said.

David nodded and they kept walking.

At the Bazaar, Radha and David were seated side by side on a plush, white sofa and Radha excused herself to go to the bathroom while they waited for their bone marrow appetizer. From the bathroom, she called Tina but got her voicemail. She left her a message saying she was sorry she couldn't speak earlier and she hoped she had a good evening tonight and would she like to come over for dinner on Monday night? They could order sushi.

On Monday night, Tina asked her, "Did you get some sun? You look darker and kind of glowing. What's your secret?"

"I went to a tanning booth," Radha said. "It's supposed to be good for anxiety."

The next day Tina went to a tanning salon behind NYU. She didn't lock the door well enough and the receptionist came in while she was lying in the bed wearing her underwear and a small pair of dark glasses. She heard the door open and tried to sit up fast and banged her head against the top of the tanning booth. The small glasses toppled off her face and she squinted her eyes in the brightness.

"Lock the door, lock the door," the receptionist muttered angrily as she backed out of the room. "What do these people think this is? A massage parlor?"

SHE COULDN'T BELIEVE HER mother had gone to Miami with David. Tina and Marianne had been to Miami for spring break their senior year and she couldn't imagine her mother in that setting. Granted, her mother probably wasn't doing Jägerbombs at Señor, but still. South Beach wasn't for Indian mothers.

Tina looked around the lawn at everyone so beautiful, so flawless, guzzling bottles of mineral water and expensive alcohol. She looked at her mother, taking risks and looking happy. What was the last risk Tina had taken? Getting on the East River Ferry without a ticket?

She texted Sid. *This party is dull. What are you doing?*

She received a reply within seconds. *Thinking about how much I enjoyed seeing you again. Bunk the party. Run away. Come find me.*

Tina looked up at the people, all the beautiful people in their beautiful clothes and thought, Marianne was right—they could be anywhere in the world tonight. She wanted to be in India.

Where does one find you at this hour? she texted back.

Sid gave her cryptic instructions to the middle of a flyover near the Red Fort and told her to find him there on the side of the road in thirty minutes.

Tell your driver to just drop you off and that you'll call him when you're ready to be picked up. He won't have anywhere he can wait on the flyover.

"Where are you going, Cinderella?" Rocco caught her near the exit.

"Jet lag," she said. "I'm going to go sleep."

"I'll walk you, I need a cigarette," Rocco said.

Tina let Rocco walk along with her as she headed toward the car park. He didn't seem to register that she wasn't going in the direction of the cottages.

She took his cigarette from him and took a drag. She coughed and handed it back, "Nope, I can't do it. I don't know how I even pretended to enjoy the occasional one in college."

"Why are we going to the car park?" Rocco stopped and looked around. The dim fairy lights that were scattered through all the trees made Rocco's eyes glisten blue. No wonder she had run around London with him that night.

"I'm going to meet someone," Tina said. She pulled out her phone and called Sunil and told him to pull up.

"Lucky guy," Rocco said. "You look beautiful."

"Thanks," Tina said. "But it's not romantic."

"Good," Rocco said. "Go, go. Disappear into the night and do your thing. You're on holiday."

He grabbed her hand and kissed it.

Somewhere in New Delhi:
Tina's Not Really Sure—Is This Even Safe?
Probably Not

"THERE," TINA SAID TO SUNIL. SHE COULD SEE SID ON THE SIDE of the overbridge, the headlights catching him standing on the edge of the narrow pavement leaning on his elbows and looking out over the railing. Cars and trucks rattled past, lighting up his frame. "Stop right over there."

"Ma'am," Sunil said. "This is not a suitable place for you."

Tina met his eyes in the rearview mirror and said, "I'll call you when I need you, Sunil. Thank you."

She had seen the way Shefali communicated with her staff and tried to channel the same sense of authority. Shefali always said, "Remember, if you treat your staff like family, they'll treat you like family, and more family is the last thing you need."

Tina wrapped her shawl tightly around her to hide her bare midriff and pulled off her diamond earrings and dropped them into her purse.

She walked up to Sid and saw what he was looking at. Laal Qila, the Red Fort, rising up above the city, the view unobstructed from this point on the overbridge. Below them, cars, trucks, bikes, autos, and even a bullock cart went by. Behind them, more vehicles. But if they ignored all that, in front of them was the majestic fort and above it, the moon. Tina stood next to Sid in silence. He turned to face her, smiled, and looked back at the fort with reverence, the rest of him still. The sound of the traffic fell away, the chaos of Delhi was silent. Too silent. The darkness and the beauty in front of them were making Tina uncomfortable so she said, "How did you discover this?"

"The World Wide Web, Tina," he said, smiling. "I looked up things to do in Delhi."

"So did I, but I got a list of designer shops to visit in Shahpur Jat. What did you google?"

"Ah, even our search terms are from different worlds," Sid said. "Now, stop worrying and enjoy. Who cares how I found it?"

From there Tina followed Sid along the narrow sidewalk to the bottom of the bridge. The traffic was less there, and they managed to walk side by side. Tina had only ever seen this side of Delhi from inside an air-conditioned car and she had always been a little scared of it. But now it didn't seem so terrifying. They stepped past two men sleeping on the sidewalk, wrapped up in dirty shawls, their chappals under their heads as makeshift pillows. The men were curled into tight balls to protect against the cold and the world. Sid was talking about one of his training clients who had flown him to Goa and then not exercised once while they were there.

"It was my first time on an airplane," he said. "I loved it so much. I didn't expect it to be quite so magnificent. My client was flying in business class and he apologized to me about economy class. But I saw his seat and it was much farther away from a window than mine was. If anything, I was the one who should have been apologizing to him."

Sid had stopped walking and pulled out his wallet. He took two hundred-rupee notes and secured one near each sleeping man.

"Merry Christmas," he said and kept walking. The thought hadn't even crossed Tina's mind and she was sure she had much more money in her purse. But if she added to it now it would look offensive so instead she said, "And a happy New Year," and they kept walking in the darkness of the November night.

"And a happy Valentine's Day," Sid added with a smile.

"And a blessed Republic Day," Tina added.

"And a prosperous Holi," Sid said.

A man sat in a wheelchair, a dirty turban wrapped around his head. He looked at Tina and Sid walking past. In front of him, a woman squatted on the ground reading from a newspaper.

"Look at these two wandering around looking for drugs," the husband said, pointing his chin toward Sid and Tina, who were outside hearing range. Tina caught his eye and smiled at him.

"Chalo, okay, let's do it, it's been a while," the man said to his wife in a mix of Hindi, English, and Punjabi.

The wife got up, looked over at Tina and Sid, and screamed at the man in Punjabi, pushed him over, covered her face with the pallu of her sari, and walked away in the opposite direction. She hid behind a pillar and watched. Her husband looked over at her and stood, shaking, both hands grasping the sides of his wheelchair, and fell to the ground clutching his turban and saying, "Oh heavens, oh lord, oh dear, my legs."

Tina and Sid ran over to the man and helped him up. The man looked at the concern in Tina's eyes and almost felt guilty but then he saw a stone sparkle on the ground. Something had fallen out of the woman's purse. Something shiny and probably expensive. As they settled him back into his chair, he used his foot to kick the bauble under the chair where she wouldn't notice it.

"Is there anything we can do for you?" Tina asked.

"Nothing, nothing at all. You've already helped," he said. "Go on your way, enjoy your evening. God bless you both."

Behind the pillar his wife laughed and laughed. Her husband would have been a brilliant actor if he'd been given the opportunity.

The man watched Tina and Sid disappear. When they were out of sight, he bent down, picked up the earring, ran to find his wife behind the pillar, and opened his hand to reveal the glistening earring.

The wife picked it up and smiled at her husband.

"I've never owned a diamond before," she said.

"I told you this wheelchair would bring us luck," he said. "And you should have seen the girl's face—so proud of herself. Bless her."

"You still really shouldn't steal wheelchairs," she said, giving him a kiss on his cheek and walking back over to their belongings to find something to thread the earring to in order to wear as a necklace.

A few yards ahead, under the bridge, Tina and Sid approached what looked like a family gathered around a small pushcart. The father was lying on a mat holding up a small transistor radio to his ear, listening to a cricket match. Two small children were squatting beside him stacking rocks on top of one another. The mother, a worn shawl covering her head, stood at the pushcart cooking corn over hot coals. Tina pulled her shawl tighter.

"Are you cold?" Sid asked. "Bombay doesn't have seasons. Not like this, anyway. In Bombay we have hot, hotter, and wet."

"I wouldn't miss the New York winter," Tina said. "But other than that, I love seasons."

"I don't think I could handle seasons every year," Sid said. "It would make me too aware of the passage of time. Bhutta?"

Tina looked at the woman making the corn. It was filthy all around her, actual heaps of garbage lying near the roadside. The children weren't wearing pants and one of them had snot running out of his nose.

"Actually, I need to get back to the club before anyone realizes I'm gone," Tina said. But she looked up to find a street name and intersection quickly. Maybe she could come back and film this family. But what would the story be? She couldn't make an entire show simply documenting filth and poverty. That felt somehow icky, voyeuristic, not hers to tell. But then who could tell it? If Tina didn't tell their story because it wasn't hers to tell, wouldn't the next person in her job do it and work her way up to an Emmy nomination?

Sid smiled a knowing smile and said, "Yeah, you probably wouldn't want to eat this anyway. Not sure if your stomach could handle it."

"No, it isn't that," Tina said quickly. "It's not that at all."

"I shouldn't be making you wander around Delhi in the middle of the night."

"No, this is amazing," Tina said.

"So is that club you're staying at," Sid said.

Tina shook her head.

"This is the Delhi I wanted to see, not just the club. But I really do have to go," she said. "I've got a full day tomorrow and I need to sleep."

She called Sunil and then looked back up to Sid's face. Even with her in heels, he was quite a few inches taller than her and his height gave him a slight slouch that made him look forever casual. A car drove past, a remixed version of an old Bollywood song she recognized playing loudly.

MR. DAS WAS LISTENING to the same Bollywood song, but it was the original version, not a remix, and he was not under a bridge or in the Goldenrod Garden of Colebrookes, but on Mrs. Sethi's balcony with the cool Delhi air filtering in as they sat drinking tea and chatting.

"You're sure you don't have to go to that cocktail party?" Mrs. Sethi asked.

"They've invited a thousand people, they'll never notice I'm not there," Mr. Das said. "And there's nowhere else I want to be right now."

Mrs. Sethi smiled and Anita came out carrying a tray with a plate of hot, fried vegetable pakoras and two small glasses of sweet port wine.

"Why did I ever leave India?" Mr. Das asked.

"Why did you?"

Mr. Das picked up a spinach pakora and said, "This wasn't my India. I didn't know this could be India. This wasn't my America either. My parents worked and worked and worked and we lived well but they were never that interested in relaxation or pleasure."

"That word sounds too indulgent," Mrs. Sethi said. "Pleasure. I don't see it as that. I see it as appreciation. Of the little things, you know? Appreciating the cool air despite the pollution. Enjoying the pakoras despite how unhealthy they are. Actively seeking out pleasure can feel a bit selfish in this world filled with cruelty."

"To the art of appreciation, then." He lifted his glass of port and sipped. "This is delicious."

"I bought that in Portugal. Minal and I took a holiday there last year. Actually, that was purely for pleasure," Mrs. Sethi laughed. "Sometimes pure pleasure is hard to resist, indulgent or not."

"I'm worried Tina also doesn't know how to enjoy herself," Mr. Das said. "She lives like me. For work and for others, rarely for herself. Does your daughter have a boyfriend? You've never said."

"A boyfriend, no," Mrs. Sethi said. "But she has a roommate, as Minal always says, with an emphasis on the word. A female roommate."

"Roommates are good but not the same as a husband at the end of the day," Mr. Das said. "What if this roommate goes off and gets married? Then your daughter also will end up alone."

Mrs. Sethi laughed and said, "Not a roommate, Neel, a girlfriend. My daughter doesn't use the word yet but she has a girlfriend. She has a roommate, in the same room, in a two-bedroom apartment in San Francisco. My daughter is gay."

"Your daughter has a two-bedroom apartment in San Francisco?" Mr. Das asked.

"Her roommate runs a tech company. I don't quite know what she does but it lets them live in a two-bedroom apartment near Dolores Park."

"Tina also lives in a two-bedroom apartment but with no roommates of any sort. I worry about her," Mr. Das said.

"That's our job."

"And she worries about me. That worries me even more."

Mr. Das took another sip of his port.

"Can I see you again tomorrow?" Mr. Das asked. "And every single day that I'm here after that?"

"Let's start with tomorrow," Mrs. Sethi said. "And take it from there."

Colebrookes, New Delhi: The Chef's Assistant Just Dropped a Whole Crate of Eggs on the Kitchen Floor and Then the Chef Slipped on It and Fell

EARLY THE NEXT MORNING, MR. DAS SAW HIS WIFE WALKING toward his cottage in her tracksuit and sneakers.

"No David Smith today?" he called out.

"He went out early to see the Qutab Minar," Radha said.

"And still you're exercising? So it isn't all just an act for his sake?" Mr. Das said. "Forget that. Come sit and have a nice milky cup of tea and some buttered toast. No matter how many times I tell them to bring the toast without butter, they don't listen."

Radha hesitated for a moment, tried to tell herself she would feel good if she went for a brisk walk but the idea of buttered toast dipped into hot, sweet tea was much more appealing than a long walk. She joined her ex-husband on his porch and said, "I suppose you're right. That was always my favorite thing when we visited in winter."

"It was your second-favorite thing," Mr. Das said. "Your favorite thing was staying in bed under the blanket. I'm impressed that you wake up early and go for walks these days. I should learn from you."

His Fitbit was attached to his shoelace and he had his legs crossed and was kicking the one with the Fitbit up and down.

"Hitting your ten thousand steps a day?" Radha asked.

"And more," he said. "It's quite a challenge doing it without taking too many steps. Isn't Delhi beautiful this time of year? I think I've missed it."

NEEL AND RADHA HAD not been back in Delhi together since the summer Neel got malaria, since long before their divorce. Radha herself had only been back once since then—alone, to Calcutta, when her mother had died. That trip was when everything fell apart. But only because the marriage was already on the brink and just needed a big bad wolf to blow gently. She had spent a day with another man in Delhi after cremating her mother. Ashok De, her mother's doctor, the man who had held her outside the crematorium while she waited for the ashes, the man who caused her marriage to fall apart, had flown with her to Delhi to keep her company. Saying he held her was taking it too far actually. He had stood next to her and patted her shoulder. What he didn't know was that Radha was crying more out of guilt than sadness. Guilt that she was relieved that her mother had died—relatively painlessly, in her sleep, with her beloved maid sleeping on a chataai on the ground next to her, at the appropriate age of ninety-one—and freed Radha from having to constantly worry about her and feel bad that she lived so far away.

Who really was to blame for the divorce? Radha had wondered this often herself. For some reason she had always taken the blame on herself but she wasn't sure it was her fault.

It all fell apart at an IKEA, of all places. Radha had returned to Columbus after cremating her mother, after her near-affair with Ashok De, after being certain that her marriage was not worth fighting for, to Mr. Das standing at the airport holding a flask of her favorite green tea. How silly it seemed to even use the word "affair," or "near-affair," when nothing physical had happened, no intimate words had been exchanged, nothing worthy of a confession had actually transpired. But did an affair need any of those traditional markers? Was it not enough that Radha had felt a pull? Would she not be upset if she knew another woman had booked a flight to accompany Mr. Das somewhere for comfort? That felt more like betrayal than the simple, mindless exchange of bodily fluids.

Mr. Das took her luggage from her, handed her the flask, kissed her forehead, and said, "She's at peace now. And you can be too."

He said little else as they walked to the car park toward their Honda Accord. In the car he said, "You've been wanting a new bed for a while now. Why don't we get one tomorrow? Remember how much Ma hated American mattresses? Always said Indian coir mattresses were the best for her back."

"But always complained about backaches," Radha said, smiling.

"We should buy a new bed and raise a toast to her tomorrow," Mr. Das said.

Radha was tired from the long flight, the cremation, the electrifying hours spent with Ashok De, but she couldn't stand the thought of going home now, of needing rest. At the funeral someone had said that the belly button doesn't burn during cremation, but remains hard and in the same shape as it is on the living person. The idea of sleeping made her feel sad.

"Let's go now," Radha said. "I slept on the flight. Let's have a glass of wine and go buy a new bed."

Mr. Das was being so gentle, so kind. She had missed him while she was in Calcutta. Only now was she realizing she wanted him by her side.

They had two glasses of wine with a prosciutto pizza for lunch and then Mr. Das suggested Restoration Hardware. Radha paused and said, "That's too much for a bed. IKEA will do. They have surprisingly good beds. And you know I like the minimalist design."

Was that the first hint, Radha now wondered. Did she know that this bed was not going to be shared for long? Why had she pushed for IKEA when she so loved Restoration Hardware?

But they had been having a nice time at IKEA, Radha remembered. Mr. Das made Radha sit down on a black swivel chair and pushed her past the office section. Radha laughed.

"I shouldn't be laughing," she said. "My mother just died. You know, when you walk to the back to collect the ashes, you can feel the bones of bodies crunching below the soles of your shoes."

"I cremated both my parents, remember? And my aunt," Mr. Das said. "Your mother spent too many years not laughing. Now you have to make up for that."

Then he spun the chair and hit the ankles of an overweight white woman who was bent over checking the price on a filing cabinet. She fell forward and Mr. Das rushed over to help her up. She shouted at him to be more careful, then asked him if he worked there because she couldn't figure out the price of the piece. Mr. Das said no, he didn't work there and she shouldn't assume that just because he was wearing a blue shirt. But since he had knocked her over, he felt the least he could do was help so he found the price of the filing cabinet for the woman.

Radha sat in the swivel chair and watched the interaction, feeling guilty that she had thought her marriage was floundering. She just hadn't been paying any attention to it—neither of them had been. They had been busy.

A few rooms later, they were lying side by side on a king-size bed holding hands—something they hadn't done in nearly two decades.

"I thought we were falling apart," Radha said. "We were barely talking."

"Life gets busy," Mr. Das said.

Radha propped herself up on one elbow and looked down at Mr. Das. They were two middle-aged Indians in a suburban IKEA. The American dream.

"I almost made a mistake," Radha said, feeling more connected to Mr. Das than she had in years. Feeling the need to confess to her almost-affair thinking it would bring them closer, thinking it would scare them into holding on to each other tightly because that's what they knew and wasn't it more comfortable to stick to what they knew at this point?

Mr. Das turned his face slightly to look at her.

"Meaning?" he asked.

"In India, in Calcutta. I was so lonely and so depressed, I almost touched another man. But, Neel, I didn't. I didn't touch him because it was you I wanted, you I missed. We had stopped talking but look at us, look at this—it's still us. It always was us," Radha said. She thought Neel would respond the same way.

"You had an affair? At your mother's funeral?" Mr. Das asked, sitting up.

"No. I didn't have an affair, that's my point. I realized that I'm still . . . I still . . . I realized that you and I belong together," Radha said. "And don't sound so incredulous about the timing—funerals are when people are at their most vulnerable."

"So you didn't have an affair?"

A Chinese couple came to check the price on the bed. They had also obviously been fighting, the woman speaking in Mandarin through clenched teeth. The husband bent down to check the price while the woman stood over them, still talking. The husband couldn't find the price tag and walked over to the other side.

"Four hundred and ninety-nine," Mr. Das shouted at him. "Four hundred and ninety-nine. Move on."

The wife shouted something more in Mandarin and walked off as the husband scrambled to get up and follow.

"No! Don't you see?" Radha asked. "I came close to destroying what matters to me and it made me realize how wonderful our relationship is."

"Why are you telling me this, then?" Mr. Das asked.

"Because we'd been drifting apart, Neel. And we need to acknowledge that. But not all is lost. What we have is good. Thinking about losing it scared me."

Radha saw the back of Mr. Das's head nodding. He leaned over and looked at the plastic-covered tag attached to the bed.

"This one is good enough," he said. "We don't really need a new bed anyway. Let's get this one."

He took a small pencil and scribbled down the number of the bed and got up and followed the sign for the exit. Radha was up on both elbows, looking at him. When they got down to the warehouse to pick up the box for the bed they had chosen, it was out of stock.

"What a waste of a trip," Mr. Das said.

Three months later, by the time they went to Yale for Tina's graduation, the divorce papers were on the kitchen counter and Radha had signed the lease for an apartment in Manhattan.

In her Manhattan apartment, the bed was from Restoration Hardware.

"IT'S NICE ALL BEING back here. Even though Tina will barely talk to me," Radha said. She picked up a slice of toast, folded it in half, and dipped it in the tea.

"Don't keep it in there for so long, the toast will get too soggy," Mr. Das said.

"Yes, yes. I know your obsession with not letting soggy toast fall in the tea," Radha said. "Did you enjoy the party last night? Quite a flashy wedding your sister is throwing."

"It was beautiful," Mr. Das said.

"I didn't see you all night," Radha said.

"I know, it was quite crowded, wasn't it?"

"You met that woman?" Radha asked.

"I had lunch with her yesterday. Mrs. Sethi," Mr. Das said. "Jyoti. She's kept her late husband's name, which got me thinking—how come you never changed your name back?"

"My career. I'm known as Radha Das; it would be too confusing."

"David Smith doesn't mind?" Mr. Das asked.

"You all really don't need to say his full name every time. Anyway, it's never come up," Radha said. She drank some more of her tea. "Do you mind?"

"Of course not," Mr. Das said. "There are millions of people named Das in the world. It doesn't have to connect you to me."

Tina came out of her cottage then, saw her parents sitting on her father's porch like normal parents, and was about to immediately rush back into the comfortable darkness of her room when her mother shouted out, "Tina! Come sit with us. I'll call for some black coffee and extra toast."

Radha reached forward and called for Rajesh. Tina walked the fifty feet or so to her father's cottage wondering where everyone else had vanished. Marianne's bed was still made from the previous day.

"Did you just wake up?" her mother asked. Tina nodded and her mother continued, "Don't waste your days sleeping, darling. This trip is hardly a week long."

Tina ignored her and looked at a short, skinny woman in a brown sari watering the plants. A small baby was attached to her back in a sort of sling, a monkey cap covering most of its face. The woman was wearing earmuffs and humming loudly and watering the plants. She looked young, in her early twenties at most. The baby behind her freed a hand and grabbed at her hair that was pulled back into a bun. The woman laughed and removed the baby's fingers from the tangle of her hair and called him mischievous over her shoulder. The baby settled on holding her gold necklace and she went back to watering the plants, both of them smiling.

"I hardly saw you last night either," Radha said. "Where did you vanish?"

"I stepped out. I got sick of the wedding and the flashy display of wealth."

"Our communist," Mr. Das said.

"Our communist who lives in an apartment with dimmers," Radha said and both her parents laughed.

"This"—Tina waved her hand around the grounds—"isn't all there is to India."

"Nobody said it was, darling," Radha said.

"I spoke to a homeless man in a wheelchair last night," Tina said.

"There was a homeless man in a wheelchair at the reception?" Mr. Das asked.

"Never mind," Tina said.

"It's nice to get a moment to be just the three of us sitting here," Radha said, looking out at the Colebrookes lawn. A small group of sparrows skittered around on the gravel driveway.

Rajesh came over with three coconuts with straws in them.

"Good morning, good morning, lovely family," Rajesh said. "I thought you might like some fresh coconuts. Mrs. Das, you look so beautiful."

Radha smiled as Rajesh placed the coconuts down in front of them.

"Are you married, Rajesh?" Radha asked.

"No, ma'am. I'm not interested in marrying," Rajesh said. "Not my thing."

"A girlfriend then?"

Rajesh smiled and lowered his eyes and shook his head.

"Are you gay?" Radha asked.

"Radha!" Mr. Das said.

"I love all humans, male and female, ma'am," Rajesh said.

"So you're bisexual?" Radha asked.

"No labels, ma'am. I fall for who I fall for, if you know what I mean."

"I do," Radha said.

"Enjoy the fresh coconuts. Coconut water is better for the skin than any facial," Rajesh said. "Pure hydration."

He looked at Tina closely and added, "But for you I would also recommend once a week yogurt, honey, and turmeric on the face for half an hour."

"Okay, I did not ask for skin-care advice," Tina said. "How much turmeric?"

Rajesh smiled at her and said, "Just a teaspoon. Half an hour only."

A stray dog barked from the center of the lawn. Rajesh turned around in a panic.

"How on earth did that get in here? That Pushpa, I bet she let him in. Pushpa!" he shouted at the woman with the baby who was laughing in the direction of the dog and pointing it out to her baby. "Pushpa! You know we can't let the dogs in here."

He turned to the Das family and said, "That woman is determined to get fired. Just last month she was caught putting food out for the crows. Just imagine."

Rajesh ran off toward the lawn shouting at the dog, trying to shepherd it off the lawn as Pushpa stood with the baby on her back and laughed at Rajesh chasing the dog around.

"I can't believe we never came back after your malaria. If I'd known that would be our last trip to India together, I would have insisted we take a holiday to the Taj or to Goa or Cochin," Radha said.

"I wasn't going to go anywhere except back to America after being released from the hospital," Mr. Das said. "That was a nightmare."

He leaned back and looked in the direction Rajesh had gone.

"I was so glad to leave," Tina remembered. "I just wanted to get back to America and go to the mall with my friends."

"I remember that stage. You wore those awful pants from the shop with all the bare-bodied men on the walls," Mr. Das said.

"Abercrombie and Fitch," Tina said. "Track pants."

"All your classmates had the same pair," Radha said.

"You used to wear similar pants when I first met you," Mr. Das said to his ex-wife.

"Good memory. Except mine were a pair of export reject ones from Lajpat Nagar," Radha said. "At one-tenth the price."

RADHA THOUGHT BACK TO the first day she met Neel Das, at Wooster college in August of 1979 in the cafeteria on campus. Neel was in the second year of his program and Radha had just arrived from Delhi, her first time in America. Radha had no interest in dating or getting married and had, since as far back as she could remember, wanted nothing more than to study and be independent and live life on her own terms. But then she took her orange plastic tray with her bland turkey sandwich and glass of milk and followed her friend Tanvi—second-year master's in philosophy, originally from Bombay, assigned as a mentor to Radha— and sat down at the same table as Mr. Das and was immediately charmed.

He slid down the wooden bench to make space for them and looked at Radha and said, "A newbie. Fresh off the proverbial boat. Welcome to America. The portions are the size of your head here."

He pointed at her huge sandwich and added, "My appetite has grown accordingly so feel free to give me whatever you can't finish."

Then he turned to his right and continued his conversation with Gautam, another Indian student from Chennai who had come to do a master's in electrical engineering. Gautam, Tanvi, Radha, and Neel quickly became close friends. Gautam and Tanvi, always the two cooler ones with their bell-bottoms and their cigarettes, started dating while Radha and Neel tagged along. The four of them took a bus trip to Niagara Falls, during which Radha insisted on getting a separate hotel room for herself, despite her limited finances, because she didn't want to share a room with Neel. Neel himself didn't seem to care much, Radha remembered. He was too busy reading philosophy in a youthful bid to distinguish himself from all the other Indian men studying practical subjects. He didn't smoke cigarettes but somehow this made him even cooler than the ones who did. Radha never had that confidence, and by the end of her first semester she was smoking an average of ten cigarettes a day.

One cold winter night, Tanvi and Radha were sitting in Tanvi's kitchen having a glass of wine when Gautam tried to jokingly startle them. He banged his gloved hands on the window and with a loud crash the window shattered. The kitchen floor looked covered with icicles and everything froze for a moment. Tanvi sat motionless with her wineglass halfway up to her mouth, Radha turned to look out of the window where Gautam stood, hands still up where the window should be, cigarette dangling out of his mouth, eyes wide, and a few feet behind him, Neel stood, with no gloves and no hat, watching.

Then suddenly everything moved fast as the men rushed into the kitchen and Tanvi dropped her wineglass to add to the mess and blood poured out of a wound so close to Tanvi's eye the others were certain she was going to go blind. They had to get to the hospital but none of them had bothered getting American driver's licenses and the thought of calling an ambulance never even occurred to them. Gautam held Tanvi's face and shouted apologies in a state of panic, while Radha lit a cigarette and then rushed to gather up the shards of glass to avoid more injury. Only Neel seemed to know what to do. He called a local taxi company and then he went to the bathroom and found a large towel that he soaked in water and brought out to Gautam to hold against Tanvi's eye.

The car pulled up in front of Tanvi's apartment. The driver put down the passenger-side window, looked at the four of them and the blood-soaked towel, and said, "Fuck, no, I don't need any trouble from a group of curries," and started his car again. But Neel went around to the front of the car and slammed his hands down on the hood and shouted, "We need to go to a hospital right away. Do you fucking understand? I don't care that you're too much of an asshole to have a shred of empathy, and I don't care that you're so fucking terrified of working for one of us someday that you call us curries. It's cold and my friend's face is bleeding and you will get us to the hospital right now."

Radha remembered watching his face lit by the glow of the headlights, wondering how he didn't feel cold while the rest of them shivered in their gloves and hats.

"And because I'm not an asshole like you, I'll tip you extra," Neel said, his tone slightly softened. He motioned for the others to get into the backseat and he took the front passenger seat. The driver's bag and coat were there so Neel had to sit holding them in his lap, and this intimacy between him and the driver made Radha smile.

They ended up at the hospital for over three hours and Tanvi got five stitches along her eye. At some point Radha and Neel fell asleep in the empty waiting room huddled under her jacket, her head on his shoulder, his head on her head.

"YOU WERE WEARING THOSE track pants on the night we went to the hospital with Tanvi," Mr. Das said.

"I wore them all the time. I had a pair of sweatpants on under them that night because I was not equipped for winter in America," Radha said.

"Whatever happened to Gautam?" Mr. Das asked.

"He moved to Cairo, I believe," Radha said. "It's still hard to believe Tanvi died so young."

Mr. Das shrugged and said, "It's sad but it's not like we were in touch with her recently. Didn't you two constantly fight about politics anyway?"

"A blind hatred of Muslims isn't politics," Radha said. "And the way she spoke disparagingly about India always bothered me, remember? She saw America as an escape. The last time I spoke to her she said I shouldn't let Tina go to India in case she got raped. And then she invited me to a puja session in her house in Dallas."

"And God still didn't spare her the stomach cancer," Mr. Das said.

"You told me to be careful in Delhi too," Tina said. "And you always criticize India."

"That's different," Radha said. "I say it affectionately—the way a child can criticize a parent."

"But you never come here."

"That's because my life is in America," Radha said.

"And you always wanted me to be American," Tina continued. "You let me start wearing a bra way earlier than any of the other Indian girls."

"That's because I wanted you to be happy, Tina. I wanted you to fit in. We were raising you as a brown girl in America and those were the pre–Priyanka Chopra years. There was no Mindy Kaling. Or that You-Tube woman. Nothing, nobody. I didn't want you being made fun of. Adolescence is difficult enough."

"Even Priyanka Chopra somehow has different accents on American television and Indian television, have you noticed?" Mr. Das asked.

"And who can blame her?" Radha said. "What's wrong with doing that? She wants to be understood at home and everywhere. Fair enough, I say. We praise people who speak French and English, why can't people have different accents for different audiences? It's quite a skill to do it well."

"I have a wonderful British accent," Mr. Das said. "I watched an episode of that *Peppa Pig* cartoon on the flight. Did either of you see it? Clever concept. So simple and so engaging. Actually, I ended up watching three episodes."

"Ma," Tina asked Radha. "Are you going to marry David?"

Tina was surprised to hear herself ask this question. Certainly, she had thought about it ever since she had first heard about David, and her father must have as well but nobody had asked it out loud.

Mr. Das was so surprised that his daughter had suddenly asked this that he let his toast soak in his tea for too long and it had broken off and fallen into the cup, ruining both his tea and the toast. He looked at his ex-wife to see how she would respond, and for a moment there was silence.

"Neel, your toast has fallen into the cup," Radha said.

"Peppa Pig has a baby brother named George," Mr. Das offered. "He loves dinosaurs."

Before Radha could address Tina's question, a red Jaguar pulled up. Nono, Pavan's grandmother, emerged from the backseat, wearing a starched, off-white sari and big sunglasses. Her driver turned the car off and rushed over to her side to hand her a purple walking cane and matching purple Prada purse. Her white hair was cut short and stylishly, and her diamond earrings sparkled in the early morning light. Her driver offered her his arm to help her walk and she poked him in the legs with her cane and walked ahead herself.

"Thank goodness they're doing the wedding in Delhi instead of Dubai," she said to the driver. "At least the girl's family is sensible. Getting married in Dubai would be like getting married in the middle of a shopping mall."

The driver nodded along and followed one step behind her.

"How many times do I have to tell you not to walk so close," Nono said. "I'm not going to fall no matter what my son tells you. And if I do fall, you can catch me even if you're two feet away—no need to stick to me."

She stopped and used her cane to mark a circle around her feet and said, "Stay outside this imaginary line at all times. And tell the girl's family that flowers—proper flowers, not cheap marigolds—should line all the roads inside the club at all times. Flowers from abroad, not Sarojini Nagar."

The driver took a notebook out of his pocket and scribbled down her instructions.

"What is that?" Nono asked.

The driver looked up at her.

"Where did you get that ridiculous notebook?"

"Ma'am, I just want to make sure I don't forget," the driver said nervously.

"Really? The notebook was your idea? Then why does it have my son's initials embossed on the front? Did he give you this? Does he want you to keep track of what I say so he can prove I have dementia? He just wants to dump me in an old person's home but not for one minute will I allow for that. You write that down and show it to him. Write it. My brain is more intact than his has ever been. Write that down also. Idiot son of mine, planning my funeral while I'm still breathing."

Mr. Das, Radha, and Tina watched from the porch. Nono approached their porch and said, "Are you from the girls' side?"

She let herself onto the porch, placed her purse on the table, nudged Mr. Das with her cane so he moved to the next chair, and sat down. She pressed the buzzer on the table.

"Yes, ma'am. I am Shefali's Uncle, Neel Das," Mr. Das said, not sure why he had called her ma'am.

"And I'm Radha," Radha said. "Radha Das. And our daughter, Tina."

Rajesh appeared in response to the bell and Nono said, "Bring me an iced coffee and an ashtray."

She looked at Rajesh and added, "And tuck your uniform in, young man. This isn't some fashion show."

"Radha and Neel Das," Nono said. She reached into her purse and took out a Marlboro Red.

"Ma'am," the driver said nervously. "Sir says you should not smoke."

Nono stared at him silently until he pulled a lighter out of his pocket and reached over to help light her cigarette. The driver loved Nono and personally thought she had not a hint of dementia and that she should continue living life exactly as she wanted because it obviously suited her, but the rest of her family saw her as a hurdle on the way to their massive inheritance. She was kind enough to allow his wife and daughter to live with him in the driver's chamber in the back lawn of her home, so he was willing to do whatever she asked.

"I've heard about you two," Nono said. She took a drag of her cigarette, coughed, and said, "You're the one with the American boyfriend."

Nono looked Radha straight in the eye as she knocked the ash from her cigarette onto the center of the table.

"David Smith, yes," Radha said, not wanting to use the term "boyfriend."

"David Smith. Very American. I imagine he loves grilled cheese sandwiches. I personally don't understand how anybody over the age of eight can stand those. Marvelous, marvelous, marvelous. I wish I had had an American boyfriend or two in my lifetime," Nono said, laughing.

She took another drag of her cigarette while Rajesh placed her iced coffee and ashtray down on the table in front of her. "How are you two handling all of this? It's quite lovely to see a family all together despite the presence of a dashing American boyfriend. Is he dashing? I assume he is. How lovely for you, Radha. Most people my age sit around talking about the good old days but I'm telling you, you people have it better. Tina, is it? Life will be even more fun for you."

Nono put the cigarette out on the ashtray and reached into her purse to take out a compact and lipstick. She flipped it open, touched up her lipstick, and made sure her hair had the volume she desired. She took a sip of her iced coffee and said, "Best iced coffee in all of Delhi. I'd have preferred a cocktail but this will do for now. Tina, tell me about your life. Are you married? I love that cousin of yours dearly and I'm glad she's agreed to marry my grandson. There's no chance we can fob the other one off on you, is there? You seem too sensible for Karan."

Tina wanted nothing more in that moment than to be Nono. She wanted to get old and be dramatic and chain-smoke and cut her hair short and wear lipstick and carry a Prada purse. She wanted to have the confidence of a lifetime of decisions made—whether they were right or wrong. She told Nono about her work, feeling the need to make it sound more serious than it was.

"What I really hope to do is produce documentaries about India for the streaming networks. I think it's important to give voice to the marginalized. I want to work with the children of prostitutes, for instance. Or the children at Delhi traffic lights who perform circus acts while they beg."

"That's all been done, my dear, and it's dreadfully boring. No more poor children with bright smiles as metaphors. Please, no," Nono said. "Every foreigner shows up and does that. We don't need the world to pity us. Do India a favor and show the world our other sides too. Show them this."

Nono picked up her cane and pointed around the grounds. She poked her cane at her driver and said, "Not him, though. Not this fool. Always worrying that I'm going to topple over."

Tina could tell the driver loved Nono and her constant insults. And that Nono loved him too.

"He's worse than my husband. At least my husband was considerate enough to die fifteen years ago," Nono said. "Now it's a battle to survive between me and my son. He thinks I have dementia but little does he know that I know that he has high cholesterol."

Karan's Jaguar pulled up then, music thumping as usual.

"My son, his father, bought him that car," Nono said. "And a blue one for Pavan. These boys have no understanding of the value of money. Useless. And you know who made all the money in the first place? My husband. A modern-day caste system. It exists all around the world."

"Right. But you have an actual caste system here, of course," Tina said.

Nono looked her up and down from her shoes to her hair in a way that made Tina's skin feel as if it were shrinking.

"About which you know a lot?" Nono asked.

"Well, no. But we can't just pretend it doesn't exist," Tina said.

"So you want to make a documentary about the caste system?" Nono asked.

"Well, no," Tina said, starting to get nervous that Nono could sense how little she knew. Fortunately, she was interrupted by Marianne, who emerged from the passenger side of the Jaguar wearing a red chiffon sari with a black lace blouse and red bindi. Karan popped out from the driver's side wearing jeans and a kurta, a cigarette in one hand.

"Nono!" Karan shouted. "What are you doing here? Checking on the flowers?"

"You shouldn't smoke all the time," Nono said to Karan. "And don't shout as if I can't hear."

"We went to Old Delhi for breakfast!" Marianne said breathlessly, coming over to Tina. She took a sip of Tina's black coffee and pressed the buzzer for Rajesh.

"What is that?" Tina asked, pointing at a silver ring in Marianne's now-red nose. "Marianne, what the hell is *that?*"

Marianne put her hand up to her nose and laughed.

"I've always wanted a nose ring," she said.

"No, you haven't!" Tina said. "Marianne, you belong in cable-knits. Not berets, not burqas, and not nose rings. It looks ridiculous. And infected."

Tina leaned over closer to inspect Marianne's nose.

"Did you do it somewhere safe or was this some needle-and-ice, bedroom nonsense?"

"The shop opened the needle in front of me," Marianne said. "Relax. I love it."

"Where did you go last night?" Tina whispered to Marianne. "Please don't tell me you slept with him."

MARIANNE HAD NOT SLEPT with Karan, even though she had wanted to. Instead they had left the reception and headed over to the Oberoi hotel for a cocktail. The bar was empty and looked like it was about to close but when the bartenders saw Karan, they turned the music back on and led him and Marianne to a quiet sofa at the back of the bar.

Marianne excused herself to go to the bathroom to check her phone. There was a message from Tom that said simply, "Going to a poetry reading in Gowanus tonight."

That was it. Tom wasn't one for romantic texts or gestures, and she knew that and loved that. The men who said the most usually felt the least, Marianne found. But a poetry reading in Gowanus? That sounded so . . . dull. She didn't bother texting back and instead returned to the bar and saw Karan, one arm up on the sofa back, looking at her and smiling.

"Tell me something you've never told anyone before," Karan said to her as she returned. "I want to know you."

Marianne sat down and looked at her hands in her lap. She shifted slightly, uncrossed and recrossed her legs.

"Should we get a drink first?" she asked, looking over her shoulder to see if she could catch the bartender's attention and saw him approaching with a tray with one gin martini and one whiskey on the rocks.

"You seem the kind who would enjoy a good martini and Rahul here makes the best ones in all of Delhi," Karan said as Rahul the bartender placed the drinks down on the table in front of them. Karan often showed up at closing time with a new, usually foreign, woman on his arm. If Rahul kept the bar open and the drinks flowing, Karan and his date usually stumbled out within an hour, always leaving a ten-thousand-rupee tip and often a small pouch of cocaine inside a cigarette packet as a thank-you.

"What's your best memory?" Karan asked.

Marianne laughed.

"You're right, that's a stupid question," he said. "I know what you're thinking. You're thinking I've read some guide to picking up women and I'm using tried-and-tested lines from that."

He took a sip of whiskey.

"No, no!" Marianne said. "I laughed because it was so unexpected. I didn't know how to react."

"Okay, I'll start over. If you could do anything at all tonight, what would it be?"

Marianne took a sip of her gin martini, looked Karan in the eye, and said, "This."

Karan put his whiskey down as Susheela Raman's throaty version of "Yeh Mera Deewanapan Hai" started playing.

"This song!" Karan said. "I haven't heard this song in ages. I love it. Do you know it? It played in that scene in *The Namesake* when they're both sitting on the bed in their robes."

From behind the bar, Rahul watched Karan. Now that the music was on, Karan would stand up and put his hand out to the white girl, and she would get up and he would twirl her around on the dance floor. This man was extraordinary. If he'd come in with an Indian woman, Rahul would have brought her a cosmopolitan and played "At Last" by Etta James.

"You look so beautiful in Indian clothes," Karan said as he held Marianne's waist and swayed.

"Really? I borrowed this from Tina's mother," Marianne said. But she knew she looked beautiful in it. She felt beautiful in it.

Karan stopped and looked at her and said, "What? You can't wear something borrowed. I know just the thing you need. Come on."

"It's past midnight!" Marianne said.

"The most magical time. Anything can happen," Karan said. He placed a cigarette pack on the table and winked at Rahul as they left. "Let's go."

They arrived at a small boutique filled with glittering Indian clothes. Two men in skinny jeans and tight black T-shirts welcomed them in with glasses of prosecco and plates of mini red velvet cupcakes. Empty wrought-iron birdcages hung from the ceiling around the large chandelier. One wall was decorated with bronze plates of some sort, and a heavy framed painting of a woman in a green sari with a parrot on her shoulder looked down at the room. A small white dog snoozed in the middle of the marble floor.

"That's Max," one of the men said.

"You stay open overnight?" Marianne asked.

"That's when we design," said Homi. "During the day the staff handle the store, but we like to design when the city sleeps."

"Homi and Mazer are two of the hottest designers in India right now," Karan said.

Marianne walked along one of the racks letting her fingers graze all the fabrics. Mazer disappeared to the back. Homi loved these late-night visits from Delhi's fancy people but Mazer preferred designing in peace. He shut the door to his studio, put on his noise-canceling headphones, and sat down to look at the drawing he was working on for Deepika Padukone's Cannes trip.

"Pick anything you want," Karan said. "Everything would look good on you."

"I think you need a sari. Something light, in chiffon, maybe? Show off that body. Maybe with a lace blouse, long sleeved for sure—long-sleeved blouses are very flattering. They make you look instantly taller. I mean, you're already slim and beautiful. There's not much I can do for someone short and fat, despite what magazines try to tell you," Homi said.

"But isn't that exactly what a good designer should do?" Marianne asked.

Homi and Karan laughed and Homi said, "Come with me. I have the perfect sari for you."

In the fitting room, Marianne stared at herself in the chiffon sari and black blouse. She wondered what Tom would think of her in this. With Tom she wore jeans and collared shirts. With Tom she always felt comfortable, natural, herself. She heard Karan and Homi talking outside. Marianne looked for a price tag on her clothes but found none. Her credit card had a ten-thousand-dollar limit on it.

She stepped out of the fitting room and Karan said, "Stunning. You're stunning."

He reached his hand back while looking at her and Homi placed a small glass container filled with red bindis into it. Karan took one bindi out, removed the backing of the sticker, and pressed it onto Marianne's forehead. He put his finger under her chin, said, "Let's go a bit bigger," and replaced the bindi with a larger one. He looked at her again and said, "Perfect. I could use a cup of coffee now. Let's go."

"Don't we have to pay?" Marianne asked.

"I got it," Karan said. He picked up a white paper bag with Tina's mother's outfit lying crumpled in it.

"See you next time," Homi said.

"Cheers," Karan said. "Tell Mazer to stop being so grumpy whenever I show up. My purchases probably pay your rent."

"You do this often?" Marianne asked.

"You need a nose ring," Karan said. "I know just the place. And then the coffees. And maybe some pastries. I'm hungry now too."

"I DIDN'T SLEEP WITH him but I don't see why I shouldn't," Marianne said to Tina.

"Because of Tom?" Tina asked.

Marianne leaned her head back.

"I know," she said. "But I marry Tom and then what? We move to Cambridge and buy an expensive SNOO for our baby?"

"What's a SNOO?"

"A bassinet. It vibrates and it's supposed to really help the baby sleep," Marianne said.

"See? The fact that you know that means that's exactly what you're supposed to do. Get a SNOO," Tina said. "Marry Tom, have the kids, wear khakis, and get light-pink gel manicures and take skiing holidays. He's black, you're white, that's exotic enough."

"Both our mothers carry only Dooney & Bourke purses. And anyway, he's never even mentioned marriage," Marianne said. "Did you know that Karan is one of Asia's fifty most eligible bachelors?"

"According to?"

"*Hello! Asia* magazine. He showed me the cutout," Marianne said, glancing over at Karan, who was sharing Nono's iced coffee and chatting with Tina's parents. "Okay, that part was ridiculous. He had the laminated cutout in his wallet," Marianne said. "But he's incredibly charming. And he spends half the year in Hong Kong and travels everywhere. And he knew this whole secret nighttime side of Delhi. It made New York look so tame. I thought I had this cool life because I live in a brownstone in DUMBO and occasionally take Citi Bikes, but it feels so narrow compared to Karan's life. Imagine wearing the hottest Indian designers and partying all over Asia. You know Karan hung out with Missy Elliot in a basement bar in Singapore last year? Forget the SNOO, eventually we could have a little halfsie baby who we could take along with us everywhere. She could wear headphones at concerts in Thailand and play with other olive-skinned halfsies."

"Stop saying halfsie," Tina said. "You can't name a single Missy Elliott song. You need to sleep."

"Get Your Freak On. More than sleep, I think I need to use the bathroom," Marianne said. She got up. Karan stood up and asked, "Leaving?"

"I'm going to get some rest," Marianne said.

"I'll pick you up for the party," Karan said.

"That would be nice," Marianne said.

"What party?" Mr. Das asked. "I thought tonight was a free night."

"It is," Nono said. "But my grandson is pulling out all the tricks for this girl." Nono shook her head and said loudly, "Everyone falls for him. Karan, don't cause trouble."

"She's got dementia, Marianne," Karan said in a half whisper. "Ignore her."

But Marianne felt silly because Nono was right to call her a girl, and even though she knew she was flirting, Marianne hadn't had this much energy since college. She'd been up for twenty-four hours but she felt fine.

"I'm meeting Mrs. Sethi for a walk in Lodhi Gardens in case anyone wants to join us," Mr. Das said. He was hoping nobody would take him up on his offer but he wanted to let everyone know that he also had exciting things going on this week. He wasn't here just to sit in his room and attend the events and then go back to sleep, especially if everyone else was going to be off discovering the city and forging questionable relationships.

"I'll come," Tina said.

"What?" Mr. Das asked. "Don't you have plans?"

"Nope, I'll come. She sounds nice, Mrs. Sethi. I have to go to Sabyasachi and collect my outfit and then head to Khan Market to pick up some earrings I ordered so I'll meet you there."

"Maybe I'll see if David wants to come as well," Radha said, looking sideways at Tina. It was one thing for her ex-husband to go around with this woman but it was altogether different for her daughter to start a relationship with her. "He's been wanting to see Lodhi Gardens."

"It won't be good for him to be out in the midday sun, Radha," Mr. Das said. He wasn't sure why Radha was suddenly so eager to meet Mrs. Sethi but he certainly wasn't ready for that. "White skin is very sensitive. You have to be careful. Melanoma."

"He wears sunblock," Radha said.

"The harsh Indian sun doesn't respond to American sunblock, Radha. We are in the tropics. The sun knows no rules here. I better get going. Tina, I'll see you in the afternoon. Radha, remember to keep David Smith indoors in the afternoon."

Mr. Das quickly untied his Fitbit from his shoelace, strapped it around his wrist, and rushed off toward the main dining hall with this arm swinging at twice the pace that he was walking.

Nono pulled another cigarette out of her bag and laughed and said, "You two squabble like youngsters in love. I'm off to inspect the rest of the grounds."

She stood up, cigarette in one hand, cane in the other, while her driver followed behind her holding her purse and ashtray. She turned to him and said, "Two feet distance at all times, don't forget. And put that stupid notebook away but make sure the ashtray is close."

Marianne and Tina's Cottage, Colebrookes, New Delhi: Shefali Is at the Jeweler's Getting the Shine on Her Gold Set Dulled Down So It Looks More Modern, and the Jeweler Won't Stop Hinting That She Wants to Be Invited to the Wedding

AN HOUR LATER, MARIANNE AND TINA WERE IN THEIR cottage getting ready for the afternoon. They were both wearing Indian clothes and looked like white and brown versions of each other.

"Is that kurta from the Riyaaz years?" Tina asked, pointing her chin toward Marianne in an outfit that looked vaguely familiar. She was wearing gold chandelier earrings and her hair was braided. Her nose looked red, redder than it had this morning.

"Look at us. It's like we're on our way to some South Asia Society social at Yale," Tina said.

Marianne took out a small plastic container of Neosporin powder and shook it out onto her nose.

"Ow," she said. "How can powder landing on it hurt?"

She bent down and looked into the mirror, turning her face to the side.

"Remember that Bollywood Nights party I organized?"

"I do!" Marianne said. "That was the best event you threw. You made those vodka— What were they? In those small shells."

"Vodka pani puri shots," Tina said. "I had forgotten about those."

That had been a good party, Tina remembered. And better attended than anything else she had tried to organize during her time on the board of the South Asia Society. It had been fun and glittery and glamorous and she had projected old black and white Bollywood films on the wall and made the Bhangra team choreograph a flash mob. Her next event, a roundtable discussion on whether or not English should be the official language of India, had made her fall asleep at the table. It didn't really matter since there were only seven other people in attendance because she had forgotten to publicize it until the previous day.

There was a knock on their cottage door. Marianne opened it and found Rocco standing there, wearing shorts and a T-shirt.

"It isn't that warm," she said.

"It isn't that cold," Rocco said and entered. "Girls' rooms always smell nice. Sorry, women's rooms. But then it sounds like I'm talking about bathrooms."

Rocco stopped at Marianne's bedside table and picked up a candle.

"Pine and eucalyptus? How come we don't have this?"

"I brought it with me," Marianne said. "The smell helps me sleep."

She took the Jo Malone candle away from Rocco, inhaled the smell deeply, and placed it back down on her bedside table. It really had become a comforting smell over the years. It was silly, she knew, but an expensive candle seemed like a crucial part of her post-college personality. She had started with seven-dollar ones from TJ Maxx and made her way up to the two- or three-hundred-dollar Jo Malone or Diptyque candles and had also developed a favored scent per season.

"What are you doing today?" Tina asked. She sat down on the sofa next to Rocco and pulled her feet up under her.

"That's what I came to ask you. I heard you're going to Sabyasachi to pick up your outfits. Can I come? I brought a sherwani with me but I think the Bombay monsoon got to it and it appears to be covered with mildew of some sort. I've sent it to be dry-cleaned but it won't be ready in time."

Rocco leaned forward and picked up an orange from a bowl and started peeling it.

"I'm not going," Marianne said. "I'm going to see India Gate with Karan and am banking on my outfit being the right size."

Rocco handed one slice of orange to Tina without saying anything and Tina took it and ate it.

"Why is your nose so red?" Rocco asked.

Marianne touched her nose gently and said, "It's fine."

"Is that a nose ring?" Rocco asked. "Have you always had that?"

"It's fine," Marianne said again.

Tina laughed and said, "Don't bring it up."

Rocco took out his phone and connected to the Bluetooth speakers and put on some jazz that Tina couldn't identify.

"You can come with me," Tina said. "I didn't want to go alone anyway. I also want to buy a Kashmiri shawl from this guy near INA Market but I don't want them to see you—prices suddenly go up when they spot a white person."

Rocco passed her another slice of orange.

"I bet I could bargain a lower price than you," he said.

"Tina, you're going to lose," Marianne said. She dabbed at her lips with a tissue and walked toward the door. "I'm off to meet Karan. You two have fun."

Rocco finished the last piece of orange, put his arms behind his head, and leaned back. Male armpit hair always made Tina blush but fortunately red cheeks didn't show up on brown skin.

"When are we leaving?"

"Not for another hour. Do you want to meet outside at twelve?"

Rocco kicked his shoes off and put his feet up on the table.

"Do you mind if I hang out here for a bit? Kai brought a girl back last night and she's still around so it's getting a bit awkward for me."

"Kai," Tina said. "I keep forgetting he's here. What has he been doing?"

"Somehow successfully bedding a different beautiful woman every day. He's really making the most of this wedding."

Rocco got up and walked to the kitchen. He took a bottle of water and filled the kettle and asked Tina if she wanted a top-up for her tea or a cup of coffee. He then opened their mini fridge and looked inside.

"Can I take a Snickers bar?" he asked. He didn't wait for her answer and took the chocolate, unwrapped it, and waited for the kettle to come to a boil. He opened the cabinet above the mini fridge and took out the bottle of instant coffee and some packets of brown sugar. Tina noted the ease with which he was making her cottage his own.

"Do you want a snack?" Rocco asked. "I'm starving. Should we call for some butter-cucumber sandwiches?"

"White people love sandwiches," Tina said.

"That isn't fair, really, because all cuisines have their version of dough with filling. We have our sandwiches, you have your paranthas or your samosas—tomato, to-mah-to, if you ask me. The Italians have their pizzas, the Chinese have their dumplings, and so on and so forth. And these are a Colebrookes speciality."

"I'm well aware. Rajesh has been singing their praises since we arrived but it's not a combination I'm drawn to," Tina said.

Rocco picked up the phone and called Rajesh and asked for a plate of butter-cucumber sandwiches. He sat down on Tina's bed and leaned back against her pillows.

"Do you like New York?" he asked. "I've been there a few times but never really got into the vibe of the place."

"Do I like it? Of course I like it. It's New York. Center of the universe," Tina said. "Where else would I ever want to live? It's where everything is."

TINA THOUGHT BACK TO the week before when she had seen a rat climb up the leg of a man who was sleeping in a corner of her train compartment. She laughed it off as another New York City story, that crazy city, but between that and having recently seen people come screaming out of the Bedford station because someone had jumped in front of the train, Tina found herself increasingly tense on the subway these days. Then there was the time she had been sitting opposite an Indian couple with two small children and the mother was feeding them biryani by the spoonful, and even though the smell made Tina's mouth water, she moved to the other end of the train, embarrassed. But then she felt angry at herself for feeling embarrassed and tried to push her way back. By the time she got to where they had been sitting, the family was gone and only a few yellow rice grains were left scattered on the floor.

These days she felt best on the stretch of Lexington Avenue that had all the Indian shops and grocery stores. She never thought she would like that neighborhood, with its faint smell of curry that justified why others called that part of Murray Hill "Curry Hill." Growing up, her mother had always encouraged her to act American in America and Indian in India, but she was often left feeling like neither. She knew her mother was just trying to make life in America easier for her. She remembered running into her classmate Suzie and her mother at the JCPenney in the mall, and her mother and Suzie's mother bought them matching purple leggings. After that day, her mother always suggested she invite Suzie over. But the one time she did, Suzie spread a rumor that Tina's family kept a pet camel in their basement and only drank milk from the camel.

"CENTER OF THE UNIVERSE. I suppose so." Rocco shrugged and walked over to her and held out the Snickers bar and offered her a bite. She shook her head. No matter how many years she lived in America or how many white men she dated, she would never be able to accept jhootha food. Had he offered her the first bite, she would have done it and then let him deal with her tooth marks at the start of his next bite.

Tina's phone beeped and she looked down to see a message from Andrew.

Hope you're having fun. I dropped off a box of your stuff and your keys at your front desk. It was weird being back in your building. Part of me wishes you had just ghosted me instead of us breaking up.

"How does one go about ghosting someone?" Tina asked. She put her phone back down.

"Leave the country," Rocco said.

"You've done that?"

"I've had it done to me. I was really into this actress in Bombay and she told me she was going to London for grad school. RADA, she claimed. Said she had found a great apartment in Camden. Remember, the devil is in the details. And she disappeared, but then I saw her in a restaurant a month later and she claimed it was summer vacation in February."

"That's not ghosting, that's lying," Tina said. "Ghosting is when you don't lie but you just stop messaging or calling or speaking to the person."

"Is it?" Rocco asked. "I think that's a new generation thing. That seems like a kind way to do it. I don't think the truth is always necessary, especially if it's just been something brief. Sounds like ghosting lets the person being left behind decide what they want to believe. Like I can tell myself that Mira's family told her she had to end things with me otherwise they would cut her off so that's what she did. Not that I once accidentally farted in her presence while reaching for my wallet in a cab and she mysteriously decided to lie about going to grad school immediately after."

"That's disgusting," Tina said.

"Listen, don't rub salt in the wound, okay? I was humiliated enough."

Rocco smiled and walked back toward the kitchen. He stopped over Tina's suitcase, bent down, and picked up a gold stiletto. He held the Snickers bar between his teeth and examined the shoe with both hands. He looked over at her with a crooked smile and said, "Nice."

Tina shifted slightly on the sofa and pulled her feet down and crossed her legs. She smiled at his back as he returned to the kitchen to pour water into his cup.

"You eat a lot," Tina said.

"I used to be a tennis instructor," Rocco said. "I think I still have the appetite."

Rajesh arrived at the door with a tray with two plates, one with four triangles of cucumber butter sandwiches on white bread, with the crusts cut off, and one heaped with Lay's salted chips.

"Our famous sandwiches," Rajesh announced. "I'm so glad you called for these. I instructed the kitchen to put extra butter for you."

"Thank you, Rajesh," Rocco said.

"And ma'am," Rajesh added, handing Tina a little Ziploc bag with slices of chilled cucumbers. "I brought this for you to place on your eyes. It'll get rid of your dark circles."

"What?" Tina lifted her fingertips to her under-eyes. "Damn it. Enough with your home beauty remedies. My eyes are just fine, thanks."

But she grabbed the bag of cucumber and placed it in her fridge to use later in the day.

Rocco poured his coffee and came back to the sofa to sit next to Tina. He picked up a sandwich and handed it to her and said, "You have really elegant hands. Your fingers are long."

He held her hands in his and said, "I said that to you in London too, didn't I? I remember that. We were sitting at the bar—Punch and Judy, I think—and we could see our reflection in the mirror and I noticed your elegant hands then. Am I right?"

Tina nodded at him. He was right. And his compliment had been so sincere she had loved her own hands ever since.

"And then you made fun of the fact that I was wearing a watch," Tina said. "You said you didn't know anyone under the age of fifty wore a watch."

Rocco thumbed her watch then and said, "That's true. It suits you, though."

"Do you ever want to get married?" he asked. "Not to me, I mean is that something that appeals to you—marriage? You know every single person at this wedding, any wedding, is thinking about that."

"I don't have any strong views on marriage really. I'm not militantly for or against it. I'd like to care about someone enough to think about it but that's about all. If I do get married, I want it to be to an Indian. From India. I think."

"Sure," Rocco said. "Me, I want to have kids. Two daughters. And I want to pack them and their nappies and their mashed-up peas and show them the world."

"You've given that a lot of thought. I have no idea what kids eat."

"My brother has twin daughters in Melbourne and I miss them more than I ever thought I would. They're the one reason I think about moving back—those two nieces. But they barely know who I am so I can't change my entire life for them. But if the kids were my own, I could."

He put his feet up on the sofa.

"Burritos," Rocco said. He nudged Tina's thigh with his toe. "That's the Mexican sandwich."

It was tortas, actually, Tina thought, but sometimes it was best to let men believe they were right.

THIS MAKES SENSE, SUNIL THOUGHT, as Tina and Rocco climbed into the backseat of his car. Tina was wearing large brown sunglasses and holding a flask that she was sipping out of. This woman should not be cavorting around on bridges late at night with dark-skinned men. Not that Sunil was judgmental, not at all. He believed women should do mostly whatever they pleased—in fact, he was currently in the market for a wife and his only requirement was that she not eat non-vegetarian food. He would not even mind if she used to eat non-veg as long as she was willing to give it up for him. That's what he had told Gracey, whom he had met last weekend—her aunt knew his uncle and they thought they might be a suitable match. Gracey worked as a housekeeper in Dwarka and had a bright smile and of all the women he had met so far, Gracey was the one who interested him the most. When they met she was wearing a dark blue sari and a gold chain around her neck that contrasted with her dark skin. Sunil always preferred dark

skin even though so many women were forever talking about Fair and
Lovely and skin lighteners. Anyway, when he had mentioned the non-
veg issue to Gracey at their meeting, she had laughed and said, "Here
we are having our first meeting and you're busy planning the menu for
our anniversary party."

None of the other women had spoken so freely at their first meet-
ings. Sunil was equally scared of her and drawn to her, and he had a
worrying feeling that if he ended up married to her, he would be eating
meat by the end of the first week.

"Sunil, we're going to a shop in Mehrauli," Tina said. "I'm not sure
exactly where it is but I'll find it on my phone once we get close."

"Yes, madam," Sunil said, pulling the car onto the driveway and
toward the main gate of Colebrookes.

"And this is Rocco," Tina said. She still didn't know if she was
meant to introduce people to the help. Probably not other Indians, she
reasoned, but white people were forever trying to pretend the help
were friends. It was something to do with their guilt, she figured.

"Can we stop for a coffee on the way?" Rocco asked.

"No, I have an appointment. I'm sure you can find somewhere to
have coffee while I'm getting fitted," Tina said. "And I told you to take
a flask."

"That's not the same. I like the ritual of buying a coffee even if it's
a waste of money," Rocco said.

Tina nodded. They were paused at a traffic light. Outside Rocco's
window, a large DTC bus stood filled to the brim with people. A young
woman with headphones on was staring blankly out of the window immediately behind him. Her hands were covered in fading henna.

"Are you seeing anyone?" Rocco asked.

Tina looked straight ahead and said, "I was. Andrew. In New York.
But we decided to go our separate ways. It wasn't really working out.
Although I knew that from the start. I think I got stuck in it because I
was kind of bored. I should have taken up skateboarding instead."

Above, the red-light numbers counted down from 120. Traffic signals in Delhi were long. And it wasn't entirely out of boredom that

Tina had started dating Andrew. It was, at least partially, because his stubble reminded her of Rocco.

"Most relationships develop out of boredom. But it's true, skateboarding would have been a better option."

"See, but skateboarding comes with so much baggage. Like you can't just be a skateboarder and wear normal clothes and listen to pop music and not have skateboarding become your whole identity. Why is that? Why does skateboarding have to replace your entire personality?" Tina said.

"True," Rocco said. "I would be absolutely shocked if you told me you were an avid skateboarder but I'd just nod along if you told me you went biking on the weekends. Or what if you were really into hacky sack?"

"I am," Tina said. "On the weekend I wear one of those metal chains and keep my wallet attached to my belt loop at all times."

"I can picture it." Rocco laughed. "But I say fuck the whole package that comes with skateboarding and just do it. Apparently, learning new things makes new paths open up in your brain—the actual architecture of our brain changes—and your usual anxieties and thoughts and stuff have new directions to move in so you get a real restart. I've been trying to learn Hindi ever since I got here. And I also took a pottery class."

The numbers were down to the single digits now, and Tina made fleeting eye contact with the woman with the headphones as the bus pulled ahead of them. The lights turned green. The car started moving right as a cow ambled onto the street and Sunil honked and swerved around it. Stupid cow. If he hit a cow, he would definitely get pulled out of the car and beaten up. He was Hindu too and went to the temple every weekend. Well, almost. But the whole cow thing was getting a bit out of hand these days.

"Maybe I could learn how to apply henna," Tina said. "I could set up a little stall at Smorgasburg and paint people's hands and charge them twenty dollars. Or I'll wear a sari and a bindi and charge them fifty."

"You know how to tie a sari?" Rocco asked.

"I do, actually. My mother taught me when I was a teenager. I don't even need safety pins to hold it in place," Tina said.

A motorcycle was driving alongside them now, a little boy wearing sunglasses and standing in front of his father, who was driving. Behind the father, the mother sat sidesaddle, her sari pallu covering her hair, a small baby clutched in one arm. Only the father was wearing a helmet but he was using it to hold a cell phone in place against his ear, Tina noticed. The baby was wearing a yellow bonnet and a large black dot was on her temple to ward off the evil eye.

"Well, a sari is easily one of the sexiest items of clothing. Not on old aunties who secure the waist up high past their belly buttons, but on women like you," Rocco said.

"Stop flirting with me, Rocco," Tina said. "You had your chance."

"Flirting? Not a chance. I've got my eye on a model I met last night who won't talk to me. Who was the guy you were meeting last night?"

"I think I want to date an Indian guy," Tina said.

"I knew you were off doing something shady," Rocco said. "You'd be willing to move here if you met someone?"

Tina leaned her head back on the seat and took a sip of her tea. It was still hot and hurt her lip. She licked it and said, "I guess, I don't know. Maybe. I feel like I'm from here even though I've never lived here."

In middle school, Tina had calculated and figured out that she had been conceived in India. At the time, the information horrified her—not only because it meant her parents had had sex at least once but because it shook her childhood belief that she was fully American. What did it mean to have been conceived in India? That night she took a pair of scissors to her jeans and cut them into shorts, the edges frayed, like all the thin white girls in school were doing. She showed them to her mother, expecting to be scolded, but instead her mother said, "If you wanted cut-off shorts, you should have told me and I would have just bought you a pair."

"What does it even mean to be from somewhere these days?" Rocco asked. "My parents were diplomats so I grew up all over the place so I never really had a cultural identity. Australian, if I'm pressed, I guess, but I'm definitely not your usual Aussie and could never live there. London, maybe. But that's another one of those cities where you can be anything and that's too many choices in a way."

"Was it difficult for you when you first moved here?" Tina asked.

"No more or less than moving anywhere. I had to figure out the customs and how to use public transport and how to buy moisture absorbers for my cupboards every monsoon but that's all part of the fun of moving to a new place," Rocco said. "Every place is kind of similar in ways now anyway. Like, I often grab coffee at Starbucks in the morning and meet friends at Soho House at night. I'm on Tinder. I don't use it much, though."

"Are you dating anyone?" Tina asked.

Rocco looked over at her. He pulled out his phone, opened his pictures, and showed her a picture of a beautiful older Indian woman, thick black hair, red lipstick, large solitaire diamonds in her ears.

"I do my fair share of ill-advised dates because of boredom. Including one with the mistress of a builder in Bombay. Being the mistress to a mistress is a whole new circle of hell. Her married boyfriend came over unannounced one morning while I was there and Ramona told him I was her trainer. Never mind that I had a cigarette dangling out of my mouth."

"I wish I at least had stories like that," Tina said.

"You should come to Bombay. Ramona constantly complains that her boyfriend has multiple other girlfriends in addition to his wife," Rocco said. He put his phone away. "I'm kind of hoping this week away will naturally end things with her. It's starting to feel a little gross. Does your mystery date from last night seem promising?"

They were on an open road now, trees lining the whole street. Big, white homes with huge lawns ran along beside them. Rocco looked out of the window and Tina watched him, so at ease in this car and in himself, and she felt—what?—admiration, maybe? Envy? It was similar to what she had first felt for Andrew. Andrew was so sure about who he was—he played lacrosse in high school and his college girlfriend's name was Stephanie and she played soccer. Once, when talking about his father's ideas about immigration he had said, "My parents can be pretty conservative about immigrants. I tried to explain to him that people come here because they're desperate—like how you're here because you can't be in India, you know?"

"That's not why I'm here," Tina said.

"But he doesn't get it. People should be allowed to apply for legal asylum here, you know. Just follow the rules but it should totally be allowed."

"But that's not why I'm here," Tina repeated. "That's why some people are here, but I'm just here because I'm here."

Tina had never understood why white people in foreign countries had the luxury of being called expats while brown people were all labeled immigrants. Seeking asylum was one thing but what if you were dark skinned and wanted to live in America because of a preference for the country? Like her parents, who came over to study and stayed, the way people often stay on in places they study and associate with their entrance into adulthood. Or because that was where you were born and it was the only home you'd ever known. Like Tina herself. Sometimes she'd envied the narrowness of Andrew's world. She was always daunted by the choices life presented, whereas his were limited to a much smaller number.

Tina looked over at Rocco again. He held his palm out of the window, fingers spread wide to let the breeze flow through.

"You could have moved anywhere in the world but you moved here?" Tina asked.

"I did indeed. And I question it all the time, don't get me wrong. I'm not some hippie India freak who does yoga. Every few months I think I'll pack up and move somewhere else but then I don't and I get more and more settled. And work is going well. At some point, if you haven't found the wife and the kids and all the other traditional markers, work becomes your idea of home."

"My work is about India but based in America," Tina said.

"The perfect metaphor," Rocco said.

"Made even more perfect by the fact that I'm not accomplishing anything at work."

They stopped at another traffic signal, and on the sidewalk near them, a brass band of about a dozen men in white uniforms were gathered, holding their instruments, a big white horse at the front, making their way to some celebration or wedding, no doubt. Stray percussion sounds rang out.

"Look at that," Rocco pointed at the band and said. "I love Delhi— the roads in Bombay are so congested. In Bombay all the sexiest cars just inch along next to rickshaws. I swear the fruit sellers push their little carts along faster than the traffic moves."

They left the band behind and started moving again, and Rocco opened a small bottle of Bisleri water that Sunil had kept for his passengers and poured the water into his mouth without touching his lips to the bottle. He had mastered the Indian art of drinking water without contaminating the bottle; he even knew how to swallow with his mouth wide open and facing up.

"You drive here?" Tina asked.

"I used to. I bought a used BMW that I drove around in for a while but it got so banged up from small bumps and the AC kept conking out and the maintenance was just a disaster. It wasn't even worth the hassle of selling so I gave it to this guy in my building who had a baby but no car. They were taking the baby everywhere on their little two-wheeler and it didn't look safe. At the time I thought it made me a hero but now that car's a real hassle for them. It's like gifting someone an elephant and then expecting them to be grateful," Rocco said. He put the window down and the wind ruffled his hair. He continued, "The other day I saw them all getting on their two-wheeler and I swear they looked like they'd been caught out and tried to avoid eye contact as they swerved out of the building and down the road. I probably put them in a more dangerous situation by trying to gift them the car."

* * *

AS THEY EXITED THE Sabyasachi showroom with two assistants behind them carrying bags, they came face-to-face with Sid and a young
woman.

"Tina ma'am?" Sid said. "Sorry, Tina."

Tina felt silly about the two men standing behind her holding large
carry bags with Sabyasachi embossed onto them. She turned to them
and quickly said, "Just put them in the trunk or the front seat or wher-
ever."

"I got it. We can probably hang the longer ones up in the front and
carefully put the rest in the trunk," Rocco said and walked off toward
the car with the two assistants following.

Prem, the assistant carrying the more cumbersome of the bags—
the woman's purchases—was irritated. He wanted to be a designer but
he knew he was going to remain stuck being the assistant made to carry
the bags. He had once suggested changing the embroidery on a lehnga
and the assistant designer had rejected the idea to his face, but then
made the changes and claimed they were her own. But then the lead
designer took credit for her changes and the assistant designer had been
furious so at least there was that karmic justice. Ever since then he had
stopped sharing his clever design ideas, but he didn't know how else to
prove his worth. Another year of this and he'd have to apply for a gov-
ernment job. His parents were going to stand for only so much and no
woman would marry an aspiring designer with no real prospects.

"You were shopping there?" the woman next to Sid asked, staring at
Rocco going to the car.

"This is?" Tina asked Sid, looking the girl up and down.

"I'm Divya."

Divya had eyes that sparkled with ambition. She was wearing black
pants and a black, long-sleeved T-shirt. She was skinny, with long
black hair, a portion of which was dyed red. She was wearing a black
backpack and looked, in many ways, like she belonged on a train in
New York City. She had the swagger of knowing the streets of Delhi in
a way Tina, or even Shefali in her driver-driven cars, never would.

But she also looked, obviously, like she belonged to Sid's world.

How did she know this, Tina wondered. How could she tell by looking at Divya that they had grown up with different means? Was it the material of her clothes that gave it away? Or the skinniness of her limbs that revealed that her body had matured without enough full-fat milk? Tina, on the other hand, was what Indian aunties condescendingly called "healthy." That same deprivation could turn this Divya woman into a model if the right person saw her.

Divya, meanwhile, was busy watching Rocco and Sunil help the two store assistants put the bags into the car. She had heard that each lehnga at Sabyasachi cost as much as a house, and here this couple were filling a car full of bags. The white man must be rich, Divya thought. She looked at Sid. Sid made her laugh but jokes don't pay bills. They had met on Facebook when Sid had commented right below Divya on a picture of two stray dogs, beaten and bloodied. Sid had liked her comment calling for an investigation and added a comment saying the perpetrators of this crime should face the same fate as the dogs as punishment. Divya wasn't sure she agreed but when Sid sent her a private message, she replied and then he replied and then they kept messaging each other, and gradually moved the conversation to WhatsApp, and Divya had sent him a topless picture one day, and now they were meeting in real life for the first time.

"How do you both know each other?" Tina asked Sid.

Divya snapped out of her reverie and said, "College. Sid is the cousin of one of my friends from college and I'm showing him around while he's in Delhi."

Her parents would never allow her to date so she had decided to maintain this lie no matter who she spoke to because you never know who knows whom. For all Divya knew, this woman was visiting the home where her mother worked as a maid and somehow her mother would overhear something or other and piece things together and get furious and work even harder to get Divya married off to someone else. Her mother was forever piecing things together and getting furious.

"How do you know each other?" she asked Tina, pointing her chin in Rocco's direction.

"London," Tina said. "Where's his cousin?"

"Who?" Divya asked. "Right, his cousin is out of town. Visiting Jaipur."

"We should get going," Sid said. "Tina, I'll see you soon. Right now we're rushing to the Delhi Zoo."

"Unless you want to first join us for a cup of chai," Divya said to Rocco, who had rejoined the group after placing all the bags in the car.

"I could use a good cup of chai tea," Rocco said.

"That's redundant," Tina said.

"Don't be *that* person," Rocco said. "Just accept that it's become the language now. I also love naan bread."

Tina shook her head at him and laughed.

"And I love latte coffees," she said.

"As do I," Rocco said. "They're delicious."

"Let's go, then," Divya said to Rocco. "There's a little place just around the corner. We'll walk."

Rocco walked alongside Divya and Tina followed behind with Sid. A stray dog with a small puppy beside it fell into pace with them. Tina stiffened, as she always did around stray dogs, but Divya bent down and picked up the puppy. She held it up in the air and brought it down to her chest and nuzzled its head.

"Isn't she cute," Divya said. "I'm dying to get a dog."

She held the puppy out to Tina and Tina stared into its eyes. It was cute enough, but surely it had fleas or lice or something. Her shawl was pure pashmina. Still, with Sid watching, Tina gave the dog a gentle pat on the head. The puppy closed its eyes and leaned into Tina's hand and for a moment Tina was willing to sacrifice her shawl for the puppy. Divya placed the puppy back down on the ground and they continued walking along the dusty path.

They arrived at what was nothing more than a shack on the roadside, a blue tarp tied with rope on two tree limbs. Under it, two men had set up two large cauldrons over flames in which they continuously stirred large amounts of milky tea. On a rickety shelf were packets of Lay's and Parle-G biscuits. Over one of the sides of rope hung packets of Gems chocolate, and in a dirty-looking plastic container with a red lid, there was coffee candy for sale. On a shelf behind the two men were packets of open cigarettes for people to buy singles. On a scratchy radio, the latest Bollywood song played. Tina recognized it only because she had already heard it more than a dozen times since arriving in India—outside the airport, in the car, on the gardener's phone this morning, in a car that drove past them earlier in the day, and other places she couldn't remember. But now she liked the song because of the familiarity. She liked that the whole country was moving to this one song.

Three plastic chairs and one wooden bench stood in front of the shack. Two other men squatted with earthen cups of tea in the shade of one of the trees. The stray dog and her puppy hovered around the periphery, licking the broken pieces of previously used cups and empty chips wrappers. It was a small lane and few cars went by, the occasional bicycle, and it was quiet and calm.

Sid ordered for them all—four cups of chai, two packets of Lay's—Magic Masala and Spicy Tomato—and four coffee candies. Tina reached into her pocket to pay but Sid brushed her off. As they sat, Tina's eyes met Sid's. He was clearly looking at her. They exchanged a hidden smile and then Tina sat down.

They all listened as Divya did most of the talking, asking Rocco questions about himself then following up with lengthy stories distantly connected to her own life.

"My cousin's friend's brother went to Australia to study. I saw all the pictures when he came back," Divya said. "What a beautiful country. He said people walk around on the road wearing bathing suits there. That's how I want to live. Some of the women don't even wear tops on the beach."

"Did he go to Bondi?" Rocco asked.

"Australia," Divya said. "Here you wear jeans that are slightly too tight and all the men will climb up the walls to get a better look at you. Look all you want, I always say. But you touch me and I'll break your finger off. I'm not scared of them."

"Bombay isn't like that," Sid said.

"I want to go to Bombay too, but mostly because I want to see all the film stars. Sid says he'll show me Shah Rukh Khan's house. You know, once I was walking near the Oberoi hotel and three black cars with tinted windows pulled out, one after another. I heard it was Amitabh Bachchan in the car. You couldn't see anything inside. I don't really like his acting these days but it was still quite exciting."

"You're going to visit Sid in Bombay?" Tina asked.

"I'm going to travel the world," Divya continued. She pulled out a small atlas from her bag. "I carry this with me everywhere I go. And if I ever get lazy or think about taking some time off from work, I look at the maps of countries far away that I want to go to and how much money it will cost to travel. I'm training to be a makeup artist. Right now the money isn't great because I'm just starting out, but eventually I'll work for one of the big magazines and make enough in one night to buy a plane ticket. That's my plan. Or Sid will become a world-famous star and take me along with him."

A reality show based on a group of young women working in a local beauty salon, Tina thought. All with their own private hopes and dreams and stories.

"That depends on Tina," Sid said with a laugh. "I certainly hope so. I'll take everyone along with me. Rocco, we'll all come and visit you in Australia."

A motorbike pulled up in front of the chai stall and a man whistled at the two men making the tea. One of them took a cup of tea and two Parle-G biscuits on a steel plate over to the bike. The man drank his tea and ate the biscuits wordlessly, handed the cup and plate back to the tea seller, turned his bike on, and drove off.

Sid leaned over to Tina and said, "You'll have to send me a picture of yourself in the outfit you bought this morning. I bet you'll look beautiful."

Tina could feel his breath against her neck. She looked sideways at him and he smiled at her and said, "I just hope you get bored again tonight and you can sneak away. I know of a night market in Chandni Chowk where we can eat kulfi and watch hijras dancing."

"I've got to go," Rocco said, standing up. "I told Kai and Karan I'd meet them for lunch. Although I think this is more fun."

"I agree," Tina said, smiling at Sid. "I don't want to go either. But I told my father I'd meet up with him and Mrs. Sethi and I need to grab lunch before that."

"What wedding activities are there today?" Sid asked.

"Nothing," Tina said. "It's a day off. Shefali wanted to get her nails redone and extensions put in and all kinds of other things."

"How much is she paying her makeup artist, do you know?" Divya asked.

"I don't, sorry," Tina said.

"Some of the makeup artists charge thirty or forty thousand rupees for just one evening. Can you imagine? And they have their own assistants who carry their makeup boxes and clean up and wash the brushes. And they buy all their makeup at Sephora."

A lizard was crawling along the tarp behind the two men and fell to the ground. Tina had never seen a lizard fall before. Had it died? Maybe it was sick. Or just got tired and let gravity win for once.

Lodhi Gardens, New Delhi:
A Young Boy Is Sitting under the Shade
of a Tree Going Through an Old *Playboy*
He Bought in Daryaganj and Will Have
to Throw Out Before Going Home

MR. DAS WAITED FOR MRS. SETHI NEAR THE INDIA International Centre at the Lodhi Gardens entrance. It was a lovely afternoon, the dust and pollution adding a haze to the air that was quite romantic and diffused the afternoon sun. A fat street dog wearing a sweater lay lazily in the sun near the entrance, its tail swatting away flies every few seconds. Mr. Das was tempted to have a similar afternoon—something about India always made him want afternoon naps. It was a habit that started during the long summer afternoons in Calcutta when he was a little boy. He would come home from school and have lunch, usually rice and daal with steamed potatoes followed by a fish curry and dessert, always dessert. His father used to have a spoonful of sugar after every meal, even breakfast, if there wasn't dessert at home. His father was a family doctor who had his clinic attached to the house so, on the one hand, his father was always around but, on the other hand, he was really never around and always at work. He had regular clinic hours from 10 A.M. until 7 P.M. and he reserved his evenings to do house calls and hold free clinic hours for poor people. Mr. Das used to resent those poor people lined up outside their gate with their illnesses and ailments that would keep his father in his clinic until long after he had gone to sleep. He never saw his father take time off. On most days, the servant, Karthik, would take a tray of food to the clinic for lunch and Mr. Das would look at the empty tray return an hour later. On occasion, his father came into the main house for lunch, his stethoscope hanging off his neck but he spent most of lunch on the phone diagnosing patients who were too old or too sick to come and see him. Once his father left or the empty tray returned, Mr. Das would take a bath and have a long afternoon nap before waking up to do his homework and play cricket with the neighboring children.

He thought of that as he waited for Mrs. Sethi. A young couple pulled up on a motorbike, the man with a helmet on, the woman sitting behind him sidesaddle in a salwar kameez with her dupatta draped around her hair and face to protect it from the pollution. She jumped off the back of the bike and untied the dupatta as the man put the bike into park and removed his helmet. He smiled at her and she turned away from his smile as if they were in the middle of a conversation. She went off a few steps ahead of him and he tossed his motorbike keys in the air, caught them, put them in his pocket, and rushed to catch up with her. He grabbed her elbow and spun her around and they both disappeared into the gardens. That was what new love was supposed to look like, Mr. Das worried. What kind of future could he have with Mrs. Sethi when most of their years were already in the past? What were her afternoon rituals, he wondered. What was her childhood like? What did her parents do? Were they alive? Did it matter? Are those questions you even ask someone over fifty? And would he ever know her as well as he knew Radha? Was this all a fool's errand?

"Neel," came Mrs. Sethi's voice from behind him.

He spun around and said, "Do you sleep in the afternoons?"

Mrs. Sethi laughed and said, "Hello to you too. And no, I don't usually sleep in the afternoons. I find it depressing. It can be so tempting, especially in the hot summers and also in the cold winters here, but I don't like it. I like to keep my days occupied. These days I'm volunteering at a school for poor children. I should be there today as well, but that's the problem with volunteering, isn't it? I take days off whenever I want to. I really ought to be more disciplined. That's a long answer to an easy question. Why do you ask? Do you usually sleep in the afternoon?"

"Not since I was a child. In Calcutta, my father was a doctor. Where do I begin to tell you about a life that's so old?"

"I think we've been doing a good job so far," Mrs. Sethi said. She pointed to her wrist and said, "I've started wearing a Fitbit—do you mind if we walk?"

Mr. Das smiled and showed her his wrist as well and said, "Let's walk. Although I find it much more challenging to try and maximize my step count while minimizing my steps."

Mrs. Sethi laughed loudly and Mr. Das decided it didn't really matter what her parents used to do or whether or not she slept in the afternoon. For now, he was going to enjoy Lodhi Gardens and the autumn sun and a walk with a woman who seemed to enjoy his company.

"Tina is going to join us this afternoon. I hope that's okay."

"That's wonderful. I'm looking forward to meeting her."

Mr. Das looked up at the ruins in the middle of the garden and marveled at how majestic Delhi could be. It always amazed him that centuries-old tombs could exist, scattered in the midst of chaotic, crowded Delhi, surrounded by acres and acres of green grass and walking paths open to the public free of charge. When they had visited here when Tina was young, Mr. Das always suggested picnics in Lodhi Gardens but Radha thought it was more hassle than it would be worth—packing all the food and drinks, the plates, Tina's toys, a sheet to sit on, water bottles, napkins—and for what? To sit out in the sun and the dust and worry about flies settling on their food? And yes, that was all probably true and fair, but Mr. Das thought it was worth the hassle, worth the worries about the dust and the heat. One group of men and women was celebrating a birthday and the remnants of a large cake lay in an open cardboard box. There were several flies on the cake but none of the people seemed to mind or care and they continued to eat from their plastic plates and laugh and talk.

"That looks nice," Mrs. Sethi said.

"Picnics seem like such a hassle," Mr. Das said. Why had he said that?

"It certainly is easier to eat at home without all the flies buzzing around," Mrs. Sethi said. "But my husband loved picnics and I learned to start enjoying them as well. But my rule was always that we don't bring sweet food and we bring food that won't have any remnants, like a sandwich. Nothing with chicken bones or big lemongrass leaves that need to be left aside at the end of the meal. And it was always an argument because our maid used to make the most delicious pomfret fry and my husband loved that but I never agreed to bring those because of the hassle. So we would stop at Sugar and Spice in Khan Market and pick up sandwiches only. It was still fun and the cleanup was much easier but I suppose the pomfret fry wouldn't have been so hard either. I would have just had to pack one extra plastic bag for all the garbage and some wet wipes for our fingers. Anyway, never mind now."

Mr. Das tried to picture a young Mrs. Sethi sitting on a sheet and eating a sandwich with the dust particles moving down toward her in the rays of the sun. It was an easier image than picturing her sifting through a whole pomfret to free the flesh of the fish from the bones. But he wondered if Colebrookes did a good pomfret fry; he could use a tandoori pomfret for dinner.

The fresh smell of marijuana wafted toward them and Mrs. Sethi inhaled deeply and said, "I always love that smell."

"Of drugs?" Mr. Das asked, unable to hide his shock. "You like drugs?"

Mrs. Sethi laughed loudly. She shook her head and looked over at Mr. Das looking wide-eyed at her.

"America makes everyone so conservative," she said. "Marijuana is hardly a drug. It's better than the anti-anxiety drugs everyone is hopped-up on all the time. But I sound like an addict. I rarely smoke but come on, Neel, we're children of the sixties. Don't tell me you've never done any drugs."

"I haven't," Mr. Das said. "I've never even smoked cigarettes. Well, no, I did once but I hated it."

"I tried ecstasy on a cruise in Halong Bay last year," Mrs. Sethi said with a laugh. "I loved it. Can you imagine? I went on an organized tour of Vietnam for single Indian women and at first that sounded like just about the saddest thing I've ever heard of but I went and it ended up being one of the best two weeks of my life. There were twenty-five-year-old women and one seventy-plus-year-old spinster, and everything in between, and it was so refreshing. No more ecstasy for me but my gosh, it was fun. That's one of the few things I've never told Minal about."

Mr. Das looked over at Mrs. Sethi not sure how to respond. None of this was the India he remembered. When he had first heard of Mrs. Ray's Matchmaking Agency for Widows he had expected to be set up with some old lady wearing a synthetic sari and orthopedic shoes and maybe sprouting a chin hair. But here was Mrs. Sethi, glamorous in her raw silk kurtas, drinking port from Portugal, and confessing to having tried drugs on a cruise and not hiding any of it. And here was Mr. Das coming across as the conservative old man from New Jersey. A bee buzzed near Mr. Das and he frantically tried to move it away from his face. He knew there was nothing less manly than a man trying to escape a determined bee.

"Papa!" Tina shouted from across the small bridge over a pond on the other side of the garden. She waved in his direction. Mr. Das watched her trying to dodge the bee that had made its way over to her.

"Damn it," Tina shouted. "Do I run? Are you supposed to run when you see a bee or play dead?"

"It's not a bear, you don't play dead," Mr. Das shouted.

"So I run, then?" Tina asked, her hands waving around in front of her face. "I hit it, I felt I slapped it."

"Just leave it alone and walk away," Mrs. Sethi shouted. "Have you two never been outdoors before?"

Tina looked at the bee and then ran, reaching her father and Mrs. Sethi flustered.

"Hello, Mrs. Sethi, I'm Tina. It's nice to meet you," Tina said as she showed her palm to her father. "Do you think it stung me?"

"You would know if it had," Mrs. Sethi said. "It's nice that you could join us. I've been so keen to meet you."

"You know, bees can fly at speeds of up to fifteen miles per hour," Mr. Das said.

"And the buzzing sound is actually just their wings moving at a fast pace," Mrs. Sethi added.

The three of them continued walking down the path talking about bees and the weather and the Delhi air because to talk about anything else was too uncomfortable and too intimate.

A man walking four dogs of various sizes walked straight into their path and made Mr. Das, Mrs. Sethi, and Tina scatter. Mr. Das caught himself up in the leash of a golden retriever. The dog walker, wearing headphones, mumbled an apology but kept walking. Mr. Das brushed off his pants and said, "People have no business keeping dogs like that in Delhi. Imagine how it survives in the summer with so much fur. And none of the houses here are big enough for what a dog like that needs."

"We used to have a golden retriever actually," Mrs. Sethi said.

"Oh, sorry, I—" Mr. Das began, unsure what his apology was going to be.

"No, no. It was a terribly foolish idea but I had always wanted a golden retriever, ever since I was a small girl, and my husband bought it for me after our wedding. I loved that dog so much. It probably wasn't ideal for him but we took him up to the hills as often as we could."

"How long were you married for?" Tina asked.

"Tina!" Mr. Das said.

"No, it's okay, you can ask," Mrs. Sethi said. "Thirty-four years. A long and mostly happy marriage, one daughter. She lives in San Francisco. And one golden retriever who died twelve years ago. That's my history in a nutshell. And now back at zero, trying desperately to find what's next."

"Tina Das! Incoming!" a voice shouted from the middle of the green to their right. Tina turned around in time to see a Frisbee heading straight for her. She hadn't caught a Frisbee since her days at Yale and she wasn't sure if she was still capable of it, but this one was expertly thrown and landed almost directly in her hand. She held it and looked up and saw Rocco waving from across the field.

"Come here!" he shouted. Karan, Kai, Marianne, and David were all standing around him and they waved. A blue sheet lay out on the ground in front of them, littered with bowls and bottles and plates and glasses. Two women in matching saris sat a bit of a distance away under the shade of a tree. Even though they sat separately, they were very clearly part of this same group. Karan's help, Tina assumed.

"At least throw it back, Das," Rocco shouted. "Stop staring at us blankly."

Tina threw the Frisbee back toward Rocco.

"Is that David Smith?" Mr. Das asked. "Did he see me trip on that dog? Because that dog's leash was particularly long. In any case, it's really animal cruelty to keep dogs like that in India. It wasn't my fault. Who expects to run into a golden retriever in the middle of Lodhi Gardens?"

"Animal cruelty is pushing it," Mrs. Sethi said.

"Come join us," Marianne shouted. She waved them over. "All of you."

"We have beers," David added on. "And fried potato tikkis with coriander and mint chutney that's absolutely delicious."

The two women who were sitting under the shade came rushing over with a large blue cooler that they had been sitting next to. They took out proper white ceramic plates and beer glasses and wineglasses and set them all out for Tina, Mr. Das, and Mrs. Sethi. They served them the fried potato patties crushed with the chutney on top and garnished it with leaves of fresh coriander.

"Drinks?" Karan asked.

"These aren't quite the picnics I had in my youth," Mrs. Sethi said. She lifted her glass of wine to Mr. Das's bottle of Bira beer and said, "Cheers."

Mr. Das and Mrs. Sethi sat on the sheet and Tina kicked her sandals off to throw the Frisbee around.

"What did you mean when you said you were desperate?" Mr. Das asked Mrs. Sethi. Mr. Das had never been comfortable sitting cross-legged on the ground and with age this had only become more difficult.

But he didn't know how else to sit. It would look too dainty if he sat with his legs together under him and he wasn't flexible enough to sit with his legs straight out. He was sitting uncomfortably, cross-legged with his knees practically up at his chin, looking around for a solution, when one of the women with the cooler came over and handed him a plump pillow. He gratefully accepted and sat down on it and placed his beer on the ground next to him.

"Never could sit well like this. I don't know why Americans call it Indian style," he said.

"Do they?" Mrs. Sethi asked. "Indians like us or Indians like Native Americans?"

"Hmm, maybe the latter. I never thought about that." Mr. Das shrugged. "So you meant what, exactly?"

"About what?" Mrs. Sethi asked.

"When you said you were desperate," Mr. Das said. "Like to meet a man?"

"Gosh, no, absolutely not. I didn't say I was desperate. I think I said I was desperately trying to figure out what's next for me. As in, I still feel young, you know. I can't imagine this is it. It isn't about a man but something feels missing in my life and I'm desperate to figure out what that is. That's why I volunteer, that's why I've joined a book club, that's why I traveled to Portugal with my daughter. But everything has felt like a temporary fix so far and I'm worried that someday in the not-so-distant future, I'll wake up one morning and not find a reason to take a shower and put on proper clothes. That makes me panic."

"But—" Mr. Das started but was interrupted because the Frisbee came flying in his direction and landed a foot away from his face. He groaned at the thought of getting up and throwing the Frisbee with David and Mrs. Sethi watching. But before he did that, Mrs. Sethi jumped up gracefully, picked up the Frisbee, and tossed it back toward David. It was a perfect wrist flick and Mr. Das looked up in awe. Mrs. Sethi looked at him and said, "I even briefly joined a Frisbee club for senior citizens! Come on. We'll get older faster just sitting here."

Mr. Das hesitated. He had watched some Ultimate Frisbee videos on YouTube and thought it looked like a silly sport but it also looked rather difficult. Mrs. Sethi comfortably kicked off her sandals to play but Mr. Das couldn't imagine his bare feet touching the grass and the dirt and, in all likelihood, that awful golden retriever's feces. But he also couldn't continue to sit here while David looked about four minutes away from tearing off his shirt and leaping into the air to catch the Frisbee.

He got up and joined everyone. His daughter tossed him the Frisbee and it fell about six feet away from him but everyone cheered and he ran over to it and picked it up and tossed it to Rocco and it didn't land nearly as far and everyone cheered again and Mr. Das, for the first time, was excited about his Fitbit count increasing naturally.

A full forty-five minutes later, as the sun was starting to set, one by one they dropped out of the game. David first went to get a beer and stayed sitting, chatting with the two maids under the tree. Then Rocco and Tina came back to where the sheet was and refilled their wineglasses and sat down together. Marianne, Kai, and Karan followed.

Tina was flushed from the game, her shawl off her shoulders. She rummaged in her purse and pulled out a black hair tie to tie up her messy hair.

"Where are the bride and groom?" Rocco asked. "I've barely seen Shefali since I've been here."

"And you probably won't much more except for a brief handshake and picture on a stage on the wedding night," Tina said.

"How many people have they invited? More than a thousand, would you say?" Marianne asked.

"Easily," Tina said. "Shefali always wanted a huge wedding but I think she's regretting it now. She messaged me this morning that she's checked into the Taj to be by herself for a night."

A newlywed Indian Christian couple—long white dress for the bride, black tuxedo for the man—posed for a picture on the crumbling steps in front of one of the tombs from the Mughal Empire. Was it the Mughal Empire? Maybe not. But if she said it confidently enough, people would believe her. The photographer looked Hindu. Although how did one look Hindu? Tina thought. Why did she assume he was? Because he didn't look Muslim or Sikh or Christian so he was Hindu by default in India.

Could she make a documentary about different religions in India? Tina wondered. No, she answered herself quickly, she knew absolutely nothing about that. It would be one episode at most and even that would just be filled with every single stereotype she could think of.

"I'm enjoying seeing what a normal Indian family is like," Marianne said.

"Shefali's family is anything but normal," Tina said.

"Pavan's mother asked me if I wanted her to arrange an elephant painting afternoon—real, live elephants," Rocco said.

Tina looked over at Rocco, now shirtless. Of course, why wouldn't he be? Around them Indian men were already in sleeveless sweaters for their evening walks, preparing for the coming winter, but Rocco was shirtless. He reached across Tina to pick up a bottle of water and Tina could feel the heat coming off his body.

She flashed back to that night in London, how drawn she had been to Rocco from the start. Her body had leaned toward him and then, to make matters more complicated, he had been funny and charming and interesting. She remembered standing beside him on the road across from Liberty, his face lit up with passing headlights and his own laughter as he told her about—what was it?—how the one bad habit he had picked up in India was the tendency to stand too close to others in lines.

"I really nuzzle my belly into the lumbar of the person ahead of me," he had said. "So nobody else can squeeze in. It's terrible but it's necessary for survival in India. Otherwise I'd never get to the front of the line."

Tina laughed and then there was a break in traffic so they ran across the street and into the cobbled streets of Carnaby and Rocco had pressed up behind her and held her hips with his hands and whispered, "See? Nobody can get in front of me now."

* * *

THEY ALL SAT TALKING and drinking as the sun dipped first behind the ruins across the park and then out of sight completely. As darkness fell, the voices around them seemed to get louder even though the world seemed to disappear around them. Small lights lit up the paths around the garden and the monuments were aglow in the distance. Tina wondered what it would be like to get up from here and go home instead of to Colebrookes. To go to a one- or two-bedroom rented apartment in Hauz Khas or Defence Colony. Maybe her full-time staff would be there making dinner.

"Do you have a cook in Bombay?" she asked Rocco.

"I have someone who comes in the morning to clean and cook lunch but I usually make dinner myself," he said. "Why?"

"Is that nice?"

"I guess. I don't think about it that much, it's just sort of how things work here. She's nice, though—Jessie. She does all my shopping and keeps the fridge stocked and the apartment tidy. It's weirdly intimate. I once noticed her smelling my clothes to figure out if they were dirty or clean. But we only overlap for an hour or so in the mornings. I pay for both her kids to go to school."

David got up and walked over to the sheet where the rest of them were sitting.

"Well, I'm off. You kids have fun. Neel, you too," he said.

"Where's my mother?" Tina asked.

"At a textile exhibition of some sort. Not my thing so I decided to explore the city, and then Rocco and Kai invited me along to the gardens. But I have the car so I have to go pick her up."

"Radha and her textiles," Mr. Das said. "Good luck carting back everything she probably bought today."

"From an exhibition?" David asked.

"There are always sales," Mr. Das said. "David Smith, I still have boxes full of her textiles in my garage because she insists her apartment is too small—I can barely squeeze the car in. Do me a favor and come get those boxes sometime."

"No, sir," David said. "I have boxes full of my ex-girlfriend's hobbies still sitting around my spare bedroom. For a while she was really into cross-stitching feminist slogans so until she comes to get those boxes, you're stuck with the textiles."

Mr. Das raised his beer and said, "To exes and their hobbies."

"Nevertheless, she persisted," David said and pretended to doff a nonexistent hat at Mr. Das and went off in search of the exit. Mrs. Sethi stood up and said, "I should really head home as well. If I leave any later, I'll be sitting in traffic for hours."

Mr. Das quickly got up with her and said, "Come, I'll walk you to your car and leave from there as well."

"The adults are gone, who wants to smoke pot?" Rocco asked.

"We're all in our thirties," Marianne said.

"Actually, I'm forty-one," Rocco said.

"Not for me. Pot slows you down," Karan said. "I'm off too. Marianne, I'll pick you up around nine."

The two maids rushed around filling the cooler and putting the trash in large plastic bags and started yanking on the sheet they were sitting on until Tina, Marianne, Rocco, and Kai had to get up so they could fold it and put it away and hurry off behind Karan. Tina slapped her hands close to Rocco's leg to kill a mosquito.

"Got it," she said. "My mosquito-killing skills are unparalleled."

She brushed the back of his calf and added, "Sorry, I think the carcass got caught in your leg hair."

Rocco looked down at her and smiled.

"Just any excuse to touch me," he said.

"What?" Tina felt caught off guard. Was he flirting? Was *she* flirting? Of course she was. He was so handsome and so effortless and that night in London needed a fitting conclusion of some sort. Or maybe it was the wedding and the newness and the nostalgia of India all mixed together throwing her off. Weddings, especially destination ones, were never about wise choices; they were about panicky introspection. That's all it was. But still she smiled and locked eyes with Rocco for an additional moment and said, "Any excuse at all. There wasn't even a mosquito."

A bhel puri seller walked over wearing a metal table like a necklace. On it were steel containers with puffed rice, tomatoes and cucumbers, and coriander and onions, the various spices, and a little bag with his money. He stopped and looked at this group. No, he decided, they weren't the type to buy bhel puri on the street; they looked the type who would pay ten times what he would charge to eat the same snack in a fancy hotel. He had become good at reading people over the years and very rarely missed a sale. That, combined with his perfected price discrimination, meant he had recently bought a scooter for himself and his wife.

"You're forty-one?" Tina asked Rocco.

"Forty-two next month," Rocco said.

"That's not so old anymore, is it? I still think I'm twenty-two sometimes," Tina said. "Although apparently my elbows no longer look twenty-two. Has Rajesh been offering everyone beauty secrets?"

"No," the others said.

Tina rubbed her elbows.

"I, for one, am glad I'm no longer twenty-two," Marianne said.

"I guess it does sound old. What are you supposed to be doing at forty-two?" Rocco asked. "Aren't you supposed to have three children and a tucked-in T-shirt?"

"You'd look good with your shirt tucked or untucked," Tina said. Then she peered into her empty glass and added, "That's probably my cue to stop drinking. Off I go."

She picked up her purse without looking directly at Rocco.

"Same. I've got to get ready. Karan's taking me to a party," Marianne said.

"Everyone knows, Marianne," Tina said. "But I don't think everyone's as worried as me because everyone doesn't know about the time you disappeared for five days in college with that Saudi prince. Are you sure you don't want to be twenty-two again?"

Marianne picked up her purse and said simply, "He was Pakistani. And everyone's a fool in college."

*   *   *

TINA AND MARIANNE SAT in the car in silence. Finally, Tina said, "It's never a good idea to drink during the day."

"Right," Marianne said. "Especially in the hot sun."

They lapsed back into silence. Tina caught Sunil's eye in the rearview mirror and quickly looked away and out of the window. Could he smell the alcohol on them? Did he care?

Marianne looked down at her phone and opened the favorites in her contacts list. Her parents, her brother, the landline to her office, Tom, Tina, and the bodega at her street corner that would deliver for her if they weren't too busy. What a comforting list of favorites, she thought. Tom would still be asleep, the light starting to creep into the apartment. He would be wearing a pair of boxers and sleeping on his stomach, his arms above his head.

Outside, traffic was starting to get heavy and the car inched along, the lights of other cars lighting up Tina and Marianne's faces. Tina looked out of the window. Suddenly, a dirty face pushed up against her window, a boy's hands shading his eyes so he could look into the car and ask for money. Sunil noticed and drove forward a few feet. The little boy followed the car. He looked past Tina and registered Marianne's white skin and rushed around the car to her side and pressed up against Marianne's window. Marianne looked away, looked down at her feet, looked out past Tina's side of the window. The same thing had happened in Karan's Jaguar this morning and when she put the window down to hand the child twenty rupees, the car had suddenly been surrounded by little faces and little hands begging for more and she had been terrified. She focused hard on looking away.

"For God's sake," Tina said. She reached into her purse and pulled out a five-hundred-rupee note, leaned across Marianne, put her window down a few inches, and slid the note out to the little boy without letting her hands touch his. The little boy let out a large whoop and came over to Tina's side of the car and did a little dance for her. Tina kept looking at him as the car drove through the intersection and back to Colebrookes.

Colebrookes: Across Town, Alone
in Her Bedroom, Shefali Is Googling
Every Man She's Ever Kissed

"DID YOU TRY THE COCONUT OIL?" RAJESH ASKED AS TINA AND Marianne returned to the cottage. "Here, I've brought you beet juice. I call this special juice my unbeatable glow. You can drink this instead of sleeping and look well-rested."

"I'm not tired, though," Tina said.

"I am," Marianne said. "I'm going to go take a shower."

Tina watched her go inside and said to Rajesh, "Fine, give it to me."

"Are you liking Delhi?" Rajesh asked. He stood on the stairs leading up to Tina's patio. Behind him, two men carried a large metal pole across the lawn. The sun was setting and Tina could see the tube lights on in the club offices across the lawn. Sparrows chirped loudly.

"I'm from here," Tina said. "Sort of. I mean I know the city. Are you from here?"

"Born and raised," Rajesh said. "And trapped. If I could afford it, I'd move to Pondicherry in a minute."

"I've never been," Tina said.

"You must go. Fresh air, seaside, streets named in French—it's the best part of India, I think. But I also love the grime of Delhi, you know. If I could afford it, I would spend half the year in Pondicherry and half the year in Delhi."

Rajesh looked out at the lawns and asked, "Why has nobody turned the lights on yet? It's getting late. I have to do everything around here and I have plans tonight. Would you like anything before I go?"

"Wait," Tina said. "Listen, what do you do after your shift ends? Can I come out with you?"

"I would get fired in a minute if Colebrookes ever found out I had taken you out after dark, madam," Rajesh said.

"I'll follow you. Just tell me when you're leaving and I'll follow along ten feet behind you."

"There you are!" Bubbles Trivedi shouted at Rajesh. "I have been looking all over for you. What? They pay you to just sit around and chitchat all day?"

"I was working. I brought Tina madam a glass of beet juice," Rajesh said.

Bubbles looked over at Tina and said, "Yes, that's a good idea. Drink it every day, Tina. You won't look so tired then."

"I'm not tired, though!" Tina said but was ignored.

"Look at my nails." Bubbles came over and held her hands out to Rajesh and Tina. Each nail had a tiny, little red rose drawn on it. "Laila really knows what she's doing. Next time we're doing a Dubai theme. The thumbnail will be a tiny replica of the Burj Khalifa. And we'll do the Palm Islands, of course, and we're still brainstorming the other eight fingers."

She lifted one rose-painted nail to Tina's face and said, "Darling, go see her at the salon and tell her to do your eyebrows. You won't find a husband walking around with eyebrows like that."

Bubbles and Rajesh nodded at each other.

"I'm not looking for a husband," Tina said. "And I don't like to have my eyebrows perfectly done. It's become such an expectation for women."

"Oh ho, here we go," Bubbles said. "Now it's become societally acceptable for all of you to pretend you don't want to thread your eyebrows. Your generation now puts as much opposing pressure on women as we did, telling them they aren't supposed to want to have smooth arms and legs and wear high heels. Well, the high-heel thing is good, anyway. My sciatica pain gets so bad with high heels my whole bottom feels numb. My doctor says it's because of my weight gain but what does she know?"

Bubbles opened her purse and took out a box of motichur laddoos and offered one to Tina and Rajesh.

"Have, have. My cook makes the best laddoos in town. Using only pure ghee and I even have my sugar brought in directly from the Triveni mills."

She placed the box on the table, pulled out four fake flowers, set them aside, and took out a packet of wet wipes and handed one to Tina and one to Rajesh. She put everything back in her purse and said, "I told the family fake flowers would look lovely and we can spray them to look real but they got so angry at the suggestion. I'm carrying these to show them how nicely it will work. We'll only use them for the flowers that nobody can touch and inspect, of course. And in any case, fake flowers cost more than real flowers so it wouldn't even be a bad thing if people knew. Rajesh, now, you come with me. I need to speak to you."

"I really should turn the lights on," Rajesh said.

Rajesh and Bubbles walked away from Tina's cottage and Tina wished she had asked for one more laddoo from Bubbles's purse. They were rich and dense and crumbly and delicious, and Tina was thinking about how wise Bubbles was for always carrying desserts in her purse when Radha pulled up in a taxi. She got out looking uncharacteristically harried, her hair frizzy, her clothes crumpled, holding several bags.

"What happened to you?" Tina asked.

"Where's David? He was supposed to pick me up from the exhibition. I waited more than an hour but he didn't show up. Was he with any of you? I've been trying to call him but his phone is off because he's on roaming and he says it costs too much. I told him we got his roaming activated for emergencies so he should leave it on at all times, but of course it isn't on. Where is he?"

"I'm sure he's fine. He's a capable man." Tina walked over to her mother and took the bags from her and brought her back to her patio. In the darkness, her mother looked old. Tina had never seen her mother looking old before. In fact, her mother's refusal to age left Tina feeling forever like a child in her presence. Her mother had taken to divorced life with such ease, doing up an apartment in Manhattan tastefully, walking everywhere, and getting in terrific shape. It was her father who she always saw as old. She remembered the first day she visited him in his new apartment in New Jersey. He had brought tea out to the balcony overlooking the Manhattan skyline, and although the apartment was modern and new and beautiful and surprisingly tastefully done, Tina felt so sad for him that she had to rush away.

A car pulled into the driveway and they all looked up. Radha got up and stood on the edge of the patio. The car stopped and Mr. Das stepped out, whistling.

"Why so glum?"

"David is missing," Tina said.

"He'll be back. Probably just some mild sunstroke," Mr. Das said with a laugh. "I need to go take a shower; I haven't thrown a Frisbee around in years. I feel young again. Cheer up, Radha. Nobody ever goes missing when you want them to."

Mr. Das walked off and Tina shifted in her chair. She thought she'd say she was going in for a shower too but she didn't.

"I'm losing you while trying to find other things. God knows what things. I know you're itching to get up right now. You hate being alone with me," Radha said to her.

Radha walked to the edge of the porch. She put one hand against the wooden railing and looked out. Tina looked at the moonlight and artificial light from the driveway hitting her mother's face. She knew she looked just like her mother.

"Where on earth could he be?"

Radha sat down on the step leading down to the driveway, her back facing Tina.

"You don't seem to resent your father for the same things. You met Mrs. Sethi today?"

"Ma, Papa's been talking to her for months. I met David after you had known him for only a few weeks."

ACTUALLY, TINA HAD FIRST seen David with her mother at the Whole Foods at Columbus Circle. She had never admitted this to her mother.

After the divorce, Radha had moved into a one-bedroom apartment in a doorman building on Fifty-Eighth Street between Ninth and Tenth avenues, close to where her new office was, and Tina often stopped in if she was in the neighborhood. That day, she had a meeting with Rachel and a producer from Montreal at Caselulla on Fifty-Second Street and she decided to see if her mother was around for a quick hello. She knew she had been unfair to her mother ever since the divorce but she didn't know how else to be. She didn't know details of the divorce but she assumed it was her mother who was behind it because her mother had always seemed more beautiful, more successful, more worldly, and more intelligent than her father. It had been easier to blame her mother but Tina felt bad about that and tried to reach out to her. It was raining when Tina stepped out of Caselulla, full on an endive salad followed by a duck confit and a shared pistachio-and-ricotta cheesecake, all washed down with one-third of a bottle of white wine. Rachel and the producer got into a taxi headed to Tribeca for their next meeting while Tina stood under the awning of Caselulla trying to stay dry and called her mother.

"Ma, are you home?"

"I'm at Whole Foods right now, darling," Radha said. "And then I have to rush back for a Skype consultation with one of my clients who is in Taipei for work this week."

"I'll come say hi at Whole Foods," Tina said.

"No, Tina!" her mother started but Tina had hung up and then rushed, head bowed against the rain, up toward the Whole Foods.

On the escalator down to the Whole Foods main floor, Tina shook off the raindrops from her shoulders and her hair. As the escalator descended, she looked to see if she could spot her mother and she did, suddenly, in line for the cashier, standing next to a tall white man who had his hand on her mother's upper arm. Between them, they had only one shopping cart and Tina could see her mother's eyes darting around toward the escalator. Tina ducked behind two young women wearing brightly colored backpacks and squatted down as the escalator reached the bottom. She pulled the hood of her jacket over her head and quickly got back on the up escalator and looked the other way, scared to see her mother standing there with a strange man's hand on her arm, scared to let her mother see her. Tina called her mother as she entered the train stop. Radha answered after one ring and said, "Tina, I was just saying today isn't—" But Tina interrupted her and said, "Today isn't a good day. The rain is getting heavy, I better get back to Brooklyn."

And they both put the phones down and Tina got on the downtown A train, a crowded A train with nowhere to sit. So she stood holding a pole and cried for the first time on a train. She didn't even quite know why she was crying; she rarely cried. She had sworn she would never be that person crying on a train, yet here she was. Seeing her mother have her own life, a personal life, made Tina feel like an abandoned child even though she was an adult. Was it possible it also made her feel jealous? She pushed that thought away and dug her fingernails into the palm of her other hand, the way she had always done to stop herself from crying.

At the Fourteenth Street station, as Tina moved toward the train doors with most of the crowd, a young black woman with pink-lacquered nails handed her a piece of paper that had the name of a church in Harlem and said, "I'm Angie. Join us sometime, let Jesus dry your tears."

The act of kindness made Tina cry harder at first and then she crumpled the piece of paper and threw it into a large trash can on the platform and walked toward the L train.

*　*　*

"ARE YOU ALWAYS GOING to be angry with me?" Radha asked now, still sitting on the step leading down and looking out. "Do you even know what you're angry about?"

Tina wondered if she should ask the question she had avoided asking until now. Why? Why did you leave Papa? Why did you meet David? Why are you trying on a new life so late in life? And more importantly, how? How can I make decisions as boldly as you? But she said nothing instead.

"Don't be angry with me for trying to be happy, Tina," her mother continued. "Sometimes we end up making decisions that become other decisions that become a life we didn't want. It's nobody's fault. And that fear shouldn't stop you from making decisions of your own. And, in an ideal world, that shouldn't make you angry at me either."

"Sometimes it's like you can read my mind," Tina said.

"Between having given birth to you and my profession, I should certainly hope so."

"What else am I thinking?" Tina asked.

"This is a risky game," Radha said with a smile. "You're . . . you're thinking how we should really spend more time together and how wonderful it is to have a happy and fulfilled mother who wants all of the same for you."

"Close," Tina said. "But I was actually wondering if I can start wearing clothes from Eileen Fisher even though I'm not even forty yet."

"No," Radha said. "Absolutely not. Maybe every so often but don't start draping fabrics all over yourself yet. You'll only realize when you look back five years from now."

"That's probably true. I already get shocked when I look at pictures of myself from college when I thought I had gained weight."

"And you know me, I always think a bit of extra weight looks good."

"It's my elbows I'm worried about," Tina said.

"That's genetic!" Radha said. "See? We have things in common. I've always hated my elbows."

"Wait here," Tina said. She went into the cottage and found the vial of coconut oil that Rajesh had given her. Marianne was sitting on the edge of the bed in a towel, looking at her laptop. She barely looked up at Tina.

Tina handed the vial to her mother and said, "Rub this on your elbows for fifteen minutes before you shower."

"Coconut oil?" her mother asked. "How I wish it were that simple."

"You're happy with David?" Tina asked, still standing. "Truly happy?"

"I didn't say that. I said I'm making decisions to try and find what makes me happy and you need to do the same."

"So you aren't happy with him?"

Radha stood up and turned to face Tina. The light was behind her now so Tina could only see her silhouetted.

"Why did you leave us?" Tina said.

"Tina, don't be absurd. You haven't lived at home since you were eighteen. I did not leave you. I did not even leave your father. Stop seeing only what you want to see. You have to stop living this narrow life in which you're the victim, the unrecognized star. That isn't reality. That isn't even one of your semi-scripted reality shows."

"You don't approve of my career?" Tina asked.

Radha dropped her head and shook it in frustration.

"You would be a challenging client, Tina," Radha said. "I better go have a shower."

THE DAY SHE MET DAVID, eight years after getting divorced from Mr. Das, Radha felt like she had finally found her rhythm. She lived in a spacious apartment in Hell's Kitchen with high ceilings and had an equally spacious, all-white office for her psychiatry practice in a building just off Columbus Circle. Her home was expensively furnished from Restoration Hardware and her closet was filled with Eileen Fisher. It turned out that being single in New York was wonderful, no matter what your age.

She worked long hours and went to museums by herself, sometimes with her daughter, sometimes with her ex-husband. She went to plays and book launches and dance performances. She used her (large, open-plan) kitchen only to get cereal and make tea and coffee and she didn't feel guilty about it. She had lunch out nearly every day, trying new restaurants on her lunch break, and in the evenings, she picked up food from Whole Foods and ate on the couch while watching the BBC World News.

The day she met David was a Wednesday in late March, she remembered clearly. It was just starting to get warm in New York City and her 2 P.M. had canceled, sending a message saying he knew he ought not to cancel but he wanted to take a bike ride through Central Park instead of talking to his psychiatrist and he felt that was acceptable for his mental health. He would pay anyway, of course, and he would see her next week. A wise man, Radha thought, and she decided to reschedule the other two appointments she had that day—for an emergency, she said, and she did not feel guilty because she never canceled appointments, not even the day she had had an abnormal mammogram at lunch that turned out to be a calcium deposit—to take the rest of the afternoon off to enjoy the weather.

She locked her office door a little after 1 P.M., left her beige cardigan draped on her ergonomic chair, and stepped out into the sunshine in her brown slacks and white tunic. It felt like the rest of city all had the same plan. Radha loved the crowds in New York City. She loved seeing all the families, the couples, the lovers, and the friends and then she loved going home by herself. She knew that her daughter, even though she wouldn't admit it, felt alone in the crowds of New York but Radha felt exactly the opposite. New York made her realize that everyone ultimately died alone, even if they were surrounded by family and friends, and that realization brought her great peace. Near the southwest entrance to Central Park, a group of dancers performed to a Michael Jackson medley. Radha stood and watched their break-dancing version of "Thriller," dropped two dollar bills into the black hat at the edge of the crowd, and continued on. Horse carriages lined the street, waiting for passengers. New York City sparkled.

Radha made her way to Fifty-First Street where India Fare had opened two months ago. She had been reading rave reviews about their contemporary take on Indian food. It was run by a chef from Bombay who also ran an Indian restaurant near the Tate Modern in London. Radha didn't often eat Indian food in America because she found all the gravy the same and too heavy for her tastes but India Fare was supposed to be different.

A handsome white man in dark jeans and a black button-down shirt stood behind a podium at the entrance to India Fare. David, Radha would learn soon.

"Reservation?" he asked, not looking up from his book.

"Reservation? I don't have one," Radha said.

"No walk-ins until September, I'm afraid. And our next available reservation is for June seventh at 3 P.M. Would you like to book that?"

"June?" Radha asked. "That's absurd."

"Did you see our review in the *New Yorker* last week? Even the June seventh reservation is only because I had a cancellation just this morning. Otherwise it would be July twenty-third."

Radha looked past him through the two heavy black curtains and said, "It's just me alone. The bar is empty, I'll eat at the bar."

"We don't serve at the bar," David said. "Listen, ma'am, if you don't mind . . ."

He took off his reading glasses and looked up at Radha. She was breathtaking. Obviously, David had a soft spot for Indian women. Working at India Fare he saw some of the most stunning Indian women walk through the door. Padma Lakshmi had been one of their first patrons. But this woman was something else altogether. "Well, if you don't mind eating at the bar, I can make an exception this one time, just for you. We happen to have barstools at the back that we use in the evenings from 5 P.M. to 7 P.M. only but I can bring one out for you."

David had a date that afternoon. He had been online dating and was scheduled to have his second date with Bonnie, a history professor at Hunter, over coffee at 3 P.M. on the Upper East Side but he messaged her saying the restaurant was busier than expected, people lingering over drinks, could they please postpone. Bonnie, who got this message while applying lipstick in the bathroom at Hunter, dropped her shoulders, pulled out a rough paper towel from the dispenser, and wiped her lipstick off. Dating in this city was awful. She couldn't stand it. Her face was stained with the coral remnants of the lipstick.

David poured two glasses of Riesling and took them over to Radha and said, "On the house."

Radha stayed at the bar until 5 P.M. and David sat with her. They talked about everything, they laughed, they finished the bottle of wine, and at 5 P.M. the staff brought the rest of the barstools out and David refused to let Radha pay.

"Could I take you out for dinner sometime?" he asked.

"On a date?"

"A proper date," David said.

"I've never been on a proper date," Radha said.

"Well, then your expectations will be suitably low, which makes it easier for me. How's Friday? That gives you tomorrow to get a little anxious and, hopefully, excited. I promise I'll make it fun so even if we don't ever see each other again after that, we'll at least have one terrific evening. Say yes."

"Okay, then. Yes. How does this work? Do you pick me up at eight?" Radha asked.

"Radha Das, lesson number one of dating in New York—do not have a man pick you up and discover where you live on the first date. What if I'm a murderer? I'll message you about where to meet."

And David did make it fun. He made everything fun. And since there was no chance of having children, and the ever after in a potentially happily ever after was much shorter now than it had been when they were twenty or thirty or forty, there was very little pressure. Everything with David was the opposite of how it had been with Neel Das.

* * *

LIKE EVEN NOW, RADHA wasn't really worried about David. She assumed he was safe—he was a strong, perfectly capable man—and she didn't need him the way she had always needed Neel, or at least thought she always needed Neel. The anxiety she'd suffered with for years had started when she was in her third trimester in Ohio when there was a huge snowstorm one night and Neel was three hours late getting home. Radha had worked herself into a state of complete panic that night, thinking she would have to have and raise this child on her own. It was never panic or sadness about Neel himself, she admitted to herself years later, but it was sheer terror at having to navigate motherhood alone. Would she move back to India? But America was home by then and she loved it. How would she handle the start of her career while also raising a child on her own? She didn't like cooking and didn't know how to separate her laundry. Neel did finally get home, and then Tina was born, but Radha remained anxious and worried about Neel because she needed him more than ever.

But she never needed David. She had fallen in love with him and had great fun with him but never felt that need and that freed her to love him even more deeply. She never knew a relationship could be fun.

AFTER RADHA LEFT, TINA STAYED sitting alone on the dark porch when Marianne walked out wearing a short black dress that sparkled at certain angles. A black blazer was draped over her shoulders, her bare arms not in the actual arms of the jacket, and a small black clutch in her hands. The only thing true to the current Marianne were the black ballet flats on her feet.

"I remember that dress," Tina said. "From a long, long time ago. Many boyfriends ago. Or many personas ago."

"Stop being irritated with the world."

"What are you doing with Karan? This isn't you. How do you not see how great Tom is?"

Marianne leaned over and scratched at a point near her ankle.

"Stupid mosquitos," she muttered.

"I have some organic citronella oil in my suitcase. Go spray it on your legs. Mosquitos are attracted to dark clothes," Tina said.

When Marianne went in, Tina texted Sid asking where he was. She wanted to get out of here, wanted to go to Chandni Chowk and eat kulfi and see hijras dancing as he had promised. Tina stepped out into the dark grounds of Colebrookes before Marianne could come back out.

Tina was walking aimlessly along the driveway when David came walking down the drive holding two large bags.

"Where have you been?" Tina shouted. "My mother is going mad."

"Tina? Is that you?" David squinted down the driveway. His eyesight at night was no longer quite what it used to be. "How's your mother?"

"She's not thrilled," Tina said.

"Neither was the driver. He dropped me off at the gate," David said. "The security at the front gate is very serious. They were not happy about me walking in looking, I imagine, a little worse for the wear."

Tina looked at him, his beard scruffy, his skin bronzed from the sun and no, he was still handsome.

"I can help you with your bags," she said. "Did you go shopping?"

"Carry the light one—it has boxes of something called dhokla inside. I ate the most delicious dhokla and they insisted on giving me five boxes full."

"Who?"

"This bag is much heavier. It has papaya and coconuts," David said. "Can we go have a drink?"

Tina had never spent time alone with David but she needed another drink so she agreed and they walked over to the Fountain Bar that was nestled away in a back corner of Colebrookes. As the name suggested, it was a small bar near a fountain that was fitted with colored lights.

Only one other table was occupied, by an Indian couple sitting in silence with two glasses of white wine and a small bowl of peanuts. Tina led David to the table farthest away from them to give them some privacy.

"Any Indian whiskey, please," David said. "Something middle of the range. Double shot with no ice."

He turned to Tina and said, "I find I'm developing quite a taste for Indian whiskey on this trip. What are you drinking?"

"I'll just have a glass of your house white wine," Tina said to the waiter.

The waiter nodded and turned away, annoyed that this new couple had sat down right as he was hoping his shift would end. After 10 P.M., if there were no orders for twenty minutes, Amit was allowed to shut down the bar. The other couple had stopped ordering fifteen minutes ago and stopped talking twenty minutes ago so he thought he was free for the night but now he had to open another bottle of wine and wait. He texted Pravishi again and told her to go ahead and go back home to her husband. Pravishi was a nurse, very much married, who had lied to her husband and said she had to work late at the hospital tonight but was actually waiting for Amit outside the back gate of Colebrookes as she often did. She was holding a box with a slice of Black Forest cake and two plastic forks. Pravishi was tiring of the unreliability of this relationship but her husband had been diagnosed with ALS two years ago and she was so sick of being his caretaker. She would wait, Pravishi texted back. *Take your time.*

"As I was leaving Lodhi Gardens, I saw a young couple sitting on the sidewalk and the woman was crying. Sobbing," David said. "And the man was hunched over her."

"Did you get cheated, David?" Tina asked.

"On the contrary. I went to their home and had dinner with them," David said. "They were crying because her sister had just had a miscarriage in Udaipur and the young woman wanted to go be by her side but they couldn't afford it. Something like that—there was a bit of a language barrier."

Amit placed their drinks down in front of them and whispered, "Anything else? It's last call."

They didn't need to know the club rules and Pravishi had said she was still waiting. But the management watched and listened to everything on the club grounds so he had to make it subtle.

"I'm sorry, what?" David asked.

"Last call," Amit said, leaning in to whisper it into their faces.

"That's all for me, thanks," David said. "Tina?"

"I'm done too, thank you."

Amit texted Pravishi that he would be with her in exactly twenty-five minutes and he would bring her favorite chicken lollipop from the main kitchen on his way out. Outside the back entrance, Pravishi sat down on the sidewalk and opened the black forest cake and took a bite and put on YouTube on her phone. She would watch some Bollywood songs while she waited.

"Anyway, one thing led to another and I ended up going back to their home—a slum, really—and had dinner with them and two glasses of Pepsi and my phone ran out of charge but I didn't want to be rude and their home didn't exactly look like it would have an iPhone charger."

David waved Amit over and asked for a bowl of peanuts.

"You look so much like your mother," David said. "And you have quite similar personalities too, don't you?"

"I really don't think we do," Tina said.

"She always says you're like her, fiercely independent," David said. "And she told me not to dare ever treat you like a daughter because you would bite my head off and then she would bite my neck off."

"That part she got right." Tina smiled.

"Do you want children?" David asked. "I never wanted children."

"Have you ever regretted that choice?"

"An evening here, an evening there of regret but that's about all. No more or less regret than all my other choices made or not made."

They both sat in silence and sipped their drinks. Sudden, loud laughter broke out from the couple at the other table.

"Weddings are exhausting, aren't they?" David said. He set down his whiskey, rubbed his eyes, and cracked his knuckles.

"I've barely seen Shefali and Pavan," Tina said.

David ate some more peanuts and stared at the fountain changing colors from red to blue.

"I commend you for trying to capture this country for the screen," David said. "It's a complex place."

He stared ahead again.

"I'm in over my head," he said.

He exhaled loudly.

"Me too," Tina said. "Although I feel like I'm always in over my head. Does my mother complain about that? I feel like she's disappointed that I'm not as secure as her."

"Are you disappointed by that?" David asked. He paused briefly and added, "What am I doing? I'm turning into your mother, answering every question with a question. I'll tell you one thing—she's a brilliant psychiatrist. But as for you, I've never heard her do anything except praise you to the heavens. I was quite nervous about meeting you the first time."

"That's nice of you to say, hard for me to believe," Tina said.

"I took a creative writing class soon after my last breakup and the teacher used to harp on about writing what you know," David said. "I never agreed with that. The reason I took that class was in order to get away from everything I knew, you know?"

"Okay," Tina said.

"Is it similar for finding content to produce?" David asked. "Or is it easier to actually create what you know? Like the couple who took me home—they were lovely and kind and their home was so small and so cramped, and I can see how they'd be fascinating, but you aren't one of them. Right? Would you get the nuance or would it just be another voyeuristic perspective of poverty? By 'you' I mean 'anyone.' I've been genuinely wondering about this. I'm not sure how to even talk about India when I get back to America."

"I'm Indian, though," Tina said. She paused. She looked over at the couple at the other table. The woman had slipped off her sandal and her toe was grazing the man's ankle. A silver chain glinted against the woman's ankle. The woman leaned her chin into her hand and smiled.

"But I understand what you mean, I think. Like the home you're describing right now—I don't know the details, I don't know what kind of plumbing or access to water they have. How do they cook? Do they have stoves?"

"They did," David said.

But Tina barely heard him as she continued, "But if I now have to admit that I don't know all this, then who am I? What am I? I'm not sure I fully belong in America but what if I don't belong in India either? But I get what you're saying—maybe I'm not giving India the credit it deserves. It's not just about poverty, right? I mean, that's exactly the kind of perception that needs to change. Is that what you meant?"

"Sure," David said.

Tina looked over at him and smiled. "It's like you're inside my mind; I don't know if I like it."

"I am inside your mind. 'Who is this buffoon who hangs around my mother' is your usual thought," David said.

"Right again. What did you end up writing about?"

"A divorce story. But from the wife's perspective," David said. "I've never told your mother this. Can you imagine what a wild time she'd have if she read it and analyzed it? I thought it was pretty good. And for the record, I did not place all the blame on the wife. Anyway, I quit the class soon after that and haven't written anything else since. I thought writing would be therapeutic but it's too difficult."

"You're going to have another breakup story on your hands if you don't go and find my mother now and explain where you've been," Tina said.

ACROSS COLEBROOKES, MARIANNE PEEKED out the window to see if Tina had left before she went back out to meet Karan. Her phone flashed with a message from Tom telling her he missed her, he was on his way to a book launch in Park Slope, and he would speak to her later in the day. Marianne pictured him with his gray backpack on, slouching slightly, cigarette in hand, walking down his tree-lined lane in DUMBO. In the backpack would be an issue of the *New York Review of Books* or the *Times Literary Supplement,* a bottle of water, and a small tin of Altoids that had opened up months ago and spilled all the little white mints.

The patio was empty so Marianne rushed out and toward the main entrance, where Karan was waiting for her, his headlights on, windows rolled up, a low, thumping bass coming from the car. Marianne had to walk in the bright headlights to get to the passenger-side door and knowing Karan was in there, invisible behind the bright lights, watching her, thrilled her. Forget what Tina said about the dress; she wished she had been more honest with herself and carried a pair of heels. She had saved four pairs of her favorite heels and kept them in boxes on the top shelf of the shoe closet in the hallway of her apartment. She got in the car that smelled faintly of aftershave, cigarette smoke, and beer— the smells of college. Karan leaned back in his seat, looked at her, and said, "Didn't expect you in a dress like that. You should show off your legs more often."

He didn't wait for her to respond and pulled the car into reverse and then pulled forward toward the Colebrookes exit and the Delhi night streets. Marianne leaned back into her seat and put her feet up onto their toes, as if she were wearing heels, to accentuate her leg muscle. Tom would be on the train now, sitting down, reading, completely unaware of anyone around him. He was easily the most intelligent man Marianne had ever met. And he looked at her with the same intensity that he read—as if nothing else existed other than her.

Karan drove in near silence with music playing, Marianne unable to tell what the music was, only that the bass was overpowering. She remembered the days she had spent holed up at the Pierre hotel with Riyaaz her junior year at Yale. He was Pakistani, grew up in Dubai, and was devastatingly handsome. He drove a silver BMW 3 Series and

loved cooking. Marianne and Riyaaz were in the same English literature class the previous semester and their flirtation had started then but
never turned into anything more until that Thursday night when he
asked her if she wanted to go and watch *Monsoon Wedding* at the campus theater. Marianne skipped her lecture on the poetry of Plath and
went to an afternoon show. It was the first Indian movie Marianne had
ever seen and the dancing in the wedding scene had made her feel high.
It was the end of February so when they came out it was already getting dark outside and Marianne was going to suggest getting a drink
when Riyaaz said, "Want to go to a hookah bar and go dancing? That's
what the movie put me in the mood for. Some good Bollywood dancing."

Marianne smiled and they got into Riyaaz's car and she had no idea
where in New Haven you could smoke hookahs and dance to Bollywood. But it turned out it was nowhere in New Haven at all because
Riyaaz drove, and then kept driving, and two hours later, they pulled
into Manhattan, and on the narrow streets near NYU, Riyaaz parked
his car on MacDougal Street, and as they stepped out, a blond girl in
dark jeans and a black top suddenly vomited onto the pavement and
Marianne had to dodge the vomit but she didn't care. She couldn't believe she was here and she couldn't believe that in nearly three years of
being at Yale she hadn't come to New York City even once. Three Indian men wearing suits and eating rolls walked past, none of them
bothering to make space on the sidewalk so Marianne had to momentarily separate from Riyaaz. She was hungry but she worried that eating would ruin the magic of the day.

Riyaaz walked with a swagger, a cigarette forever between his fingers, his wealth giving him confidence beyond his twenty years. Marianne felt immature and inexperienced. Riyaaz did most of the talking
and she did most of the listening. A homeless couple sat on the ground
with tarp and sheets and dreadlocks and a large dog by their feet. A
cardboard sign sat in front of them next to an empty coffee cup with
coins. The sign said: *Lost everything, expecting a baby, anything helps,
God bless you.*

"Maybe getting a job would help," Riyaaz said and Marianne laughed and they walked past them and straight to the entrance to Falucka.

Ten, fifteen, thirty minutes into sitting in Falucka, drinking gin and tonics, and smoking a hookah, Marianne couldn't stop feeling guilty that she had laughed. She excused herself from Riyaaz, slipped out of Falucka, and gave the homeless couple ten dollars, more than she had ever given away before, and came back into the club and kissed Riyaaz while he was mid-sip. They ended up spending four nights at The Pierre Hotel on Fifth Avenue, Marianne surviving on cosmetics and deodorant bought at the Duane Reade on Lexington and some clothes she bought at Bloomingdale's one morning when Riyaaz disappeared for a meeting. He never said what the meeting was and she never asked. On that trip, Marianne first snorted cocaine and loved it, she wore all black and loved it, she had sex with Riyaaz at least twice every day (including once in the bathroom of Jules while a live band played jazz right outside) and she loved it, and she learned to walk on the cobbled streets of the Meatpacking District in stiletto heels (the trick was to lean forward until your calves burned).

They returned to New Haven at 4 A.M. on Sunday, straight from a night of partying. They had been drinking in the back room of Spitzer's when Riyaaz suddenly said, "Well, this is all getting a bit too repetitive. Let's go back." She thought he meant to the Pierre and was looking forward to a quieter glass of wine in the dark hotel bar but instead they went upstairs, packed their things wordlessly, got in the car, and drove back to New Haven. With anyone else, this would have been annoying but with Riyaaz she found her lack of say and independence absolutely thrilling. On the car ride back, Riyaaz barely spoke, this time listening to Tupac on a low volume, muttering along to some of the rapped parts. Marianne had a feeling of impending doom about returning to Yale, returning to her normal backpack and classes, returning to a life outside the Pierre, outside Manhattan, and even though a strange unease and sadness was creeping up on her in the car that night, she vowed that she would move to New York the minute she graduated.

* * *

SHE THOUGHT OF THAT now as Delhi sped past the darkened windows of Karan's car.

"This seems far," she said. "Where are we going?"

Karan lowered the volume and asked, "What?"

"This is far," Marianne repeated. "Where are we going?"

"It's my friend's farmhouse right outside the city. It won't take much longer and the cops rarely cause trouble out there. Plus he has a huge pool, you'll see."

Marianne felt a little scared by the mention of cops and why they should be a cause for concern at a party but she said nothing. Certainly, nothing about the party looked frightening when they got there. Fairy lights sparkled in the trees and heat lamps and bonfires were scattered around the rolling lawns of the party. The pool glistened, empty but filled with rows of small candles, and well-dressed people in boots and jackets and scarves stood around drinking champagne and wine and smoking cigarettes and reminding Marianne of Riyaaz in a way that made her ache.

"Come, let's get a drink," Karan said and grabbed Marianne's hand.

Two drinks later, Marianne excused herself and went to the bathroom to rinse some mouthwash through her mouth. She hated mints and gum so she always carried a small bottle of mouthwash in her purse. She swirled it around her mouth, spat it out, rinsed the light blue tinge off her teeth, and reapplied her lipstick.

Two beautiful Indian women came in, both wearing fur coats draped over their shoulders, their slender arms with gold bracelets on them clutching small purses. They smiled at Marianne and placed their purses on the bathroom counter. One of them leaned back against the sink and sipped from a glass of wine while the other one leaned into the mirror and examined her face.

"Have you seen how great my pores look? I've been doing vampire facials," she said.

Her friend glanced at her and asked, "Do you go to Fatima?"

"Of course," her friend said. "Despite what she's done to her own forehead. Have you noticed?"

"It's impossible not to. She is not currently her own best advertisement," her friend said. She opened her clutch and took out a little Altoid tin.

"I want a mint," her friend said, reapplying her lipstick in the mirror.

"It's E," her friend said. "I'm just going to do a half. Do you want the other half?"

Marianne watched them both place the half pills in their mouths and swallow them down with quick sips of wine. In the past, whenever she wore this dress, she was always offered whatever drugs were available. She looked down at herself now. Maybe it was the flat shoes that made her look like an unlikely candidate for E. She would have accepted half a pill, she thought, and walked back to the lawn. Karan was standing alone by the edge of the swimming pool. Marianne walked straight up to him, the way she had to Riyaaz, and she kissed him—except, unlike Riyaaz, Karan pulled back with a laugh and said, "Drinks went to your head pretty fast. Do you need some water? And here, come, I'll introduce you to the hosts."

He took her hand again and technically nothing he had said or done was offensive but Marianne felt her stomach sink and she felt a hot embarrassment that he would have smelled her fresh, mouth-washed breath and known that she had prepared herself to kiss him. She followed him through the crowd and stopped to pick up a vodka shot from a white waitress dressed like a nurse who was carrying around two trays with different-colored test tube shots.

"Easy, tiger," Karan said. Marianne downed her shot and continued after him. She wanted to leave but how could she? She didn't have a car, and Delhi at night in a little black dress wasn't safe. So she picked up another glass of wine and told herself she would enjoy this because surely she hadn't changed that much since the week in New York with Riyaaz.

* * *

AFTER RIYAAZ AND MARIANNE had returned to New Haven, they continued seeing each other off and on for the remainder of her junior year. She never messaged or called him first but whenever he called, he picked her up in his car and drove her to his off-campus apartment and cooked her elaborate meals and then she spent the night. He introduced her to the world of competitive cooking shows and taught her how to pair her wines with her food. One night he took her to the local grocery store and they spent an hour in the produce section working out which tomatoes would be the juiciest, which cucumbers the crunchiest, and which avocados would be the perfect shade of green that very day, and Marianne swore she had never experienced anything so erotic. He told her all his business plans with the confidence of a man who would never have to work for his money.

"So much product gets wasted," he said to her over a simmering pot of minestrone soup one night, the smell of bacon wafting through the air. "Like lotion or shampoo or conditioner. Right? Like you just use it as long as it's easy to get out of the bottle and then you probably throw it out. So I'm designing this rotating piece of plastic that will help scrape out the small bits left in the bottom of bottles. It'll end up saving people millions."

"I don't think anyone spends millions on lotions and shampoos," Marianne said.

"Whatever, thousands," Riyaaz said. He pulled a spatula out of his kitchen drawer and said, "See, the edge would be something like this."

He went to open all the windows. His parents didn't know he ate pork and they were coming for graduation the following weekend. Marianne stayed on campus for graduation because she had a part-time job at the library but also because she hoped maybe Riyaaz would introduce her to his family. He didn't. He didn't call her that whole weekend even though he knew she was there. She saw him across the quad with his family one day and waved but he just nodded back in her direction. The night before he left campus, he came to her dorm for the last time and they had sex on her creaky single bed. He gave her his juicer and his portable DVD player, kissed her on the forehead, and left. She never heard from him again. She still checked his Facebook every so often so she knew he was married to a woman named Arzoo, had one son who looked more like Arzoo than like him, and was living in Dubai, but she knew nothing else.

She especially didn't know that in Dubai, Arzoo often looked at Marianne's Facebook page because whenever she had an argument with Riyaaz, he would talk about Marianne as if she was the one that got away and now he was stuck with Arzoo.

Her senior year, Marianne started hanging out with the rich Indians and Pakistanis of her year and took Tina along with her. These South Asians had all grown up in South Asia and planned to return there as soon as they finished studying. Marianne never found another Riyaaz and missed him continuously her senior year. Soon after she graduated, she met Samuel at a Starbucks in Union Square and traded in her South Asian shawls and bangles for the infamous beret and zipped off to Paris to eat escargots and smoke cigarettes and pose nude for Samuel to draw. He was a terrible artist, and despite the romance and glamor of being stretched out nude for him, she had cringed when she saw the final sketch and quickly put her clothes back on. And then there had been Sven and Minh and Seydou, and Archie, and with them Marianne had gone to Amsterdam and Hanoi and Timbuktu and a sprawling manor in Essex. And after all that, there was Tom and his apartment in DUMBO and his parents in Newton and they spoke the same language and they had watched the same television shows and read the same magazines and attended the New Yorker Festival every October and both had glasses from Warby Parker. It was wonderful, it was safe, but was that really it?

TONIGHT, ON THIS FARMHOUSE LAWN on the outskirts of Delhi, senior-year Marianne was waking up again. Now, with the alcohol warming her blood, Karan's hand still holding hers, Marianne started to wonder which Marianne was a performance, which Marianne was true, and perhaps more important, which Marianne made her the happiest. The party was picking up, the crowds getting fatter, the room to move scarcer, and Marianne was pressed up against Karan as they chatted with his friend Kavya and her fiancé, Faisal. They were talking about their upcoming wedding in Bali but all Marianne could concentrate on was the smell of Karan's cigarette mingling with the smell of his cologne, the loud music, and the feeling of Karan's hand that had dropped hers and moved instead to her hip. He squeezed her hip; she smiled and leaned into him. Kavya and Faisal noticed and smiled at each other and Kavya said, "I think we'll leave you two alone instead of boring you with all our wedding talk."

Kavya reached into Karan's shirt pocket and pulled out his pack of cigarettes. She took two, put the cigarette pack back in his pocket, patted it twice, kissed him on his cheek, and walked away with Faisal following.

Faisal stared at Kavya's body from the back and decided he would follow her to the end of the earth if she asked. She was magnificent, that small mole on her ear, her slender fingers, her vicious sense of humor, and her willingness to overlook the fact that he had once kissed her sister. He still couldn't believe Pearl had told Kavya. What a betrayal.

Colebrookes: Today's the Haldi Lunch, but First Tina Wants to See Sid; She Wants This to Be Something—Anything

E ARLY THE NEXT MORNING, SUNIL WAS DOZING IN THE SUN outside but jumped up and dusted himself off when he saw Tina approaching. She waved him down and said, "I'm just going to take a rickshaw today, Sunil. You relax."

A rickshaw came to a loud clattering stop outside Colebrookes and Tina got in and said, "CP, M Block, Nirulas ke paas," as confidently as she could, Google Maps open on her phone in case the rickshaw driver took her off in a completely different direction. She noticed he hadn't flipped the meter down so she added, "Bhaiyya, meter se." But he looked at her in the rearview mirror and said in English, "Madam, what meter? You pay what you think is right."

Tina looked back at him and adjusted the collar of her kurta so even the sliver of skin down her neck was no longer visible. The middle of Delhi early in the morning in the middle of autumn was beautiful. Despite all the headlines about the pollution, the air felt fresh—Tina knew it wasn't, of course, and that was clear when she washed her hands at the end of a day out—but here, driving through the leafy lanes of central Delhi, it felt fresh and healthy.

The rickshaw took a left turn away from the main road that Tina's maps showed. She watched her rickshaw go in the wrong direction for almost a minute, wondering if she should say something. They were on a quiet road now, with big houses with tall gates and hardly any cars. A woman in a yellow sari and brown blouse raked leaves along the wide sidewalk. Two dogs wrestled around in a dusty spot under a tree. Tina looked at her phone again—they were on a road perpendicular to the road they were meant to be on. She looked out of the open side of the rickshaw and as she was looking back in, she made eye contact with the rickshaw driver again. She pulled out her sunglasses from her purse, put them on, and pretended to be doing other things on the phone, trying to act uninterested in the roads because of their familiarity.

Still, she did what she often did anywhere out of New York City and went to the sounds settings in her phone and pressed Ringtone and clicked on Default to make her phone ring. She turned it off and held the phone to her ear and said loudly, "Yes, I'm on the way. I'll be there in a few minutes. I'm just off Barakhamba Road. I'll be there soon."

She pretended to turn the phone off and dropped the phone back into her purse and decided instead to look ahead and try and keep track of her general direction. They drove past a man sitting beside a push-cart piled high with green grapes and guavas. A school bus was stopped on the side of the road and dozens of small girls in red-and-black-checkered uniforms milled about near the bus, their hair tied into braids with red bows. Two women, teachers, presumably, in saris, drank tea from flasks and chatted. The rickshaw stopped at a traffic light near them and Tina watched one of the teachers shout, "Stop pushing each other this instant. Anyone who starts a fight is being sent straight back to school and isn't going on any other field trips all year."

"It's a shame we can't slap them anymore," one of the teachers said to the other.

The rickshaw took a sharp left, the road curved gently to the right, then he took another right, then that road curved left but more sharply than the previous road had, and finally Tina gave up and admitted that she had no idea whether or not they were going in the right direction. She was trying to find the right sequence of words in Hindi to casually ask the driver which route he was taking when he took a right turn at an intersection with no traffic lights and the large, imposing white structures of Connaught Place suddenly loomed up in front of her.

In front of Nirula's, Tina pulled out two five-hundred-rupee notes from her wallet. She was going to stand firm and not pay a rupee more than that, she decided. She wasn't going to be charged foreigner prices by this rickshaw driver who thought he knew her so well that he refused to answer her Hindi with Hindi.

The driver took the two bills and handed one back to Tina.

"Madam, even this amount that I'm taking is too much because I know you aren't from here," he said. "But one thousand I would feel bad taking."

A documentary on rickshaw drivers in Delhi?

DESPITE THE SLIGHT WINTER CHILL in the air, Sid insisted on getting sundaes because his mother always talked about the famous Nirula's sundaes in Delhi. He ordered a vanilla one with chocolate syrup and Tina got a black coffee, and they decided to stroll through the arches of Connaught Place instead of sitting in Nirula's, which was dimly lit and depressing and empty.

Tina looked at Sid and was annoyed with herself for still seeing him as a casting choice instead of a potential romantic partner. He was so attractive, she told herself. Why wasn't she drawn to him the way she ought to be? She would make herself be. Sometimes these things needed a little nudge, even if it was forced at first.

Sid was wearing a dark blue sweater and looking at him made Tina feel hot but the very first thing he said was that he wasn't used to even slightly cold weather after a lifetime in Bombay.

"Then you'll never survive in New York," Tina said.

"I'll learn. I'm going to teach myself snowboarding once I move there," Sid said. And Tina tried to picture him on the slopes. "Do you know how to make sushi?"

"No," Tina said.

"Me neither. So I'm going to take a class on sushi-making in New York. I was at one of my client's houses one day and her daughter was watching some documentary on a sushi chef and it was brilliant. What perfection, what an art. I bet sushi chefs live longer than others on average. That documentary was based in Japan somewhere but I looked it up and there are all kinds of sushi-making classes in New York too. Sushi-making and snowboarding—two more things you have the power to make happen for me, Tina."

A woman in a blue synthetic sari and gold jewelry walked past them and turned to look at Sid. Tina turned as well and locked eyes with the woman, who quickly turned away. Sid didn't seem to notice. He crumpled his empty coffee cup and dropped it at the side of the road. He stopped at a man sitting with a large tin box open in front of him and squatted down to buy a fistful of beedis to smoke later. When he stood back up and they continued walking, Tina asked, "When you auditioned, your brother was about to get married, is that right?"

"He had a girlfriend but it ended. She was Muslim and her family said no. My mother wasn't going to say yes either but they said no first so now my mother marches around proudly talking about how tolerant she is and how the Muslim girl's family refused."

"Right, I remember now. Your audition tape said your story comes ready with Hindu-Muslim tensions."

"It sells," Sid shrugged.

"Is your mother putting pressure on you to get married? How does it work? Do you have a girlfriend or would you have an arranged marriage? Like, to someone like Divya? Would that be suitable for your mother?"

Sid stopped walking and looked at Tina and smiled.

"So many questions. And without a video camera even," he said. "So you can't pretend these questions are for the show."

"How was your night yesterday?" Tina fumbled to change the topic.

"Uneventful. Sorry I didn't reply to your message," Sid said. "My battery had died and my charger wasn't working properly."

That didn't sound too believable to Tina because two blue check marks had appeared near her message so she knew he had seen them.

"Did you do anything fun?" Tina asked.

"Nope," Sid said. "Just worked out, watched some TV, had dinner, went to bed early."

Tina had also checked his chat tab this morning and noticed that he had last logged on at 3:14 A.M.

Around them, Connaught Place was starting to get busier with people in office clothes milling about, sipping hot chai out of small earthen pots and some sipping hot coffee out of paper cups. A group of white tourists walked toward them. British, Tina could tell immediately by the accents. She watched Sid step aside near the wall in order to make room for them to walk past. When they were again shoulder to shoulder he said, "How come you aren't married?"

Tina shrugged.

"Your parents must be worried about you. You are over thirty already?"

"Yes, but that's hardly old these days," Tina said, her usual response to questions like these that she had grown accustomed to in India.

"But it will be harder to have children if you wait too much longer," Sid said, sounding concerned instead of annoying. He wasn't saying it because he was some catty auntie or smug newlywed; he was saying it because it was true. Tina wasn't even sure she wanted to have children but, along with everything else, this was something she needed to decide soon. Maybe she didn't need to get pregnant right away but she needed to decide whether or not she ever hoped to. Living alone in New York had allowed her to stay twenty-five in her mind but her body had moved along. Unlike a lot of her friends, she had never achingly wanted a child but neither had she ever felt the need to loudly call herself child-free and commit to a life without babies. It suddenly felt like everything had rushed up and caught up with her and now Tina had days left to make decisions that should have been spread out over a decade.

"I can marry you for a Green Card," Sid said.

"Or I can marry you to get Indian citizenship. Does it even work that way? Everyone knows how to go about trying to get American citizenship but what if I want to do it the other way?" Tina asked.

"I really don't know," Sid said. "I suppose you're right."

"It's about passport privilege, isn't it? It's so arbitrary but if you're born in a certain country, you automatically have the privilege to see pretty much the whole world but if you're born elsewhere, like in India, or Iran, you have to apply and pay and beg and shout just for a chance to visit most countries. Damn it. Now, on top of all the other privilege I have to think about and try and correct for, I have to add passport privilege," Tina said. "How much would it cost you to get a UK visa for instance?"

"I have no idea. Divya told me there was a website where you could see which all countries will give Indians a visa on arrival. Definitely not the UK, though. But I can't even afford a flight yet," Sid said.

"It feels like the world is flipping upside down right when I need to figure things out and now I don't even know which world I'm supposed to inhabit," Tina said, barely listening to him. "It was easy for my parents. They wanted to live in America when America was the clear choice, they wanted to get married when marriage was the only acceptable option, and then they wanted to get divorced right around when divorce became socially acceptable. The times rolled with them. Now there are no rules. I can do whatever I want, be whoever I want, and I don't know if I want that freedom."

"Your parents are divorced?" Sid asked. "I don't think I knew that. I'm so sorry."

"Don't be," Tina said. "It happened years ago and it's been best for everyone. They're both happy."

"See, my world is still the same, still small," Sid said. "Divorce still isn't acceptable. Your world is so big that you have more options. You're lucky."

"Come on, I want to get a bottle of water," Tina said.

They walked past a fancy jewelry showroom with gold displays in the front window. A man in uniform with a large mustache and larger gun stood guard outside the door.

"I can't afford any gold, I'm afraid," Sid said. "I'll buy you something artificial if we get married."

"You'll be able to afford diamonds set in platinum once I turn you into a global superstar."

"That's what I needed to do? Propose? See, the audition was misleading," Sid said.

He touched her arm and Tina, hearing Marianne's voice in her head, Rachel's voice, her own mother's voice, decided to make a decision and slipped her arm through Sid's arm. Maybe their differences didn't matter; she earned enough for them both. Could she handle a house-husband, though?

They stopped near a man standing at a corner near a fridge and paid twenty rupees for a bottle of water. On the ground near him, a stray dog lay with three puppies nestled against her. As Tina and Sid walked away with the water, the man squatted down and pet the big dog and refilled a metal bowl of water near her head. Tina took a sip of water from the bottle and offered it to Sid. He took it and held it up high away from his mouth and let the water fall in without touching his mouth to the bottle. They continued walking. Sid asked her about the wedding and how her family was doing. He said he had looked up Colebrookes on his phone the previous night and it looked fancy.

"I've decided I could never live in Delhi," Sid announced. "I'm enjoying myself here but I think I'll always stay in Bombay. I feel poorer here somehow."

"Should we have another cup of coffee?" Tina responded, unsure how else to.

"I have a better idea," Sid said and dropped Tina's arm. He pulled out his phone from his pocket—not an iPhone, Tina noted. Of course not an iPhone. She was one of the sheep who was tricked into believing that was the only phone that existed. But the rose gold was so lovely.

And the phone was so convenient. Wasn't it equally silly to be a sheep who was against it for no real rhyme or reason?

"It's only nine forty-five. Come with me," Sid said. He banged his phone against his fist. "Stupid, cheap phone keeps crashing. But come with me to East Delhi. Come meet my friend Suraj. He's an electrician at a housing complex there but really he's a writer, a lyricist. He writes only in Hindi and some Punjabi, but a lot of what I perform is his. We've never met in person, only over the Internet, but I've told him all about you. You'll like him. Come, please. I want you to meet him. I want you to be with me."

Tina looked around as if perhaps the answer were somewhere in the long, narrow walkways of Connaught Place even though she knew the answer immediately. India, with Sid by her side but also as her guide, was where she wanted to be, she was fairly certain.

And that decision was validated when the rickshaw driver automatically flipped the meter down when Sid said to him, "Mayur Vihar, phase one." The rickshaw driver who took directions in Hindi from a confident Sid, even though Sid opened with the confession that he was from Bombay and knew nothing about Delhi. In the rickshaw, as they rattled through central Delhi onto busier, faster roads with more large trucks and buses and fewer shiny cars with tinted windows, the cool autumn air sliced across their faces. Tina and Sid huddled together at the back, their knees pushed against each other. Tina held her arms tightly around herself and turned her face into the side of Sid's face to avoid inhaling the fumes from the trucks that overtook their small rickshaw. He wore no cologne, nothing on him smelled artificial. Sid put his arm around her shoulders, his hand resting against her right shoulder, and Tina could feel its warmth through the cloth of her kurta. They sat in silence, entwined, not even trying to speak because it would be futile over the loud sound of traffic and the city and wide roads.

They crossed a bridge and the horizon looked dustier than what they had left behind. At Sid's instruction, they turned off the bridge onto a small road that led to a smaller road on which the cars were smaller, older, dirtier, and more dented. There were no sidewalks and not many trees. As the rickshaw slowed its pace, Sid smiled at Tina and removed his hand from her shoulder and said, "Almost there."

Tina smiled back and turned away to face out of the rickshaw and saw a cow grazing along some low bushes. Bells clanked around its neck. A cluster of women in saris squatted in the sun at the side of the road and chatted while one oiled and combed the hair of another.

The rickshaw slowed down as Sid gave more instructions, poking his head out to try and make sense of the roads even though none were marked.

"Suraj said we had to take a left at the yellow schoolhouse. Did you see a yellow schoolhouse?"

Would a yellow schoolhouse show up on Google Maps? Tina wondered. Probably, actually, but she let Sid deal with the navigation while she also looked out of her side. They were stopped in front of a handful of five-story apartment buildings with all the windows protected by bars. Clothes dried on balconies and ropes attached outside windows.

They weren't even entering the buildings with the protected windows. They were entering the lane of small shacks that stood in the shadow of those buildings. Tina followed behind Sid, who had even more swagger in this lane than he usually did. A short, dark-skinned man with bright-white eyes and teeth came around a corner and waved at them. He looked about fifteen but a small child wearing an oversized sweater and no pants stood behind him and tugged at him.

They entered Suraj's home, which was one windowless room with a small lofted space at the top. Every inch of space was used. A corner of the main room served as a kitchen, and a small TV sat on the top of the fridge. Near the fridge was an aquarium with dirty glass and a turtle inside. They all sat on the floor, the little boy pushing a small wooden toy truck with only three wheels between them.

While Suraj and Sid chatted in faster Hindi than Tina could follow, a pretty young woman—girl really—in a salwar kameez came in the door that was propped open with a tray with two water glasses, one plate of oily samosas, and one plate of silver-coated kaju barfi. She placed the plate down in the middle of them and Suraj didn't introduce her.

"Chintu, come, leave Papa alone," the woman said in Hindi, and the little boy wandered off behind her.

Sid kept talking in Hindi and reached over and drained a glass of water and started on a samosa. Suraj, who had barely acknowledged Tina so far, now nudged the tray a bit closer to her and looked at her. Tina wanted to refuse, wanted to ask if the water was filtered, wanted to say she wasn't hungry but instead she took a few sips of water and picked up a kaju barfi. The small, diamond-shaped sweet seemed like it would be easier to digest. But it wasn't. Or maybe the water in the glass wasn't, because twenty minutes later, Tina felt a deep rumble go through her stomach. Her eyes widened in terror and she said, "Um, sorry, Sid, could I use the bathroom?"

Sid looked at her and looked out of the door and then looked at Suraj and said, "Bathroom?"

Suraj thrust his chin out toward the door and said in careful English, "Right side."

Tina thanked him and hurriedly got up and walked out of the door and to the right. She looked around in search of the bathroom. Suraj's wife and son were sitting on the ground outside, the son still pushing the truck around, the wife flipping through a magazine. The wife looked up at Tina and pointed to a wooden door behind her.

Tina smiled at her and rushed toward the wooden door and opened it to find an empty room with a mud floor that certainly smelled like a bathroom. But there was no toilet, no sink, no toilet paper, no mirror, nothing except a small bucket of water in the corner with a plastic pink mug bobbing on the surface.

Tina backed out of the bathroom and hurried past Suraj's wife and son and back into their home.

"I have to go," she said to Sid. "The haldi lunch. It's today, it's now. I have to go right now."

"Did you find the bathroom?" Sid asked.

"I'll speak to you later, okay? I really enjoyed our morning."

Sid got up and said, "Wait, I'll walk you out and make sure you get a rickshaw." But Tina waved to him and rushed back toward the main road.

"Cinderella," Sid said loudly behind her. "Leave me a glass slipper."

Tina didn't have time to be charmed because she knew her insides were a ticking clock and she needed to get back to Colebrookes and the clean bathrooms with toilet seats and water guns and toilet paper and large mirrors and flattering lighting before her body betrayed her.

Haldi Lunch, Hyacinth Haven,
Shefali Wanted the Alliteration,
Colebrookes

"OKAY, THAT'S ENOUGH NOW, UNCLE," SHEFALI SNAPPED. "I thought only women applied the haldi on the bride."

Shefali used the back of her hand to rub the turmeric off her eyebrow and squinted at the uncle.

"Do you even know us?" Shefali asked.

"Shefali," Pavan whispered. But he loved Shefali's refusal to worry about social codes. "Don't be rude, babe."

"He let his hand linger on my neck," Shefali said. "I'll be as fucking rude as I want. I can't stand old Indian uncles who think they can get away with being sleazy because everyone's forced to respect their elders regardless of whether or not we even know them. Disgusting. He is definitely not related to us."

The uncle backed away quickly. The bride was right. He wasn't invited to the wedding. He didn't even know who these people were. He was on his way to use the gym when he had seen the haldi ceremony in progress and he couldn't resist giving this young woman's swan-like neck a little stroke. His own wife's neck had long disappeared under her multiple chins. But he had to be careful now. Last week he had stroked the arm of a young woman on a flight to Hyderabad and she turned around, shouting, and took a video of him. He quickly, reverentially did a namaste and acted as if he were old and senile and had done it by mistake, but she was furious. The simple days of being able to pinch a girl's bottom were quickly slipping away, he worried.

This may have been a mistake, Shefali thought, still fuming. She had always liked the image of the haldi ceremony—she had pictured the yellow turmeric making her brown skin glow, sitting as the center of attention, looking disheveled but beautiful. But she was looking and feeling like a marinated piece of meat and she wanted to scratch her eyes but her hands were a mess so she just blinked rapidly. She should have done a mehndi ceremony instead. She had reasoned that sitting with her arms out for three hours while the henna dried would be the boring option but now she craved that boredom.

"Where the hell are all our friends?" she asked.

"Hungover, probably," Pavan said.

Marianne approached the couple, seated on a white cloth under a large white canopy.

"This is so beautiful!" she said, taking a picture with her phone. "What exactly does the turmeric signify?"

"God knows," Shefali said. "I just thought it would make for good pictures."

"Turmeric is a very auspicious color. It's known to keep the evil eye away," Bubbles said from the sidelines. "And, of course, it makes the skin glow. So many good properties. Come, come. Let Shefali touch some to your skin also; it'll help you find a suitable partner."

Marianne leaned forward and Shefali removed some of the paste from her forehead and rubbed it onto Marianne's.

"Where's Tina?" Shefali asked.

"Food poisoning," Marianne said.

"Gross," Shefali said. "From something she ate here? Is our food making people sick? I will die of embarrassment."

"No, she had gone out somewhere this morning," Marianne said.

"Tell her not to come out before she's fully better. I don't need someone vomiting all over the bushes and diverting all the attention."

"Where's . . . where's everyone else?" Marianne asked, looking around. "Hey, Pavan, where's your brother?"

"Are you sleeping with him?" Shefali asked.

"What? No!" Marianne said quickly. She looked around to see if she could find Rocco or Kai but nobody seemed to be at the lunch yet. She decided to walk back to the cottage for a little while so Karan wouldn't see her wandering around alone and aimless.

Shefali shrugged. An elderly couple approached and lifted the haldi paste up with their hands and went to apply it onto the couple.

"Auntie can put it on me and Uncle can put it on Pavan," Shefali said. "Those are the rules now."

"No," Bubbles said. "Shefali, that's not how it works."

"That's exactly how it works," Shefali said. "I'm not here to get felt up."

"HAVE YOU DONE THIS sort of thing often, then?" Radha asked Mrs. Sethi, about twenty feet away from the bride and groom. They were sitting around a large, wrought-iron table on the main Colebrookes lawn for the haldi ceremony lunch.

"Been on dates around Delhi? Not too many," Mrs. Sethi replied. "I've had two other setups but one of those didn't even progress past an initial first phone conversation and the other one fizzled after a first date. Actually, it fizzled during the first date when the gentleman said he didn't think women should date after being widowed. Not sure why he was working with a matchmaker for widows, in that case. Sometimes I think I should do one of those *50 Dates in Delhi*–type of experiments and write a book about it. All of the twenty-, thirty-year-old girls are writing books like that but they all have the same experiences. A widow should write that story."

David used both hands to tear a naan in half and then pushed open the middle like it was a pita and put a spoonful of black daal into it followed by two pieces of paneer tikka and two slices of tomato and two slices of cucumber.

"You work at an Indian restaurant?" Mrs. Sethi asked, frowning at the naan in his hand.

"Contemporary fusion Indian," Radha said while David took a large bite of his Indian pita. She looked over at him and smiled. Last night, when he had returned to the cottage, disheveled and carrying bags of dhokla, she was so relieved, so happy, she couldn't even be annoyed. She depended on him less than she had Neel, so she also got annoyed with him less, and that was wonderful, unencumbering.

"They do things like Indian tacos," Radha added as David chewed and nodded.

"And gulab jamun cupcakes," he added, having swallowed enough to be able to speak again. "Those are my favorite. Although after this trip, I think your classic hot jalebis with vanilla ice cream may be the winner."

David set about using a fork to refill the pita with the daal and half-bitten paneer tikka that had fallen out onto his plate.

"I think your book sounds like a wonderful idea," Radha said to Mrs. Sethi. "*A Widow's Guide to Dating in Delhi.* Sensational."

Mr. Das returned to the table holding his plate filled with food from the stalls that lined the edge of the lawns. He sat down at the table near Mrs. Sethi and looked over at David's pita.

"What a brilliant idea to stuff the naan with the food," he said. He tapped his finger against his temple and said, "You can tell this is the manager of a top Indian restaurant. Always innovating."

"Mrs. Sethi was just telling us about the book she's writing about dating in Delhi," Radha said, putting a forkful of slow-cooked mutton curry and rice into her mouth.

The speakers suddenly screeched loudly and a momentary silence fell over the crowd in response.

"This paneer is far better than what we serve at our restaurant," David said. "How do I go about meeting the chef of this place?"

"This is such a lovely place," Mrs. Sethi said. "I'm so glad you invited me along, Neel. I've only ever been to Colebrookes once for a Diwali celebration. I kept meaning to look into getting a membership but I never got around to it. I've heard they only open up the membership once every two years."

Nono came over to their table, her driver standing two feet behind her holding her red Prada purse, identical in every way except color to the one she had the previous morning, and her gin and tonic. She was wearing a red handloom sari with a dark red blouse and large red sunglasses that covered half her face.

"I'm worried they're serving Bombay Sapphire out of the Tanqueray bottles but other than that, this is a lovely afternoon, don't you think?" she said to the table. Without waiting for a response, she continued, "Ah yes, the strange family with all kinds of new partners. And the daughter with the plans to expose the caste system."

"Nice to see you again, Nono," Radha said, preemptively silencing Mr. Das. Nono would eat Mr. Das alive if they got in an argument over Tina and she wanted to protect him. "Did the flowers arrive like you expected?"

"Did you know that Ethiopia is the world's biggest exporter of roses? I'd never have guessed. Anyway, that's where they've come from. We chartered a refrigerated plane so do take special note of the roses tomorrow night."

Nono turned to her driver and took a large sip of her drink and handed the glass back to him. She stood still, savoring the sip and looking at the four of them. Nobody spoke but David continued to eat.

"You people warm my heart," she said. She waved her cane in their direction and added, "Not everyone here approves of you but I do. My only objection is this fool stuffing his daal into his naan. That's not how we eat, my dear."

"Well, Nono," David said. "Then you're missing out."

"You may well be right, young man," she said and David laughed and said, "Nobody has called me young man in a very long time."

"It's all relative," Nono said and turned again to take another sip of her drink and look out over the lawns.

"Weddings celebrate new beginnings," Nono said. "But they also mourn the passing of the old. They'll never be unmarried again—the only remaining options now are divorced, widowed, or dead."

"Or married," Mr. Das said.

Nono leaned forward and stroked his cheek with her wrinkled hand, patted it twice, and said, "Our resident optimist. I like you."

She pointed at Mrs. Sethi and said, "And who are you?"

"Mrs. Jyoti Sethi," Mrs. Sethi said, holding her hand out for Nono to shake. "I'm a friend of Neel's."

"A friend?" Nono said with a smile. "Delightful. Tell me, how did you meet each other?"

"Through a friend," Mr. Das said as Mrs. Sethi said, "Through a matchmaker."

Nono laughed and said, "Bring me up to speed while I smoke a cigarette. Do any of you mind if I smoke while you eat? If you do, you can sit at that empty table just over there. My son won't let me smoke anymore. He won't let me do anything for this wedding except the flowers and even that I've heard him whisper to his wife to double-check everything I do."

Nono hated how invisible old age had made her. At least she still held most of the family's money but she knew her son was determined to get a power of attorney and lay claim to the family fortune and stick her in a home, but she was not about to go down without a fight. She hated being old—people either walked on eggshells around you, worried that you would be easily offended, or they simply didn't see you.

Nono lit a Marlboro Red, took a slow drag, and said, "So, Mrs. Sethi. Tell me everything."

"We met through a matchmaking agency for widows," Mrs. Sethi said. "I prefer not to hide it. I think it's quite wonderful that such services now exist. In fact, Nono, if you're interested—"

"Absolutely not, darling. That's a wonderful thought but I don't ever want another man in my life, thank you very much. Being alone is the best thing to ever happen to me. But continue, how did you find this matchmaker?" Nono asked.

"She herself is a widow," Mr. Das said. "And she's married to my sister's neighbor's brother-in-law. My sister insisted on putting us in touch."

They all turned to Mrs. Sethi. Mr. Das realized he had never actually asked her how she found Mrs. Ray's Matchmaking Agency for Widows.

"I'm quite pleased to say I was the very first client to reach out to her. I was googling options . . . and Mrs. Ray has a very basic website up with her phone number and I called her."

"What exactly did you google?" Mr. Das asked.

"Oh, online matches for our . . . our generation, or something like that," Mrs. Sethi said quickly. As loud and proud as she was about her life, she didn't want to admit that she had googled "Delhi lonely widow" and, worse still, that a lot of porn had come up.

Nono pressed her cigarette out and stood.

"All of you enjoy your lunch, then. I must go find my son before he makes another horrid décor decision without me. He wanted a flower wall with the couple's initials on it. Tacky. I'll see you all tomorrow. Same people, same setting, slightly different clothes."

The four of them watched Nono walk away and Mr. Das frowned and said, "You're writing a book about dating in Delhi?"

"I'm not, actually," Mrs. Sethi said. "I was just saying I ought to because at least it would be original. Haven't we all had enough of hearing twenty- and thirty-year-olds go on and on about their love lives?"

"Why does anyone need to go on and on about their love lives? Why can't some things just be done in private?" Mr. Das said. "I don't think I'd be comfortable with you writing a tell-all book about your personal life."

"Well, Neel, I'm afraid your comfort would not be a huge concern of mine in this case. No longer needing permission to do anything is one of the best things about growing old, don't you think?" Mrs. Sethi said. "If I write the book, I'll give you a different name and I'll make sure there's a disclaimer in the front that certain names and identifying factors have been changed."

Radha laughed loudly at that while her ex-husband frowned.

"Make sure you write about his Fitbit, though," Radha said. "Drop a few crumbs."

"I've eaten too much," David announced. "Radha, are you done? Let's get a coffee and walk off all this food."

Radha was tempted to sit and watch her ex-husband have an uncomfortable conversation but walked with David to the café counter instead. She wondered where Tina was and why she wasn't at the haldi lunch.

Tina wasn't at the haldi lunch because she was lying in bed, stuck between rushing to the bathroom and curling up in bed and clutching her cramping stomach. Rajesh had dropped off Electral, a fresh coconut, and a plate of toast for her. Sid texted to ask her if she got home safely and she couldn't bear to tell him she was rolling around on the bed, miserable.

"One more gulab jamun?" Mrs. Sethi asked Mr. Das. She would never write the book. She liked Mr. Das, she liked his whole family, she was enjoying the midday sun and Colebrookes, and she had made her point about not needing his approval and she wanted to return to the pleasant afternoon. She missed having family around.

"You never told me how your husband died," Mr. Das said suddenly.

"Heart attack," Mrs. Sethi said. "His third. Nothing terribly notable. We had gone for an evening walk and when we came home, he sat down and clutched his chest. He knew what was happening. He told me not to bother calling an ambulance or a doctor and to stay near him. He collapsed to the floor and then he died. That's all there was to it and I hate talking about it or thinking about it."

"I'm sorry," Mr. Das said.

Mrs. Sethi nodded.

"Calling Minal was almost harder than watching him die," she said.

She looked across the grass at families of all shapes and sizes sitting around their tables. In unguarded moments Mrs. Sethi often had panic attacks and she could feel one coming on. She knew she was supposed to honor her husband's memory, think about him often, but for her, survival meant trying to never think about him. She refused to be made to feel guilty about this. Her mourning was her own.

"I'm going to get one more gulab jamun," she said and got up.

Minal told her to always change her physical state when she needed to change her emotional state—"Stand if you're sitting, sit if you're standing, squat if you need to, do a push-up, a jumping jack, anything"—so she walked briskly to the dessert counter and asked for another plate of gulab jamuns with extra syrup. When she returned to the table she felt calmer.

"I'm sorry I asked. I shouldn't have," Mr. Das said.

Mrs. Sethi smiled at him.

"You have every right to ask. I still have a hard time with it, it's silly. But he was a good man."

"Tell me a nice memory," Mr. Das said.

"Are you sure?" Mrs. Sethi asked.

He nodded.

There were so many, Mrs. Sethi thought. He had never bought her jewelry or held doors open but he always made her laugh. But how do you tell someone about the small moments of laughter? Mrs. Sethi used to be an anxious flier and her husband knew that. He always held her ears shut tightly during takeoff because that was the hardest part for her and he had read somewhere that avoiding listening to the sound changes of an airplane could help some fearful fliers. She came to love that ritual. She would clutch the arms of her seat while he held her ears shut, no matter what time the flight was or how tired he was. Once they had enough money to start flying business class, he would still lean over the large space between them, his back straining and hurting, and hold her ears. Then they would both order a cocktail and settle in for the flight. After his first heart attack, when he was only forty-two, he bought her a pair of Bose noise-canceling headphones and said, "Put these away in the cupboard. You won't need them yet but when my heart goes, you can put these on your ears to block the sound. You better not stop traveling."

Mrs. Sethi had been annoyed at that, his attempt at humor just days after a heart attack. But now she used those headphones every time she traveled.

"That sounds like a nice marriage," Mr. Das said. "You were both lucky."

"I didn't always recognize it," Mrs. Sethi said.

She looked over at Mr. Das, his face handsome in the afternoon sun, his hair still thick, his skin not yet shriveled. His eyes were kind, lines forming around the edges that made him look like he was always smiling. Even though she was searching, she hadn't really expected to like anyone but here she was, falling in love with a man who lived across the world.

"I cheated on him once," Mrs. Sethi said. "I'm not proud of it but I'd like you to know. It was brief, hardly a few weeks, with Minal's school principal."

Mr. Das put down the glass of water he was drinking from. His body suddenly felt hot and heavy. He removed his blazer and placed it behind him on the chair.

"It was awful. I hated the affair, I hated myself," Mrs. Sethi said. "When it was over, I made Minal switch schools and hated myself for that even more. It's one of the few things about me that Minal doesn't know. I told her we changed her school because her old school still allowed corporal punishment. Minal had been slapped once by a maths teacher. But I didn't move her until after the affair. You know how it was back then—teachers occasionally slapped kids. In my day, there was still caning. Seems so crazy now, doesn't it?"

"Did you tell him?" Mr. Das asked.

Mrs. Sethi pushed the plate of gulab jamuns aside and said, "I did. And he forgave me eventually. I don't know if I ever forgave myself but he did. Like I said, he was a good man. And, listen, not to defend myself, but I had the affair when things were going dreadfully for us. He had been traveling for work and was not at all present and had left the lion's share of parenting on my shoulders and I was exhausted and tired and had no support and I was angry. Minal was going through a difficult phase at the time."

In fact, it had started, like some silly movie, in the school principal's office when Mrs. Sethi had been called in because Minal had been caught stealing a classmate's scissors and then been caught using those scissors to cut the skirt of another classmate's uniform. Mrs. Sethi had met Apaar Pathak, the school principal, in the past and always found him very dashing, and that afternoon, before she knew it, they were kissing atop his large wooden principal's desk. In a way she was glad it had happened because it saved her marriage. Mr. Sethi stopped traveling as much and he started taking Minal to see movies on the last Sunday afternoon of each month. For a year following the affair things were fragile but they gradually filled the cracks of their marriage and ended up stronger than ever. Apaar Pathak had died soon after in a car accident on Nizamuddin Bridge but Mrs. Sethi didn't know that for many years.

Mr. Das looked at his watch and said, "I should go check on Tina."

"The BRAT diet for upset stomachs," Mrs. Sethi said. "Bananas, rice, apples, and toast. I also have some Digene in my purse."

She pulled out a foil strip from her bag and handed it to Mr. Das.

"Should I wait for you here?" Mrs. Sethi asked. "I have to go vegetable shopping at INA. You could join me. And then we could even hop across to Dilli Haat for a cup of tea and maybe some momos even though I've eaten so much I can't imagine eating anything else."

"I should probably take a short nap. Jet lag," Mr. Das said. "I'll give you a call later, though."

"Am I seeing you for dinner tonight?" Mrs. Sethi asked. "There are no wedding activities, right?"

"Right. Actually, I'm not sure. I may have to see my sister, Shefali's mother," Mr. Das said. "I'll be in touch."

He pushed his chair back and walked toward his cottage, leaving Mrs. Sethi sitting alone at her table watching him walk away.

She took a deep breath. She was too old to hide things, she told herself. If her late husband could handle her affair, a prospective new partner should be able to also. She felt her eyes fill with tears and pulled her sunglasses off her head and onto her face. How silly, she told herself—she barely knew the man, he had made it clear he could never live in Delhi, and she knew she could never live in America. She didn't even know why she had felt compelled to share the truth about her past. Mrs. Sethi blinked hard and fast and walked out toward her car. She looked back once over her shoulder and saw Mr. Das turn a corner and disappear.

Marianne was sitting on the porch of her cottage drinking a sweet-and-salty fresh lime soda and playing with her phone. She didn't want to go back to the haldi until Rocco or Kai joined her and she could throw her head back and pretend to laugh at their jokes if Karan saw her.

A black Range Rover pulled up and she watched Karan step out, followed by his parents and Nono. Marianne dropped her phone down on the table and picked up *The God of Small Things* and pretended she was deeply absorbed. She looked up from behind the book. Karan's mother was beautiful, she noted, wearing a cobalt-blue sari with a matching shawl draped around her shoulders. She was slim and tall and her hair was pulled into a low bun. Karan's father, on the other hand, was wearing a plain, white kurta pajama set, stained with yellow haldi, and had a large paunch and a receding hairline. The standards were so much lower for men, Marianne noted. She hoped Karan would take after his mother or his grandmother.

"I don't know why she wanted to do a haldi," Marianne heard Karan's mother say. "It's a mess, a complete mess. And turmeric doesn't wash out of anything. Shefali and her whims. Not one part of this wedding is following proper traditions. She's just picked a riotous mishmash."

"I like the way she's made it her own," Nono said.

"Mummy, stay in the car," Karan's father said loudly. "You're too old to be walking around. We'll quickly check the setup for tomorrow and go back to the haldi."

"I can't believe Colebrookes thought they were going to get away with patchy grass for the final reception," Karan's mother said. "Standards have really gone down here."

"I told you I also want to confirm the lighting is being done properly," Nono said. "And you don't need to shout, son, I can hear perfectly."

"Let her come," Karan's mother whispered. "It's good for her brain to be engaged."

"Yes," Nono said. "Let's slow down the dementia."

She put her arm through Karan's and they walked in the direction of Marianne's cottage toward the lawn. Marianne stood up and waited to say hello. She pulled her back up straight and tucked her hair behind her ear. She was wearing the outfit Karan had got her and she hoped he'd notice.

"Hi!" she waved. "Karan, this is your family? Auntie, you look so elegant."

Karan's mother stopped and looked Marianne up and down. She gave a half-smile and said, "And you look lovely as well, my dear."

"Thank you," Marianne said. "This outfit, actually, Karan—"

"That outfit is nice," Karan interrupted quickly. "Enjoy the wedding."

They kept walking past Marianne and she heard Karan say to his mother, "Some friend of Shefali's, I think. By the way, I told Bubbles to tell the bartenders to switch to the Chilean white for anyone who looks drunk enough that they won't notice it's cheaper. Save the expensive Marlborough for the sober guests at the start of the night."

Marianne watched them go and sat down on the step of her cottage. She thought back to Riyaaz, who had ignored her over his graduation weekend. She thought back to Minh, with whom she had gone to Hanoi, and how he sat next to her at a coffee shop and talked to his friends in Vietnamese and how she smiled and nodded. She thought about Seydou telling her he thought black African women had much better bodies than white American ones and how she laughed as she agreed.

She picked up her phone again and looked at a picture from her first visit to Tom's parents' house in Cambridge. That day, Marianne was wearing skinny jeans and a beige sweater, black New Balance sneakers on her feet, and had her hair pulled into a ponytail. Tom's sister, Jenifer, was wearing something almost exactly the same, except her sneakers were yellow and her sweater was brown. For lunch that day they had roast chicken, biscuits, an avocado-and-kale salad, and deviled eggs. Marianne made the salad, Jenifer made lemonade. They all sat in the backyard and Tom strummed his old high school guitar and then Marianne picked it up and played a slow version of "You're Just Too

Good to Be True," and Tom's mother had said, "Marianne, it's like you've always been part of this family. We're so glad you came to visit," and Marianne had felt so safe and so comfortable and so happy. As if she were at home with her own family.

She wondered what Tom would be doing at the moment. He might be watching *Narcos* on Netflix. Or, more likely, reading. When she first met him, when she first went to his home and saw his wall of book-shelves exploding with books—books stacked on the ground, books stacked on the kitchen table, books stacked in the bathroom, books everywhere—her immediate thought was that he was the one. But then she got scared. A lot of the books were the same as the books on her shelves.

When reading, Tom would often stop to quote a passage to Mari-anne. Recently, he had been reading aloud from a long academic article on the literature surrounding motherhood when he paused and said, "I wish there was more writing on fatherhood. I get that the physical and emotional brunt falls on women but by excluding fathers from the con-versation, we're giving them a free pass to not be involved. Not that I'm even sure I want kids, you know?"

Marianne had responded by saying she felt like sushi for dinner.

She saw Mr. Das coming around the corner by himself and watched him undo his belt and refasten it on a looser hole. Mr. Das noticed Marianne standing on the patio of the cottage she was sharing with Tina.

"Marianne, dear, where has my daughter disappeared?"

"Food poisoning, Uncle. Where are you off to? Where's your date? I think you're very brave, Uncle," Marianne said. "Being willing to try again at your age. It's impressive that you're putting yourself out there again and I'm cheering for you."

Mr. Das stopped at the steps to the patio and looked at Marianne.

"You tell Tina to give me a call when she's awake," Mr. Das said. "And to drink plenty of fluids. Poor girl. I wonder how she got food poisoning—everything seems very clean here. Marianne, what is wrong with your nose? Why is it so red?"

He leaned forward and squinted.

"Is that pus?"

"I'm fine," Marianne said. She touched her nose ring gently again. She needed more Neosporin. It would heal soon. Nose rings probably just took longer to heal than earrings.

Mr. Das nodded and continued on his way. He had always liked Marianne but found her a little unnerving. He had seen Marianne go through many huge changes since she became friends with Tina at Yale and every change was made with such commitment and dedication that Mr. Das marveled at her sense of self. Or was it her lack of sense of self? She never seemed to question, remember, or mourn the person she had been the previous day—she simply was who she was, or was it that she wasn't who she was? He had a lot to learn from her.

He pulled out his phone and called Mrs. Sethi.

"Have you left?" he asked.

"I'm just getting to my car," Mrs. Sethi said.

"Wait there," he said. "I'll nap when I get back to America."

In his cottage, Mr. Das quickly brushed his teeth, picked up his wallet and phone, and walked back out to find Mrs. Sethi. Should he have invited her to join him in his cottage? he suddenly wondered. But he wasn't ready to be in an enclosed, intimate space with her, even though their very first date had been at her home. There had been no expectation of intimacy then, but would there be now? Despite their ongoing interactions, Mr. Das hadn't really given this much thought. He had never been driven too much by lust or sexual desire. It had always upset Radha that he saw sex as a necessity to release stress or to procreate because she thought it meant he was not attracted to her but it was never about her. And now he had to think about this again. And as he was walking to find Mrs. Sethi and thinking about his sex life, he saw Radha walking toward him, holding a small earthen pot of hot chai.

"Going back for more food?" she asked.

"I'm sorry about my sex drive," Mr. Das said.

Radha coughed a bit of chai and cleared her throat.

"You're beautiful," Mr. Das continued. "You know that, I hope? Even at your age, you're quite striking. I have to run."

Radha watched him walk away with a smile. She'd hated his compliments accompanied by insults until suddenly she started loving them. She remembered the day it happened. They had been married for about two years and had started discussing the possibility of having a baby. They were in the airport waiting to board a flight to Delhi for the summer holidays and it was crowded and loud. Mr. Das was sipping from a can of Coke and saying, "Remind me to stow away some of the mini cans from the plane."

Radha, the way Radha did, was methodically going through the pros and cons of getting pregnant at this stage of her career. Mr. Das, never the kind to say a pregnant woman was glowing, said, "Well, we're young now so you can get fat and then get slim again and go back to being pretty. But hopefully you won't get too slim because you look better with a few extra kilos."

But then when had it started to go wrong? Radha wondered now. Was it when she first said that she didn't want more children? Or was it when she agreed to one more child but then couldn't get pregnant again? Mr. Das seemed convinced that she couldn't get pregnant again because she wasn't putting her mind to it. He believed it depended on the intention they brought to their lovemaking—his term, not hers—and while she agreed that that maybe played a small role, she also didn't think you could deny science. And in any case, if it was about the mindset you brought to the sex, it hardly helped that her husband charted her ovulation to time their sex. And then, before she knew it, things started to unravel. And they did nothing to stop it.

Radha watched her ex-husband turn the corner and disappear from view.

Mr. Das stopped and called Mrs. Sethi.

"Why don't you come to my room?" he said. "You said you've always wanted to join Colebrookes so you should come see the cottages. And then I'll have the car get us from here."

He told her how to get there and rushed back to his cottage to make sure it looked presentable. He pushed all his shirts and pants and underwear and undershirts into the cupboard and shut the door. In the bathroom, he took a hand towel and wiped down the countertops and even scrubbed the dry toothpaste off the mirror above the sink. The rest of the cottage looked fine because he wasn't the kind to spread out in a temporary situation. Most of his clothes were still in his suitcase and he had just a small toilet case on a shelf in the bathroom. What more did a man his age need? He was always shocked when he looked at Tina's suitcases filled with boxes of shoes and smaller boxes of jewelry and mesh bags of brightly colored underwear that embarrassed him, and bottles of potions and lotions for her skin that still had the elasticity of youth even though she didn't think so. Radha wasn't like that. Radha was old enough to have curated items and neutral underwear and little else. Everywhere they went, a small bottle of Chanel No. 5 appeared on a shelf in the bathroom.

There was a knock on the door. He opened it to Mrs. Sethi and said, "What's your favorite perfume?"

"Chanel No. 5," she said without missing a moment. "You really start with intimate and urgent questions."

"Chanel No. 5?"

He picked up her wrist and took a deep breath of the heavy floral scent. Maybe he didn't have a good sense of smell after all because this evoked nothing at all. He was relieved.

"It's nice," he said.

And he held on to her wrist for a few extra seconds and then let go and stepped away from the door to let her in.

"I need to know how many other men you're seeing. And I need to know what you'd write about in this book. Even if we never see each other again after this week, I need to know everything," Mr. Das said.

Mrs. Sethi looked at her reflection in the full-length mirror on the cupboard and said, "Well, that's a lot."

She sat down on the edge of the bed and said, "Let me call Anita and tell her to pick up the vegetables for dinner so we can talk in peace. My New Zealand avocado can wait."

Colebrookes: The Pedicurist at the Salon Prefers Male Clients Because They Rarely Get Pedicures So They Have Low Expectations

AFTER MRS. SETHI WENT HOME, MR. DAS DECIDED TO TAKE his daughter's advice and get a pedicure. He hadn't kissed her—no perfect moment had presented itself and then, despite his tall claims about napping when he got to America, he started yawning and Mrs. Sethi smiled and touched his hand and said, "Get some rest, Neel. I also better go," and left his room.

Mr. Das had incredibly soft feet and had always prided himself on them even though, as a man, he rarely had the chance to show them off to the world. But Tina had said it was more about the soothing aspect of the whole pedicure so he agreed to go to the Colebrookes salon. Did one wear shoes to a pedicure? What was the etiquette? He had washed his feet more thoroughly than usual, sitting gingerly on the edge of the tub to really scrub in between the toes and on the heel. He didn't want the staff to judge his feet, these feet he was so proud of.

He and the pedicurist were the only men in the salon but he quite liked the cold, clinical smell—it reminded him of his father's clinic. He settled into the soft black chair with a cup of ginger tea while a woman massaged his shoulders from the back. Near the row of mirrors, two women sat, one clicking away on her phone while two women worked different colors through her hair, and the other staring straight into a mirror while one woman cut her black hair. Both the women had black capes draped around their shoulders. To his right another woman was leaning back on a chair holding her eyebrows while a woman ran a thread to pull out the extra hairs. Mr. Das was glad he was a man.

Soft Bollywood music played and Mr. Das thought this was the perfect time to call Mrs. Ray, the matchmaker, and fill her in on his dates with Mrs. Sethi. He was ready for the next step but he wasn't sure what the next step was or how to go about taking it.

Mrs. Ray was still on holiday in Goa when she saw Mr. Das calling. She was sitting on a large, round swinging chair on the hilltop in Vagator drinking coconut water from a coconut and watching the sunset with her husband, Upen Chopra. She didn't particularly want to answer but Mr. Das was her first American client and she was charging him in dollars so she couldn't exactly ignore his calls. If she managed to set him up successfully, she would be able to consider opening a branch in Edison, New Jersey, or maybe even Silicon Valley. Imagine. The widow from Mayur Palli, the wrong side of the river, the CEO of a multinational dating agency.

"I have to get this, darling," she said to Upen, who was reading *The Economist* and drinking a glass of white wine. "It's Mr. Das again."

Upen looked over at his new wife sitting on a large white chair wearing white linen pants and a long pink kurta, large brown sunglasses on her head, a laptop on the table in front of her. She was glamorous and being a widow only made her more so. A woman who had suffered, Upen thought, was more beautiful than the rest. He smiled at her and said, "My businesswoman. Answer all the calls you need. I'd be happy to retire and be a house-husband."

"Tch," Mrs. Ray said. "I could never be married to a house-husband. Don't go getting any ideas or I'll shut down my business."

"How can I help you, Mr. Das?" Mrs. Ray said on the phone, still smiling over at Upen.

"Mrs. Ray," he said, watching the bubbles around his feet as they soaked in a tub of hot water. "I like Mrs. Sethi quite a lot."

"Yes, I thought you would," Mrs. Ray said. She leaned forward and took another sip of her coconut water. She opened her laptop and opened her notes on Mrs. Sethi and Mr. Das. She minimized the document in which she was working on her memoir and opened their files. Yes, yes, she was not surprised that this connection was working well. Mrs. Sethi had been difficult to set up so far—men seemed intimidated by her—but Mr. Das's ex-wife had clearly trained him well.

"So now I need to know, what next? I have only a few days," Mr. Das asked. "What does a man my age do when he's interested in a woman?"

The woman who was staring into the mirror broke eye contact with herself and looked back at Mr. Das. He lowered his voice a little and added, "I haven't even, you know, done anything physical yet."

Mr. Das took a sip of his tea and noticed the woman who was getting her hair colored was leaning back with her hair wrapped in little pieces of foil—what was that for, he wondered—while someone started painting some sort of white substance on her face.

Nono walked in then and stopped and looked at Mr. Das sitting in his chair with his khaki pants folded halfway up his calves. Mr. Das nodded hoping she would move along but she stopped in front of him, shook her head, and said, "Feminism has gone too far. Is this why your wife left you?"

"No," Mr. Das said. "No, no. This is my first pedicure ever. My daughter insisted. I would never do this. My feet are naturally soft as can be."

"What do your feet have to do with this, Mr. Das?" Mrs. Ray asked on the phone.

"Nothing, nothing," Mr. Das said. "I was talking to someone else."

He gestured toward his phone hoping Nono would continue on her way but she stood there watching the pedicurist at his feet and muttering about men no longer being real men.

"So what do I do, Mrs. Ray? About my situation?" Mr. Das asked. Nono didn't move.

"What did you do with your ex-wife?" Mrs. Ray asked.

She thought back to the start of her own relationship with Upen

Chopra. It had involved long walks and hot tea and glasses of wine and romantic dinners in dimly lit restaurants.

"That was a long time ago, Mrs. Ray," Mr. Das said.

"Who is Mrs. Ray?" Nono asked, still standing by Mr. Das.

Mr. Das shook his head at her. Why wouldn't she leave? He cupped the phone with one hand and said, "Nono, if you don't mind. I'm on an important call."

He gestured with his chin toward the rest of the salon.

"Romance, Mr. Das," Mrs. Ray said on the phone. "Romance. Flowers and wine and fancy restaurants and long walks and hot cups of tea."

He wiggled his toes around in the bubbling water.

"Romance is for the young," he said.

"Romance is for everyone," Nono said loudly.

She waved to the receptionist and said, "Bring me a chair, dear. I'm going to sit here and have a little chat with Mr. Das."

"Mr. Das, I don't know who else is chiming in over there but she's right—romance is for everyone. That's what I'm trying to teach all my clients. Stop thinking like an old divorced man—think like a young man in love for the first time."

Mrs. Ray closed her laptop again and stood facing the breeze coming off the ocean and over the cliff.

"Make it fresh, Mr. Das," Mrs. Ray continued. "I have faith in you. Think like a youngster."

She put the phone down and walked over to Upen Chopra, pulled the magazine away from him, kissed him on his mouth, and said, "Let's go for a swim. And then maybe some time alone in our cottage before dinner."

Upen Chopra stood up, pulled Mrs. Ray toward him, and said, "Forget the swim."

Mrs. Ray smiled and led him back toward the cottage. Think like a youngster. Maybe that would be the title of her memoir.

"Think like a youngster, she said," Mr. Das said to Nono. "When I was young I was busy studying. How do young people think?"

"Ma'am," a young woman wearing black pants and a black collared shirt nervously approached Nono. "Ma'am, your massage was scheduled for twenty minutes ago. Would you mind coming now? We have a very full schedule today."

"Rearrange things then, dear," Nono said, placing her bag down on the ground near Mr. Das. "And bring me a ginger tea and two Marie biscuits on a plate."

"Ma'am," the woman repeated. "Ma'am, your son called. I understand you may be a bit confused."

"You tell that son of mine that I'll shut down his bank accounts if he doesn't stop telling people I have dementia. Now, go get me the tea and biscuits. Extra hot."

The woman nodded and quickly backed away.

"Sometimes I think maybe I should just give in and retreat in silence to an old people's home," Nono said. "But old people are so dreadfully boring, have you noticed? Their stories have no arcs. I refuse to be surrounded by that. And I love the comfort of my own home. I'm used to a certain lifestyle and those homes are all made for monks, what with the vegetarian food and early bedtimes. I've always preferred whiskey and late nights."

"When were you first diagnosed?" Mr. Das asked.

"Never. I've never been diagnosed," Nono said. "Dementia is just what my son has decided on because he has no interest in caring for me. We're stuck, here in India, my generation. We no longer live in joint families where the children have to look after us but we also don't have good senior communities or assisted living centers."

Mr. Das nodded.

"I don't have a solution," Nono said. "Ultimately we all have to face our old age or trade it for the tragedy of dying young. There's no winning on your way out of the world. Old people turn into babies again, but we're hardly cute. Nobody wants to clean an old person's bottom. I'm not at that stage yet and I can only hope I die before I am. Anyway, let's not get too morbid."

The same woman who had tried to get Nono in for her massage returned with the ginger tea and Marie biscuits.

"Whenever you're ready," she said softly and backed away.

"Now tell me, Mr. Das. What is it you need to think like a youngster for? I may be old but my mind is still young, no matter what my son tries to tell the world."

Near his feet, his pedicurist held up something that looked like a small brown brick and said, "Sir, your heels are remarkably soft. I barely needed to exfoliate."

"You're welcome," Mr. Das said with a sigh.

He turned to Nono and told her all about Mrs. Sethi.

"Have you kissed her yet?" Nono asked. She placed her cup down and opened her purse and took out her compact. "Look how my skin wrinkles. I get Botox done every six weeks but it has no effect beyond a certain age."

"I haven't kissed anyone in about twenty years. Maybe Radha once or twice, but barely. I'm just trying to work out what to do. I want to do something special for Mrs. Sethi in case I never see her again after this."

"Well, then you must kiss her. Here's what we will do. I happen to have a lovely little backyard with a greenhouse filled to the brim with pots and pots of flowers from all over the world. I have a small, climate-controlled, all-glass room built inside of it. I use it to read, eat meals, have a drink, or sometimes just to sit surrounded by the flowers. It's really quite lovely and tonight, it's yours. My staff will prepare a meal. I'll handle it all. I love doing this kind of thing, especially for young lovers. But it's all on one condition—before the clock strikes midnight, you have to kiss Mrs. Sethi. I have closed-circuit cameras all over my house, including in the greenhouse, so I'll be watching."

It was all going fine until that last bit of the deal, Mr. Das thought. But why not? It didn't sound like she was saying it in a kinky way. An intimate greenhouse dinner sounded like a perfect grand gesture, and besides, if anything were to progress beyond kissing, they would return to Colebrookes or Mrs. Sethi's home. The pedicurist was wiping his feet down with a warm, damp towel. Mr. Das rubbed his feet together. Oh, my. But what about the rest of him? His arms and legs had grown skinny with age and lately he had noticed a little bit of extra skin that flopped over the band of his underwear. His skin, though wrinkled in places, had taken on a disconcerting softness. He had a handsome face, he knew that, but his body was aging. Parts of him were becoming like a chubby baby—the smoothness, the softness. Would his soft feet alarm Mrs. Sethi? He would have to leave his socks on if clothes came off. But Radha always laughed if he did that. So much so that he had got in the habit of removing his socks before removing his pants so he wouldn't have even a moment of standing there in only his socks. How did all this work with a new person? Mr. Das was feeling tired just thinking about it.

"Now, don't overthink things and don't worry," Nono said. "This will be fun. I'll have a wonderful dinner prepared. Dress nicely and arrive by eight."

"Wait, why are you doing this for me?" Mr. Das asked.

"I always wanted to be a theater director," Nono said.

She put her cup down on the table and waved over the girl in all black.

"Are you ready for the massage now, ma'am? That would be very helpful in terms of our scheduling."

"Cancel my massage and tell the driver to pull up. I have an important show to run tonight. Mr. Das, don't forget—a kiss before midnight. I'll be watching. What fun."

Nono picked up her purse and walked out of the beauty parlor, the girl in all black rushing to apologize to another woman who was sitting near the entrance looking angry about a scheduling change.

Mr. Das picked up his sandals and walked out of the beauty parlor back toward his cottage barefoot to try and get his feet a bit rougher and manlier before he had to remove his socks. He sent Mrs. Sethi a message saying he had a surprise planned for this evening and would pick her up at 7:30 P.M.

On the way out of his pedicure, he bumped into Tina heading to the beauty parlor to get her eyebrows threaded.

"My feet have become too soft," he said to his daughter.

"That's what a pedicure is supposed to do," Tina said.

"How are you feeling?"

"Miserable but at least I've regained control of the whole vomiting situation," Tina said.

She could still feel clawing in her stomach and her entire core hurt from the exertion. Her skin felt sallow and dry, the effects of Chon's face mask all gone from one round of food poisoning and the accompanying dehydration.

"I wonder where you picked it up," Mr. Das said. "Don't you think usually when you vomit you deep down know the source of what caused it?"

"I'm going to vomit again if we keep discussing this," Tina said. "Where are you off to?"

"I've got a big evening ahead. What does a youngster wear for a big night out?"

"Jeans, I guess. Are you seeing Mrs. Sethi again?"

"You said my jeans looked like dad jeans," Mr. Das said.

"Actually, I said they looked like mom jeans. Even worse," Tina said.

"I'll wear a suit," Mr. Das said.

Colebrookes, but across Town Shefali Is Wearing a Face Mask and Researching Whether or Not Stopping Birth Control Will Make Her Break Out Because She Wants to Get Pregnant but Not If She's Going to Get Acne

TINA HAD HER EYEBROWS THREADED, HER NAILS POLISHED, AND a head massage, hair wash, and blowout, and was strolling slowly back toward her cottage, finally feeling a bit better after the food poisoning. Two small boys ran around the lawn holding fake guns and shouting at each other.

"I'll kill you," one said.

"I'll kill you first," the other shouted. "Bang, bang."

"I have a bulletproof vest on, you didn't know that!" the first boy said.

"But my bullet hit your head, you died," the other one said.

"But I also have a bulletproof helmet on so now I'll kill you," the other one said.

The boy breathed out loudly, clearly tired, and said, "That's not fair. That's not allowed. You can't suddenly have a helmet."

"Bang, bang, now you're dead! You should have a brought a bulletproof helmet, you idiot."

"Mommy, tell Sahil he can't do that."

Tina could see two women wearing tight jeans and tight tops and high heels, having a drink near the pool. The mothers, Tina assumed. One of them looked over at the boys and said, "Uff, Rahul, please don't be such a sissy."

Like most outdoor pools in Delhi in the winter, this one was empty but Colebrookes had filled it with mud pots full of colorful bougainvillea with fairy lights woven through them and around the edges of the pool. In the middle of the pool was a grand piano, and a man in a tuxedo was playing an instrumental version of—yes, it was—Celine Dion's "My Heart Will Go On." Indians loved that song.

At the table next to the two mothers sat two women who looked like sisters with a handsome older man who looked like he could be their father or one of their partners. Men were rarely seen with women who could be either, Tina noted. They were all drinking colorful drinks and snacking from a bowl of peanuts in the middle of the table. One of the women was in the middle of telling an animated story about, from what Tina could gather as she slowly walked past, something that had happened to her on a chartered flight to Mallorca the previous week, something about an emerald earring gone missing.

Tina smiled at them. What a normal family they looked like. The mother was probably at home today, maybe getting a massage or reading a book or watching a movie. Maybe every Thursday night the father took his daughters out to Colebrookes for an evening drink. Tina imagined them doing this since they were young—going out for ice cream first, then a cup of coffee, and now, as adults, a cocktail.

Rocco emerged from around the corner, his hair damp, his skin glowing, a towel draped around his neck.

"There's an indoor pool too, did you know that?" he said.

The gray T-shirt he was wearing was wet in places he hadn't bothered drying carefully and was clinging to his muscular body. He was wearing jeans and a pair of blue-and-white Indian chappals. He rubbed the towel in his hair. A pair of wet swimming trunks dangled off his elbow.

"I love Indian weddings—this is basically just an excuse to take a holiday. We aren't actually expected to be anywhere or do anything boring," Rocco said.

"I don't think this is most Indian weddings. I think this is how Shefali gets married—on her own terms, none of the boring traditional stuff, only the things she can take perfect pictures of."

Rocco lifted his shirt and rubbed his stomach and Tina got a glimpse of his abs and a fine trail of brown hair.

"Aren't you cold?" she asked.

Rocco looked down at his chest and said, "Why? Are my nipples showing?"

Tina laughed.

"I should have called," Rocco said.

"Stop it, don't worry about it. It hardly matters."

"No, it does matter. I had an amazing time with you. And I've thought about you often since then."

"So then why didn't you call?" Tina said. "Ow, fuck."

One of the two little kids had slammed straight into her, his fake gun piercing her thigh.

"Sorry, Auntie," he shouted and ran away.

"Did that jerk just call me Auntie? I should be Didi at most. I don't look like an Auntie."

She rubbed her thigh.

"Wait, Shefali never told you?" Rocco asked.

"Told me what?"

"You're going to hate me," Rocco said. "That is, if you don't already."

"I don't hate you. It was a long time ago. We didn't even have sex. I'm just curious."

"I slept with Zahra the next night. Remember her? The comedian?" Rocco said.

Tina felt a heavy, hot weight tumble down her body and her mouth went dry. She could barely hear Rocco continue.

"I shouldn't have told you. Shit, I am so attracted to you, I should have said I lost your number. But you're off with some mystery man here at night anyway."

"No!" Tina said. She closed her eyes for a moment. Not because she was going to cry but because she needed a moment to not be looking at him. "I really wish you had just lied. I don't want to hear you didn't call me because of the tall, hot Pakistani comedian. And that mystery guy thing isn't actually, I don't know. I feel even worse now. Why would you even think you should tell me the truth?"

"I thought women appreciate the truth," Rocco said.

"Not when the truth is mean," Tina said. "I had all my own ideas— you had a steady girlfriend but you couldn't resist me that night. Or, you know, the one we always tell ourselves—that you just felt too strongly about me but knew that it wouldn't work. Anything, anything other than you hooked up with the hotter girl the next night."

A ball hit Tina in the back.

"Damn it," she shouted looking back.

She picked up the ball and flung it in the opposite direction of the kid.

"That's what he gets for calling me Auntie," Tina said.

"You're much hotter than Zahra," Rocco said.

"No, don't tell unbelievable lies, you idiot," Tina said. "That's even worse. You need to learn when to lie."

"I really thought you knew. I bumped into Shefali when I was having breakfast with Zahra the morning after and I figured she told you."

"Shefali doesn't notice anything that isn't directly about her," Tina said.

"I really wanted to call you. I thought we had the most amazing connection. But then I figured you wouldn't want to hear from me because of the whole Zahra thing. Which was really a regrettable choice because you have never seen anyone more boring in bed. She just mostly lay there like a stick."

"Okay, that's enough," Tina said.

The little kid went running past, panting, holding the ball. Tina watched him run to his mother, who held a cup up to his mouth. She then kissed his forehead, wiped her lipstick mark off, and returned to her cocktail and conversation.

"Are you heading back to the cottages?" Tina asked.

Rocco said yes and they both walked away from the lights and down the dark road along the main lawn toward the cottages on the far side. Two women workers in matching brown uniform saris walked past them and folded their hands and said "Namaste." Tina nodded; Rocco folded his hands and said "Namaste" back. Tina kicked some pebbles with her shoe. But the pebbles didn't roll away.

"Is that poop?" Rocco said. "Did you just kick poop? I think that's dog poop."

Tina looked down at her shoe and tried to scrape it onto the road.

"Why did you kick poop?" Rocco asked.

"Obviously, not on purpose," Tina said, laughing despite everything. "I thought it was a pebble."

She continued walking, scraping her foot along the path.

"Have you noticed it's never really silent here?" Rocco said. "Like the kind of silence that hurts your ears. You don't get that here."

"Tina?" Radha called to her daughter. Radha was sitting on a yoga mat in the middle of the lawn in the darkness.

"Ma?" Tina said, squinting to look. "What are you doing out there?"

"Yoga, meditation," Radha said. "Do you want to join me?"

Tina looked over at Rocco and said, "I should. I've been pretty unfair to my mother on this trip. And for the last decade. Am I a shitty person?"

Rocco looked at Tina standing in the darkness, her face lit only by the small lamp beside her and he said, "You seem pretty magnificent to me. Listen, about Zahra and London and—"

Tina put her hand on Rocco's hand and said, "It's okay."

Tina didn't expect an apology. The night was what it was, and yes, she had googled Rocco repeatedly since, always curious about what he was doing. But it was nothing more than mild interest. Although she had come across a picture of him at a movie premiere where he was wearing dark jeans and a black button-down with the sleeves rolled up and holding a whiskey glass in one hand, and that picture had made her google "Rocco Gallagher girlfriend," and she did then briefly think about what it would be like to explore India with him. But that was all. She had truly never expected to see him again.

"I'm glad we got to see each other this week," Tina said. And even though she was sad, she meant it.

"Me too. You should move to Bombay. I'm not joking—from everything I've heard you say this week, you belong in India. Not just this week—from everything you said that night in London. And in Bombay you could keep doing the work you're doing."

"I need to go," Tina said. She gestured vaguely onto the lawn.

"Your mother's cool, by the way," Rocco said.

"I'll see you," Tina said and climbed over the low wooden fence, past the poinsettias, and toward her mother sitting on a yoga mat in the darkness.

Radha was wearing a long, cream-colored dress with a shawl draped over her shoulders. Her feet were bare, a pair of bejeweled jootis lying side by side near the yoga mat. On a tray there was a copper tumbler and glass of water. Radha shifted over on her mat and said to her daughter, "Come, sit near me. The grass is getting wet with dew."

Tina sat down, her feet in the grass, her knees pulled up to her chin. She could hear cars honking and trucks rumbling past in the distance, dogs barking, and two women talking at the far end of the lawn.

"That fellow is very charming," Radha said. "Rocco, right? I saw him very patiently playing table tennis with an old man yesterday. And then his equally old wife kissed Rocco square on the lips and Rocco took it well."

Tina watched Rocco walk away and smiled into the darkness.

"Where's David?" she asked her mother.

"In the main kitchen," Radha said. "With the chef. He wants to learn how to make the paneer tikkas from lunch the other day and in return is teaching the chef how to make his mother's meat loaf. Imagine Indians eating meat loaf."

"I don't think I've ever eaten meat loaf," Tina said. "Did you ever make meat loaf for us?"

"I doubt it," Radha said.

Most nights they'd had takeout or microwavable meals or, at most, a basic khichdi, but it was generous of her daughter to ask this.

"Is he enjoying being here?"

"Loving it," Radha said. "I'm enjoying seeing it through his eyes. It's nice to sometimes see something familiar from a fresh perspective."

The two women who had been talking on the edge of the lawn were walking past them, unable to see Tina and Radha sitting in the dark. It was Bubbles Trivedi with a friend. Both women had big, brown hair and were smoking cigarettes as they walked.

"You've outdone yourself with this one," the friend was saying to Bubbles.

"It's a much higher budget than I needed," Bubbles said. "But don't tell anyone that, obviously. I've given them the impression that this is peanuts—as if it's basically volunteer work for me. I didn't know what I was getting into until the grandmother said they wanted to give everyone those fancy Bose noise-canceling headphones as favors."

"The grandmother with dementia?" the friend asked.

"That's the one. Her son told me to humor her and let her pick out the flowers and the favors so she'll feel important."

"So everyone's getting those headphones?" the friend asked.

"They're getting iPads! Just to test the waters I told her nobody gives anything less than iPads to the guests these days and next thing I know that grandmother ordered seven hundred and fifty new iPads. One for me also."

Both the women laughed and continued down the path.

"I guess we're getting new iPads," Radha said.

"Bubbles Trivedi," Tina said. "Now, that's a reality show character. *My Big Fat Indian Wedding.*"

"That's a terrific idea," Radha said.

"Give her a good catchphrase. Put her in different animal-print outfits for every episode. Let her go scouting for white people in the youth hostels around town," Tina said. "Have her bribing the local police commissioner to keep music going past the allotted time. Send her to Bombay in search of Bollywood stars to attend the wedding, for a price."

"This is not the Delhi I once knew," Radha said.

She reached beside her and opened her water bottle.

"I don't know the real Delhi. I keep thinking I do. I keep thinking I'm finding it under bridges or at street corners but I'm not. And I can't find one of my diamond earrings," Tina said.

"Did you check all your shirts? I must have lost a dozen earrings while pulling shirts off. Delhi is like New York in that sense. Those real housewives of New York tell you more about New York, poverty and all, than a tour of the outer boroughs."

"I can't believe how much you watch those shows," Tina said. "Your clients would lose faith in you if they knew."

"Imagine something like that set here. It would be madness," Radha said.

She reached over to the tumbler next to her and poured out a glass of water.

"Do you want some?" she asked Tina. "Water kept in copper tumblers is supposed to be good for the health. I bought two of these at Cottage Industries today. Would you like one for your apartment?"

Tina looked at the mottled copper glass. It wouldn't go in her Williamsburg apartment that had no traces of anything Indian.

"I like it," Tina said. "I'll take one if it's extra."

"How's Marianne?" Radha asked.

"Marianne is Marianne. Good old Marianne the chameleon," Tina said. "She thinks she should marry some rich Indian guy and live in Hong Kong or Dubai. I don't know how she doesn't see how lucky she is to have Tom."

"Forget Tom. You girls are lucky to have each other. Female friendships are difficult. Female relationships in general are difficult."

"Do you think you could ever live in India again?" Tina asked.

Radha exhaled and looked into the distance. She'd had this question on her mind since she arrived. She loved India—the sights, the smell, the feeling of home, the food, the people, even the crowds. The reason she had moved to Manhattan right after her divorce was that Manhattan reminded her of India—the chaos comforted her. She had never liked the suburbs.

"What would I do here?" she asked. "I love this country but home is where you make your home, not necessarily where you were born."

Tina looked over at her mother again, the moonlight catching the small diamond nose ring in her nose.

"I think this Bubbles idea is terrific," Radha said. "I bet she would also round up a nutty cast of characters."

"Do you think I could make India home?" Tina asked.

"I'm surprised to hear you ask that. Your whole life you've wanted nothing more than to be American," Radha said.

"Because you encouraged it," Tina said.

"Of course I did, darling," Radha said. "Because nobody wants to see their daughter feel like an outsider. We lived in a different time. And you are an American. As much or as little as Marianne is, or I am, or even your father is."

"That's all fine to say but if I'm in line at a gas station anywhere outside New York, I'm still an outsider. Especially the way America is now," Tina said. "Here at least I look like the billion other people around me. But then there's the traffic. How on earth am I supposed to fit in if I scream in terror every time I need to cross the road?"

"Tina, you'll never get anywhere if you keep thinking of yourself as an outsider. You've never let yourself fit in or belong and I don't know why. You don't have to be American or Indian or even Indian-American. You just have to be you. Did I really forget to teach you that all these years?"

"Your being you seems to not include Papa and me," Tina said, feeling all the anger that had ebbed and flowed over the years. "You seem so much happier now."

Tina looked away and Radha put her hand around Tina's upper arm and leaned into her daughter.

"Tina, you don't need anyone's permission to be happy," she said. "I am happier now but I'm still your mother and I'm still your father's partner in many ways, just not romantic ones. But please understand that you don't know, or need to know, the details of our separation. You just need to understand that it wasn't about you."

"Maybe I do need to know the details," Tina said.

"No," Radha said. "You don't need the burden of deciding who was right or wrong between your parents. That isn't your role. That was and is for us to figure out, and we did, and if we can get along now and move on, so can you."

"I've always blamed you," Tina said. "I just assumed I should always blame you because you so quickly seemed so happy and David is . . . David is everything Papa isn't."

"Don't be so sure," Radha said. "David may be white and Papa brown but they're more similar than you realize."

Radha shook her head with a smile.

"I'll always have a soft spot for Papa," she said.

"Was it his fault? The divorce?" Tina pushed again.

"I want to say yes so you'll forgive me, Tina, but it was nobody's fault. It just didn't work and we were fortunate enough to live in a time and place where divorce was acceptable. That's all there is to it."

Tina looked over at her mother as she heard a low hiss beside her. She was looking for the source when the sprinklers suddenly turned on full blast, cold water coming at them from all directions. They jumped up, her mother grabbed her shoes and yoga mat, Tina grabbed the copper tumbler, and they ran toward the dry pavement.

Bubbles Trivedi and her friend were walking back toward the lawn, both still smoking cigarettes, now with wineglasses in hand as well. Tina and Radha came to a stop in front of them, water dripping from their clothes and hair.

"Dear, dear, dear," Bubbles said. "Look at you two. What a mess. Here, take my wine."

She handed the wineglass over to Radha who took it despite the pink lipstick mark on the edge and drank it down.

Bubbles looked at Tina and said, "I hear you were ill today. Nice to see you up and about. Silver lining—I think you lost some weight." She poked Tina's stomach and continued, "I always say a little bit of food poisoning is the best pre-wedding ritual. I encourage all my brides to step out for a little street food the day before the reception. You have to time it well, though. You can't be rushing off to the toilet when you need to be shaking hands with the finance minister, am I right?"

Then Bubbles placed her hand on Radha's wrist and said, "Now, you're the one with that handsome American boyfriend. Come, walk with me. We'll get you dried off and you tell me your wedding plans. I'll organize every last detail for you. I work with only the best clients. An interracial second marriage? The possibilities are endless."

"You could have the wedding somewhere in the UK—hints of Camilla and Charles," Tina said with a laugh. "And what if my father walked my mother down the aisle?"

"Stop that," Radha said. "You're both mad."

"Come, come," Bubbles said to Radha. "I agree the Camilla–Charles idea is a bit bleak. I was thinking more along the lines of raw silk saris in shades of gold for you and your dearest friends. A matching bandhgala for that handsome husband. Something modern, something multicultural. Catered by Dishoom, of course. Have you been?"

"David has."

Bubbles dropped her cigarette on the ground and crushed it underfoot as she continued.

"They've changed the face of Indian dining in the UK. It's no longer bright orange curry masquerading as chicken tikka masala. I went to the one in Carnaby last time I was there and a small dog urinated right near my chair, can you imagine? That's exactly why I hate outdoor eating."

"Terrible," Bubbles's friend said. "The only thing worse is live music in restaurants."

"Don't even get me started," Bubbles said. "If I want to go to a concert, I'll go to a concert. I don't need the concert brought to my dinner table, forcing me to smile politely at the loud saxophone player blowing my wig off."

"That's a wig?" Radha asked.

Bubbles touched her beehive hair and said, "A lady never reveals her secrets."

"But you just did," her friend said.

"I'm going to go change and check on Marianne," Tina said, going in the opposite direction toward her cottage.

"Be gentle with her," Radha said, touching Tina's shoulder.

TINA ENTERED THE ROOM and saw Marianne asleep in her bed, even though it was barely dark outside. She was on top of the sheets in her pajamas, a glass of water and her Kindle on her bedside table. Tina remembered Marianne falling asleep early and on top of her covers at Yale whenever she had done badly on an exam. Marianne always took her classes more seriously than Tina did and a low grade broke her heart and left her without enough energy to even get under her sheets. Whenever Tina found her like that, she would cover her with a red HSBC blanket they had got for free during orientation week freshman year.

The black dress Marianne had worn last night was lying in a heap in the corner of the room. Her small Livia daily journal was also on her bedside table with a pen inside. Marianne was usually faithful about penning down a few sentences about her day before bed every night but Tina hadn't noticed her doing that on this trip until now. A bottle of Neosporin powder stood beside the journal. Marianne's suede Tod's loafers were neatly lined under her bed, the cream-colored heels jutting out.

Mrs. Sethi's House, New Delhi: Lavina
Is Making Carrot Cake That Mrs. Sethi Will
Eat a Slice of and Then Declare Too Rich
and Then Lavina Can Eat the Rest

AROUND THE SAME TIME, IN ANOTHER PART OF THE CITY, Mrs. Sethi poured herself a glass of white wine topped with soda. She needed something to take the edge off but she didn't want to be drunk. This all felt so crazy—this dating, this man, these butterflies. Until now she had only been on dates with men she'd met once, at most twice, and never spoken to again. There was never a question of anything physical or intimate but all of a sudden that was all there, hanging in the air, with this man who lived across the world.

She sat down on the new vintage armchair on her balcony—it had arrived this morning and she already loved it. She had spotted it in Chor Bazaar in Bombay when she was there visiting her cousin a few months back. Her cousin, who had made plenty of money as an advertising executive and now ran a design store in Kamala Mills that made no money, had offered to have the armchair reupholstered in a mustard-yellow vegan leather and shipped to her in Delhi. Mrs. Sethi shouted for Lavina to bring her a bowl of salted peanuts, pulled her feet up under her, and reached for her phone.

"Hi, Ma," Minal answered. "You're calling from home."

"Hi, beta," Mrs. Sethi said. "Yes, I'm at home. Just enjoying the Delhi weather. Having wine and peanuts on the balcony."

"I want to see. Should I call back on video?" Minal asked.

"No, no," Mrs. Sethi said. She didn't want to be looking at her daughter's face for this conversation. "Let's just chat. I paid for unlimited free calls to the United States and Canada and I don't even know anyone in Canada."

Mrs. Sethi took a sip of her wine for strength and then quickly, before she could overthink it, said, "Minal, I think I've met someone."

And then she told her everything. She had been dreading this call. Minal was so attached to her father and so heartbroken when he died. It was because of Minal that Mrs. Sethi still kept all her late husband's clothes exactly as he had left them in his cupboard. She had given away some of his ties but everything else was still on the same hangers and the same shelves. When Minal came to Delhi she often wore her father's shirts and sweaters and left traces of her perfume on them.

Maybe Mrs. Sethi also kept the cupboard that way a little bit for herself. She missed her husband. Not with the same ache that she had for the year after he had died but she still missed him every day—until this week when she suddenly realized she hadn't thought of him for a day. She would never forget him; she could never forget him—but maybe she could honor his memory and finally, nearly ten years later, also move on.

"He has a daughter?" Minal asked when Mrs. Sethi had finished.

"Yes, your age. And she's lovely. I think you'll get along," Mrs. Sethi said.

"You've spent a lot of time with her, then?"

"Some, not a lot. She lives in New York. They're all here for a wedding. Even the ex-wife with her new boyfriend."

"Ma," Minal said. "This is going to sound petty, but—"

"No, no, dear. You say whatever you need to. I wanted to tell you before taking things any further. I don't even know what further means anymore at this age. But this is just something I'm exploring. If you're not ready, I'll call it off."

"Ma, stop, stop. I'm so happy to hear this. I've been wanting you to do this. Remember when you came here and I introduced you to my friend's father—Mr. Dogra? That was meant to be a setup."

"That man? Minal, he was nearly eighty and overweight," Mrs. Sethi said. "Have some standards for me."

Minal laughed and said, "I know! My friend kept saying how handsome her father was. I had never seen a picture."

"And remember he kept talking about what good Indian food he had eaten on holiday in Japan?" Mrs. Sethi said.

"And then he complained about how he had missed two trains in Japan because they ran on time there."

"So you're okay with this?" Mrs. Sethi said.

She looked out at Delhi in front of her, twilight settling in, the dust creating a romantic haze. How she loved this city.

"It's the daughter," Minal said. "I don't want you to mother another daughter. Or son. That's what I meant when I said I might sound petty."

"I could never mother another daughter," Mrs. Sethi said. "One hardheaded lesbian is enough."

Mrs. Sethi heard her daughter spit out laughter.

"Did you just say 'lesbian'?"

"Well, you don't say it so I may as well, right? LGBTQ. I marched in the Delhi pride parade for you this year."

"Ma, he's a lucky man, this Mr. Das. Don't replace me with the daughter but other than that, I'm cheering for you."

"Then tell me, Minal, what does 'think like a youngster' mean? That's what his message to me about tonight said."

AT 7:30 P.M., MRS. SETHI was wearing a Benarasi silk sari and had tied a string of jasmine through her bun and picked up an off-white pashmina shawl. It wasn't how young people dressed but it was her favorite sari and it made her skin glow. And she wasn't a fool—she knew how sensual it was to remove a sari and then, perhaps even more so, to let a man watch her re-drape it. Even though she usually wore kurtas these days, saris still felt like armor. And the process of removing the sari, then the petticoat and the blouse, gave her a bit more time to process and protect herself. A kurta or a shirt was on and then it was off, stomach visible, bra out, nothing to shield, nothing to prepare. Or a dress—a dress was the worst offender when it came to getting unclothed in front of someone after a certain age. But a sari would allow her to ease into her nudity and her body. *Nudity.* Mrs. Sethi turned away from the mirror at the thought of that word and sat down at her dresser. She brushed some bronzer onto her cheeks and lined her lower lids with kohl. She pushed in a small pair of solitaire diamond earrings and dabbed Chanel No. 5 onto her wrists and neck right as her doorbell rang.

Mr. Das was standing on the doorstep of Mrs. Sethi's home wearing a black suit that he had brought for the final wedding reception. He was holding a bouquet of a dozen red roses. He had considered a bouquet of orchids but the classic red roses seemed more fitting for tonight.

Mr. Das and Mrs. Sethi took a moment to just stare and smile at each other.

Nono's House, New Delhi: The Guard Is Smoking a Cigarette and Reading a Dirty Magazine Wrapped in the Cover of an Old Issue of *The Economist*

MR. DAS GASPED AS THEY ARRIVED AT NONO'S HOUSE. A man wearing a blue-and-gold turban met them at the gate and escorted them to the greenhouse in the backyard. Everything was twinkling with fairy lights and a small but heavy rectangular mahogany table was set up inside the glass room within the greenhouse. Soft piano music played. Of course Nono didn't want to get pushed out of her home, Mr. Das thought. Two chairs were placed side by side and Mr. Das and Mrs. Sethi sat down while the man poured still and sparkling water into chunky green glasses.

"What is this place?" Mrs. Sethi whispered to Mr. Das.

"I wanted to do something special for tonight," Mr. Das said. He turned to face Mrs. Sethi and added, "I've enjoyed meeting you so much."

"Nono recommends you begin with two glasses of prosecco," the turbaned man said. "If there are no objections, I'll return shortly with those and your amuse-bouche."

"This doesn't feel like Delhi," Mrs. Sethi said, looking out at the colorful flowers filling the greenhouse, small lights sparkling everywhere, a mist forming above the plants.

Mr. Das looked around to see if he could find the camera. One vase in the corner looked a bit suspicious, with a round black design on it. He got up and walked over to it and turned it around, pretending he was examining the flowers in it. A few minutes later, the turbaned man re-entered with the two glasses of prosecco and small plates with single pieces of beetroot ravioli. He then walked to the same corner and turned the vase back around, bowed, and promised to return with their appetizer and an assortment of wine, unless either Mr. Das or Mrs. Sethi would like to order a cocktail.

"I wouldn't mind a martini," Mrs. Sethi said at the same time that Mr. Das said, "Nothing for me, thanks."

"No, no, then nothing for me either," Mrs. Sethi said.

"No, please go ahead," Mr. Das said.

"I'll get two martinis," the turbaned man said and backed out of the room silently.

Mrs. Sethi was embarrassed. Her husband never liked it when she drank hard alcohol but she loved a good gin martini and got the feeling this place, whatever this place was, would make a perfect one.

"I do love these flowers," Mr. Das said, standing again near the vase he suspected was a camera and turning it around.

"Calla lilies, I believe," Mrs. Sethi said.

She walked over to Mr. Das and placed her hand on his arm. He turned to face her.

"I'm so happy we met," Mrs. Sethi said. "I hadn't expected to get along quite so well."

Mr. Das squinted over her shoulder to see if there were any other cameras visible. Then he said to her, "I feel so lucky."

They looked at each other, faces inches apart. Mr. Das touched the string of jasmine in Mrs. Sethi's hair and said, "No smell makes me more nostalgic for India than jasmine."

Mrs. Sethi removed her hand from his arm and touched her hair. Mr. Das dodged around her to check the vase at the other end of the room. Even this one had a black design on it. He was turning that one around to face the wall when the turbaned man returned with the martinis and two leather folders containing the menus for the evening.

Mr. Das opened his to a note from Nono that read *That's not where the camera is. You're not going to find the camera and you're going to lose your chance. She wants you to kiss her. Do it.*

"Tuna tartar? And pork belly salad? Is this a restaurant? What is this? Neel, I am so impressed by your planning. I've lived in Delhi for decades but somehow you've discovered a secret dining option that nobody knows about. I thought Colebrookes was fancy."

She removed her shawl and placed it on the back of her chair. Mr. Das looked at the inside of her right arm where there was a small line tattoo. He reached forward and touched it with his fingertip and said, "You have a tattoo?"

"Gosh, I forget it's there sometimes," Mrs. Sethi said. She looked down at her arm and Mr. Das's finger pressed against it. His finger was slightly rough but his hand was not an old man's hand. It was large and the fingernails were perfect ovals, short and tidy. "Minal and I got it together. It's the gate of my house, our house. My husband had designed the gate to look like a supply-and-demand curve and he loved it so much. Last year when I was visiting San Francisco, Minal and I decided to get them done late one night after dinner. Do you have any?"

"Tattoos? Definitely not. I can't think of anything I'd want to live with for the rest of my life," Mr. Das said.

"Well, that probably isn't that long anymore so the commitment doesn't have to be so great. Getting a tattoo at eighteen would be riskier."

"An origami swan," Mr. Das said. "If I had to get one, gun to my head, I'd get an origami swan."

"That was a quick answer," Mrs. Sethi said. "Why an origami swan?"

"Tina loves them. She got really into origami for half a week, perfected the art of swans, and then lost interest. I don't think I actually could do it, though."

"You should. Getting old is so inherently unfashionable," Mrs. Sethi said. "This little transgression makes me feel—"

Mr. Das cut her off. He stood up over her and leaned down, hitting his hip against the edge of the table. That would bruise, he just knew it. Never mind. He bent over toward her and held her face in his hands and kissed her on the lips.

Mrs. Sethi sat still holding the menu open in her hands, her face reaching up to this man, his mouth on her mouth, happy. It didn't feel so strange or so unknown or so frightening. It felt remarkably familiar, she noted. Except for the ache in her neck from the awkward angle. She tried to pull herself up to standing but Mr. Das was wedged in between the heavy table and her so as she stood she was pressed up against every bit of him and could feel his erection pressing against the pleats of her sari. That was perhaps too much for the moment. She slipped away from him to the other side of the table, put the menu down, and reached her hands up to his shoulders and kissed him again. When she pulled away, she smiled at him and said, "Finally."

Right then the turbaned man returned with the tuna tartar and a trolley of different wine options. Mrs. Sethi turned to Mr. Das and said, "What timing. It's as if they're watching us."

She gave Mr. Das's hand a little squeeze and looked at the bottles of wine and asked to try a Chenin Blanc from Australia. Behind her back, Mr. Das gave a small thumbs-up and smiled around the whole room so Nono would see, no matter where the camera was.

"He has no idea where the camera is," Nono said with a laugh to her driver. They sat side by side on velvet armchairs in Nono's television room with the live feed playing in front of them. In front of Nono was a teakwood box filled with her gold jewelry. She picked up a pair of gold earrings with mirrors on the inside and squinted at it closely. She was sick of these—she set them aside to send to her jeweler tomorrow to have melted down and turned into something else, a pendant per-haps. Nono sipped on a Campari soda, her driver had a cardamom tea, and in between them on a small wooden table was a plate of Afghani chicken tikka.

"Cameras," the driver said, picking up the remote control and flipping angles. "Plural. I even put one on the actual dining table in case we ever decide to edit this and turn it into something."

"This is for personal enjoyment, not some creepy art project," Nono said. "Pass my ashtray. Why is it so far?"

The driver walked over to the bookshelf and brought Nono her ashtray and held up a lighter for her to light a cigarette.

Nono put an Afghani chicken tikka into her mouth. She spat it back out into a napkin and handed the napkin to her driver and said, "Take this to the kitchen and tell the cooks it's overcooked. The chicken should melt, not taste like rubber. And make them send me a large serving of the dessert they've made for Mr. Das."

Dessert was a flourless chocolate cake with a scoop of cinnamon ice cream on the side. In the greenhouse, it was served on only one plate with two spoons side by side. Mrs. Sethi touched Mr. Das's hand and said, "Of course the one man I like lives around the world. Mr. Mehta lived in Gurgaon and I thought that was too far."

"Otherwise he was a good option?" Mr. Das asked.

"Not at all," Mrs. Sethi said. "The next day he sent me something called a Venmo request for my half of the meal. This after he had spent the entire meal talking about how rich he was."

"So it's better if I ask you for your share now?" Mr. Das asked.

Mrs. Sethi smiled at him.

"I don't think I could ever live in America, Neel," Mrs. Sethi said. "It's a lovely country to visit but this is home for me."

"I got malaria the last time I spent a long stretch in India," Mr. Das said, thinking back to that awful summer spent weak and exhausted.

"Malaria? That's a shame," Mrs. Sethi said. "Touch wood, I've never had it. But I'm very particular about screens on the windows and burning camphor at dusk."

It was nearing midnight and the turbaned waiter returned to the greenhouse with a small brown ROYCE box with two squares of dark chocolate and an envelope for Mr. Das. In it, a note from Nono said *Enough now. I don't like people on the premises past midnight. Well done*

tonight. You were charming. I wish you both luck for the future. You seem
well-suited for each other.

"I should get home," Mrs. Sethi said, the high of the evening wearing off as the reality of their situation was settling in. She visited her daughter every year, and she loved Niagara Falls and the Grand Canyon and even Manhattan but she didn't see herself living in America. As an Indian, she worried she would never feel at home. And, more crucially, she would have to make her own morning tea and load her own dishwasher. Mrs. Sethi belonged in Delhi. She wasn't sure about too much about the rest of her life, but of this she was sure.

Mr. Das followed Mrs. Sethi out of Nono's yard and into his waiting car. He held the door open for her and came around to the other side. The Delhi autumn air smelled of fires burning to keep the night watchmen warm. An occasional crackle broke through the steady hum of traffic. Mr. Das and Mrs. Sethi sat side by side, his hand on top of hers, and they both looked out of their windows. Mrs. Sethi flipped her hand and laced her fingers through his. It didn't matter what the future held, she decided. This moment was what mattered. She had taken two weekend-long workshops on mindfulness last year and this was exactly the kind of situation she had to use that in. She had to only think about the moment. After all, she had always believed that any years she got to live past sixty was borrowed time.

She didn't invite Mr. Das to come upstairs. She wanted this evening to stand alone in its perfection. And Mr. Das, as he kissed her hand on her doorstep, felt similarly. Sex—whatever that looked like at this point—was easier left to the imagination for now.

Colebrookes: Across Town Shefali Is Nervous, Looking Up at the Ceiling—Is This It? Is Pavan the Only Man She'll Ever Be with Again? If She Doesn't Go to Sleep Right Now, She's Going to Look Tired Tomorrow

"A CIGARETTE?" MR. DAS SAID AS HE GOT OUT OF HIS CAR and saw Radha sitting on the front porch of his cottage. "Quite a throwback, as they say. How does this fit in with David Smith and his morning walks?"

"Why do you think I'm sitting on your porch? And I'll be coming in to use your mouthwash before I return to my cottage."

Radha took a long drag and looked over at him.

"Bubbles Trivedi is keen to plan my wedding. She thinks it should be a destination wedding in Mallorca so it's about halfway between India and America and she wants to book Malaika Arora's yoga instructor to hold yoga sessions with the guests every morning."

"Who is Malaika Arora?" Mr. Das asked sitting down across his ex-wife.

"That's what you're concerned about? Not that I'm planning my wedding?" Radha said.

"You won't marry David Smith," Mr. Das said. He leaned back in his chair and looked out across the lawn. "This country has changed, Radha. In ways I never could have imagined when I left."

Radha leaned forward and crushed her half-smoked cigarette in a small metal ashtray that sat on the glass table in between them.

"We've changed too," she said. "I can't believe how heavily I used to smoke. Half a cigarette now and my lungs feel blackened. Why do you assume I won't marry him?"

"You just won't," Mr. Das said. "I say this as a compliment—I don't think you were made to be married. A partner, yes. And maybe you and David Smith will end up together until death does you part and so on. But that piece of paper, that formality, that legal binding—all that isn't you."

"Where are you coming from so late at night?" Radha asked.

Mr. Das took his wallet from his back pocket.

"You need a new wallet. You've had that for at least twenty years," Radha said.

"It does the job," he said. He opened the coin pouch and pulled out his gold wedding band.

"Is that ours?" Radha asked.

"I never knew what to do with it," Mr. Das said. "And then the day I found that gorgeous Jersey City apartment, it fell out of my wallet as I went to pay for a coffee, and I started seeing it as some kind of good luck charm and kept it."

"I had mine melted down and turned into a pendant," Radha said.

"See?" Mr. Das said, pointing his ring at Radha. "Not the marriage type."

He put the ring back into his wallet and put the wallet back in his pocket.

"I feel as though I ought to have some big revelation this week," Radha said. "A week in the country of my birth with my ex-husband and my new American boyfriend. But I'm pretty happy. I was happy before this trip and I'm going to return and continue being happy. How dull. I can't even pretend to be shocked by your statement that I'll never marry David. You're right, I won't. I love him and will stay with him but I don't want another marriage. But I've known that all along; that's nothing new."

"Well then, I'll have the revelation for us both, Radha. I think I want to see where things go with Mrs. Sethi," Mr. Das said.

Colebrookes: Across Town, Half a Sleeping Pill
Later, Shefali Has Woken Up Happy; She Slept
Beautifully Last Night and Her Eyes Look
Bright Today and Pavan Is Perfect for Her

"MARIANNE," TINA SAID. "ARE YOU AWAKE?"

There was no answer so slightly more loudly Tina again said, "Are you awake?"

"Tina, when you ask me that it wakes me up, you know?" Marianne said. "What is it? It's really early."

"A reality show about Bubbles," Tina said. "And lavish Indian weddings in general."

She propped herself up on her elbow and looked over at Marianne in her bed.

"I'd watch hours of Bubbles Trivedi doing pretty much anything," Marianne said, stretching her arms up and out. She reached over and looked at her phone and placed it back down on the table and took a sip of water from a Bisleri bottle.

"Right? And think about the settings—castles, palaces, this—Colebrookes, farmhouse parties, seven-star hotels, yachts off the Bombay coast glittering in the Arabian Sea, and private jets to Umaid Bhavan. Bachelorette parties in the Maldives. But also conservative aunts and uncles, love marriages versus arranged, coded words for sex, brides smoking cigarettes in secret with mehndi up to their elbows, and taking swigs of whiskey from the groom's flask before walking in with their eyes lowered to the floor demurely."

"And handsome bodyguards with earpieces," Marianne said, flipping over onto her stomach and pushing her hair behind her ears. "You have so much energy! I take it the food poisoning has left your system."

"I spoke to Rachel last night and she's already enthusiastic about it," Tina said. "I need to go find Bubbles. This is it."

She got up and threw on a pair of jeans, a black, long-sleeved T-shirt, and a pair of brown boots and rushed out of the cottage. Marianne touched her finger to her nose. It still felt tender. She tried to gently twist the small diamond stud but it hurt too much. It was stuck—what a metaphor—too painful to take out, too painful to leave in. She dropped her head back onto the bed and closed her eyes to snooze a little bit more.

"I'm looking for Bubbles," Tina shouted to Rajesh on the lawns outside. She got closer to him and said, "Do you know where she is? Are you wearing fake eyelashes?"

Rajesh reached up to his eyes and said, "Oops, forgot to remove those."

He pulled them off and dropped them into his shirt pocket with a laugh.

Tina looked at him closely, his lips stained red, bits of brown makeup caked into the laugh lines around his eyes.

Rajesh held his finger up to his lips and said, "Shhh," and winked at her.

"Why are you wearing fake eyelashes?" Tina asked.

"Practice," Rajesh said. He checked over his shoulder and leaned into Tina and whispered, "At night, I'm not Rajesh, your butler, I'm Raat Kumari, your night goddess."

"What?" Tina said.

"I perform. And tomorrow night, Tina, I am Zara, Bollywood superstar, item-girl extraordinaire, thirty-seven-year-old who pretends to be twenty-four years old. My biggest performance to date."

"You're going to pretend to be Zara?" Tina said.

Rajesh laughed and said, "Isn't it brilliant? Don't tell anyone. Bubbles is in a bit of a bind and I've been doing drag for the last five years. I can transform into Zara spectacularly. Wait and see. You won't even know it's me. Bubbles is a genius. You were looking for her? I think she's in the sauna sweating out all the champagne she's been drinking."

"You're moonlighting as a drag performer for Bubbles?" Tina said. She shook Rajesh by the shoulders and laughed. "No, no, this is too much. This is spectacular. This is made for television. Rajesh, thank you, I have to go."

Tina ran in the direction of the main clubhouse and the women's saunas. She quickly said hello to the woman at the front desk, shouted out her cottage number, and went straight into the sauna.

Bubbles lay on the top bench of the sauna on a zebra-print towel in a leopard-print, one-piece bathing suit. Her hair was spread out in a halo around her and her long, lacquered nails were clacking against a flask filled with water and sliced lemons that she had balanced on her belly. She was wearing large, round Fendi sunglasses and had wireless headphones in her ear. All her various pieces of jewelry were carefully placed around her on the bench.

A young Indian woman sat on the perpendicular lower bench, naked except for a pair of white bathing suit bottoms, her brown hair pulled into a topknot. She was flipping through an issue of *Vogue India*. Her abs were tight and slim, her breasts round and firm, a thin gold chain with a moon pendant lay against the glistening sweat of her chest. She looked up right as Tina, still fully dressed, was staring at her and said, "Can I help you?"

"Um, no, sorry," Tina said.

"You're not supposed to wear so many clothes in the sauna, you know?" the woman said.

"How are your abs so toned?" Tina asked, still staring.

"Pole dancing and Pilates. There's a new studio in South Ex called Shine. It's run by Ilya from Russia. You should try it," the woman said. "Could you maybe stop staring at me? It's making me rather uncomfortable."

"Sorry, so sorry. You're very beautiful," Tina said.

Bubbles took one of her headphones out, pushed her sunglasses onto her head, leaned up on one elbow, and said to Tina, "Why thank you, darling."

"No, not— Never mind. You're welcome, Bubbles. I've been looking all over for you." Tina could feel her pants starting to stick to her. Two drops of sweat dripped down her back. "Gosh, it really is quite hot in here," she said and pulled at her shirt collar and blinked twice to stop feeling dizzy.

"Bubbles, are you interested in television?" Tina asked.

"I don't watch too much," Bubbles said. "My favorite one is where all these washed-up stars live in a house together and behave badly. But I also love singing competitions and talent competitions. You know, there's a seven-year-old boy in Chennai who can play two pianos at the same time. I also love cooking competitions, especially the ones where children compete. And you know that American show in which people claim they're in love to get Green Cards? Genius. And those housewives all over America, love them. I also managed to illegally download the show about those huge, fat, fat people who get gastric bypass surgery and they eat only McDonald's food and one-liter Pepsi Cokes and cry. And that RuPaul woman. Or man? I don't know but she is so beautiful, I could watch her for hours. Anyway, like I said, I don't watch too much."

"Would you want to be on a television show?" Tina asked. She was worried she was about to pass out. She used her palm to wipe her forehead dry.

Bubbles sat upright now, pulling both her headphones out, and said, "Be on one?"

"A wedding-planning show. Where you plan and execute expensive, lavish, over-the-top Indian weddings in exotic locations with fake

British soldiers and imported flowers and Bollywood stars," Tina said. She wiped her brow again. "I don't feel so good. I think I'm still dehydrated from the food poisoning."

"You don't look good," the young woman said to Tina, setting her magazine aside. "I think you should step out of the sauna and drink some water."

She got up and pulled the sauna door open and helped Tina out.

"I was born for the screen," Bubbles shouted. She tried to get up to follow Tina out but her bathing suit strap had snagged on a broken piece of wood on the bench. "Damn it. Tina, wait!"

Tina sat down against a locker while the Indian woman got her a small bottle of water.

"Have you had your arm hair lasered off?" Tina asked in between sips.

"Drink the whole bottle," the woman said. "And yes. I've had everything below my eyelashes lasered off. You should try it."

The woman from the front desk came into the locker room and said, "Ma'am, are you okay? We just saw you on the cameras and you really are not supposed to enter the sauna in street clothes. It can be very dangerous. You need to get some fresh air."

The woman gave Tina a Parle-G biscuit and helped her out of the clubhouse.

"You should go and lie down for a while," she told Tina. "You're the one who had loosies yesterday, aren't you?"

"Loosies?" Tina asked. "That's a disgusting word. I had a slight upset stomach, yes. Why does everyone know about it?"

"Go get some rest," the woman said. "I'll have my colleague bring you Electral."

A few minutes after Tina left, Bubbles flew out of the locker room, still trying to put on all the jewelry she had removed in the sauna. The clasp of her most expensive diamond bracelet was so fiddly she always regretted removing it.

"*Where did she go?* What television show was she talking about? I want to be on television. I'll come up with a catchphrase! Something about a good catch—is that good?" she asked the woman at the front desk.

"Ma'am." The woman jumped up. "Ma'am, you aren't allowed on the grounds in just your bathing suit. Ma'am, please return to the locker room."

FIFTEEN MINUTES LATER, BUBBLES TRIVEDI stood outside Tina and Marianne's cottage in her sunglasses, wearing a dusty pink kaftan with a beige fur shrug around her shoulders. A white suede Fendi purse dangled off her right shoulder with a beige fur ball keychain attached to the external zipper. Her skin and hair were still slick with sweat. She knocked on the cottage door. Marianne opened it.

"I, darling child, am your subject," Bubbles announced.

"Excuse me?" Marianne said.

Bubbles lowered her sunglasses and looked at Marianne.

"No, not you. Your friend. Where's Tina? My entrance was for her sake," Bubbles said, shaking her head. She looked over Marianne's shoulder. "I'm going to be a television star."

"Come on in. Tina's lying down but she can barely contain her excitement," Marianne said. "I'm off to have breakfast and a facial but please try to keep her calm. She had a rough day yesterday."

Bubbles grabbed Marianne's left hand and said, "Unmarried. Perfect."

"You know that already," Marianne said.

Bubbles ignored her, pulled out another business card, and handed it to Marianne. "You message me when you're ready to get married. I'll put up the best show you've ever seen. You seem the kind who would want to get married in some ramshackle barn outside Manhattan."

Marianne studied her card and said, "You're not completely wrong. Do you know a good barn?"

Bubbles tapped her card with a long pink fingernail and said, "Just call when you're ready. I'll find you the best barn in all the land."

"You've found your star, darling child," Bubbles said again, this time to the correct person. "*The Wedding Planner. My Big Fat Indian Wedding. Destination*, colon, *Wedding*. The options are endless."

"You're interested?" Tina asked. She had stripped down to her underwear and bra and was lying in bed with a damp cloth on her head.

"Sauna heat just stays with you, doesn't it?" Bubbles said. She leaned down close to Tina's bed. "It does not smell great in here."

Bubbles walked over to the windows and opened them up and propped the front door open with a chair.

Tina sat up in her bed and said, "This works, right? I mean everyone's already done the documentaries on India's truck drivers or, I don't know, pesticides in local alcohol, or sex workers' children."

"*Born into Brothels*. A thousand times over," Bubbles said.

Tina was surprised Bubbles had heard of that documentary.

"Even I've heard of that documentary," Bubbles said, reading her mind. "But a grand extravaganza of a show about elaborate Indian weddings is exactly the need of the hour. And whether you like it or not, that's what you know. That's what you have an understanding of. And social commentary can also be made by turning the lens on wealth, you know."

Tina pulled at a cuticle on her right thumb and stared at Bubbles. Bubbles tapped at her own temple and said, "Not just a pretty face."

She was wearing a heavy gold necklace that looked like a lizard wrapped around her neck. Its eyes were large red rubies.

"We could give you a catchphrase," Tina said.

"You'll be surprised to hear I don't hold back on camera," Bubbles said. "I have lots of raunchy jokes to share."

"I could have jump cuts of street scenes—a husband in a wheelchair under a bridge, a woman roasting corn, a little girl begging—as a white limousine drives past with the bride shouting at her makeup artist," Tina said. "India, the land of contrast."

"You know, my niece married a New Zealander and for their wedding, we flew in the entire Indian and New Zealand cricket teams to

Andaman for a cricket match and then they attended the wedding as guests. And last year at a wedding in Udaipur, Rihanna came," Bubbles said.

"You brought Rihanna to India?" Tina asked, getting out of bed. There was too much to do to waste time recovering from food poisoning. She walked over to her suitcase and took out a dress and pulled it on.

"Not exactly but I was at the wedding. My point is that weddings are so over-the-top these days, especially Indian ones. My neighbor's son's wedding—not even one of the more lavish ones, it was done just in Neemrana, but the white horse that he was riding in on got scared when one of his uncles fired a gun and took off galloping with my neighbor's son sitting on his back. Imagine if you had managed to capture that on camera," Bubbles said.

"And people would agree to this," Tina said. "I mean, look at Shefali—she would jump at an opportunity like this. And why should India only get poverty if other countries are allowed complex and varied representations? Look at Japan! First it was only anime and porn but now they've got Marie Kondo."

"You know, that Marie Kondo first told everyone to throw everything away and now she's gone and opened a shop to sell things. And she's so small and tiny and cute, nobody even thinks to question her for one second. Now, that's a brilliant businesswoman," Bubbles said. She continued, "One family, they didn't allow the widowed grand-aunt to attend the wedding because they thought she would bring bad luck to the young couple. Just imagine. And they were quite shameless about telling everyone about it."

"Did you do anything about that?" Tina asked.

Bubbles hadn't. Mostly because it wasn't a family she actually knew; it was a news article she had read but that wasn't the point.

"I plan weddings, dear. I don't interfere in personal politics."

"I could show the world this India," Tina said. "Show them all this madness, the contradictions, the beauty, the chaos."

Tina sat down on the bed and picked up the water bottle.

"I never realized food poisoning could knock you out so badly," she said.

Bubbles reached into her purse and took out a little silver container and passed it to Tina and said, "Ajwain. Take a pinch and put it in your mouth and chew it slowly to really get the juice out of the little seeds. It'll settle your stomach."

"What is ajwain in English?"

Bubbles took the container back and smelled it and said, "I'm not sure. Aniseed? No, that's saunf—also good for digestion, by the way. Ajwain, ajwain. I really don't know what it is in English."

Bubbles put it back in her purse and said, "And end of season one, we'll cut to you being proposed to by that handsome Australian fellow. And we'll start season two gearing up to plan your wedding in Bondi Beach."

"Rocco?" Tina asked. "No, he isn't, we aren't—"

"We'll break the fourth wall, show you as a producer. So along the way, during the season, we'll make sure we catch glimpses of your romance."

There was a knock on the open door and Rajesh leaned in holding a tray with a red Gatorade on it.

"Delivery for you, Ms. Tina," Rajesh said. "From your dear friend Miss Marianne."

He placed the bottle on the coffee table and handed Tina a note.

Found a Gatorade at the Colebrookes shop. It's red flavored and about to expire and cost me an arm and a leg so you better drink it and recover soon. Try an NYC hangover cure for Delhi Belly. PS. I think the show sounds brilliant.

"Rajesh, what's ajwain in English?" Bubbles asked.

"Carom," Rajesh said.

"I thought that was a game," Bubbles said.

Tina looked down at the note from Marianne, dear Marianne. Lucky Marianne who couldn't see how perfect Tom was for her. Or maybe she could and she pretended she couldn't because it hadn't crossed Tom's mind to propose. Marianne had always been stubborn and prideful. But Marianne belonged with Tom. Marianne knew it, Tina knew it, and Tom knew it, but Tom had no idea how close he was to losing her. Tina would fix it, she decided.

"I have another brilliant idea," she said to Bubbles and Rajesh. "Look at me, I'm on fire. I'm ready to fix the world today. Where's my phone?"

She pulled the sheet off the bed and found the phone.

"You should use headphones when you talk on the phone," Rajesh said. "Holding the phone close to your face too much can increase acne."

"Okay, thank you, Rajesh," Tina said. "That's quite enough."

Rajesh turned to leave and Tina squatted down near her suitcase and said, "Damn it, where are my headphones?"

Bubbles snickered behind her.

Tina rummaged around and said, "Bubbles, could you excuse me now, please? There's something else I have to do."

"Yes, dear," Bubbles said. "And I'm due for a manicure anyway. I'll speak to you this afternoon about next steps."

"TINA?" TOM SAID, JOLTING awake in his bed in DUMBO. His glasses were still on his face. He could still smell the remnants of the last cigarette of the night on his breath. He squinted over at the clock and saw that it was nearing 2 A.M. He must have fallen asleep while reading.

"Is everything okay? Is it Marianne?" he asked, sitting up and straightening his glasses, his plaid comforter around his skinny waist.

"She's fine. You're flying to India tonight. I'm buying you a ticket—it's in coach and you'll pay me back so don't try to take some stupid communist stand. I googled you when you first started dating Marianne, and I know you were in the Black Republicans at Penn."

"What? That's like seven pages into my Google search," Tom said. "I only went to one meeting. It was college, everyone experiments."

"Relax," Tina said. "You're going to show up here and you're going to surprise Marianne and you're going to make sure you don't lose her because she loves you and you love her and you're perfectly suited for each other. Do you hear me?"

"Did you see the *Spectator* piece about the debate championship that I won?" Tom asked.

"Tom!" Tina said. "Do you hear me? You're coming to India."

"Tina, I miss her. I woke up with my glasses still on my face. She usually removes them for me," Tom said.

"Stop it. If you want someone to take your glasses off for you when you fall asleep, train a cat," Tina said. "This is about you and Marianne. Tom, get here."

"You can train a cat to take your glasses off?" Tom asked. He reached for his phone to google this. She was probably right. Cats were very intelligent creatures.

Colebrookes: One of the Gardeners
Is Repotting a Bougainvillea and Looks Up
and Sees the Pink Sky and Takes a
Moment to Gasp with Gratitude

THE OFF-WHITE LANDLINE PHONE RANG IN TINA AND MARIANNE'S cottage and the unfamiliar, low sound surprised Tina at first. She couldn't find the offending object but then discovered it on the ground, under Marianne's bed. Marianne must have moved it down there in order to have space for her candles on the small table between their beds.

"Yes?" Tina answered the phone.

"Madam, so sorry to trouble you but there is a young man at the gate who is saying he is here to visit you," the voice on the other end said.

"Right, Sid," Tina said. "Just send him here."

"Madam, it would be most helpful if you could come and receive your—guest, your visitor—for club rules," the voice continued.

"But everyone walks in—what's the problem?" Tina pressed.

"He'll be waiting at the gate. Thank you, madam. Have a lovely evening," the voice on the other end hung up the phone.

Tina stepped out of the cottage and walked out toward the gate. A man in a Colebrookes uniform was watering the pots of flowers that lined the lanes. Tina smiled at him but he didn't smile back. Tina stepped into the space between two flowerpots to allow a silver Mercedes with dark-tinted windows to drive past her. She turned her head away as the dust from the wheels coated her face. Near the entrance two male tennis instructors in all white were chatting, their large bags hanging off their backs. Tina apologized as she walked past them, even though they didn't bother to move even an inch to let her pass. Tina always muttered an apology when she walked past someone and mostly she saw the "sorry" like an "excuse me." But social media was telling her that she was conditioned to do this only because she was a woman and by doing this she was playing into the patriarchy so now Tina always felt guilty when she apologized to anyone. She got to the gate and saw Sid to the right of the exit, leaning back against the brick wall of Colebrookes with one foot up against the wall. She looked over her shoulder at the security guard who was leaning out of his booth watching her walk toward Sid. He ducked back into his booth when she made eye contact and then poked one eye out more discreetly but Tina could still see him clearly.

"I should have met you somewhere else," Sid said. "Let's just go for a walk or something. We can get a tea."

"Don't be silly. You'll like it here. I've ordered tea and some pastries to my porch already; we don't have to go anywhere. They have a strict entrance policy for anyone who isn't a member or a guest or staff. That's all."

"Right," Sid said. "An entrance policy."

"It's ridiculous, I know. As if they can judge by appearances. Mark Zuckerberg wears only those horrid T-shirts every day. But he's white so I guess that's different. The point is these policies are really silly."

"I don't want to be your political statement," Sid said.

"What? No, you aren't. That's not what I meant," Tina started. "If you're not comfortable—"

"Stop, you're making things worse," Sid said. He pointed toward the entrance. "Let's just go. You lead the way."

Tina walked back in through the entrance, the security guard now openly staring at them. They continued down the walk. A car came toward them and Tina stepped aside but Sid didn't. He was looking down at his shoes as he walked. Tina nudged him by the elbow but felt uncomfortable having any more physical contact. Sid looked up, looked at the car, and squinted in through the windshield. He still didn't move.

"You should—" Tina didn't finish her sentence and the driver honked loudly at Sid.

"What are pedestrians supposed to do? Climb into the bushes?"

"There aren't many pedestrians here," Tina said. "And yes, I basically did climb into the pots earlier when a car came."

Sid slowly stepped aside. He turned and watched the car drive away before continuing to follow Tina down the path.

By the time they reached the patio, Tina decided it would be best to sit inside the cottage to avoid the obviously curious eyes all around the club.

"We can just sit inside," she said. "Evening pollution levels are the highest supposedly."

"Right, sure," Sid said.

They went into the cottage and Tina turned the lights on and looked around at this space that was bigger than Suraj's whole home that they had been to two days ago. Clothes were strewn all over the beds and chairs and furniture and Tina and Marianne's jewelry glinted on the dresser. A pile of shoes of different colors and styles lay all over the floor.

"You travel heavy," Sid said.

"It's also a lot of Marianne's things. I told you about her, right? We're sharing this room."

"I'm being grumpy today, I'm sorry," Sid said. "I hate places like this."

And he hated not being able to afford places like this. He hated that a whole part of the world was inaccessible for him. Not that he was dying to get into this place but earlier today he wanted so desperately to have sex with Divya, and she had finally agreed, but they couldn't find an affordable private place and he was still angry and frustrated.

But it was time to shake that off, he decided. Nobody wants to cast an actual angry young man.

"But would you watch a show about places like this?" Tina said.

"What?"

"Never mind. I should have suggested meeting you somewhere else. It's just that everyone always seems to want to visit Colebrookes so I thought you might enjoy it."

Sid sat down on the sofa with his legs splayed apart and leaned back with his right arm behind his head. Now Tina was grateful that the armchair was full of clothes and she sat down right next to him and tucked her legs up under her so her knees were leaning against one of his knees. He put his hand down on her knee, patted it, left it there, and said, "Don't feel bad. I hate being here but I'm definitely going to go back to Bombay and tell everyone I know that I came here."

Rajesh knocked on the door. Tina was about to get up to answer it but Sid got up before her and said, "Sit. I'll answer."

He opened the door and exchanged a few quick words with Rajesh in Hindi that Tina couldn't understand and came back in the room holding a tray with a pot of green tea, two cups, and two small plates of assorted sandwiches and pastries.

Sid put the tray down and poured two cups of tea.

"When I tell people in Bombay, this will be champagne," he said.

"Let's make it really champagne. I have something I'm sort of celebrating tonight. I don't know if they have real champagne but we'll get some sparkling wine," Tina said, reaching for the butler call button.

"Isn't that what champagne is?" Sid asked.

"Well, actually, real champagne has to be from— You know, never mind. I actually started that sentence with 'well, actually,' so I'm going to stop there. It's basically the same these days." Tina said into the phone, "Two glasses of Sula sparkling, please. Make sure it's very cold."

Rajesh returned soon with the two glasses and, clearly curious, poked his head into the cottage even though he had nothing else to deliver.

"Anything else, madam?" he said, staring at Sid who was standing near the table holding the tray with the two glasses. He raised his eyebrows at Tina and winked. "I brought you a little pot of organic ghee that works better to moisturize the lips than any expensive balm."

"You stop or I'll reveal your little secret," Tina said.

Rajesh looked back and forth from Tina to Sid and nodded and slowly edged out of the door.

"I know him," Sid said.

"What? How?"

Sid laughed, put the tray down on the table, handed a glass to Tina, and said, "Relax, I was joking. I don't know everyone in my income bracket."

"Cheers," Tina said.

They quickly worked their way through repeated top-ups while Sid asked her for details about her life in New York.

"Have you ever been to one of the live recordings of those morning shows? Do they really do that in front of full windows overlooking Times Square or is it green-screened in?"

"I walked past a line waiting to see Prince at 8 A.M. in Bryant Park for a morning show once," Tina said. "Does that count?"

"Please don't tell me you shop at farmers markets, though," Sid said. "I see that on so many TV shows and I just don't understand—all markets in India are farmer's markets."

Tina watched Sid walk over and pick up Marianne's candle.

"Do you have electricity outages here?" he asked.

"No, they have generators," Tina said. "Marianne likes the smell of those; they're not for electricity outages."

"Does the smell keep away mosquitos?" Sid asked.

"No," Tina said. "Nothing. The candles do nothing. They're just for pleasure, I guess."

Sid smelled it and put it back down on the bedside table.

Side by side on the couch again, Sid said, "So you think you may ever end up living here? Or Bombay? Personally, I think you should come live in Bombay."

"Do you? So I can be close?"

Tina looked over at him and smiled. This was the moment. It had to be. By this point she was leaning into the side of his chest, both of them dangling their third, and empty, champagne flutes in their hands. Tina turned around and faced Sid and reached her hands up to his face and shut her eyes, ready to kiss him. He held her face in his hands, his strong hands, and said, "Make the show, Tina. Give the world something new."

Tina leaned forward, pushing his hands back—was he resisting? she thought for a fleeting second. No, he just had naturally strong hands—and kissed him. He kissed her back and said, "Imagine it, Tina."

He stood up, quickly placing his glass down on the table and moving across to the other side.

"We can take over Hollywood!" he said.

"And then Bollywood," Tina added. "It's much easier to move culture from West to East."

Tina leaned back on the sofa and smiled at his enthusiasm.

"I'm thinking of making a reality show about lavish Indian weddings," Tina said. "Isn't that a brilliant idea? People will just eat up Bubbles."

"What?" Sid said. "Who the hell is Bubbles?"

"Bubbles Trivedi," Tina said. "The wedding planner."

"But what about me?" Sid said.

"What about you?" Tina could sense the mood had changed in the room. "Can you come sit down again?"

"I'm just supposed to go back to Bombay and personal training despite everything this week? Everything I put myself through?"

Tina's glass slipped out of her hand and hit the ground but didn't shatter and Tina wished it had so it would give her something to do, somewhere to look.

"You kissed me for . . ." Tina couldn't finish the sentence. She groaned, "You thought . . . Oh my God, you felt you had to."

Sid paced back and forth across the table, far out of Tina's reach.

"You came to Delhi by train just to see me," Tina said. She was sitting on the edge of the sofa now, looking down at the champagne glass by her feet, watching it lie still on the black-and-white rug beneath the table.

"I would go anywhere for opportunity, Tina. You know that about me. For the show. For the fame and the money and everything else you said was going to be a possibility. I would do anything for that."

She was, very literally, sitting on a casting couch, Tina thought.

"I'm the sleazy television executive," she said. "Who brought you to my room, got you drunk, and tried to hook up with you."

"I'm going to go," Sid said.

"No!" Tina said. "Wait. I'm not even attracted to you. I've been trying to be all week because you are just so objectively handsome that I felt I ought to be."

"How is insulting me making this situation any better?" Sid said.

He sat down on the edge of Marianne's bed.

"I feel like a complete idiot. You maybe didn't give me all the right signals but we come from different worlds and this was my responsibility," Tina said. She picked up her empty glass from the floor and placed it back on the table.

"Signals?" Sid asked.

"Well, we've been pretty intimate this week," Tina said.

"I barely even know what that means. I just went along with everything you were suggesting because this felt like a weeklong audition," Sid said.

"I made a mistake," Tina said. "That has very little to do with you and more to do with what I wanted from India."

"I don't have a proper bed—I sleep on a mattress that stays rolled up during the day so we can use our one room for other things. This, this whole cottage that you're staying in for a holiday, is bigger than my home and when you used the word 'cottage' I pictured something very different. I don't know a lot about the world but I know enough to know I don't want to be someone's fetish. And if we were ever to be together, it would just be that—both ways! I'm perfectly aware that I wouldn't fit in in your Bronx apartment."

"Brooklyn," Tina corrected.

"What?"

"Never mind."

Sid walked out of the door. Tina stood up and rushed behind him.

"Wait!"

"Tina!" Bubbles was rushing toward Tina's cottage. "My husband has prostate cancer."

"What?" Tina said. Sid also stopped on the porch. "You just found out? I'm so sorry to hear this. Don't worry about the show at all. This is dreadful news."

"No, no. We've known for ages but it'll be perfect for the show. He won't die—it's very slow-moving and his diabetes will probably get him first—but imagine if you have me, this lovely, bubbly wedding planner—even named Bubbles, don't forget—who is also dealing with her tragic personal story. We'll have all the ingredients for a hit show."

"Bubbles Trivedi?" Sid asked. Tina nodded.

"Who is this handsome young man?" Bubbles asked. "And where's your Australian fellow?"

"Who?" Sid asked.

"Never mind," Tina said. "Bubbles, this is my friend Sid. He's a personal trainer."

"And a very attractive one at that. We should get you to get all our brides to be in shape for their weddings. Stir the pot a little. The dark-skinned poor boy seducing the wealthy brides-to-be. Look at how good I am at this. Could I get a co-producing credit?" Bubbles said.

"Bubbles, please don't use terms like 'poor,'" Tina started.

"Why not?" Sid said. "That's what I am."

"But you're right, though," Tina said. "Bubbles, you're right! Sid, Sid, listen. I can still do this. I can cast you. You can be in this new show."

"I'm going to go," Sid said. "I don't want to get my hopes up again."

Bubbles rubbed his triceps and said, "You'll be perfect for this role.

You can stand behind the brides and hold their elbows firmly against their bodies while they lift the weight for a tricep curl. And then it'll get too hot so you'll take off your shirt, and use the same shirt to wipe your muscular torso."

"Bubbles! Please stop rubbing his arm," Tina said. She turned to Sid, "I'm so sorry for all the . . . all the objectification you've been facing tonight."

"I'm going to go, Tina," Sid said. He wouldn't look her in the eye.

"Sid, please just give me a night to think and check back in with my New York office. I really think I have a role for you this time."

"Come, Sid, walk with me," Bubbles said. She held Sid's arm and they walked off down the Colebrookes drive. "And Tina, don't forget the prostate cancer bit in your pitch."

Colebrookes: Mr. Das Is Awake and Watching an Exercise Video on YouTube as He Drinks His Morning Tea

"I CAN'T GO," TINA SAID IN THE DARK. SHE ROLLED OVER AND pulled the sheets up to her chin and said to Marianne, "I sexually harassed someone I had power over."

"You didn't sexually harass him," Marianne said. She put a bottle of Bisleri, two packets of Parle-G biscuits, and a small bottle of hand sanitizer into her Herschel backpack.

"I tried to kiss him," Tina groaned. "And he was trying to audition."

"Bullshit," Marianne said. She pushed open the curtains but it was still dark outside so the room remained dark. She walked over to Tina's bed and put her bedside lamp on. Tina covered her eyes and rolled away.

"He's not innocent in this, Tina. He was leading you on."

"He was asking for it?" Tina said.

Marianne couldn't help but laugh. She got up and poured a tea for herself and a coffee for Tina and took them both over to Tina's bed.

"Would you feel this guilty if he wasn't poor?" Marianne asked.

"What?" Tina rolled back to Marianne, sat up, and took the cup of coffee. "You can't say that."

"No, seriously. If he were some rich banker guy in New York, you'd be pissed and maybe a little embarrassed but you wouldn't feel guilty."

"I'd be furious," Tina said.

"Exactly," Marianne said. "So the best thing you can do is afford Sid the same thing. He doesn't want your pity now on top of you sexually harassing him."

"I didn't sexually harass him!" Tina said.

Marianne laughed and said, "Anyway, now you may actually be able to get him a role on a show and he didn't even need to have sex with you for it."

"I'm not even attracted to Sid," Tina said. "The one I really want to be kissing is Rocco."

"Really? Even though he didn't call you after London?" Marianne said.

"God, I'm pathetic," Tina said. "At least I'll have my career while I watch my personal life go up in embarrassing flames."

Marianne returned with the plate of milk rusks Rajesh had brought and set them on the quilt on Tina's bed. She sat down next to Tina and looked at her phone.

"Tom's phone has been off since yesterday," Marianne said. "I can't reach him. I'm worried. This is really unlike him."

"What about Karan?" Tina asked.

"I was behaving like an idiot, wasn't I? Can you imagine me moving to Dubai or Hong Kong or Delhi? I wouldn't survive a week."

"International playboys are exhausting," Tina said. "We're too old for them."

"But I think I've pissed Tom off," Marianne said. "I've barely had any contact with him the last few days and now I can't reach him. Right when I'm having my revelation of him maybe being the one."

Tina stretched her arms overhead and kicked the sheets off and rolled to the side.

"I guess I have to face the world," she said.

"Come on, let's go. I can't wait to see the Taj Mahal," Marianne said. "Maybe it'll get my mind off things. There's nothing I can do about Tom until I get back anyway."

A loud knock on the door interrupted them.

"Can you get that? I have to use the bathroom," Marianne said.

Tina opened the door to Rajesh standing there holding two small Colebrookes tote bags personalized with Tina's and Marianne's initials on them.

"Agra lovers bag deliveries for you, ma'am. Please hurry and get out to the bus so you are all back in time for tonight's reception. Have a wonderful day today," Rajesh said.

He peered over her shoulder into the room wondering if that same handsome fellow as yesterday might be hiding in there. He wasn't.

"The bus is already here. And remember to drink lots of water with the champagne so you don't get a chin wobble when you're older," Rajesh said to Tina as he exited.

Each bag had a small marble Taj Mahal replica, a pressed rose encased in glass, a champagne flute with their names on it, a bejeweled hair clip, and a small bottle of Dom Pérignon. A note said *To love. Don't worry—there's an ice box with actual cold champagne in the bus. To the Taj Mahal we go.*

Everyone gathered around the driveway at 6 A.M. and started climbing onto the bus. Bollywood songs played as the driver sat with his feet on the steering wheel, watching something on his phone. He laughed as Tina walked on and said, "This cat dances."

He held the phone out to Tina and added, "And it's wearing a black hat. This is too much."

Tina looked at the phone and nodded and walked on. Mr. Das, who was sitting in the front passenger seat along with Mrs. Sethi so as to not get carsick, looked up and said to the driver, "Is that the one where the cat ends up in the kitchen sink and then the camera gets blurry?"

"Sir," the driver took his foot off the steering wheel and turned to face Mr. Das. "Why would you give away the ending?"

The driver muttered to himself while all the other passengers boarded. His wife hated the stray cats he fed every morning and he was certain she would "accidentally" forget to put milk out for them today. She was forever harping on about him loving the cats more than he loved her.

And indeed, his wife, Bharti, was at that moment sitting on her haunches outside their front door with her tea and biscuits and a spray bottle filled with water in her hand. Every time one of her husband's little pet stray cats approached searching for milk, she sprayed it with water and shooed it away. If he took enough early morning shifts, she would be able to get rid of the cats within a week.

Pavan and Shefali, in matching yellow outfits, climbed onto the bus at 6:15 A.M. and everyone cheered.

"We aren't coming," Shefali said. "I have no interest in battling the crowds. I'm going to get a mani-pedi."

"Didn't you just do that?" Pavan asked.

"And I should just have the same nail polish for all days of my wedding?" Shefali said. "Do you not care about me at all?"

"I'm sorry," Pavan said. "Listen, why don't we get some more sleep and then eat something."

"I am not going to eat today and look bloated for tonight, Pavan. What is wrong with you?"

Shefali walked off the bus.

"I'm going back to bed. Hopefully, someone will let me know once she's eaten something," Pavan said. "Anyway, we just came to tell you all to have a fun day. Akshay is the photographer who will be with you, and he will take pictures that we'll have printed and ready for you by the time you leave tomorrow. Susanna, Kritika, and Pallavi"— he pointed to three women sitting in the back row in matching cotton saris—"have snacks, tea, coffee, and drinks packed and ready for you. Kritika makes terrific cocktails as well. If you need anything, just ask them but we've also booked all of you lunch at the Taj Hotel in Agra."

"Hold on," Nono announced. "If you two aren't going, no way in hell I'm going."

"No, Nono, please go with everyone. You'll be a good guide," Pavan said.

"What? With the dementia? Not possible," Nono said. She stood and looked at everyone else on the bus. "You don't need a guide. If there's anything you need to know, you've all got phones in your pockets—just google it. And yes, it's true, they cut off the hands of all the workers."

Nono also got off the bus and her driver quickly followed.

"This is optional?" Karan said. "Pavan, you said you were coming. Fuck it, I'm getting off too. You hear about all those accidents where a busload of people attending a wedding plummet into a ravine and everyone dies."

"There are a lot of accidents?" Marianne asked.

"No, it'll be fine," Pavan said. "Karan, you promised. Sit back down."

The bus driver looked into the rearview mirror and said, "Anyone else getting off? Speak now or complain later."

"I'm going to go sit up front behind the driver," Marianne said to Tina. "That's the safest spot in case of an accident because drivers subconsciously protect themselves."

"Not subconsciously," the driver muttered.

And then, in a large sputtering of Colebrookes dust, the bus took off for Agra.

"A mausoleum," David said loudly to Radha. "Can you believe it? Built in 1632 by Shah Jahan. My friend Marshall had a dog named that when we were in high school."

"Please stop reading Wikipedia pages to us," Tina said.

"Actually, do continue," Mr. Das said from across the aisle. "I knew it was sometime in the sixteen hundreds but I didn't know it was 1632."

"How does the actual year affect what you think of it?" Radha said. "It's early, David, darling, why don't we keep the facts for later?"

Mr. Das got up and stood in the aisle and said to Radha, "Here, I'll sit here for some time. I just took an anti-nausea medicine. You go sleep at the back. Anyone else need an Ondem?"

Mr. Das stood up, waving a strip of medicine around.

"Anti-nausea pills always make me a little loopy," he said.

"I'll take one," Karan said. "I don't mind feeling a little loopy."

"I'll take one too," Rocco said.

Radha pushed her sunglasses up on top of her head and said, "Neel, stop handing out anti-nausea medication for recreational use. And go sit with your date—what an absurd word."

"Radha, you really could use some more sleep," David said. "And I'm wide awake. Let me have a chat with Neel here while you get some rest."

As the bus rumbled down the highway toward Agra, there was a silence as most people slept. Even Mr. Das had fallen asleep against David's shoulder and David had fallen asleep against the window. The silence was suddenly, briefly, broken by a large bang and the bus careening this way and that before coming to a jerky stop with one wheel off the road in a ditch. The only sound was a mechanical hiss coming from the front of the bus.

The driver stood up, disoriented, and came rushing through the aisle asking if everyone was okay. Tina stood up, shaking, her right elbow hurting. It had hit against the hard armrest on the side of her chair. And then she saw her father sitting near the window across the aisle with blood pouring down his forehead. Tina didn't say anything but fell back into her chair. Rocco shouted to the women at the back to bring a glass of water for Tina.

Radha pushed to where Mr. Das was and grabbed his face in her hands. Behind her, David pulled off her dupatta, shouted for more water, soaked the cloth, and used it to gently wipe Mr. Das's face clean and hold the cloth against his forehead. Radha sat cradling Mr. Das while David shouted instructions at everyone.

"He'll be fine," he said, looking straight at Tina. "He's fine. There's always more blood than we expect. Hey, rich kid, brother of the groom—you need to get an ambulance or a car or whatever you use in India to get Neel to a hospital. It's not an emergency but it's urgent. There's a difference—process that and make decisions wisely. Bus driver—I am so sorry, I learned nobody's name; I swear it isn't racism—get out and make sure the bus isn't suddenly going to explode."

"He used to be a volunteer EMT," Radha announced to the whole bus, smiling.

"Tina, are you hurt?" David said. "Why do you look like you've had a concussion? From what I can tell, that side of the bus had no impact."

"I'm fine, I'm fine. Just tell me if my father's fine."

"I'm fine," Mr. Das said weakly. "Just a little shocked, but David Smith here seems to know what he's doing. Is Mrs. Sethi okay?"

Mrs. Sethi, in her ongoing search to find more meaning in her life, had also taken classes at Sunder Nagar's Emergency Preparation Centre, and she was busy using Karan's phone to call for a replacement bus. She was standing on the side of the road with the driver directing traffic away from the stalled bus so that no other vehicle would ram them. At least they would return to Delhi and have a more peaceful day. She couldn't believe they were trying to fit in a Taj Mahal visit on the same day as the main reception and she had agreed to go only because she wanted to spend every possible minute with Neel Das before he left for America. Things were going well between them but they hadn't discussed his impending departure. Mrs. Sethi wanted to but she was too scared of ruining the time they had. She was too old to chase a man across the world. A blue Maruti van pulled up next to her and an elderly couple put the window down and looked out.

"Need any help, ma'am?"

"No, I think we're all okay," Mrs. Sethi said. "We were on our way to Agra."

"Is everyone okay?" the man asked. "Your family is on the bus?"

"My husband," Mrs. Sethi said just to hear the word again. Just to feel how it would sound. She had always liked the word. "But everyone is fine, thank you."

"You're really okay, Neel?" Radha said to him, kneeling in the aisle of the bus, cradling her ex-husband's head in her arms while her boyfriend applied pressure to the bleeding wound on his forehead above his right eye.

"It's like that night—" Mr. Das started.

"—with Tanvi's cut," Radha finished. "When you shouted at the taxi driver and told him he would work for us someday."

"I felt terrible about saying that," Mr. Das said. "But I could tell you were impressed so it was okay."

Radha stroked his hair and smiled down at him. Mr. Das reached up and held her wrist and kissed her hand.

"David Smith is a good man."

Over Mr. Das's bleeding head, Radha looked at David and smiled.

"You're a good fellow yourself," David said to Mr. Das. Mr. Das nodded. "What a fitting start to a day exploring history's most magnificent monument to love."

"Start and end," Radha said. "We're going back to Delhi. It was absurd to try and fit this in today."

"Stranded in a broken-down bus half in a ditch on the side of the road outside Delhi is more of a monument to long-term love than the Taj Mahal," Mr. Das said. "I hope all the youngsters are taking notes. For the early part of love, think like a youngster but then to make it last, think like an old person."

"It's true," Radha said. "I tell all my clients that love is never about flowers and diamonds and endless romance. Love is about running a really boring business together. Love is about being in a broken-down bus in a ditch."

She looked up at David and met his eye and smiled. Mr. Das saw them looking at each other and smiled.

"David Smith, she doesn't like flowers and she always tips thirty percent, even when the service is mediocre," Mr. Das said. "And she enjoys a good dirty martini, and even though she'll tell you she's watching the BBC, she'll change channels on the ad breaks to watch some nonsense reality show and not return to the BBC. She's always wanted to own a telescope but never bought herself one and I foolishly never did either so maybe you can get that for her next birthday."

Mrs. Sethi climbed back on the bus and said, "Another bus is coming to pick us up. We're going back to Delhi and, Neel, you will be met at Colebrookes by the club doctor. Does anyone else need any medical attention?"

"Marianne's nose," Tina said.

"It's fine," Marianne said. "Healing well."

She touched her finger to it and pulled it back. It still really burned.

"Jyoti," Mr. Das said. "Will you, would you . . ."

He sat up in the aisle of the bus.

"Do you . . ." he said.

Everyone stood around looking at him, waiting to see what he would say. Tina looked at Mrs. Sethi looking at her father and smiling, waiting.

"Would you bring me a glass of water?" Mr. Das said. What had he meant to say? He wasn't too sure himself; it was meant to be something more meaningful than that but he didn't quite know what.

"Papa, you're sure you're okay?" Tina said.

Mr. Das nodded.

"Just thirsty," he said.

Colebrookes: Mr. Das Hopes He Gets a Permanent Scar; He's Always Liked Scars but Never Had One except from Where He Hurt His Hand on His Mother's Knitting Needle

AN HOUR LATER MR. DAS AND MRS. SETHI STEPPED OFF THE replacement bus at Colebrookes first and a skinny man was standing in front of them holding a small wheeling suitcase and looking confused.

"What is this?" Mr. Das said. He squinted at the man. "Do I have a concussion? You look familiar. Thomas?"

"Mr. Das," Tom said. "Nice to see you. Would you happen to know which one Marianne's cottage is? I'm here to surprise her when she gets back from Agra."

"You're already here?" Tina stepped off next, followed by Rocco.

"Who is this?" Rocco said. "How many men are you planning to have visit you?"

Tina turned around and said, "Don't let Marianne get off yet. Stop her. Rocco, go stop her."

Marianne was behind Radha when Rocco shouted, "Hey, Marianne. Tina left her phone behind—could you go look for it at the back?"

"What?" Marianne asked. Karan was right behind her and Marianne wanted to get off the bus. "No. Tell her to get it herself. I need to get off this stupid bus."

Rocco shrugged and let Marianne push past him as he asked, "Is that Tina's boyfriend?"

"Tom?" Marianne said.

Tom and Tina both turned to face Marianne getting off the bus. Tom looked over at Tina and said, "It's now or never, I guess."

He got down on one knee as everyone got off the bus and gathered around and said, "Marianne Laing, will you marry me?"

"Marry you?" Karan said, stepping up near Marianne.

Tina walked over and pushed him back and whispered "Do not get involved" through her teeth.

Tom reached into his backpack and took out the box from Bergdorf's with a thin platinum ring.

He looked up at Marianne and said, "Is your nose bleeding?"

Marianne kneeled down near him in the dusty driveway and whispered, "What are you doing? Are you sure?"

"Yes, of course I'm sure. Look, you know I'm not the kind to make some huge romantic gesture but I flew across the world to ask you to please marry me. I've missed you this week. Is that a piercing?"

"You can barely even see a diamond on that ring," Karan said.

"She doesn't like diamonds. Who the fuck are you?" Tom said.

Marianne looked over at Tina with panic in her eyes. Tina turned to everyone standing around Marianne and Tom kneeling in the dust and said, "We should all give them some privacy. Let's go, let's go."

"Not before Marianne says yes!" Mr. Das shouted, his head still bleeding into Radha's dupatta.

"Uncle, you need to go to the doctor," Marianne said, looking up at Mr. Das.

"Karan, can you please get my father to the doctor?" Tina asked, nudging Karan away. "Go. Don't get in the way of this. You barely even know her."

"Fine," Karan said. "But he's way too skinny. Uncle, let's go. The club doctor should be able to see you now."

"Marianne, what's the answer?" Mr. Das asked again.

Marianne looked over at Mr. Das and said, "It's a yes, Uncle."

As everyone clapped, Bubbles Trivedi arrived as if out of thin air, wearing a cream-colored sari with large red roses all over it and a red velvet blouse. A red chrysanthemum was pinned to her hair.

"Did I hear a proposal?" Bubbles asked. She rushed over to Marianne and Tom as they were standing up, Tom placing the ring on Marianne's finger. "Nice to meet you, young man. Bubbles Trivedi, wedding planner and television star. Tina, our first subjects!"

"They aren't even Indian," Tina said.

"Wedding planner?" Tom said. "I don't want a big wedding with some planner. Marianne, can we just do a city hall thing?"

"I could wear a white pantsuit and a small veil," Marianne said. "Maybe with blue suede pumps. And the whole feel can be reluctant-wedding chic. You know, like it matters so little but we just decided to do it anyway because why not? That kind of vibe."

"No, no, that won't work at all," Bubbles said. She looked around and added, "Never mind. You two do your city hall thing. Tina, I think our season should start off with an Indian wedding on Lake Como. Come, walk with me."

Bubbles and Tina walked back toward Tina's cottage. David slipped his hand into Radha's and said, "Should we go have a coffee?"

Radha nodded.

"I don't think I want to get married again, David," she said.

"Good, neither do I," David said. "I've never been the marrying kind."

"The fact that we both said that makes me want to marry you," Radha said. "I say we skip the wedding and do a honeymoon anyway."

"Lisbon," David said. "I've been wanting to go to Lisbon."

"I have many Lisbon tips," Mrs. Sethi said behind them. She wasn't sure where to go while she waited for Mr. Das to get back from the doctor.

Colebrookes: Shefali Now Wishes She Hadn't Planned the Two for the Same Night; She Feels Like She's Missing Out on Fun

NONO PEERED THROUGH HER OPERA GLASSES AND SAID, "That isn't Zara and Zarina. Bubbles! Who is that onstage?"

It was Rajesh, wearing a heavy green lehnga and a short gold blouse, a green dupatta draped over his wig, big chandelier earrings, a maang tikka in the part of his wig, his makeup applied expertly, swaying his hips in time to the drumbeat of the latest Bollywood song. Next to him was his friend Vaibhav, a newer performer, Rajesh's mentee in the drag scene, wearing the inverse of his outfit—a gold lehnga and a green blouse with a gold dupatta over his head. Behind them was a row of eight backup dancers wearing short gold-and-green dresses. A large disco ball rotated above them, making everything sparkle. Behind them was a wall of colorful flowers. The lights were flashing across their faces, and Bubbles hoped nobody would catch on that these were impersonators.

She came running over and grabbed Nono's glasses and said, "Of course it is. Stars look different in person is all. Come, come, take a look at all the orchids we got in for today. Your son says you shouldn't stay standing for long stretches. It probably adds to your confusion."

She pulled Nono in a different direction while whispering into her earpiece, "More backlight onstage, more backlight onstage! I told Rajesh *not* to find his light but that's of course exactly what he keeps doing."

She walked past David and Radha standing near the bar, waiting to be served their drinks. She paused briefly to hand them her business cards again.

"A spare, just in case," Bubbles said.

"Don't bother," David said handing back the card. "We're not the marrying type."

He reached down and grabbed Radha's hand. She intertwined her fingers through his and held tight.

"That's what everyone says," Bubbles said.

"But we know," Radha said.

Bubbles grabbed her cards back and said, "Well, in that case you don't need these. They cost twenty rupees per card to get printed with the glitter."

Radha looked down at her fingers, now covered with fine gold glitter.

"We could do a non-wedding celebration," David said.

"That's the same as a wedding," Mr. Das approached and interrupted. "Though you get to act superior as if you've come up with some brilliant, anti-establishment idea."

There was a Band-Aid above his eye. He pointed to it and said, "No concussion but three stitches."

"Scars look good," David said.

Mr. Das nodded and said, "A Manhattan, please. Make it strong."

He pointed to the Band-Aid again and added, "We've had a rough day."

The bartender—the same South African one who was atop the horse the first night—was not actually a bartender. He was a gardener from Johannesburg and had been spending the last hour drinking whiskey himself and had absolutely no idea how to make a Manhattan. The first night, he had hooked up with Aarti, Shefali's friend who had gone to Pratt, and was now drunk enough to look for her again. He wouldn't make his ten thousand rupees if he vanished but he had probably already drunk that amount in free liquor and he was heading back to Johannesburg next week and didn't really need much more money. He poured Mr. Das a whiskey with a splash of soda and two spoons of Campari and passed it over and ducked out from behind the bar to find Aarti.

"Hey, hey, hey," Bubbles shouted. "Where do you think you're going? You—Jeff, David, Rocco, damn it, what is your name? Where do you think you're going? You're working until midnight."

Bubbles rushed after him, shouting into her earpiece, "One bartender has disappeared. Send a replacement. Send a replacement immediately. And send one of the guards to come and stand behind the bar and make sure no more of these hippies gets drunk; it's like managing children."

"You have an assistant?" Tina asked, running into Bubbles.

"It's that handsome fellow, Sid. I told him I'd pay for his flight back instead of him wasting a day and a night on a train in exchange for him helping me tonight," Bubbles said.

"Sid is here? I'm not ready to see him yet," Tina said, looking quickly behind her. She saw couples standing in front of a wall made of flowers with a metal *S* for Shefali and *P* for Pavan entwined in gold lettering within a gold circle.

"This is like an audition for him. Do you think I should kiss him? Maybe after one wedding, while we're drinking some leftover wine and discussing how everything went. Would that be a good storyline? I'd be willing to," Bubbles said with a wink.

"No," Tina said.

Across the lawn, Sid was ignoring his earpiece so he could enjoy the mutton biryani in peace for ten minutes before returning to help Bubbles.

Standing near the biryani counter next to him, Aarti, Shefali's friend said, "That's not really Zara and Zarina, is it? Isn't Zara the taller one in real life?"

She squinted toward the stage. "I'm not a hundred percent sure but it does not look like them."

Oops, Sid thought. He needed this wedding to go well so Bubbles would get the show and he would become a star.

"Of course it's them. All the stars look different in real life. I live in Bombay and I once saw Kareena Kapoor and let me tell you, she has two nannies for that one baby," Sid said.

Aarti looked over at him suspiciously and said, "What does that have to do with how she looks in real life?"

"That man looks like he wants your attention," Sid said, pointing behind her.

The South African bartender was stumbling toward Aarti.

"No, I cannot repeat that mistake," Aarti said as she rushed off in the other direction.

Bubbles came charging behind the South African man.

"Out, out," she shouted at him. "It's bad enough you're drunk but you're not going to stumble around ruining this wedding. Sid, where have you been? Is your earpiece off?"

Sid shoveled the last spoonful of biryani into his mouth, put his plate down, grabbed the bartender by the arm, and said to Bubbles, "I will escort him out. Meanwhile, you need to either change the lighting or get those men off the stage—people are starting to catch on that it isn't Zara and Zarina up there."

"I'm down a bartender," Bubbles said. "There's a line forming."

"I can do it." Rocco had heard her as he was entering the lawns. "I used to bartend in Adelaide. I'm a little rusty but I can google whatever I don't know."

Bubbles grabbed his face in her hands and kissed him square on the lips and said, "Go, go! Bar number six—it's all yours. You're a savior. I'll set aside two iPads for you if you want. And I'll give you and Tina a discount when you're ready. But don't wait too long—despite what they say, even the male biological clock has a deadline. Now, go! Make everyone's drinks extra strong. I need to get Zara and Zarina off the premises before anyone catches on."

Bubbles rushed to the stage while shouting into her earpiece, "Dim the lights, dim the lights. Start lowering the volume on the music."

Tina saw her rush past and looked behind her for Sid. She saw him entering the main lawn area, looking handsome in black pants and a black T-shirt. Tina thought about disappearing into the crowd, maybe even going back to her cottage and reading a book, nobody would notice. But no, she decided, she was no sexual harasser. She walked toward Sid and said, "This is a good idea, this job."

"Do you think the show will happen?" Sid asked.

"Yes," Tina said. "But, listen, I don't want to get your hopes up again and I certainly don't want you to think you have to kiss me. But yes, I'm hopeful about this show."

"Show or no show, I think I want to work for Bubbles anyway," Sid said. "It's more fun than being a personal trainer to people who have no interest in working out. I spend half the shifts sitting around and watching my clients drinking coconut water and having phone conversations. And my most regular client, Mr. Singh, insists on exercising in only a pair of underwear and his turban."

Tina wondered if Sid would have kissed her back if the circumstances were different, if there had never been any mention of a show in the first place. But then she decided her ego didn't need to hear the answer to that because she already knew the answer to that.

"I'm going to go get a drink," Tina said.

"Bubbles says I'm not allowed to drink until the guests leave," Sid said.

"I wasn't inviting you to get one with me," Tina said.

"I have to be careful with you now, Tina ma'am," Sid said with a smile.

Tina smiled also and said, "Rachel thinks this idea has legs. It's looking good so far but as we both know, it's never final until it's on-air."

"Can I confess something?" Sid asked. "I thought about kissing you the very first day I walked in to audition for you and you shouted at someone that you had said no sugar in your coffee."

Tina laughed.

"I remember that. And then I didn't drink the coffee because I was certain they had spat in it."

"They didn't spit in it but they did make it with unfiltered water to get you back," Sid said with a laugh.

"That was a stressful audition," Tina said. "I think I knew even then that the show was falling apart."

Sid nodded. He looked straight at Tina.

"Tina. America and this," he said and gestured around the lawn. "They're similar in many ways. This and my life . . . more different than cats and dogs. My home floods every monsoon because the city repaved the lane outside and now it comes up higher than the entrance to our door so all the water runs in. You live here, I live there. That's how the world is divided."

"I guess that is more how it's split these days," Tina said. "Borders of money, not countries."

Sid shrugged his shoulders.

"For some of us it's always been split like that," he said.

"I hope this show happens, Sid. I'm going to really try. I promise."

"I know," Sid said. "I know this matters to you as much as it matters to me."

Tina walked away toward her father, who she saw standing across the lawn fiddling with his watch.

"I have typical Indian-man wrists," Mr. Das said to his daughter. He held up both his hands and twisted his wrists. "So thin, nothing fits properly."

He shook his head.

"That's why I'm not sure it's worth buying an Apple Watch," he continued. "But it's nice to want to spend money on material goods sometimes, isn't it? It's so attainable. For a while there, I couldn't think of anything I wanted to buy."

"Do you want a drink?" Tina asked.

They approached the bar and saw Rocco behind it. The bar was lit from below and small vases with one flower each lined the edge.

"What are you doing back there?" Tina asked. "It doesn't matter. I'll take a vodka martini, please."

"Coming right up. And for you, Uncle?" he asked.

"Uncle. I like that," Mr. Das said. "I'm fine. This isn't a Manhattan but I'm loving whatever it is."

Mr. Das looked down at his phone and added, "Mrs. Sethi has just arrived. I better go get her from the gate. You two enjoy yourselves."

Aarti came over to the bar and said, "A large vodka tonic, please. Fast."

She looked over her shoulder for the South African man but couldn't see him anywhere, so she took her drink and went back into the crowd. Two men approached the bar and rapped on it with their knuckles and one said, "Two whiskeys, make it quick."

"Do you need some help back there?" Tina asked.

"I'd like that," Rocco said.

Tina joined him behind the bar and poured the whiskeys for the impatient men, then two glasses of prosecco for two slim women, one fresh lime soda for an old lady. Then Nono pushed through the others waiting at the bar and said, "A Campari soda with a splash of orange juice for me. And a whiskey shot while I wait. If my son is going to go around telling everyone I have dementia, I may as well at least be drunk."

"Hi, Nono," Tina said. "Are you having a nice evening?"

Nono surveyed the grounds with her opera glasses and said, "You know what? It's lovely. And I like Bubbles's idea of having friends bartend. I was skeptical about her wedding planning skills but she has my stamp of approval. Not a marigold in sight."

Nono's driver stood two feet behind her and nodded.

"Get him an Old Monk and Coke. He pretends he doesn't drink but I can smell it on him. Fortunately, he drives even better after a drink."

Nono smiled at Tina and then smiled at Rocco and then back again at Tina and said, "Enjoy your evening, you two. And enjoy everything the world has to offer."

"Want a drink?" Tina whispered to Rocco as the bar cleared for a moment to make way for Nono to exit, followed by her driver. Tina squatted down behind the bar and pulled him down next to her. She reached into the mini fridge and pulled out a bottle of prosecco. They could hear people murmuring at the bar, looking to get served.

A cover band sang "Can't Take My Eyes Off You" onstage, and small lights twinkled in the trees above them, the pollution creating a gentle haze.

Rocco popped the cork open, angling it into the bushes in front of them. He passed the bottle, liquid fizzing over, to Tina, who took a large sip and passed it back to him. He held the bottle up and said, "To us."

And he leaned forward and kissed Tina who fell back onto a case of beer. But she didn't care. She reached her arms around Rocco's shoulders and kissed him back.

"I googled you too," she said when they separated. "And I looked for you on social media."

Rocco looked down at her and smiled and said, "I didn't call you, it's true, but I was briefly in Williamsburg. I was hoping I'd run into you so we could have done this sooner."

"What?"

Tina sat up and pulled her sari pallu straight. Rocco was on his knees in front of her.

"I didn't come just to look for you. An advert I was working on was shooting in Queens so I kind of had an excuse. I rented an apartment in Williamsburg."

"When?" Tina said.

"In April."

"I was there," Tina said.

"I know. You're pretty active on social media so I went to all the places you posted from, like a trail of crumbs. But I never saw you. And in one of the pictures there were two wineglasses and an empty tray of oysters so I gave up. I was only there for a week anyway."

The song changed to a modern version of "Khoya Khoya Chand," and a large paper lantern was released into the sky above them to resemble the lost moon. Tina looked up at it floating into the darkness.

"Do you think I could live here?" Tina asked at the same time that her father asked Mrs. Sethi the same question near the main gate of the lawns.

Mrs. Sethi and Rocco both smiled in response.

"I think you'd love it here," Mrs. Sethi said to Mr. Das.

"Good," Mr. Das said. "Because I've booked a one-way ticket back here for next month. If, Mrs. Jyoti Sethi, you might be interested in seeing where this goes."

"I think maybe it's time I started calling myself Ms. Jyoti Kaul, don't you think? My maiden name. And you know, you can get really effective mosquito repellant plug-ins these days; I don't even use a mosquito net anymore."

"Can we give this a real try?" Mr. Das said.

"We have less to lose and fewer days ahead," Mrs. Sethi said. "But even if we were twenty, I'd say yes."

"Yes, you would love it here," Rocco said to Tina, still on the ground behind the bar. "And maybe I could take you out for a proper dinner and call you the next morning."

Lights suddenly erupted in the sky. Tina looked up and said, "More fireworks."

This time a three-dimensional, all-white Taj Mahal formed in the heavens above them. And then exploded into bright lights that made the sky flash like mid-afternoon for some moments.

"We got to the Taj anyway," Mr. Das said.

"We'll get to the real Taj soon," Mrs. Sethi said. "No words or pictures or movies or even fireworks can ever capture the beauty of the Taj."

"Okay, that's pretty cool," Tom said to Marianne from the porch of their cottage. They had been so busy having sex they were running late for the reception. "Want to go tomorrow? We can get on a morning train."

"I can't believe you flew across the world to propose to me. I figured if you ever did it, it would be over a lobster dinner at some restaurant overlooking the East River," Marianne said. She sat down on Tom's lap and kissed his cheek.

A mosquito landed on Marianne's knuckle. She looked down at it for a brief moment and then slapped it dead with her other hand.

"Just when I'm getting the hang of killing mosquitos, it's time to go back to America," she said.

"I found two cockroaches in my kitchen as I was leaving," Tom said. "If that helps."

Marianne stood up and said, "Wait here. There's something I need to do."

She went into the bathroom and leaned into the mirror and slowly removed her nose ring. It was definitely infected. But if she removed it now it would likely heal completely and not leave a mark. She dabbed at the hole with a square of toilet paper and sprinkled some more Neosporin powder on it. Good thing her skin was so pale, the white powder was barely visible. She dropped the tissue and the small stud into the trash can. The bloody tissue looked very dirty so she took a few more squares of toilet paper and let them drift into the trash can to hide all traces of the nose ring.

"Let's go," Marianne said, coming back to the porch and holding her hand out to Tom. "I've barely seen Shefali and Pavan all week."

They walked toward the main lawn where Bubbles approached them and said, "You're the ones who want a court marriage. Listen, if you have any of my business cards, be a dear and give them back to me, will you? I was too enthusiastic about giving them to everyone, no questions asked, and now I've run out. They're expensive to print with the glitter."

Marianne and Tom walked to the left through an arch of pink and red roses.

Tina and Rocco joined them from behind. They walked toward the stage on which Shefali and Pavan sat around a small fire. Shefali's parents sat on the ground behind them on one side, Pavan's parents sat on the ground behind them on the other side, and a priest in a white dhoti sat near the fire, shirtless, his belly bare to the world. Shefali looked stunning in a red silk sari, her head covered, with red lipstick, heavy gold jewelry, and her arms hennaed up to her elbows. Next to her, Pavan sat in a cream-colored silk kurta pajama. Their feet were bare and they were looking at each other and smiling. Shefali wiped the sweat off her upper lip and Pavan reached forward and pushed a hair back from her face. The priest saw it, frowned, and cleared his throat. People these days had no understanding of ceremony. And they had insisted on getting married in the evening while the party, with alcohol, raged on in the adjacent lawn.

"That'll be much more fun," Shefali had said during their meeting. "Our friends can sneak us shots."

"And keep the religious stuff to a bare minimum," Pavan had added. "People get bored with all that."

Shefali nodded and the priest was about to walk out of this meeting but he had quoted double his usual rate to the wedding planner and she had easily agreed so he had to stay put and do as he was told. That, and he found Bubbles Trivedi so inexplicably beautiful he would do anything to be around her. He noticed her now, entering the ceremony area with a throng of people, and puffed his belly out and made his Sanskrit even louder. He paused for Shefali to repeat what he had said but she was tickling Pavan's toes with her toes and giggling and not paying any attention to the priest. The priest decided to skip the next section and instead handed a small white sweet to Shefali. Fine. Let these two get on with it. They may not have any respect for the ceremony but at least they seemed to really like each other. He told Shefali to feed a small bite of the sweet to Pavan.

"Is that soap?" Rocco asked Tina.

"No," Tina said. "Why on earth would you think that's soap?"

Although she could understand the confusion and she certainly had no idea what the priest was saying in Sanskrit.

"Like as a metaphor for washing your mouth out," Rocco said.

"It's a dessert. Like a metaphor for a lifetime of sweetness," Bubbles said. "I told that priest to say all those parts in English."

She shook her head and walked up to the main podium and bent down and whispered to the priest. The feel of her breath on his neck gave him goose bumps all over his bare torso. He looked at Bubbles as he said, "Shefali, you are giving him the gift of a lifetime of sweetness. And you, Bubbles, are giving me the same."

"Focus on the couple and make the interesting parts in English, like I told you. There's lots of foreigners here. And stop staring at me with those googly eyes. I'm happily married. But do a good job and I'll hire you again."

The priest nodded and looked back at the couple and pulled a coconut out of the basket behind him and placed it in the tray in front of them. Bubbles nodded at him and returned to all of Shefali and Pavan's friends and family standing near the stage.

"Everyone is here! This is perfect. Everyone gather around. We'll take a picture. Come along, come along."

"I'm staying," Tina said.

"I wouldn't," Rocco said. "Bubbles will be furious and I'll get yelled at for leaving my future wife behind the bar."

"No, I'm staying in India," Tina said again, hoping she would sound believable. "I'm staying and setting up an office and I'm developing a show about big Indian weddings. I'll re-evaluate how things are in six months but for now, this is what I'm doing."

Rocco leaned forward toward her but Tina leaned back and said, "Are you nuts? You can't kiss me in front of my family. Even if we were to someday get married, I'd probably just pat your arm when the priest says you can now kiss the bride."

They got up and moved toward Poinsettia Point, just in time to see Kai emerge with a skinny Indian woman on his arm, both looking glamorous.

"This is Mitali," Kai said.

"Minakshi," the woman corrected him.

"Right," Kai said.

"That's where you've been the last two nights," Rocco said.

Radha and David came out of their cottage and merged with the group.

"Ma, I'm staying in Delhi," Tina said. "I'm finally making a decision."

Radha dropped David's hand and put her arm around Tina.

"You'll love it here."

"You're staying?" Mr. Das rushed up behind them and asked.

Tina nodded.

"I'm coming back at the end of the month," Mr. Das said. "On a one-way ticket. I'm giving it a go with Mrs. Sethi, née Miss Kaul, at least until malaria season. I've been inspired on this trip. In fact . . ."

Mr. Das suddenly grabbed Mrs. Sethi's hand and dropped down to the ground.

"Mrs. Sethi. Sorry, I mean Ms. Jyoti Kaul."

He looked up at everyone gathered around him. "I never got down on one knee when I proposed to Radha but I liked how that Tom fellow did it. Of course, Marianne said yes."

"Neel, please get up," Mrs. Sethi said.

"Is someone capturing this on camera? I bet it would go viral. *Tina!*" Mr. Das shouted.

"Tina!" Bubbles added on, equally loudly. "Start filming, start filming. This could be our season opener. Here, hold this."

Bubbles slammed her purse onto Rocco's stomach and positioned herself right behind Mr. Das.

"Shoot from the right, that's my better angle," Bubbles said.

"Mine also," Mr. Das said. "What a coincidence."

"No, Papa, don't be ridiculous," Tina said.

"Neel, one thing at a time," Mrs. Sethi said. "Someday, maybe, but let's start with you moving here. Let's start with a month, even a night together."

Rocco whistled.

"That's my father," Tina said.

"Sorry."

"What is going on?" Shefali shouted from the stage. "You should all be looking over here at us."

She went to stand and the priest gasped and said, "This is a mockery of a wedding. Young lady, please sit back down."

"It's too soon, isn't it?" Mr. Das said. "Fair enough, fair enough."

He looked over at the stage and shouted at Shefali, "Nothing to see here, darling niece. Continue on with your wedding."

Mrs. Sethi reached down and helped Mr. Das up.

"See?" Mr. Das said to Radha. "This is why I want to be married again—to have someone help me up after a failed proposal."

He stood up and put his arm around his daughter's shoulder even though he had the Fitbit on that wrist.

"Maybe we can rent an apartment together since I'm not getting married yet," Mr. Das said.

"No," Tina said.

Mr. Das nodded and smiled and the camera clicked.

ACKNOWLEDGMENTS

| | |

As always, my agent, Adam Eaglin at the Elyse Cheney Agency.
My editor, Hilary Rubin Teeman.
Taylor Noel.
Caroline Weishuhn.
And everyone at Ballantine Books and Penguin Random House.
Alice Lawson at the Gersh Agency.
Alexandra Pringle, Faiza Khan, and Meenakshi Singh at
    Bloomsbury Publishing.
Rachael Merola.
Paramita Das, Monika Gupta, Geetika Prasad, Jenn Kamara,
    Alexandra Watson, Crystal Kim, Nikhil Mehta, Soha Ali Khan,
    Simar Kohli, Rajiv Menon.
Maria, Gracie, Sharlotte, Jessie, Patricia, and Auntie Melba.
The city of Bombay. In particular, the neighborhood of Bandra West.
The McClearys.
Mai, and the memory of Appa, Mani, and Dadai.
Karna Basu, Shabnam Faruki, and Avaaz.
My parents, Kaushik and Alaka Basu.
My husband, Mikey McCleary.
And our two daughters, Sky and Ivy.

DESTINATION
WEDDING

III

DIKSHA BASU

A BOOK CLUB GUIDE

QUESTIONS AND TOPICS
FOR DISCUSSION

1. How does this novel push back at traditional notions of what love looks like?

2. Why do you think Tina assumes her mother was responsible for the divorce? How does her relationship with her mother differ from that of her father?

3. Was there anything about this book's depiction of India that you found surprising? Did it change your perspective on Indian culture at all?

4. Why do you think Tina is so set on marrying an Indian man? How does her struggle with her Indian-American identity inform her choices?

5. Which character did you identify with most and why?

6. How does the novel reflect class and privilege in India? How do class systems differ from or mirror those in the United States?

7. After she helps a man who has ostensibly fallen out of his wheelchair, Tina wonders what the best way is to interact with poverty and make a difference. How does Tina attempt to be charitable, and how do her efforts occasionally backfire? What does this reflect about her own intentions and views of India? With Sid?

8.   Tina says Rocco fit in in India so easily "when it seemed Tina didn't fit in anywhere" (76). Why do you think this is? What do you think it means to really belong somewhere?

9.   Tina spends much of the novel searching for the "real" India while Mr. Das reflects at one point, "This wasn't my India" (99). How do characters prescribe personal meaning to India throughout the book? What does this say about how place impacts our memory and identity?

10. What do you think of Marianne's relationship with Karan, and with Tina's decision to book a flight for Tom? Do you think Marianne and Tom are right for each other?

Q: *Destination Wedding* is similar to your debut, *The Windfall*, in that both grapple with class differences and paint vivid pictures of India's upper echelons. Why are you interested in writing about class?

A: I spoke about this a lot when *The Windfall* was published and it all holds true for *Destination Wedding* as well. People tend to dismiss writing about the one percent as being somehow frivolous or trivial (unless, of course, all the wealthy people you write about are evil capitalists who eventually get their comeuppance). And to be clear, I write about a cross-section of society—my characters are never sitting in ivory towers. They live and breathe and interact with the bustle and cacophony of cities where it's impossible to stay separated. One of the reasons I love writing about and (currently) living in an urban Indian city is that you have to be part of the complicated fabric of the city. The crossroads of poverty and wealth, the haves and the have-nots, the blurred line where the marginalized meet the mainstream is what I'm most drawn to in my work. There are many windows through which one can look at the world and this is the one I choose.

Q: Like Tina, you have close connections to both India and New York City. How are your own experiences in these two cities reflected in *Destination Wedding*?

A: I have always felt like I belonged in both and belonged in neither. Now I split my time between NYC and Mumbai but my real feeling of home comes from my family. I understand that now. Home is an idea, not a place.

Q: *Destination Wedding* illuminates generational clashes as Tina, her parents, and Marianne navigate romance in very different ways—from matchmaking to post-divorce dating. How do you approach writing about dating and love across generations?

A: I find second chances at love very interesting because our first chances at love define us so much. Who are we when we come out of that? I've always been intrigued by the idea of romance later in life. So much media focuses on that first "happily ever after" but with higher life expectancies and the idea of middle age changing, many people may end up having more than one great love and I wonder what that will look like.

Q: *Destination Wedding* features several interracial relationships, including Mrs. Das and her new white boyfriend, and Tina and her ex-boyfriend Andrew (with his intolerance of spicy food!). Could you talk about what it's like to write about two cultures colliding?

A: This is one space where I'm writing what I know, I suppose. I'm Indian, born in Delhi, raised all over, and my husband is a New Zealander, born in Chennai, raised all over. We met in Mumbai and now have two daughters who are going to navigate this complicated identity. I want them to learn bharatanatyam and ballet, the shehnai and the violin. It's something I deal with on a daily basis. And not just in my married or home life; this is a topic I've been thinking about subconsciously ever since I was young—living as an Indian in America. But I was never lost—my parents took us to India twice a year; I speak Hindi, Bengali, Marathi. I could feel lost but instead I feel fortunate to be able to call to places home.

Q: What is your writing routine, if you have one? Has it changed at all since you wrote *The Windfall*?

A: I started writing *Destination Wedding* about three years ago and I've also had two babies in the last three years so time has shifted shape for me. I no longer have the luxury of long hours of staring into space so I now write in short bursts with laser sharp focus and I think that's infused this book with energy and a sense of urgency.

PHOTO: © PHOTO CREDIT

DIKSHA BASU is the author of
Destination Wedding and *The Windfall*.
Originally from New Delhi, India,
she now divides her time between
New York City and Bombay.

authordikshabasu.com

Twitter: @dikshabasu

This book was set in Fournier, a typeface
named for Pierre-Simon Fournier (1712–68),
the youngest son of a French printing family.
He started out engraving woodblocks and large
capitals, then moved on to fonts of type. In 1736
he began his own foundry and made several
important contributions in the field of type
design; he is said to have cut 147 alphabets of
his own creation. Fournier is probably best
remembered as the designer of St. Augustine
Ordinaire, a face that served as the model for
the Monotype Corporation's Fournier,
which was released in 1925.

RANDOM HOUSE BOOK CLUB

Because Stories Are Better Shared

Discover

Exciting new books that spark conversation every week.

Connect

With authors on tour—or in your living room. (Request an Author Chat for your book club!)

Discuss

Stories that move you with fellow book lovers on Facebook, on Goodreads, or at in-person meet-ups.

Enhance

Your reading experience with discussion prompts, digital book club kits, and more, available on our website.

Join our online book club community!

 randomhousebookclub.com

 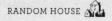